D1081842

BAD NEWS
TRAVELS FAST

by

Maureen Milliken

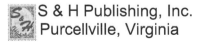
S & H Publishing, Inc.
Purcellville, Virginia

Maureen Milliken/S & H Publishing, Inc.
P. O. Box 456
Purcellville, VA 20134
www.SandHpublishing.com

Bad News Travels Fast / Maureen Milliken. -- 1st ed.
ISBN 978-1-63320-064-7 – print edition
ISBN 978-1-63320-065-4 – ebook edition
   Fiction: Mystery: Amateur Sleuth: Woman Sleuth: Maine

PRAISE FOR THE BERNIE O'DEA MYSTERY SERIES:

"Bernie O'Dea is the rarest kind of fictional detective -- a crime-solving journalist who thinks and acts like an actual journalist. Resourceful, intelligent, and charming, she is someone you very much want to spend time with. " -- Paul Doiron, author of *Stay Hidden*

DEDICATION

While journalism is a noble calling, one of its great ironies is that newsrooms are often quagmires of duplicity, ego, and unearned entitlement. This book is dedicated to those journalists who, despite the odds, maintain their professionalism, good humor, and humanity. I've been lucky enough to work beside many. An extra special dedication to the few who never forgot the value of friendship under fire, the News Chicks: Carol Robidoux, Lorna Colquhoun and Sherry Wood; and two comrades in arms, Chris Duffy and Matt McSorley.

CHAPTER 1

Bernie O'Dea stood in the dirt parking lot in the early evening heat. It was too damn hot for Maine in June. Humid and buggy. But she noticed those things out of habit, they didn't bother her the way they usually did. She stared at the trail that crossed the meadow where Lydia Manzo's body had been carried out three days earlier as though it would tell her what she needed to know.

It was the same time of day. That was a coincidence. She'd gotten in her car and roared north as soon as she heard the voicemail from Pete. She knew he wouldn't be there—he'd sent it hours earlier. But she was there anyway.

The meadow was a riot of early summer wildflowers, delicate yellows and purples, some bright orange. The mountains beyond, lit by the setting sun off to the west, were green and dark-blue humps, covered with forest. They looked cool and welcoming. It was all a lie. The mountains, the thick woods and unforgiving terrain, had taken Lydia's life. Now they had Pete. She had an awful feeling he was never going to come out.

Her cellphone rang. She didn't want to answer, but it was Sandy and if she didn't, he'd probably come after her.

"Are you up in Carrabassett?" he asked.

She didn't want to say. This was going to be the rest of her life, she could see that. A bewildered daze punctuated by unwelcome blips of life that she didn't want to deal with.

"I'm at the trailhead by the Sugarloaf Airport."

She could picture him in his office behind the firetruck bay, his feet on his desk, twirling the phone cord as he tried to figure out how best to talk the crazy woman back into the safe embrace of reality.

"What're you doing? It'll be dark soon. It's too late to go after him." His voice was careful, too soothing. It annoyed her. The annoyance felt good, though, a break from the panic.

"I'm just here. Don't worry."

"Come back to Redimere. We can have a beer and hash things over."

"Not tonight."

"I don't mean that," he said. "I know you two are back together. But you're upset and need to talk to someone."

"Don't worry." She hung up. Sandy didn't have to worry. She wasn't going to wander into the woods. She had a newspaper to put out, a dog and cats to feed. She wasn't going to vanish, like Lydia did.

Like Pete had.

Okay, he hadn't vanished. He'd intended to go on the hike for months, but he was supposed to leave Thursday, not this afternoon, three days early.

Her phone buzzed. She ignored it, willing the mountains to tell her something. Anything. She could hear cars pulling off Route 27 into the parking lot of the Lazy Logger Café, but the lot at the trailhead behind it, where she was, was deserted. Aside from the occasional car, it was quiet. If the mountains had anything to say, she'd hear it. They were dead quiet.

She got back in her car, defeated. Her phone buzzed again.

"What?" she said.

"Bernie, Pete's fine. Please come home," Sandy said.

"I don't understand anything." She started crying.

"It's just been a bad few days."

Bad year, more like it.

"I shouldn't have told you about Lydia," he said.

"That doesn't have anything to do with it." It did, but the facts of Lydia's death—the secret, unprintable facts—were trumped by Pete leaving.

"Bernadette, sweetheart."

"Don't sweetheart me," she said. "I'm pissed off. Lydia's dead. It was bad enough when it was suicide, but Friday you said it was murder, and that pissed me off more. Then you said I couldn't say anything until the medical examiner's report came out. Well, it did, and it didn't say anything about murder. Now you've gone back on the whole thing. And guess what? The police chief, who happens to be my boyfriend, has taken off with barely a word into the same goddam woods. Sweetheart doesn't do it for me."

"I'm sorry," he said. "I'm upset, too."

"I just had to get away to think," Bernie said. She flipped her phone shut and leaned back against the seat. The real explanation of why she'd raced up to the woods wouldn't make sense to Sandy. It barely did to her. She just wanted to see if she could look at where Pete had gone and understand why. It was getting dark now—the longest day of the year had come and gone a week ago. The days were going to get shorter, darkness would come faster, it would squeeze from both sides until there was no light at all.

She started the car and bumped through the dirt parking lot back out to Route 27 and home.

*****

Bernie had a half-hour, give or take, depending on how she drove and whether she hit a deer, to hash things over. She knew the minute she crossed the town line she'd start obsessing about Pete again. For now, she tried to make sense of the Lydia thing.

She worked backwards, from when Sandy and his unofficial search crew had found Lydia Friday afternoon, dead in her bright purple tent. A spot where searchers, a month ago, in the first frenzied days of her disappearance, would have passed close enough to hear her cough, or maybe cry out, if she'd been in any condition to do either.

But the search had moved on up the Appalachian Trail. As the days turned into weeks Bernie knew Lydia probably wouldn't be found alive. Maine's northern woods were unforgiving—the terrain brutal, the vastness underrated. No cell service, no one to hear you

3

shout for help.

Friday night, when Sandy whispered to her that no, it wasn't suicide, Bernie wondered if he was wrong. No one else said anything that night, or acted like it was anything but suicide. She'd been at enough crime scenes in her two-plus decades as a reporter to know the signs when they thought it was homicide. He was experienced in search and rescue, and as a rural fire chief had seen countless bodies that had met their end in a mind-blowing variety of ways. He wasn't given to flights of fancy. Over the weekend, when she'd still been rational, she'd tried to weigh the likelihood of him being wrong against the likelihood of him being right. It kept coming back on the side of him being right.

Suicide seemed just as unlikely. Lydia getting lost, for that matter, seemed just as unlikely.

Bernie should know, she'd been writing about Lydia for five months.

A few hours earlier, when she'd gotten the email from the state police with the medical examiner's report, she'd written what she realized would probably be among the last Lydia Manzo stories her newspaper, the *Peaks Weekly Watcher*, would publish. That fact upset her, not only because Lydia was dead, but because she had too many questions and she was told they weren't going to be answered.

She didn't know as she wrote that Pete was on his way up to the mountains. If she'd known, she wouldn't have been able to write at all.

She'd tried to capture, as much as she could, the unexpected and tragic end to an adventure that had started out so well. It'd been a great story: The upbeat, tenacious hiker from Buffalo, New York, recently retired nurse, divorced mother of two grown children, hiking the Appalachian Trail. She had to finish the 2,179-mile hike in time for her son's July wedding, an added layer of drama.

If things had gone as planned, just about now Bernie would've been writing about Lydia's triumphant summit of Mount Katahdin, the northern end of the trail.

But things hadn't gone as planned. Not at all.

4

Lydia's plan went to hell the first week of June. She didn't meet her friends in Caratunk, thirty-seven miles from Wyman Township, where they'd put her back on the trail after she spent part of Memorial Day weekend in Redimere, Bernie's town.

The friends, Crystal and LeeAnne—fellow nurses, the self-proclaimed Woo Hoo Girls—had been her support staff since March. They knew after three months of it that schedules were more suggestions than anything else, but Lydia missed the twenty-four hours-before-we-panic window, something that had never happened before. They hiked back from the meeting point looking for her. They asked the few other hikers they encountered—there weren't many this time of year in the western Maine high peaks that gave the newspaper its name. This part of the world was just waking up from another endless winter. None had seen her.

Then Friday, as the wet late-spring days slid into humid, buggy, early summer, Lydia was found. She was half a mile from the trail, not far from where she'd set out four weeks earlier. The information flow that gushed from the state investigators during the weeks Lydia was missing shut down.

Then, a few hours before Bernie raced up Route 27, the medical examiner's report and the terse state police news release that accompanied it arrived. She'd expected so much more.

Sure, the details that no one would talk about Friday night were there. The report laid out in graphic prose, almost poetic in its gruesomeness, how lack of water, and to a lesser extent, food, had brought Lydia to the brink of death in the three-plus weeks she'd lived after she wandered off the trail. Bernie was stunned a healthy fifty-five-year-old could deteriorate that fast. The report detailed the state of her decomposition—green-tinged skin, particularly her lower stomach and extremities. Bloating was beginning, helped out by the warmer-than-normal humid June.

Lack of water and food would have killed her in days, maybe hours. But it hadn't.

Delirious from hunger and thirst, or maybe despondent from being lost, her dream dead when she was so close to finishing—no

5

one would ever know since she didn't leave a note—with the last of her ebbing strength, Lydia shook the trail mix crumbs out of a Ziploc bag and put it over her head.

It would be a quick and relatively painless end, most agreed as word spread—Lydia hurrying death along to avoid the slower, more agonizing one coming.

"It's like the people who jumped out of the World Trade Center," she'd said to Guy. But that was before the report had come in. "It's that or wait for death to come get you."

"Makes sense," Guy had said. "Given it didn't look like anyone else was gonna."

When Bernie didn't say anything, he added, "Come get her."

Bernie almost said, "Someone did, in a manner of speaking." But Guy didn't know. She was desperate to talk to him about it. He'd been a mentor when she first worked at the *Weekly Watcher* right out of college, and in the three years she'd been back after two decades of working away, he'd been her sounding board. She knew that they'd have a great conversation as soon as the medical examiner's report was released and she could talk about what really happened. A conversation about how Lydia could have been murdered in one of the wildest parts of the most remote state on the trail.

Then the report came.

Asphyxiation, it concluded. Then redaction, long, impenetrable lines of black, with a word here and there— "and," "the," and most tantalizing, "head"—almost as if whoever redacted it knew how much it would frustrate her.

The medical examiner left in small details that said nothing— the web of blackberry bush scratches on her ankles, calves, the backs of her hands and lower arms, for instance.

"Who cares. Friggin' blackberry scratches," Bernie said as she typed. She couldn't hit the right keys, could barely put together the mealy-mouthed non-story.

"Why redact so many things if it's suicide?" she said, her sweaty fingers slipping off the keys. Confusion turned to anger.

Could she keep a possible, no make that probable, murder a secret for the rest of her life? No, definitely not.

She hit more wrong keys, then went too far with the backspace button, deleting a sentence.

This was maybe the first time in her life she wished she didn't know the details. Wished she was just a happy vessel for law enforcement to dump information into that she could parrot out with a blissful lack of curiosity like so many reporters she'd known.

Even though she knew it was pointless, she called George Libby, the state's lead investigator. Normally she'd go through the official spokesman, but she didn't have the patience.

"This must be about the report," he said when he answered. No "hello."

She got right to the point, too. "I'm wondering about the redactions and if there's anything you can tell me that lead to the conclusion."

"You have our official statement. I know you're about to interrupt me, so I'll add this just for you: When a private citizen commits suicide, there are details that're nobody's business. The investigation's over."

"But—"

"I investigate homicides for a living, and can tell you this case is closed and there's nothing else to say. Keep that in mind if you hear any rumors up in your neck of the woods." He disconnected.

She turned to Guy. She wanted a loophole, a way to talk about it. "It just doesn't make sense," she said.

"Don't go borrowing trouble," Guy said.

"Let's pretend it wasn't suicide, or even natural causes."

"Why, Bernadette, do you do this?"

"Pretend someone thinks it's murder." She wanted to tell him so bad it hurt.

"Your problem is you have way too much imagination," he said.

"My imagination has served me well," she said. "Look at it this way, the fact Lydia was lost didn't make sense. She had a good plan, she was organized. Her friends were on top of things and helping her every step of the way. She had a GPS and took this intensive AT hiking course and everything."

Guy rolled his eyes. "It was pouring the day she was last seen. She panicked and got disoriented. She was exhausted after hiking for months and her guard was down. She'd just finished some of the worst terrain on the trail, and the part she was on is no picnic. I know, I've hiked it many times. Makes perfect sense."

"There are lots of people wandering around out there," Bernie said. "The Midnight Rambler, Danny Fuller. Other trail hikers. It's like Grand Central Station with pine trees."

Guy turned back to his computer. "It's uninhabited wilderness that has swallowed up a few unfortunate souls. Everyone else is on the trails. You're arguing just for the sake of arguing."

She'd been tempted to call Pete, but he'd made it clear earlier, before the report came in, that it wasn't his case, it was the state's. Normally, back before they broke up, she would've hounded him anyway. During the breakup, she wouldn't have even had the first conversation. Now she was trying to be on her best behavior. She hadn't said a word about what Sandy told her Friday night. She was proud of herself. Once it was public, they could talk to their hearts' content about it.

Now, driving back to town, she wished she'd called Pete. Not because of the Lydia story, but because he was gone. He sounded so matter-of-fact in his voicemail when he said he was going, not final at all. So why did she keep feeling like it was?

CHAPTER 2

Pete knew it was too late in the day for much hiking, but he could at least get into the woods. He hadn't thought much about it when he decided to leave that afternoon, he just knew he needed that dark stillness now, not three days from how. He tried to tell himself he wasn't running from something, but running to something. Bernie would have called him on that. "Cliché alert!" It made him smile as he started across the meadow, the sound of Sandy's pickup tearing out of the parking lot still ringing in his ears.

The sun was low and mid-afternoon hot. He was already sweating. He wished Bernie had picked up when he called. He didn't want to just leave a voicemail. He'd checked his phone after he put his pack on, but she hadn't called back or texted. He hadn't explained it well to her. Didn't explain at all, really. He'd been so desperate to go. He was already out of cell range, so now it wouldn't matter. He'd turned the phone off and put it back in his pack. For the next week it'd just be a useless chunk of plastic.

He'd been balancing things pretty well, but it'd all come crashing down on his head in the last twenty-four hours. He reached the edge of the meadow and let out the breath he'd been holding. It was like stepping into a cave, or a portal to another world. The temperature dropped, even the drone of the mosquitos changed.

The need to go had been building since yesterday. One little blow after another.

There'd been Sandy, pissed off, standing at Pete's desk that morning, demanding that he "do something" about the state police closing the Lydia Manzo case.

Sandy had known since Saturday that the state police were going to rule it suicide, so Pete wasn't sure what he'd been expecting. Sandy said he thought they'd wait to make it public. Wait for what?

Friday, Pete told Sandy he'd see what he could do. Now, Monday, Sandy thought Pete had turned around on that. Pete had been too exhausted, his headache building, to explain. Truthfully, too, he didn't feel like he had one good reason to make Sandy feel better.

Sandy knew that, too.

"I wonder if the fact you believed me Friday about Lydia, but not today is about something else, not about Lydia at all," he'd said. Dawna was there, too, looking on, concerned, which just made him feel dishonest and more like a jerk.

"Here's the deal with Lydia," he'd said to them. "The state police told me Saturday out of professional courtesy that they'd ruled it suicide. I appreciated it, given how pissed off they were that the town's fire chief, my most junior officer, and Lydia's two friends, who in no way should have been involved, went bumbling into the woods on a tip that they didn't even bother to tell anyone about."

"They were pissed because we found her and they couldn't," Sandy said. "We didn't go bumbling. I know what I'm doing. This is totally different from what you said Friday. Saturday, too."

Pete knew Sandy was right, but that didn't change the script. "Do you have any idea how much shit I had to eat with George Libby when I saw him Sunday? He's not a fan of ours as it is, and he sure as hell isn't a fan of yours. I wasn't going to argue with the lead investigator on the case about what the Redimere fire chief may or may not have seen."

"I know what I saw. You've seen more homicides in a year on your last job than Libby will see his whole career. You can force the issue."

"No I can't," Pete said. "That was Philly. This is Maine. I might as well be a pastry chef for all they care. The state is done with the case. Anything but suicide doesn't make sense. It's a waste of resources to pursue it when they have so many other things going on, including trying to catch an actual murderer who's been at large for weeks. I don't know how many times I can say it. We're done with this."

Pete's head was going to split wide open. Dawna had stayed after Sandy left. He could see her questions, the compassion and understanding behind them. He didn't deserve it. He knew she wouldn't let him deflect her. It's one of the reasons she made such a good sergeant. And as she talked, he didn't disagree with anything she said. He was ashamed she had to say it. Still, her last line had left him cold.

"You're in a position where a bad decision could cost someone their life."

She'd nailed it. It was one of the things haunting him the last few months, creeping into his nightmares and lately into his days. Things had been quiet since November, everything was okay. Bernie was okay. Things had calmed down after a horrific year. But he couldn't shake it. He thought time would smooth his issues out, but they were getting worse. Dawna saw it, too.

The shame of that conversation didn't ease as the woods thickened around him. It always took a while to decompress. He hoped he could get past kicking himself and start thinking about Lydia's case, the lifeline he was hanging onto to prove he was actually okay.

He turned onto an unmarked trail that followed a stream. He had an idea of where he was going, but he'd figure it out more specifically in the morning. For now, he just wanted to find a spot to camp for the night.

The final blow in a day that just kept getting worse came when he'd finally told Vicki he had a headache and was taking the afternoon off.

She handed him a package. "This came in the mail," she'd said. "Must be a late birthday present."

She had no idea she'd just handed him a bomb. Actually, he

11

wished it'd been a bomb. Because when he took it home and opened it, what was inside was worse.

He stopped at a clear spot next to the stream. It was already getting dark, and when night came in the woods, it came fast. He took out his paraffin burner and collapsible pot. He loved the neatness and efficiency of camping. He didn't even have a tent or sleeping bag, just a blanket roll. He had water from home, but that was for drinking. He scooped some out of the stream and put it on the burner to boil. He sat back against a tree. His headache had faded. He took a deep breath, counted to four, then let it out on four beats. A trick he'd learned from his counselor in Philly to keep the panic attacks at bay. He was skeptical about the Midnight Rambler, Bernie's obsessive and impressive research aside. Still, he'd often thought how good the guy had it, if he actually existed. Living like this all the time. Pete knew it was a romantic fantasy. Maybe that's why some people believed in him. In reality, it'd be a miserable, lonely existence if it was your life. Though the way his day had gone, how much more miserable could it be?

The final punch, one of his own making, the cherry on top of the shit sundae he'd made for himself, was that he'd decided maybe he and Sandy could talk after all.

By the time Sandy got to Pete's house to drive him to the trailhead, reality had seeped in and Pete was in no condition for the discussion.

As they sped up Route 27, he and Sandy squabbled like teenage boys. Sandy came right out first thing and said he knew Pete wouldn't back him up about Lydia because he'd found out about him and Bernie. Sandy made it clear he didn't have anything to apologize for. Pete normally would have agreed, but nothing was normal now.

"You guys didn't waste any time, did you?" Pete said.

"You told her it was a clean break. You didn't want to hold her back from finding someone."

"She told you that?" Pete wondered how much of that terrible inarticulate conversation of a month ago she'd repeated to Sandy.

"She was devastated and needed someone to talk to."

"And you just happened to be there."

"We're friends. Like I said, you told her to find someone else."

"I know what I told her." Pete cringed with shame now, alone in the woods, as he thought about the conversation. It was different from the shame he felt with Dawna, but shame nevertheless. He felt it then, too, but couldn't stop it.

"How'd you know?" Sandy asked.

It was such a small thing. Sunday morning, he'd tossed a wet towel in Bernie's dirty laundry basket, then thought better of it, pulled it out, and there it was. One of those faded blue Redimere FD T-shirts with "CHIEF" in white letters on the sleeve that Sandy wore all the time. It'd sent him reeling as Bernie chattered away from the bathroom.

"It doesn't matter," he said. He didn't want to give Sandy the satisfaction of witnessing his pain, his stupid befuddlement. "What matters is you took advantage of her." Out of the corner of his eye, he saw Sandy's grip tighten on the wheel.

"You've gotta be kidding," Sandy said. "I've got news for you. She's a big girl and she knew exactly what she was doing."

Pete's headache, which had grown and bloomed as the day wore on, had exploded with the contents of his father's package. As he and Sandy nipped at each other, it jackhammered in time with his heart. The dumpster-garbage smell, the companion to his migraines, choked him. Rational thinking was twisted out of shape. All he felt was anger. He didn't care if it didn't make sense. He knew Sandy wasn't his father, or his stepfather, but he was here and they weren't.

"She was vulnerable. You couldn't wait to pounce."

Sandy took a deep breath. "She needed someone to show her she was lovable and wanted. I fit the bill. She needed a man. I'm not just talking about the physical shit, right? She needed a man who'd be strong for her, who'd act like a man."

This wasn't the conversation Pete had pictured, back when he still thought they'd have a grownup-to-grownup conversation.

13

When was that? It felt like a different life. The car in front of them was going about ten miles under the fifty-five mile limit. Sandy wanted to get past, probably wanted to get Pete out of the car, get away from him. He was tailgating, nowhere to pass on the curving two-lane. He inched the pickup over the center line, then swerved back as a logging truck rounded a curve and roared toward them.

"You broke her heart," Sandy said.

They passed the sign entering Carrabassett Valley: "Once you've been here, your life will never be the same." Every time they drove past it, Bernie said, "Yeah, but is that good or bad?"

Pete breathed in, held it, counted to four.

"She still had so much faith in you that she figured if you broke up with her, your reasons were good enough that it wasn't gonna be fixed." It took a lot to piss Sandy off, but Pete had managed to. All day long. His voice had an edge Pete had never heard before. "If it makes you feel any better, we both agreed from the start it was just physical. I didn't even think we needed to keep it a secret, but she didn't want to hurt you. Now you're taking off on her less than two days after you begged her to take you back, and being a total dick on top of it. I can take it. If you're not going to support me about Lydia because of this, that's your problem. I thought more of you than that, but whatever. But Bernie doesn't deserve it. She may have slept with me, but her heart was with you. You don't even get how lucky that makes you."

The breathing exercise wasn't working. Pete dug his fingernails into his palms, trying to fight the urge to open the door and fall out. Could feel himself bouncing on pavement. Anything to get away from that hot dumpster death smell. "I don't need relationship advice from the guy with three divorces under his belt."

"Actually, it looks like you do."

They turned onto the gravel drive that took them behind the Lazy Logger Café to the trailhead. Sandy slowed and pulled aside for a Jeep full of teenagers with mountain bikes, the loud thump of bass drowning out everything else. It made Pete's head throb dark red blasts. For a minute he thought he was going to vomit, but they turned onto 27 and the noise faded away.

As the truck turned into a parking space by the trailhead Pete said, "Guys like you just do whatever you want with women, like they're nothing, treat them like garbage, hurt them, then act like it's her fault, not yours." He got out of the truck before Sandy came to a stop.

Sandy slammed on the brakes and got out, too, coming around the truck as Pete lifted his pack out, shouldered it and began adjusting the straps. He wondered if Sandy was going to deck him here in this sunny parking lot, where Friday night they'd stood together, best friends, waiting for Lydia's remains to be brought out. The lot was empty. He almost wished Sandy, who was inches taller and forty pounds heavier, would let him have it.

Sandy stopped in front of him, his arms folded tight, hands tucked under his armpits, making it clear if anyone was going to throw a punch, it'd have to be Pete. "What the hell are you even talking about? I wouldn't treat Bernie like that, or any woman. You know that. Where did that come from?"

Sandy looked hurt, confused. Pete hated himself, but he couldn't stop the monster let loose by that package from his father. "Try to keep your fucking paws off my girl while I'm gone."

Sandy's hands, still tucked in his armpits, curled into fists. "I know the pain you've gone through and I feel for you. If I hurt you by sleeping with Bernie, I'm sorry. You've been like a brother to me, no matter what, and I thought you felt the same way. But If you'd rather be this asshole, this guy I don't even know, do everybody a favor and go get lost like Lydia did."

He got back in the truck and roared out of the lot, spitting gravel.

Pete didn't like the guy he was any more than Sandy did. Less.

Now, in the cool dark, he wished he'd been able to rein it in. He wished he'd tried harder to talk to Bernie before he left.

He wished a lot of things, but there wasn't anything he could do about it now.

15

CHAPTER 3

Bernie drove down Main Street, not sure if she should go to the office and finish some of the work she'd blown off for her pointless drive, or just go home and stew all night.

The town's cruiser was in the parking lot of the Pizza Bowl. For a split second her heart soared. Less than a split second. It was a programmed reaction. She pulled up next to the cruiser and got out. Dawna rolled down the window.

"Hey, can I come in?" Bernie asked.

"Yeah, get out of the bugs," Dawna said. "I heard you went up looking for Pete."

"Not exactly. Sandy's being dramatic," Bernie said as she got into the air-conditioned car. It made her feel a little better. Less exhausted.

"Pete'll be okay," Dawna said.

From where they sat, Bernie could see down Main Street. The Watcher building was two blocks down, its peeling yellow clapboard just visible across the street from the bright and busy Country Grocer. Down at their end of the row of one and two-story wood and brick buildings, most closed for the night, it was quiet aside from faint music from the Pizza Bowl, an occasional car arriving or leaving, someone laughing or calling good-night.

"Hard to believe Fourth of July is in less than a week," Bernie said. "The calm before the storm."

Bernie had never been a summer person. When she'd lived in the cities of central New England, summer just meant it was warm out. Everyone was working. Sure, people talked about their weekend at the beach or vacation plans. Came into work with tans on top of their newsroom pallor, but it was business as usual. Back in Maine, though, in a town where the population doubles in July and August, she felt it keenly. Quiet as downtown may be, on the lakes and rivers, the pockets of camps and cabins, half of the town partied, up late, firecrackers going off, music playing. She could hear it as she lay in bed at night. She got it. They lived fifty weeks a year for the two weeks they could come up here, and she was in a parallel universe where people got up early and went to work, required sleep and wouldn't know a firecracker if it floated to the top of their morning coffee.

"I'm glad it's on a Sunday," Dawna said. "It'll keep the chaos confined to a couple days, hopefully."

That's another thing Bernie forgot until she moved back to Maine—the whole state shuts down for a week for the Fourth, the official start of summer. Don't try to get too much business done, no one's around. In fact, some of them are in Redimere, setting off firecrackers and blasting music at one a.m.

"Here's hoping," Bernie said.

"I just want a nice, smooth uneventful week," Dawna said. "No surprises."

"Why'd he go?" Bernie asked. "I know he was going on that hike. He's planned it for months. But he was going to leave Thursday. He left me a voicemail, but it didn't say much. I didn't see it until hours after he called." She was glad she sounded better than when she'd talked to Sandy, but she didn't feel any better.

"I think he just really needed a break. You know, after last year, he didn't want to be here on the Fourth," Dawna said "I told him it was fine."

"Did something happen today?"

"All sorts of things." Dawna smiled.

Bernie didn't buy it. "All he said in his voicemail was that he just really had to go, and that he was sorry. That he'd text me from the trailhead next Monday to come get him." He'd sounded so matter-of-fact, so normal.

Dawna sighed. "Okay, I don't know why he left, but here's

17

some of what happened today. He went around and around with Sandy about the medical examiner's report. Sandy wanted Pete to do something about it, make them keep the case open, look at it more. Pete just kept saying it wasn't his call."

"Doesn't he believe Sandy?"

"Wait, how much do you know?"

"Sandy told me he thinks Lydia was murdered, but he didn't tell me any details. He swore me to secrecy, and I haven't told anyone. Until now."

"Pete believes him, but I don't think he wanted to get Sandy's hopes up. I think he plans to poke around while he's up there. I mean, he was going to that area anyway, now it's like he's got a reason."

"I'm glad he has a reason," Bernie said. "Something solid to focus on."

"I have a confession," Dawna said. "I kind of read him the riot act today. He needs help, Bernie. He's good at hiding it, but his PTSD is beyond what he can deal with himself."

"How did he respond?" Deflect, deflect, deflect, was Bernie's guess.

"He seemed embarrassed and said if he didn't feel better when he got back from the hike he'd get help."

"Feel better. Like it's a stomach bug or something."

"Have you two talked about it?"

"I tried." Then we split up. She didn't want to say that part, it put her right back into the epicenter of fear and panic.

"Did he tell you about the basketball game?"

"What, the two-on-two league?"

"He and Walt were playing Sandy and Jamie last night and Pete was really rough on Sandy, like he was trying to pick a fight. I don't have to tell you, that's not like him at all."

"No, not like him." Bernie wondered if Pete knew about her and Sandy. There was no way he could, and it was over. Hopefully he never would. She didn't want to talk about it anymore.

"What did Sandy see that makes him think Lydia was killed? It

18

does seem pretty far-fetched."

"He said her face was bright red, definitely carbon monoxide poisoning. Some other things, too, but that was the big one."

"I wonder if there could be a natural cause of that. It's not like she had a grill in her tent."

"I know," Dawna said. "But Sandy knows his stuff."

"What does Pete think he's going to find?" It's almost like they weren't back together at all. What had they even talked about Saturday night into Sunday morning? Bernie couldn't remember.

"I think he just wants to get the lay of the land, think it out," Dawna said. "You know how he is. Logical, wants to see, then go from there."

They watched the street. The occasional car, people, too, walking in the warm night from the store and Pizza Bowl back home or to the Four Seasons cabins along the river.

"Do you know who she is?" Bernie asked as a woman walked by.

"Colleen Sullivan," Dawna said. "She was in to talk to Pete last week about something."

Bernie almost said, "That's an Irish name," but then didn't. It would have made her sound ignorant. She'd noticed her the day before in the Country Grocer. Redimere wasn't any different from most of the rural towns in the whitest state in the nation—you could count its black residents on one hand. One finger, actually. Walt Pecoe, who owned the grocery store. So Colleen stood out.

"What was she talking to Pete about?"

"I'm not sure," Dawna said. "It may've had to do with Lydia, though. It was a couple days before she was found, and she's from Buffalo, too."

Bernie should make Colleen's acquaintance. It wouldn't be hard. She was probably staying at the Four Seasons or one of the town's two B&Bs that were within walking distance of the store. But not tonight. She opened the door.

"Thanks for the visit. I need to get home so I can get up and do it all over again tomorrow."

19

"Listen, Bernie. Don't worry about Pete. No matter how he feels, he's got a good head on his shoulders. He'll be okay."

Bernie nodded. That's the same thing she would've said about Lydia a month ago. Lydia did everything right, and now she was dead.

*****

It was close to ten when Bernie got home. Her brother was on the couch watching a movie, the dog on top of him, the cats sprawled on the floor nearby. The smell of grilled hamburgers hung in the air.

"There's a plate with a couple burgers in the oven," Sal said.

"Thanks. I don't know what I'll do when you move out." She stressed "when you move out," but he didn't seem to notice. Probably because it was white noise after hearing it since November.

"Message for you on the phone."

Bernie pushed the button to hear the dry crackle of Gert Feeney, her tipster on the board of selectman. Gert always called her landline, which was fine with Bernie. Her cellphone was a never-ending curse, the voicemail box filling up with bill collectors and annoyances. She tended to turn it off and put it in a drawer and then not check it and miss important calls. Ones like when your boyfriend calls to say he's going into the woods.

"Want to give you a heads-up, totally off the record," Gert said. "I heard that our new young mayor had the town clerk pull Pete and Sandy's personnel files. Didn't say anything to me about it, of course. I don't know if he's told anyone else on the board what's up. Could be nothing, could be something. I let Pete know earlier today, between us again, and he's not concerned, but maybe he should be. I'm telling you in case you want to dig around. I know you two try to keep the personal and job separate, but I woulda told you if you weren't dating."

Bernie got the hamburgers, found some potato salad and a beer in the fridge, and sat down next to Sal, pushing his legs out of the way. "Why aren't the Red Sox on?" She pushed Dubya's snout

20

away from her plate. The dog, a thirty-pound Sherman tank tangle of fur, put it back. She pushed it away again.

"They're off. I hate to see them take a night off with the streak they're on."

"Speaking of streaks."

"This movie sucks." He turned off the TV.

"Have you found a job yet? It's been seven months since you quit the dump."

"You're turning into Mom. I've told you a million times, the options for a fired college professor turned artist aren't great in northern Franklin County, Maine. I thought you were pleased that I'm taking my career in the rubbish sciences to the next level, as you know, helping Eli with his hauling business."

"It doesn't sound like a great career path for a man in his forties with a Ph.D."

"I know we're only having this conversation because you had a long day and you're hungry."

"Haaaaangry," Bernie said. She finished the first hamburger and started on the second. "These are good. What did you do?"

"Little horseradish."

"Maybe you should open a restaurant. Ha."

"I do have something going on. You know Chloe Houten?"

"Oh no." Bernie's first sight of the woman, a few months before, was burned into her head. Frazzled, in a loose peasant dress and parka in the Country Grocer, a baby strapped to her chest, his bright red face twisted in full wail under an equally bright red tuft of hair and a little girl, maybe four, with coffee-colored skin and braids tied off in bright ribbons dumping boxes of Oreos and Froot Loops in the cart as Chloe searched through her bag, "Where's my wallet? Where's my wallet?" Since then, Bernie'd learned the pre-teen Chloe's question, in retrospect, seemed to be directed at as he lounged against the magazine racks reading comic books and ignoring her, was also hers.

"No, it's fine," Sal said. "She found a barn rental for me, and I'm going to work on my art. Welding sculpture."

21

"Awesome."

"Be happy for me. I'm following my muse."

"How will you pay the rent? I mean is it an actual barn, with hay and stuff? Where is it?" Bernie tried to figure out if this was good news, but she was too tired.

"Out back of her house. No hay. More of a glorified shed. Carriage house, maybe."

"Even more awesome. You know she has three kids by three different guys, right?"

"What does that have to do with anything?"

"I see that glimmer in your eye."

"As usual, who the hell are you to give me relationship advice?" He picked up her empty plate. "Done with this?" She nodded. He took it to the sink.

"Touché," she said, lying down on the couch, with her beer on her stomach. Dubya tried to squeeze next to her, then gave up and settled at the end, between her feet.

"Those kids are cute," Sal said.

Bernie pictured a fourth one, with Sal's curly black hair and Roman nose. "Oh lord, Sal."

"Just kidding. She's hardly charging me anything for rent if I do some welding for her."

Bernie closed her eyes and listened to the soothing sound of someone else washing the dishes, wondering what someone like Chloe would need welded. She was too tired to ask.

"That message you just got. Reminded me of something funny I heard today," he said.

"Funny ha ha or funny I'm not going to like it?"

"The second."

"What?"

"Fergus Kelley and Sean Speck have teamed up for some online newspaper thing and are covering the same territory as you. I heard they're asking around about your dueling boyfriends."

She took a long drink of beer, leaned back and closed her eyes again. The beer bubbled up into her esophagus. "Fantastic."

"You're taking it well, considering that slob Kelley almost got you killed last year."

"Actually, I'm not. I'm just too tired to react. I'm screaming inside."

"They're getting cozy with Lydia Manzo's friend Crystal. Chloe told me. The mayor, Ryan Grant, is her boss at the real estate company. She's also friends with Speck."

"Figures." The scale of too many things going on at once had officially tipped. Bernie was surprised she didn't fall off the couch with the weight of it. She thought of calling Gert back, but it was late and Gert was in her seventies.

"Have you walked Dubby tonight?" she asked.

"Too busy cooking supper for you."

"I'll take him."

"Come right home," Sal said.

"Too tired not to." She was tired, but she knew she was too jumpy to sleep. She'd broken the habit she'd had of going for long nighttime walks. Actually, dating Pete had broken it. Then there'd been Sandy. None of that had eased her insomnia. Walking helped her think, and she was glad she had the dog as an excuse.

She walked up the hill, Dubya stopping every ten steps to sniff, dig and pee. Maybe, she thought, there was a silver lining in the Ryan Grant situation. Maybe the mayor nosing around is what prompted Pete to take off. The silver lining being, it'd be an explanation, of sorts, as to why he did. But she couldn't see it. In fact, the last thing he'd do is take off if he thought he had a battle on his hands, especially if Fergus Kelley—the slob, as Sal had put it, who almost got her killed—was involved.

Bernie and Gert Feeney were in agreement about the new mayor. Bernie called it Golden Boy Syndrome—he'd been told all his life how wonderful he was, people just handed him things because he was an intelligent, polite male. He had no idea how hard it was to be heard, or have to fight to get ahead. Bernie had seen a few of them in the male-dominated news business, gliding along oblivious to how hard it was for those who weren't so blessed with nice manners and maleness.

Gert, who'd honed her people instincts with forty years of teaching high school, called him a good old boy in training. "I don't trust him for a minute."

The town had been shredded a few months earlier in a true crime show, *Murdertown: USA,* after what had been a tough and deadly year. Bernie and Gert both thought Grant seemed more upset about the show than the lives that were lost.

"He's just young and naïve," Pete had said when Bernie bitched about him. "He's got idealistic ideas and no real-life experience."

"Guys like that are the most dangerous," Bernie replied. "People don't realize the combination of no experience and already-formed ideas is a bad mix. He doesn't understand collaboration or teamwork, and people who don't march to his drummer can get hurt. Guys like him don't even have the balls to let you see it coming."

"People seem to like him," Pete said. "They think he's an impressive young guy. A bright light."

She knew he was just poking her. It was back when they could banter and she wasn't afraid it meant something bad. "People think he agrees with them because he never gives a straight answer. That's why they like him."

At the time, it'd been a theoretical discussion. Bernie didn't trust Grant, and knew he'd be way more of a problem than the town administrator, Dave Marshall, who'd treated transparency like it was an oath of office. But Dave and his position were out, Grant was in. She figured she'd deal with it. She didn't work for him, after all. It never occurred to her to worry about Pete. He was good at reading people. So good he'd even been recruited to take the FBI's behavior analysis course for cops at Quantico, something he'd casually mentioned one day the way she'd mention picking up a carton of milk. If he could figure out the minds of criminals, he should be able to handle the Ryan Grants of the world. But then, she'd always thought she could handle the Fergus Kelleys of the world.

When she got home, she went to bed, knowing she'd lie awake. She checked her cellphone, but nothing. She knew it was stupid. He was in the woods.

CHAPTER 4

Bernie was up before dawn. She hadn't slept all night, just like she knew she wouldn't. Although maybe, between watching the red numbers on the clock tick the minutes, then hours, away, and listening to the loons through the open window, she'd slept a little. She'd dreamed Fergus Kelley was working at the *Watcher* again and she'd stayed outside on the street, refusing to go in when she saw him through the window.

But when she got to work, mist rising off the pavement as dawn crept down Main Street, of course he wasn't there. The staff filed in as the morning brightened, everyone annoyingly chipper and talkative, doing their work and getting things done.

By mid-morning, Bernie needed a break.

"I'm going across the street." She said it fast, so no one would ask her to pick up a coffee or a breakfast sandwich. She almost made it.

Then, Annette, as if they were in the middle of a conversation, as if Bernie didn't already have her hand on the door handle, wasn't already pulling it open, said, "I was talking to Fergus Kelley—"

Bernie let go of the handle. "He was here?"

"No, I saw him at Dunkin's. He's gained weight."

"I thought he was gone," Carrie said. "Back to Massachusetts."

Annette shook her head. "He's working for that new online thingee, *Franklin On Call*. With Sean. They're doing a big story about Lydia Manzo."

Bernie walked out. She'd still been in shock about Pete last night when Sal brought it up. Too exhausted and too many things going on to deal with it. Now it hit her full-on. The dream should have been an indicator she wasn't dealing with it at all. Fergus hadn't done anything illegal, nothing he could be arrested for, but maybe tarred and feathered and run out of town on a rail if it was a century or two ago. His lack of ethical boundaries combined with a massive undeserved ego had brutal results. Now he was teaming up with Sean Speck. It made perfect sense, one awful former employee joining with another in an effort that she knew, just knew, was going to make her life hell.

At least, if what he told Annette was true, they were working on a Lydia Manzo story, not something on Pete or Sandy, whatever that would even be. She had Lydia Manzo covered and no one could beat her, even if she couldn't write about the questions about her death.

The store was crammed with summer people standing in aisles and staring at the shelves in slack-jawed befuddlement. At least that's how it seemed. Just like the leaves and wildflowers bursting out everywhere where there'd been barren ground a week before, the coming Fourth of July weekend meant it was time for the summer people. She waited to pay in a line that snaked down the bread and cookie aisle, trying to ignore the rumble in her stomach, the Oreos at her elbow, the jostling and space-hogging of people used to living in bigger towns. She'd wanted to spend a couple minutes of peace down at the picnic table behind her building with her sandwich, her coffee and her thoughts. But the minutes of the tiny amount of time she'd allotted herself were ticking away. She was considering leaving and paying later, when she felt a hand on her elbow.

"Bernie, have a minute?" It was Walt, the owner.

"Sure." She held up her sandwich and coffee. "I gotta pay first."

"It's on me. Let's go out back." He cleared a space on his desk, which was almost as messy as hers. "You can eat here."

"What's wrong?" she asked. Walt was usually smiling, but he wasn't today.

"How's Pete?"

Bernie took a bite out of her sandwich. "Why?"

"He's not himself."

"He's feeling things, I guess," Bernie said. "You're his friend. You know he's gone on his hike."

"I heard. I'm glad. It'll do him good. I'm glad the two of you are back together, too, that'll do him even better." He finally smiled.

"Geez, this is a small town," Bernie said. Their reconciliation was barely forty-eight hours old.

"He mentioned it at basketball Sunday. Actually, he'd talked to me about it before. I think he knew he made a mistake from the minute he let you go, but had to work through it."

"That doesn't make me feel better. You realize, right, it's going to take more than the love of a good woman to make him better?" The thought scared the hell out of her, but she didn't want to say that to Walt. He probably felt the same way.

"It'll help. He may seem like Superman, but he needs love and support just like anyone else."

"Thanks Dr. Phil, glad we can talk like this," Bernie said. Then she felt bad. Walt was a genuinely sweet guy who didn't deserve her rotten moods. "Sorry. He's lucky to have friends like you, too. He's not the kind of person who's going to ask anyone for help, though."

"All the more reason for us to step up."

She ate and waited. While she was talking he'd been nodding that way that people do who have a new topic when she was still on the old one.

"That's something about Lydia," he said. "Suicide. Hard to believe."

"Yeah. Very sad."

"I feel like I know her. Crystal and LeeAnne are in here all the time."

"I know. I'm still getting used to it."

"I wanted to tell you about something I heard," he said. "You may already know."

"Try me."

28

"I'm not telling anyone else, just you, and you didn't hear it from me."

"Sure."

"Friday night, I brought sandwiches and sodas up to the investigators who were up there all night at the trailhead, I think you'd left by then, and I heard two of them talking about how Lydia didn't have a GPS or a compass. That struck me funny, because I read all the stories you wrote and there was that one that explained how her GPS device worked."

"I hadn't heard that. Do you know the context, like had they heard it from someone else?"

"No, straight from the horse's mouth," Walt said. "One of them had to inventory what they'd found at the campsite as they packed it up to bring to Augusta, and he told the other guy. I figured it would've been in your story on the website Saturday or the one yesterday if you'd heard."

"Thanks for the tip."

"Don't say you heard it from me."

"Definitely." She wasn't going to ask him if he was sure. She knew he was, the same way she knew Sandy was.

*****

Bernie was just back at her desk when Dawna called.

"Was someone coming over for the police log, or do you want me to email it?"

"I can send Carrie over if there's anything we need to ask about," Bernie said. "Otherwise, email's good."

Carrie had her headphones on, furiously typing her article from the West Vineyard selectmen's meeting. Bernie hated to interrupt her.

"I kinda hoped you'd come over," Dawna said.

Bernie was there in two minutes.

"I want to show you something." Dawna led her into Pete's office.

Bernie had been trying to push her anxiety back, almost pretend that she and Pete were just busy at work, and that's why they hadn't talked that day. But she couldn't pretend standing in his office. She felt a pang when she saw the photo on his desk, her at the beach from their disastrous Memorial Day weekend trip, looking her usual mess, with a stupid smile, brushing a tangle of wet hair out of her face, her legs covered in sand.

Dawna stood next to the conference table. "Check this out."

There was an evidence bag with a dirty piece of notebook paper, the stenographer's kind with the line down the middle. "Is that something of Lydia's?" Bernie had seen her notes. Crystal and LeeAnne had shown her, she'd taken photos for the paper. Lydia used that kind of paper.

"No," Dawna said.

Bernie looked closer. The handwriting was definitely not Lydia's neat cursive. It was neat, but the block letters were strangely rounded. It said: "You can find Danny Fuller at the Lazy Logger dumpster in the early mornings."

"Where'd it come from?"

"I found it on the cruiser windshield Wednesday. The state police had it for a few days, but they don't think it's anything, so they gave it back."

"Nice," Bernie said. "A tip. Do you think it's for real?" She was happy for the distraction, something new and interesting. Something that wasn't Lydia and wasn't Pete.

"You can't write about it now, but I wanted to show you, just for a heads up for the future," Dawna said. "Pete said I could pursue it."

"What about the Piscataquis County sheriff?" Bernie asked.

"You know how it is," Dawna said. "State's calling the shots, since Fuller's wanted for murder."

"I haven't even been writing about him," Bernie said. "It's two counties over. Aren't they looking for him in Piscataquis or Somerset? How many weeks has it been since he killed his ex-girlfriend?" She counted back. "Six." A lot could happen in six weeks, Bernie knew. Relationships could crumble then be reborn. Happy hiking nurses could disappear and die.

"I know they're not looking for Fuller this far west," Dawna said. "They weren't looking for Lydia this far west, either. The state guys think the note's a hoax, that he's still near Monson, where he knows the territory, but you well know he could've easily gotten on the trail."

Bernie ran it through her head. Monson was the last stop before the 100-mile Wilderness, the last stretch of the Appalachian Trail before Baxter Park. She counted back—between Lydia and the Midnight Rambler she was an expert on the trail's waypoints. "That's what, seventy miles between Wyman Township and Monson on the AT? And the trailhead in Wyman is just a few miles up the road from the Logger."

"Exactly. But the state guys don't see it that way."

"Flatlanders," Bernie said. Most of Maine was an uninteresting mystery to those in its few relatively urban areas. The vast expanse north of L.L. Bean and west of the lobster-and-lighthouse highway, Route 1, was something they couldn't fathom. She'd seen it with cops, journalists, all sorts of people who should know better. The fact there was a huge wedge of woods and mountains and an entire county between where they were and Monson wasn't the barrier it may seem on a map. They were linked by the Appalachian Trail.

Bernie tried to picture her Midnight Rambler map. "I guess, if he's going to the Logger, that's in Carrabassett, he's taking the West Carry Trail down from the AT. I mean, that's how they got Lydia out." That's where Pete went.

"Bingo."

"You don't think Pete's looking for him, too?" Danny Fuller was a violent, angry and large man.

"No. I figure Fuller's staying out of sight, or someone would've spotted him. Pete knows better than to tangle with a guy like that. That wouldn't keep him from keeping an eye out, though."

Bernie pictured Pete with a giant magnifying glass, his curly hair sticking out from under a deer-stalker cap searching the trail Sherlock Holmes-style in his hiking shorts, boots and T-shirt. It made her feel a little better.

Dawna smiled, all dimples. "I told him to get the Midnight Rambler and he'd have the hat trick."

"Very funny," Bernie said. "He doesn't even think the Rambler exists."

"I called the Franklin County Sheriff, you know, Tom Fry, and his guys are going to keep an eye out around the Lazy Logger when they're up there, but they don't have a lot of manpower," Dawna said.

"So what're you going to do?"

"I'm figuring it out," she said. "I'll let you know when I have a story for you."

"Thanks." Bernie appreciated the fact Dawna was trying to cheer her up, or distract her. Something. It'd worked a little. "I still think that burglary at Redimere Drug a couple weeks ago was him."

"We already talked about that," Dawna said. "Looks more like someone wanting drugs. The burglar took a lot of morphine. You said the Rambler has an MO, right? That doesn't fit it."

"Let's just agree to disagree," Bernie said. "I get tired of arguing with people about him. Jamie was trying to tell me the other day that Rambler sightings are probably just hikers, hunters, other people out in the woods, that it's an urban legend. Rural legend, I guess. I don't know why people can't see the patterns. I'm not the only one who thinks so."

"Don't tell Pete, but I'm in your camp, too, except for that burglary," Dawna said. "Maybe he'll actually find the Rambler and you can say I told you so."

"Yeah, can't wait." She tried to make it sound like the words weren't coming around a giant lump in her throat.

*****

Pete had been hiking for hours, hoping for that moment, like a drug kicking in, when he crossed from the dark. He'd lain awake, listening to the owls and night rustling, the creek nearby. He'd heard something lapping water, loudly, at one point. Either a deer or a moose.

Bernie thought he was nuts to camp without a tent. "What if

32

you get attacked by a bear or coyote?"

"How's it different from being in a tent?" he'd said. "Or one of those three-sided shelters you like at Baxter? Wild animals won't attack a sleeping, live person, anyway. They only attack if you're threatening them, or if you're already dead and look like easy supper."

"What about that polar bear who attacked the guy in his tent in Greenland?"

She made him laugh. He could probably replay every conversation he'd ever had with her, but it'd just make him feel worse. He had to look forward. Think about Lydia. Investigate. He briefly followed the Appalachian Trail, then angled south on a smaller trail. There were overgrown logging roads in the area, deteriorating remnants of a past world, that would bring him deeper into the wilderness. This is where he'd planned to come when he first decided to go on the hike months ago, after looking at Bernie's map, seeing the outlines of an old world where no one went anymore.

He didn't believe in fate, or signs, but when Lydia's murder happened in the same area, it fit. He felt it four days ago when he was in the trailhead parking lot as the sun set, waiting for Lydia's remains to come out. After what Sandy told him that night, he felt like he had a plan. He'd expected they'd find Lydia dead, but it was still a sad shock

But underneath, in the part of his mind that wasn't on Lydia, he'd felt a little sliver of happiness that night. He'd also been chewing over for days, weeks really, the fact that he had to ask Bernie to forgive him, he had to admit his terrible mistake. Explain how he'd scared the shit out of himself, scared himself right out of his mind to the point he'd done the unthinkable and broken up with her. He'd done nothing but think and pick it over in the month they were apart. He was going to talk to her Friday, but then Lydia was found. That night in the parking lot, the gaggle of law enforcement, everyone from the Warden Service to the Border Patrol getting into the action, it was easy for her to avoid him. She'd been awkward and nervous when they did talk, and he felt bad, but he also felt a secret joy. In twenty-four hours it'd be okay. He'd talk it all out with her, tell her he needed her by his side as he got help. It was a new day, sharp and clear and peaceful. He hadn't felt peaceful in a long time.

When they did talk the next night, it'd been great, just as he'd hoped. Then everything went to shit.

The day was getting warm as the sun rose. The mugginess of the morning was lifting. There was no breeze and the bugs were thick in the early morning air, but they didn't bother him. He listened for bird songs, tried to identify them the way his uncle had taught him. Anything to put himself in the moment. He used to be able to do it when he ran cross-country in high school, thinking only of the run, the trail and the leaves, the wind, the smells. Or when he was on the pitcher's mound, just him, the ball, and the batter. It'd been a way to focus. It came from his grandfather's stories from the Czech resistance, how you made yourself think of something else when they were torturing you. Try to think of the name of every kid in your fifth-grade class. Start with your first memory and see how much of your life you can remember. Don't react to the pain. It's only pain. It'd worked great for sports. It'd worked for the bad things, too. It'd been a long time, though, since he'd been able to find that place.

Somewhere in the past few months, he'd lost the battle. The smell had come back, that dumpster smell. No, he was kidding himself when he said dumpster. That hot smell of death. His therapist a couple years before said it was a part of the PTSD, his adrenaline sparking the part of his brain where awful feelings came from.

He took a deep breath. Tried to focus on the real smells, another therapist exercise, a way to cement the thought. Fragrant blossoms, maybe apple, that thick grapey smell that they have in the spring or early summer. What else? Leaves, decaying. The dirt itself, thick and pungent, soft and almost springy under his hiking boots, thawed out from a wet winter, the decomposing leaves joining it.

He thought about Lydia. Where she went off the trail, how she would've gotten to where she was found.

He slapped at a deer fly. He'd put on repellent, some not-quite-effective natural stuff Walt sold, but bugs didn't really bother him anyway. He'd laughed when he and Bernie had gone hiking in May, right before everything went to shit, and she'd been eaten alive by what had to be the first mosquitoes of the season. He'd hardly been touched. Regret hit him again. He'd been such an idiot. He was now, too. Leaving her behind, no doubt confused. Probably pissed and wondering what she'd done wrong. *Nothing, baby.* He wished he could send it to her on the breeze. No cell service out here. No texting. Something someone should have told Lydia.

He stopped, took a deep breath, got his bearings. Okay, Lydia, let's see what you can tell me.

CHAPTER 5

It was one of those days when everything was against Bernie. Not just the big obvious things, either. Everything was screwed up—the pages, the ads, the computers, which kept crashing. She'd gotten such a nice early start, but she felt like she was running in quicksand and twenty-four hours from now there wouldn't be a newspaper.

It was great that Dawna showed her the note, but since she couldn't write about it now, she wished Danny Fuller hadn't elbowed his psychopathic way into her head.

The task at hand was to find someone to confirm that Lydia didn't have her GPS or compass when she got lost. That was a big deal whether she was murdered or not. It was the difference between her staying lost or finding her way out of the woods.

She'd called George Libby, the lead investigator, but it went to voicemail. She knew he wouldn't call back. She wanted to try Lydia's friends, but wasn't sure how far to press them in their shock and grief. She hadn't talked to them yet for the story, except briefly Friday when everything was so raw.

Usually, even on the most hectic days, there were a few sweet hours when her ADHD medication kicked in and the world smoothed out and irritation faded. It was usually the most productive part of the day. That hadn't happened today and it was pissing her off, because now she knew it wouldn't. She tried to decide which of the million things she should be doing right now to do next.

"How's my favorite editor?"

Eli Perry towered over her, his daughter Natalie at his side, a shorter, darker, pigtailed duplicate of her freckled, red-headed giant barrel of a father. They were both wearing turquoise polo shirts that said "Perry Rubbish Disposal," their names embroidered in script above a dump truck.

"Nice shirts," Bernie said.

"We're branding," said Natalie. "Dad let me pick out the color."

"Nice. Working with your dad?" Bernie asked.

"I ride shotgun."

"That must be fun, riding around in the truck."

Natalie shrugged.

"She's a good helper," Eli said. "I'm keeping her out of trouble this summer. She also checks the storage area out for me every day, cleans it up. Never too young to learn the business."

"People leave lots of junk lying around and don't put it in the dumpster," Natalie said. "I have to clean out the empty units, too."

"Sounds like fun," Bernie said.

"I want to be a private eye," Natalie said.

"Don't complain kid, you get paid." He tweaked one of her pigtails. "Things are taking off," he said to Bernie. "A lot of customers say they saw the ad. I want to talk to Shirley about adding one for the storage area."

"Be my guest," Bernie said.

He went over to talk to Shirley, but Natalie stayed.

"Hey, you guys pick up at the Lazy Logger, don't you?" Bernie asked. She'd just remembered his new ad had testimonials from his customers, to show he was county-wide.

Eli was busy talking to Shirley, but Natalie answered. "We go up there on Tuesday and Thursday. They're a good customer." Her big black eyes stared at Bernie with more than their usual intensity. There seemed to be some suspicion, too.

"Ever see anyone interesting up there?" Bernie asked. Worth a shot.

"Lots of people," Natalie said.

"Really?"

"Well, not lots. Some. It's still dark out." Natalie looked like she was going to add something, but now she was recalibrating. Her expression changed to bright conversation look. Bernie knew it well, because she did it too when she wanted to stop someone asking a question. "We stop at the storage units first, so Dad can check on things, then we go up there, and they're our first stop, and from there we go up to Stratton and Eustis."

Natalie and Bernie stared each other down as Bernie tried to think of a way to ask if they'd ever seen Danny Fuller diving in one of the Logger's dumpsters. The kid was good, if she actually knew something. Or maybe Bernie was seeing all sorts of meaning where there wasn't because she was so anxious.

Eli came back. "I'm taking out a quarter page for now," he said. "I've got lots of customers there, but need some more so I can do some upgrades. Place was kind of a mess when I bought it." He put his massive hand on Natalie's head. "Time to fly, puddin' pie."

Lydia's friend Crystal came in as they left. Eli bowed as he held the door open. Natalie stepped back and scowled. Bernie caught her eye and smiled. She knew what it was like to have an embarrassing father. Natalie nodded, a quick bob, but the scowl deepened.

Bernie had tried to avoid calling Lydia and her friends the Woo Hoo Girls in print, but they'd insisted. It's what they'd called themselves for years, a product of a night with too much wine and a lot of "woo hooing," the way people do. They laughed when they told Bernie about it, obviously one of those old inside jokes among close friends. When Lydia disappeared, other media latched onto it. Just like it was easier to write "the Midnight Rambler" instead of "the possibly non-existent hermit who lives in the woods and burglarizes camps," it was easier to write "the Woo Hoos" than "the friends and fellow nurses who are helping Lydia Manzo on her Appalachian Trail hike."

Redimere had been their staging area for the Maine portion of Lydia's hike, it was one of the bigger towns roughly halfway between the New Hampshire border and Mount Katahdin, though that wasn't saying much. When she got lost, they settled in. Bernie had known them ever since the initial pitch to feature Lydia in the paper over the winter. They'd become friends who could talk about other things, but Lydia had always been at the center. Seeing Crystal now was a startling reminder that Lydia truly was gone for good.

When Bernie briefly talked to Crystal and LeeAnne Friday, they'd been stunned. It was impossible to talk much with the cluster of law enforcement who'd wanted their attention. She remembered with annoyance how Sean Speck, who lived nearby in a Sugarloaf slope-side condo, had been there taking photos. Now she knew why. But Crystal was here, talking to her, not in some slimy hovel of an office talking to Speck and Fergus Kelley.

Crystal handed Bernie a Dunkin' Donuts iced coffee. "Thought you might need one."

"Thanks." Bernie had already had about three gallons of coffee since she got up. Crystal always brought her one, and Bernie wished she wouldn't, but it had gone on too long for Bernie to say no now.

"Where's LeeAnne? I'm not used to seeing one of you without the other."

"She had to go back to Buffalo," Crystal said. Her face crumpled.

"I'm sorry about Lydia," Bernie said. "I know I said it Friday, but I truly am sorry."

"Thanks." Crystal took a deep breath. "The family asked me to bring her home once she's released."

"That's good of you."

"It's the least I could do," Crystal said.

"They're lucky to have you," Bernie said. Lydia had been, too. Crystal was the organizer of the group. One of those people who could always take charge without a lot of fuss, the one people turned to in a crisis.

"Her kids are a mess, and neither of them want to come out here with the media circus," Crystal said. "Justin wants to postpone the wedding, but everyone, including me, told him Lydia would be very upset with him if he did that."

"At least the media circus is dying down," Bernie said. She'd noticed, actually, that it seemed to be gone. The TV trucks and other reporters were off to some other big story now that the Lydia case was closed. No *Murdertown: USA* for now, at least.

"The police even gave me her stuff back." She looked like she was going to cry again.

"Do you want to go down to the table?" Bernie asked. The day already seemed to have lasted a week. The rest stretched out like miles of slow, bad road. Like one of those dreams where you're running in deep mud and never get anywhere. Still, she wasn't going to turn down a chance to finally talk to Crystal

"Yes, let's," Crystal said.

The grassy patch behind the building, where the rocky river fork tumbled down from the mountains, was Bernie's favorite spot at work. Aside from the pastoral pleasure, she liked the fact no one could get within earshot without being seen well in advance. She'd talked to Crystal and LeeAnne many times there over the past month.

Crystal sat with her back to the river, her spine straight, hands folded in front of her. She was trying to keep it together, Bernie knew. She looked as put-together as ever, her bob hair-sprayed in place, a touch of lipstick, but Bernie wasn't going to push her on how she felt. She knew Crystal was probably a basket case inside. Before Lydia was found, the internet trolls were relentless, and it had skyrocketed since Friday. Bernie had turned off the comments on all her online stories, but some of the dailies were just letting it rip. Bernie'd also heard the snarky remarks of law enforcement, including about Sandy and Jamie's bad judgment letting Crystal and LeeAnne join them Friday.

"I don't believe the medical examiner's report," Crystal said.

"That she killed herself?"

"Exactly. No one even asked our opinion. We're medical professionals. I'd think our input would be invaluable."

"Did you see something at the scene that would make you believe it was anything else?"

"The fire chief and the officer wouldn't let us near the tent."

Her face crumpled again. Bernie wished she had a tissue, but at least Crystal wasn't in full-blown cry. Bernie hoped it stayed that way. She was a sympathy crier and she'd been on the edge all day.

"I remember LeeAnne saying Friday that Lydia wouldn't have given up on you guys looking for her, is that why you think she didn't kill herself?" Bernie kicked herself for putting words in Crystal's mouth. You never got quotes for a story by asking questions someone can answer with one word. She tried to relax and stop worrying about upsetting Crystal, who seemed to have steadied herself anyway.

"She was less than two hundred miles from finishing, her son's getting married in July," Crystal said. "I've known her for twenty years. There's no way."

Bernie wanted something concrete. "I've filed a freedom of information request for the search reports and all the other documents—the case file—to see if there's more information than what they're saying," Bernie said. "I won't hear back for a while. If you saw anything that even just seems off, even if it didn't then, it could mean something."

Crystal thought about it, twirling the straw in her iced coffee, then sipping slowing. Bernie drank hers too. It tasted good. Lots of sugar, which Bernie was trying to cut down on, another thing she should've told Crystal months ago, but couldn't now, after she'd gulped down dozens of sugar-thick iced coffee gifts from her.

"I can't think of anything," Crystal said. "When we saw the tent, it was such a shock, I wasn't looking at anything else."

"Can you tell me more about the tip?"

"It was from another thru-hiker, as I think I told you Friday. She was on the trail for most of the time Lydia was lost, so she didn't know anyone was looking until she saw a poster in Millinocket after she left Baxter Park, one of the ones with my cell number. She called, and I went and talked to her."

"She's probably the one those boys mistook for Lydia, why the searchers were looking in the wrong place," Bernie said. It had been one of the frustrations of the search. Teenagers on a day hike saw a middle-aged woman hiking twenty miles beyond where Lydia was eventually found and reported it a few days after the search started. It was assumed they'd seen Lydia, and the focus of the search moved to that part of the trail.

"I'm still mad about that," Crystal said, her voice shaking. "They'd been so dismissive of LeeAnne and I. So when I got the tip, I figured we'd do it ourselves."

"I'd like to talk to the tipster."

"I'll see if I can find her information," Crystal said. "I was so excited, I didn't think to get her contacts. I assumed Lydia was alive, and I was just focused on that. She was a little different, too. She didn't want to deal with the police, wanted to talk in person, not on the phone. I wish I'd paid more attention. Her trail name was Wilson. I don't even know if she told me her real name. At the time, I could care less."

"Could Wilson have been part of her real name?" Bernie knew that's not how trail names worked, but you never know. She fought the urge to say "couldn't care less." Like the iced coffee situation, Bernie knew nothing could be gained by correcting Crystal's grammar. She wasn't one of Bernie's siblings.

"The police asked me that, too, and were pretty impatient with me about it, but I have no idea. She said she was from one of the 'I' states. I know that doesn't help much. She was wearing a Yankees sweatshirt, but that doesn't mean anything."

"Oh, it means something all right."

Crystal looked blank.

"Sorry, Red Sox fan joke." Bernie had her notebook open to her notes from Friday. She needed to stay on point and stop being irreverent. Crystal was a grieving friend, not another journalist, or Pete. "George Libby told me Wilson told you that she walked the trail between Long Falls Dam Road and West Carry Pond with Lydia, but Lydia was too slow, so she left her behind."

"She also said Lydia didn't have much energy, which didn't sound like Lydia, but you saw for yourself how tired she was when she stopped here," Crystal said. "That doesn't mean she killed herself. I wonder if Wilson might have something to do with it. She didn't want to deal with law enforcement, as I said, and she was just so strange. Honestly, she was a kind of large woman, which made me suspicious about whether she was actually a thru-hiker. She wasn't lean like most of them are at this point."

"There must be an official way to find out who she is," Bernie said. "How would Wilson have gotten to Millinocket so fast, though, if she'd done something? It's more than a hundred and fifty miles of trail and Lydia wasn't dead more than a day when you found her."

Crystal flinched when Bernie said "dead." Bernie took a long sip of her iced coffee to refocus. *Remember, grieving friend.*

"I just realized that you said you did a freedom of information request for the case file," Crystal said. "The police chief has it. Didn't you know?"

"Pete?"

"Yes. He mentioned it Sunday when he gave me her belongings. He'd just been to Augusta that afternoon to get it."

Bernie wasn't sure if she should be mad Pete hadn't mentioned that. Then again, they'd barely talked since Sunday morning. He had work to do—she now knew it included going to Augusta to get the case file—and she had a family party at her sister's in Skowhegan. Also, there was the firewall between their jobs and personal life. They'd decided that when they'd started dating, and she assumed it was still in place. So no, she couldn't be mad.

"Maybe there's a list of hikers," Crystal said. "The search team must've tried to figure out who was hiking the same time as Lydia."

Bernie had thought that, too, but didn't want to say. There were firewalls between herself and her sources, too. "Let's just say something bad happened that wasn't suicide and wasn't natural," she said. "Why? Especially way out there on the trail. That's what stopped the police short. Murder doesn't make sense."

"It could've been that guy who killed his girlfriend," Crystal said. "Or the hermit."

"I thought of them," Bernie said. "It doesn't seem like Danny

Fuller's style and I don't know that the Rambler has ever hurt anyone. No one's ever even talked to him that we know of."

"Maybe he never had to before," Crystal said. "She saw him or came upon his stash of stolen goods and was going to tell on him."

"Maybe." Bernie had developed an affection for the Midnight Rambler, or, she knew, her fantasy of him. She battled with it, particularly after so many camp owners had described to her how violated and terrorized they felt by being targeted over and over by break-ins and thefts. She always kind of pictured meeting him someday. It'd be like Scout in *To Kill a Mockingbird*. "Hey, Boo." Fantasy and reality aside, she didn't envision him as a murderer.

"Is there a reason Lydia wouldn't have her GPS or compass?" Bernie asked.

"Why are you asking?" Crystal was suddenly on guard.

"I heard they may not have found them with her stuff, and since you have her stuff, you'd be the one who'd know." Bernie had just connected the dots on that.

"She lost the GPS around Rangeley," Crystal said. "She didn't know how to use a compass. She didn't have one."

"Seriously?" Bernie was shocked. You don't hike without a compass.

"The trail is very well-marked," Crystal said, annoyed. "She could never quite figure out how to use one and didn't think she'd need it. She wasn't even that concerned about the GPS, except that it cost a lot."

Bernie wondered how she hadn't known that about Lydia. Maybe because it was so basic, she'd just assumed she'd had a compass. They'd talked about the GPS, because it was so cool, but that was early in Lydia's trip, a Skype from Virginia. Bernie'd never asked about the compass. It'd be like asking about her socks.

"Did the fire chief or police chief tell you something you're not telling me?" Crystal asked.

Bernie tried to hold Crystal's gaze. "Of course not."

"You seem very accepting of the fact it may not be suicide."

Bernie shrugged. "It's what I do. Question things."

"I've always been forthcoming with you, so I hope if you know something, you'll tell me. She was my friend." She looked at her watch. "I have to go. I'll reiterate that she didn't commit suicide. Someone killed her. Maybe it was some crazy random trail hiker. I'm sure it won't be the first time that's happened. Maybe it was Wilson, or the hermit, or the girlfriend murderer. It's not up to me to find out who and why, it's up to the police. I want to know why they don't care."

"Who knows?" Bernie said. Random murders didn't happen nearly as often as people thought they did, and certainly not in the Maine woods or on the Appalachian Trail, but there was no point telling people that. Crystal didn't seem that interested in an answer, anyway.

"I have other press to speak to," Crystal said.

"Okay," Bernie said. She could guess who the "other press" was. The rest of the media had fled town. It was back to the locals. "I hope you respect our professional relationship enough to keep what we discussed confidential." She wanted to say "By all that's holy, don't tell Feckless Kelley about the case file."

Crystal sighed. "Bernie, I'm just like you. I just want to find out what happened."

CHAPTER 6

Bernie tried to focus on work and stop second-guessing every little thing, tried to bat away the doom. She'd given in and texted Pete, even though she knew he wouldn't see it until he was off the trail: BTW I lv U. She hated texting. Hated trying to figure out which number keys correspond with what letter and how many times to push it. It was like writing in Morse code. Carrie, the evangelist for the digital age, kept telling Bernie she should get an iPhone. Carrie had one, and it was pretty cool. She even got email on it and could shoot video. The thought of that much stuff to do on a phone scared the hell out of Bernie, though. She had enough trouble navigating the simple not always reliable phone she had now.

Texting Pete brought whatever momentum she'd built up over the morning to a halt. She stared at her computer, so it'd almost look like she was working, as she cycled through the rehash of regrets and second-guesses. She knew when the loop started she had to let it play until the end.

She wished they'd talked more Saturday night and Sunday morning about his PTSD. Maybe he had a different attitude about it now than before they broke up. When she'd brought it up on that miserable ride back from Phippsburg on Memorial Day, suggesting he get help, he'd said, "Quickest way to lose my job."

"Going on like you are is the quickest way to lose your job," she'd said. "They have to help you. It's the law."

He snapped back at her, so unlike Pete it left her speechless. "You of all people should know what talking to your supervisors about a mental health issue does for your career."

Hard to argue with that. That was the last time she'd brought it up, though it's not like she'd had another chance because they broke up the next day.

She took a break from the mental treadmill to make sure everyone was still on schedule with articles and ad layouts. They were. It's almost like they didn't need her at all. She had to edit stories, finish her own story. Find stuff to fill the holes. Tuesdays usually ended close to midnight, even if she left the office at suppertime and finished up on her laptop at home.

She'd felt behind earlier, but now, after reassessing, she felt ahead of the game. She probably wasn't, just another illusion, but she'd go with it.

She stepped out to the parking lot and went down to the table. It was getting close to noon, but there was still a hot morning haze, shimmering sunlit fog poking through the pines and maples. Working on the Lydia story had deepened her funk. It'd bothered Bernie ever since Lydia got lost that she'd seemed so prepared. She'd been so happy, so determined. It had still all gone to shit. Now she couldn't separate it from Pete.

Bernie'd played a game with herself as winter turned to the Maine season of less winter. When did she first know she'd fallen in love with him? She'd always felt a glow, warm and welcoming, even when they were at odds. A few weeks after they started dating, though, on an icy snow-speckled late afternoon, she was locking up the office when she heard him shout. She looked up to see him walking down the street toward her. He'd been in court in Farmington and was wearing a suit and a long black overcoat, open to the wind, blowing behind him. He was smiling like seeing her was the best thing that had ever happened to him. Maybe it was the clothes, or the way the wind ruddied his face and tossed his hair, like something out of a book about a much more romantic life than the one she had. Maybe the smile. The way he hurried toward her. She was pretty sure that was when she knew it. She'd had to hold onto the doorknob to steady herself.

In college she'd fallen for a guy because he knew all the words to "Rosalita." In the two decades since, she'd refined her criteria, though liking Springsteen still didn't hurt. Once she was teasing her ten-year-old niece about boyfriends and asked what her niece liked in a guy. She'd expected some ten-year-old answer. But Elise had said, "He has to have my back and not treat me like I'm stupid." Bernie couldn't think of a better way to put it. Pete, aside from a whole slew of positives, had her back, for real, when it counted, not just when it was convenient. And he genuinely liked her, aside from loving her—outbursts, obsessions, sarcasm, opinions, bad jokes and all.

She loved him, and it didn't match any of the things she'd expected love to be when she'd tried to figure it out before him. It was just theirs, no one else's.

Somewhere, cocooned in the snow, their love grew. She knew he had PTSD, but he seemed okay, at least most of the time. It'd been easy to discount what he wouldn't talk about: his restless sleep and nightmares, so startling to Bernie when they first started dating. His troubles faded in that cold dark closet of Maine winter.

As the days warmed up and the snow went away, though, it became obvious how precarious everything was. The snow had muffled everything, let her hope. The world began to open up and things fell apart. The *Murdertown: USA* episode accelerated things, their town exposed, laid bare in two poorly narrated hours. Pete hadn't wanted to be on it, but everyone, including Bernie, made the argument that the show was going to be made anyway, and he was the best person to tell the story.

No, not *Dateline*, she was always correcting her family. Not *48 Hours*. It was *Murdertown: USA*, a lower-tier show on some obscure channel. Even so, it seemed everyone in the world had watched it.

Pete was thoughtful and articulate onscreen, despite his reluctance. She realized afterwards reluctance wasn't the right word. He hated it. When he watched the show, at her insistence, it was with clenched jaw and white face. In the days and weeks after, he crumbled in little pieces. The quick bursts of irritability or anger, so unlike him. Migraines. His fingernails digging into his palms, even when his voice was calm. The sharp intake of breath, then holding it. He was fine. *Fine.* She wanted to believe him, so she did.

It didn't help that as winter broke, her job became chaos. Personnel issues, and, hard to believe, the problems that came with increasing circulation and record ad sales. Newspapers in 2010 were still clawing to stay alive after what may have been the worst year ever for the industry, but there'd been a lot of big news in Redimere in 2009. The *Watcher* had benefited. She was focused on work, so focused she'd made miscalculations with the relationship. She missed signals, tripped over emotional detours. She'd talked herself out of seeing reality.

As she sat at the picnic table listening to cheerful shouts from the street, the giddiness that summer was finally here, she couldn't enjoy it. Lydia's death was a giant metaphor for the demon that always hovered, reminding her not to get too happy. You could be having the time of your life, hiking along the Appalachian Trail, blogging about the fantastic, inspiring adventure, your own personal pair of handmaidens making sure you were taken care of. Everyone loving you, rooting for you. The next thing you know you're lost, lying on a damp sleeping bag in a smelly little coffin-shaped tent, no idea where you are in the thick unforgiving woods, waiting to die and no one coming to save you, wondering how things went so wrong. Then some asshole puts a Ziploc bag over your head.

Okay, in Bernie's case it was a figurative Appalachian Trail. She wasn't dying—that she knew of —but she still felt that truth. She'd known it long before the surprising, terrible end to Lydia Manzo.

Like 9/11. You're at your desk eating a bagel. It's a beautiful high-definition blue sky September morning, you're booting up the computer and wishing that annoying co-worker would stop whistling. It's eight-thirty dammit, too early for that shit. Thirty minutes later you're about to jump to your death because it's better than being burned alive, clutching the hand of the annoying whistler, who's now the most important person in your life because you're going to close your eyes and whistle along with him, hoping you die in mid-air before you hit the asphalt.

Maybe 9/11 was an extreme metaphor, but that unexpected life-shattering shock had happened in smaller ways as long as she could remember. She'd bounce off into the world, ready to meet it, life all high-definition blue sky, no warning signs, the trail seemingly well-marked, only to be blindsided. Warning signs? Her life was a daily parade of warning signs. How was she supposed to know which ones were real? So she was on guard. She'd been on guard long before Lydia Manzo. Long before 9/11, which, she admitted, she watched with disbelief from the comfort of her kitchen hundreds of miles away.

Bernie felt it now, sitting behind the Watcher when she should be in there working. She'd wandered off the trail. No GPS. No compass. She wished to hell Pete hadn't left, because the feeling had a very specific message this time, now that she'd obsessed about it for twenty-four hours. It was telling her she was never going to see him again.

*****

Pete had taken a roundabout route to get a feel for the area, but close to noon he came upon the clearing that had been Lydia's final resting place. When they were searching for her, the terrain had seemed brutal. No one knew there was an overgrown logging road that led practically to where she was, screened by a couple dozen yards of trees and brush. Too bad Lydia didn't realize it either. She could have walked out fresh as a daisy.

The dumb happenstance of the whole thing was a stunner, another thing that if anyone had connected the dots, could have led to her earlier. Bernie, apparently, had talked to Lydia about the old logging roads and where they led, the stuff she'd mapped out in her Rambler research. She was fascinated by the overgrown logging camps and fire towers, vestiges from before two towns a little northeast were flooded to make Flagstaff Lake.

Crystal's tipster said that Lydia was off to see something Bernie had told her about, old foundations of a logging camp or something.

He was surprised Bernie hadn't thought of it while they were still looking for Lydia, remembered that she'd told her. It's the kind of thing she'd normally remember. But he knew, too, that when she had a lot going on, there could be enormous, obvious black holes in what she would normally know. He knew it embarrassed her, and he wasn't going to say anything to her about Lydia and the logging road conversation. There was no point giving Bernie a reason to beat herself up any more than she already did.

The clearing where Lydia had camped was small, a treeless patch of dirt at the base of a rock fall. Big enough for Lydia's little tent and to stretch her legs. Big enough, too, for a campfire, but she hadn't made one. He looked up. Blue sky. Searchers would've seen the smoke. There were enough scattered fallen branches, pine cones and leaves around to light a dozen. He took off his pack and sat on a rock. The air cooled his wet back as he took out his water bottle and his one sandwich—the rest of the trip would be ramen noodles, trail mix, jerky and dried fruit. As he ate, he assessed the site. Aside from scuffs in the dirt from the recovery party, it didn't look like anyone had ever been here. Nothing to indicate it's where someone had spent the last days of her life. The clearing would've been hard for her to find—there was no natural break in the trees between it and the logging road. But she'd been lost, climbing, trying to get a cell signal. Hikers were taught to go downhill when they're lost. It's basic. She hadn't done that. Sandy said he'd seen it before, people forgetting logic in the panic of being lost, He'd even seen people who were certain their compass was wrong and had wandered miles in the wrong direction because of it.

Pete finished eating and circled the site, poking around the underbrush. Lydia would've dug a hole for her waste. Her friends said she was fastidious, always had tissue to wipe, which she always buried. He couldn't find a sign she'd buried anything.

He toed the bottom of the rock slide. It wouldn't make sense to bury waste there. He nudged the smaller rocks at the bottom and a flash of white caught his eye. It was a plastic bottle, the size of his thumb. The crew that cleared the campsite should've seen it, but maybe they weren't looking, just focusing on her tent. He lifted it with a stick, careful not to touch it. The pharmacy label was mostly rubbed off, even though the bottle looked new. There was enough left, though, to read the name of the drug: baclofen. He'd heard of it—it's for back pain or spasms. He dropped the bottle into the baggie his sandwich had been in and put it in the front pocket of his pack.

The area was remote, but in a way, not. He'd hiked near here with Sandy back in May. Lydia was just a name in the *Watcher* then, not yet in Maine. He hadn't been paying much attention, but he'd been here then for the same reason Lydia ended up here—Bernie's map and the promise of something exotic. The promise was kept— he and Sandy had found remnants of century-old civilization. Weathered barn boards, piled stones. A rusted pump sunk in the ground.

Sandy had just adopted Heidi, a regal German shepherd who'd flunked out of state police K-9 training. She was frantic at times, running back and forth, yipping, digging. Sandy said she was chasing old ghosts. It'd been a good day.

The first thing Sandy had said to Pete when he called him from the trailhead after he found Lydia, was that her face was cherry red from CO. Sandy did CO workshops all over Maine. He was considered an expert. If he said that's what it was, then that's what it was. Sandy had also seen a lot of suicides as an EMT and firefighter, and said even without the red face, she didn't look like someone who'd suffocated herself with a plastic bag. The shoelace around the bottom of the bag, holding it close to her neck, wasn't tight enough. She hadn't fought it, scratching at her neck, trying to get the bag off like even those determined to die do. There were always scratch marks. Sandy said if she'd had the strength to undo her shoelace, put the bag over her head and secure it with the lace, she would have also had the strength to try to get it off when suffocation panic set in. Sandy also hadn't seen any petechiae—the broken blood vessels in the eyes that indicate asphyxia. They should be there if she'd suffocated. Pete agreed with all that—he'd investigated a lot of deaths, too. He hadn't seen Lydia's body, but he trusted Sandy.

Lydia also had blisters on her face and neck. Sandy couldn't tell what they were. The medical examiner had noted them, but not as anything significant. Maybe sunburn, or allergies.

Sandy thought the scratches on her bare calves and arms meant something, too. They were fresh and looked like they were from blackberry bushes. There were no blackberries around the campsite and she hadn't been in good enough health to wander. Pete had been looking for blackberry brambles on his hike and had yet to see one vine.

The investigators thought it was all bullshit. The cherry red? More like the cyanosis that appears with asphyxia, and the beginning of decomposition. She was in a hot, humid tent and decomposition would start fast. The lack of petechiae? It'd been a Ziploc bag, not a garrote.

"Why do you people always have to screw things up?" George Libby said to Pete. It was a rhetorical question. "This time it's not even your department, it's the fire chief. I know that guy, and I wouldn't believe him if he said the sun was coming up in the fucking east."

Libby had almost spit the words. Blackberry bush scratches? The woods were full of all sorts of shit—Libby had shown Pete the scratches and bug bites on his own pale city legs as evidence. Who the hell gave a shit? Libby said it a dozen times.

Pete gave a shit. He'd been a homicide cop for a long time and knew that when something was out of place, it should be considered. Sandy had done his job as a first responder and checked Lydia for vitals. He got a good long look at her. Pete guessed by the time the medical examiner had her, the CO red had worn off as decomposition took hold. It took forever to get her out of there. They'd talked about getting her somewhere the Lifeflight helicopter could land, but she wasn't alive, so there was no rush, it wasn't worth the expense. It was hot and dripping humid out, and it took the recovery party hours to get to her, get her out of the woods, and then to Augusta in Friday night summer traffic. Then the autopsy wasn't performed until Saturday morning.

The campsite was quickly packed up, her stuff to be looked at in Augusta, too, where the lab was air conditioned, rather than in the buggy, sticky woods of the Franklin County high peaks in June. The bottle Pete found proved they rushed it, if nothing else did.

He also knew that Sandy was a country boy, much more than Pete. More than George Libby. If Sandy thought scratches from blackberry bushes meant something, they meant something.

The bottle was a nice surprise; he didn't think he'd find anything. He'd just hoped seeing the campsite and area would help things fall into place. It was his comfort zone, a good distraction. No, it was more than that. Every bad thing that had happened over the past year on his watch had rocketed out of his control. He knew checking out her campsite was a game to make himself feel like his old self. Maybe he'd figure something out, though, and then he could do something about it. Or convince someone to do something about it, more likely, and it would be a victory and he could feel like himself again.

CHAPTER 7

Bernie had to get back to work, but she just couldn't. That loop in her head wasn't played out and it kept coming to Memorial Day weekend, the key, she was sure, to when things went wrong with Lydia and where they went wrong for Bernie.

As she and Pete drove south that Friday, she kept apologizing for the rain. He kept telling her he didn't mind. Still, she felt it was her fault. It'd been her idea to go to Phippsburg, on one of Maine's mid-coast peninsulas, a three-hour drive. It was one of her favorite places, and she wanted him to see it. He'd lived in Maine for nearly two years but hadn't seen much more than their crazy little corner of the state.

She'd interviewed Lydia the night before, at the Pour House. Bernie had been looking forward to it for a long time, but it ended up feeling off, flat. She couldn't put her finger on why and lay awake all night afterwards, picking it apart.

As they drove down Route 27, cutting through Augusta, then angling toward Bath, she tried to explain it to Pete.

"She's tired," he said. "She's hiked two thousand miles."

"It was more like she was jumpy," Bernie said. "Nervous."

"You're thinking of yourself. Relax, come on. It's a weekend away. Our first." He smiled at her, but he looked tired, too.

They drove down the Phippsburg peninsula, the dark sky spitting rain as they followed the Kennebec River spreading out to the Atlantic. She tried to force herself into vacation mode. "At least it won't be crowded."

"Bad weather doesn't bother me." Pete sounded like he meant

it. It didn't bother her either. She preferred it. No sunburned crowds of tourists getting in their way. A cozy fire, books to read. Just the two of them.

The dirt road to her brother Tommy's cabin climbed through the trees, which were just beginning to pop bright green. The Maine moment—and it really was a moment—when the earth splits open and explodes lush green was still a week or two away. The drive was steep, the woods scattered with boulders, the trees tangled by centuries of ocean wind. They were driving into another world, where just the two of them existed.

"Perfect," Pete said when they walked into the cabin. He'd said from the beginning he liked that option more than a bed and breakfast or motel. "More romantic."

She knew what it really was—he didn't want to stay where someone could hear his nightmares.

"Want to see my favorite beach in the world?" The rain had stopped, though it was still misty and gray. She felt like an anxious tour guide.

"Absolutely," Pete said.

"We have to hike in."

"I love it already."

They parked in the nearly empty lot at the Bates-Morse Mountain Preserve trailhead. The beach was down a two-mile former logging road through forest and across a marsh. "It's almost like nature makes you work for it," Bernie said.

They walked in silence for a few minutes. The salt air smelled good and Bernie began to cheer, despite the misty weather.

"Did I ever tell you about my grandfather?" Pete asked.

Totally out of the blue. Of course he hadn't. He rarely said anything about his family.

"No, I don't think so."

"He was in the Czech resistance. He wanted to stay and fight the Nazis, but he was young, and his parents pulled some strings so he could come here."

"Lucky for him."

56

"He never saw them again. They died in the war."

"Concentration camp?"

"My great-grandmother, yeah, along with his sisters. They lived in a village, Lezaky. When the Nazis occupied it, they shot all the men over sixteen, including my great-grandfather, and sent the women to concentration camps. My great-grandmother and my grandfather's two sisters, who were eleven and twelve when he left, died. He died when I was thirteen."

"Lezaky." Bernie tried it out, trying to say it the way Pete had. "Were you close to him?"

"Yeah. I was named after him. Petricek. He was more comfortable talking about his family and that type of thing in Czech, but everyone spoke English most of the time. So, I would, you know, in Czech."

She wanted to ask him more about his family, but he seemed done. She wondered where it'd come from, that burst of family history. Later, when she thought about it, it seemed loaded with portent, him thinking about his survivor grandfather and the people who didn't survive.

The end of the trail opened onto a beach that stretched flat in either direction, peninsulas covered in pine trees and rock outcroppings at either end, rock rising out of the sea in front of them. The only other people in sight were a man, sitting on a towel, and two young girls, shrieking and laughing as they chased the surf, yelling "Dad! Look Dad! Did you see that?"

"The tide's coming in," Bernie said. They took off their shoes and walked toward the water.

"How can you tell?"

"The waves. See the swells and how close together they are? I always think of it like it's rushing to get here."

The cold water made her feet ache. "Yikes." She stepped back into dry sand and dug in her toes.

Pete stood in the water, up to his knees, the waves crashing against his legs, soaking his shorts. He raised his arms and stretched, then stepped forward. She imagined him walking straight into the water, walking and not stopping, until he was gone. It was so real she wanted to call out and tell him to stop.

He turned and came back, smiling.

It was a silly thought. She smiled back.

"That felt good." He sat down on the sand.

"I think there's an offshore storm," she said, sitting next to him. The ocean cooperated by crashing a large wave on nearby rocks. She tried to find the calm that a vacation was supposed to bring. It always took a couple days to kick in. A weekend, even a long one, wasn't enough. It wasn't going to happen a few hours in. She gave up.

"I'm firing Sean when we get back."

"About time," Pete said. "He can move back to OJ's mansion."

She'd referred to Sean Speck as Kato Kaelin so much sometimes she got the two mixed up. He had the same floppy hair, the same aging surfer-dude act. She suspected Sean spent most of the time he was supposed to be working actually smoking dope in his condo up by Sugarloaf, waiting for ski season.

"The difference between Kato and Sean is that Kato had a millionaire willing to indulge him," Bernie said. "I know I said I was desperate for a photographer, but I'm not that desperate."

"Atta girl."

"Thanks for not saying 'I told you so.'"

"No point."

"One of the many reasons I love you. We can just go back to doing photos the way we had before. Me, Carrie. Carol, though she's going to Costa Rica until mid-July. I can always try a freelancer, I guess, if I can find another one. When I first started using Sean, he was the only one I could find. Still, maybe there's someone. I just won't make the mistake —"

"Hey." Pete took her hand. "Hey, hey, hey." She'd been clutching the sand, digging her fingers in and squeezing. He unclenched her fist, his fingers warm and strong. The sand fell back where it belonged. He turned her palm up, and resting it in his, brushed sand away, his fingers passing over her palm again and again, even after all the sand, that coarse Maine sand, was gone.

. She watched the water, gray and roiling, churning toward the beach. His fingers passed across her palm, pressed against it, hypnotizing her. They burned with an electric current. She began to relax.

"We're not going to spend the weekend talking about Sean Speck," he said. "Or the newspaper. Or your brother, or Ryan Grant, or *Murdertown: USA,* or the police department."

She kept her eyes on the waves. "What the hell are we going to talk about?"

"We'll think of something." He kissed her palm, and then enclosed her hand in both of his. He was tender like that, something she wasn't used to. She felt that drop in the pit of her stomach, love and fear rolled into one. Maybe they'd talk and everything would be okay. She'd realize he was fine, just overworked. She snuck a glance at him. He was looking out to sea. He still had her hand encased between both of his, his warmth passing into her. She burrowed her feet into the sand. He lay back, his tanned legs stretched out in front of him, sand stuck to the wet hair. He let go of her hand, but rested one of his on her back, warm and firm. He was okay. Everything was okay. She wanted to say it out loud, ask him if she was right.

"I gave Lydia these letters people had sent to the paper for her." Bernie turned to see if Pete was listening.

"Mmm hmmm."

"She kind of read them while we talked at the Pour House last night. They were well-wishers, that type of thing. But she seemed bothered. Maybe I should have asked her about it."

"You can ask her after she summits Katahdin."

There'd be different things to ask then. "Bothered" wasn't the right word. Lydia had changed after the letters. She was distracted, maybe, but more than that. Her friends hadn't seemed to notice. Bernie caught her eye at one point and she'd looked like she was asking something, signaling, then the moment was gone. Probably Bernie's imagination. Hiking the AT can sap a person and Lydia probably had a lot on her mind.

59

The two girls at the water's edge, maybe seven and four— Bernie could never gauge age well despite her scads of nieces and nephews—shrieked and giggled as they raced the waves onto the sand, little shore birds piping and chirping over the water's crash. Their dad's eyes stayed on his phone. There wasn't even cell service out here. What could be more interesting than your kids? She saw it all the time, though. People would rather post photos of their kids on Facebook—look at me, I'm so involved with my kids!—than interact with them.

She looked back over her shoulder at Pete. His arm was flung over his eyes as though shielding them from a non-existent sun. "How you doing?" she asked.

"Fine. This is perfect." His hand flexed on her back.

She watched the girls chase each other like puppies, trying to remember what it was like to be that age, when the icy water didn't hurt and the most fun you ever had in your life was every moment.

The older one swam, a churning kid-stroke that didn't get her far, then she'd stop and jump toward the swells. She laughed as the waves lifted her or crashed past her.

"Dad, look at that one. Look at that one. Dad, watch me!"

"Okay, honey." He didn't look up.

The girl was farther out, her dark head bobbing. Bernie couldn't tell if she was still shouting. There was a noise, but was it the girl, or one of the gulls circling and diving above? The thought formed slowly, the obvious coming together in little pieces, not clear until they arranged themselves. She knew it was coming, but couldn't hurry it. It had frustrated teachers and bosses, who figured she was either dumb or playing games. It frustrated her more. She saw it, felt it, just couldn't get to it. Like now. The alarm rose with the slow-motion thought. "Um," she said, trying to get to the words. Pete stirred behind her. "Um," she said, louder.

The younger of the two girls stood on the sand, water playing at her feet, watching her sister. She turned to her father. *She's thinking the same thing.* The slow train of alarm picked up steam. The older girl was too far out, her head disappearing behind swells. Was that her shouting, or a gull? Bernie tried again to separate the sounds. "Um."

Wouldn't the dad know if there were a problem? Some kind of parental instinct? Maybe she was overreacting. The girl seemed to know how to swim. Bernie breathed in, her fog was lifting. The girl's head appeared, and Bernie heard a distinct shriek, strangled and so far away.

Bernie turned to Pete. "Should she—"

He was already on his feet, running to the water, shedding his flannel shirt, then his T-shirt. Then he was diving into the waves. He swam strong, sure strokes toward where the bobbing head had last been.

Bernie ran behind, picking up his clothes.

The dad was at her side. "Caitlin? Caitlin!" he screamed and ran toward the surf. "CAITLIN!"

"He's got her," Bernie yelled. But she didn't know that. The girl's head hadn't popped back up. She couldn't see Pete, either, the swells higher, more frequent, breaking white on top of each other. Bernie thought of the stories—there were so many—of people being swept by a rip tide to their death. Still, it was Pete. He was strong and fearless, and she knew from personal experience that there were no better hands to put a life into. If only she could see him, be sure he was okay.

"Pete!" She pressed his still-warm shirts to her chest.

Several yards out, his head surfaced. "Where is she?" His voice was thin above the crashing surf, which was getting fiercer.

Bernie scanned the swells, then farther out, where they were big, but more spread out, without as many whitecaps. There she was, way out, farther from where she'd been just moments before, an anchorless buoy. Bernie pointed, but Pete had seen her too.

The father paced, his other daughter, her hands clutched to her chest, hopping beside him, crying.

"Where is she?" he asked. "Oh my God, oh my God."

He turned to Bernie. "Why's he swimming so slow? He's not even going to her." He walked out a few more steps. "Caitlin! Over here!"

He was right. Pete seemed to be making little progress for the amount of effort, swimming perpendicular to the beach, rather than straight to the girl.

"Riptide," Bernie said, her eyes on Pete.

"Where's he going? GO GET HER!"

The two heads disappeared behind a swell, then there they were, together, moving parallel to the beach in the other direction.

"He got her," Bernie said. The heads moved together slowly, not toward them, but not farther out.

The father yelled, "Over here," as if Pete didn't know where the beach was. When Pete finally angled toward the beach, the father rushed toward them, meeting them as they came out of the surf, the girl's arms wrapped around Pete's neck. She was sobbing. So was her sister. So was the dad. Bernie was, too. Pete was the only one not crying. He was breathing hard, but looked calm. Just another day at the beach.

The father held out his arms for his child. Bernie knew a story about Pete, something that had happened to him years before. How he'd picked up a little girl covered in blood at a homicide scene, the unhurt living victim, and wouldn't let her go. It's when things fell apart for him in Philadelphia, the aftershock still being felt. His eyes met Bernie's over the head of the crying girl in his arms. She saw deep fear, just for a second, then it was gone. Maybe it hadn't been there at all, she'd imagined it because of that other girl.

Pete gently loosed the girl's grip from around his neck, and peeled her off, handing her to her father. "Riptide," he said, gasping.

"Oh my God, thank you." The father took the girl. "I just looked away for a minute." He didn't look at them as he said it.

The girl clung to her dad with the same ferocity she'd clung to Pete. Her little sister tugged at her father's shorts. "Dad. Dad."

"Get her warm, fast," Pete said, no longer gasping, his voice steady, though he was soaking wet, his skin pebbled from the cold. "Have a doctor check her out. I don't think she's hurt, but she's hypothermic."

"Should I call an ambulance?" The father looked from Pete to Bernie. "I mean, I know there's no cell service, but I could, I don't know, call or something."

"The fastest thing would be to go to the cabins," Pete said, gesturing back to the path, where there were conservation area rentals. Tenants were the only ones allowed to drive through the gate two miles away. "I saw cars. Get someone there to drive you to your car. Call an ambulance the minute you have cell service. Tell them you're going north on 209 and they'll meet you. Get her warm first. Right now."

Pete's tone, full-on police chief, got the father moving. He took the younger girl by the arm and jogged back to their stuff, wrapped a towel around his sobbing wet daughter, told her everything was going to be all right.

Then Bernie and Pete were alone on the beach, the only noise Pete's shaky breath and the gulls. The whole thing had taken less than ten minutes.

"Holy shit," Bernie said. "Are you okay?"

Pete was trembling, his lips blue. Bernie still clutched his shirts to her chest. "Dry off and put these on," she said. The father had left the beach towel. Bernie figured he owed Pete that, at least. "I'll get the towel." But she didn't move, the concept beyond her ability. Pete walked toward the towel, drying himself off with the T-shirt. He put on the flannel shirt but didn't button it. His hands were shaking.

"Let me get that," she said. He stood, like a kid, his eyes on her face as she buttoned.

A car started in the distance, then tires screeched on gravel.

"Good," Pete said.

She held out the towel. "Take off your shorts and put this on."

He took off his shorts and boxers, wrapped the towel around his waist. Bernie picked up their shoes. "We can get some coffee at that store," she said. "Warm you up."

"Coffee'd be good." The shakiness was still there, but

otherwise it was the same tone he'd have if they were walking down Main Street in Redimere.

They double-timed back to the car, Bernie skipping to keep up. The two miles seemed longer than it had on the hike out. She was stunned by the unreality, the deadly drama that had come so fast, then disappeared back into the gray mist. Her life as 9/11.

"You'll have to drive," he said when they got to the parking lot. He turned over the lump of his wet shorts until he found the pocket with the keys. "I didn't even think about these." He pulled out his wallet. "Or this."

She'd been fooled by his matter-of-fact tone, but now that the shock was wearing off, she knew better. His shaking was worse, his teeth chattering. She turned the heat in the car up as high as it would go. Fat raindrops hit the windshield as she approached the intersection with Route 209.

"Jesus, Pete."

"It's okay, Bernie. It's fine." His fists were clenched tightly in his lap, his eyes straight ahead. He seemed like he was trying, but not succeeding, to take deep breaths.

"You'd think your brand new used car would have heat," she said, checking the knob again. She'd hoped the joke, that he'd replaced his aging car with an only slightly less aging one, would get the laugh it usually did.

His fists clenched and unclenched. His trembling shook the car. At least that's how it felt.

"Are you okay?"

"Fine," he said.

"No, you're not."

He took a deep breath, as though he were going to say something big, but all that came out was, "If I'm not, I don't want to talk to about it." He turned and looked out the window.

The hot air blasted at them, finally. Rain pelted the windshield. The noise of both roared in her ears, making it hard to think. She turned up the wipers, adding rhythm to the chaos.

"Are you having a panic attack?" she asked. She'd seen the

signs before, though she never asked—he obviously hadn't wanted to talk about it.

"I'm fine. Not a big deal," he said, his voice thin and cracked, no longer matter-of-fact.

"Bullshit." She was sick of dancing around, him saying everything was fine and her letting him. "You're having a panic attack."

"I'm hypothermic."

Bernie didn't want to quit now that she'd finally started. "I love you no matter what. I want to help you. I can't if you pretend your PTSD doesn't exist. You're so smart about everything, but about this, it's like you're some cliché out of a bad TV show. The haunted cop. That guy always ends up destroying himself and the people around him, if you're not familiar."

"There's nothing to talk about. Even if there was, it wouldn't do any good."

Her urge to argue about it died as fast as it'd come on. It wasn't the right time. It wasn't fair to expect him to do anything but sit there and shake. She pulled into the store parking lot. A pile of camp wood on the porch, four dollars a bundle, was getting soaked on the crowded porch. Inside smelled like cinnamon, car oil and, yes, coffee. She navigated the shelves, too many jammed along the tilted wood floor, to the coffee station in the back. The store soothed her. The warmth, the smells, the shelves of junk food and motor oil, the wooden floor, the board on the wall with fishing lures, the large lottery display and congealing pizza in the heated glass case were touchstones. She could be anywhere in Maine. She could be in Redimere. She took a deep breath. Everything was okay. It was normal for Pete to be shaken up. Anyone would be. The girl was okay. They didn't have to solve every problem today.

She got two of the largest cardboard cups from the stack. She chose the dark roast, double-checked to make sure it wasn't decaf. The different carafes of half and half, skim milk, whole milk, soy milk slowed her down. She sniffed to see which one was the least spoiled, and settled on the half and half. She realized too late she'd put some in Pete's, as well as sugar. He took his coffee black. Chalk up another misstep for her.

Back in the car, he took the coffee with both hands.

"Got us a scratch ticket," she said. She put her cup in the holder, careful not to slop coffee the way she would in her car without even thinking.

She scratched, trying to ignore him picking at the plastic tab on the cover on his cup with unsteady hands. If he didn't have it pulled up before she was done with the ticket, she'd do it for him. No fuss.

"Five dollars," she said. "Now I can get that operation." He didn't say anything. "Whoa, tough crowd." She made a drum roll sound. He chuckled, short and quiet. She'd take it.

"Maybe invest in some new jokes," he said as he took the top off the coffee.

"If it ain't broke, don't fix it, as my old man would say." She started the car, driving slowly so his coffee wouldn't spill.

He made a choking noise.

"What?" She hit the brakes, afraid he was having another attack. The coffee sloshed onto his hand and lap.

"What's in this?" He wiped at his lap with his sleeve.

"Cream and sugar. Figured you could use some fortification." She handed him napkins—she always grabbed some when she had coffee in the car—then shifted into first and touched the gas, nice and slow.

"I'm sorry," he said. "I was being an asshole."

"You stole my apology. You're not being an asshole, I'm being self-absorbed and non-empathetic."

"You're fine." He took a long sip. "I love you. Just don't ever get me coffee again."

She laughed, relieved. The rain was still heavy, bouncing up from the pavement, drumming on the car roof. She drove slow, searching through the rain-distorted windshield for anything familiar in the woods, afraid she'd miss the turnoff to the cabin.

"I feel like Lydia was scared," Bernie said. She's not sure why it came to her. Maybe the look in Pete's eyes ever since they got in the car. "She'd been on the trail all those months, though. Why would she be scared? Is that dumb?"

She looked over to see if he was listening. He was trembling, his face white. She almost didn't hear it under the rain and the wipers, the rusty blow of the heater. "No, it's not dumb."

Now as she sat behind the Watcher, she wished she'd said more. About Lydia, because she *was* scared. About him, asked him what he was scared of.

Too late now. She went up the stairs, back into the newsroom.

CHAPTER 8

Minutes after she was back at her desk, Bernie got a text from Sandy asking if she had time for a coffee break. For a second she felt that tingle of excitement she felt the last few weeks whenever she got a text from him, but it was only for a second. She really couldn't take the time for another break, but on the other hand he was the one who'd taken Pete to the woods.

They met in the park by the mill a block down Main Street. Not as many prying ears as at Dunkin's or Choppy's, kind of an offsite version of her picnic table behind the Watcher. As she approached him where he sat at the table, she was struck, as she'd always been, at how good he looked in the white shirt and black pants of his fire chief uniform, how handsome he was, with his wavy light brown hair, those damn massive blue eyes. It wasn't love and she wasn't tempted to try to go back on their deal—their fling was just for fun, not a "relationship," and once it was over it was over—but she'd always had a lot of affection for Sandy and was glad their friendship was still intact. "See?" said the bad-girl devil on her shoulder "you *can* have sex just for fun and it doesn't hurt a thing." But the Catholic-guilt angel on the other shoulder, so humorless, so smug and self-righteous, was always there to weigh in, too. "Was it worth it? Did it really not hurt anyone? What would your parents think?" She was forty-four years old, what her parents thought shouldn't matter, but the angel still sat there, shaking its head in disappointment. She shrugged them both off and sat down.

Sandy smiled, a burst of sunshine with perfect white teeth, of course. "Look, I'm sorry about the whole Lydia murder thing, that you can't write about it."

"So am I."

"It's best to let it go."

"Why?"

Sandy laughed. "Why ask why?"

"I'm not in a good mood."

"Okay. Here's why. Because there's too much shit going on already. Because it'll be beating your head against a concrete wall for no blessed good. Because Pete's already on edge, so why poke the bear."

"That brings up another issue, with a lot of sub-issues. Why did he leave? What happened?" She hadn't realized the tears were so close.

"He just needed to get away."

"Did you guys talk?" She wiped her eyes.

"More or less. But I don't have answers for you."

"I'm worried," Bernie said. "He's not himself." How many times had she heard that in the past twenty-four hours?

"Yeah, so I told him. I wasn't very nice."

"What'd you say?"

"I told him to get lost in the woods like Lydia."

"Why'd you say that?" Bernie ground her palms into her eyes. *Make it all stop.*

"We were trading insults, and it seemed like the thing to do. Stop that. You're going to break your eye sockets."

"Why were you trading insults? That's not like either of you."

"He was being an asshole, and I called him on it. I'm annoyed about the Lydia thing, too, you know. I know what I saw. He's going to let someone get away with murder?"

"Is that all you're annoyed about?" Bernie wondered if annoyed was even the right word.

"That's all." Sandy smiled. The self-conscious one he rarely showed, but that she'd gotten to know so well. She called it his cover-up smile. To herself, of course.

"I'm worried something bad's going to happen."

"You just have Lydia Manzo fever. Her dying was a shock and

you're feeling it."

"This is more. I feel doom." The planes into the buildings on the bright sky day. She didn't want to say it out loud. He'd laugh.

"Worst case scenario, he comes back no better than he was, and we do an intervention."

"I'm worried he won't come back." She tried to say it quiet and small so it wouldn't feel so awful.

"He knew I didn't mean it seriously, to get lost."

"It's not what you said. It's him." She was afraid to say it. "Maybe he won't come back."

Sandy turned white under his tan. "Has he said anything that makes you think that?"

"He's not the kind of guy who'd announce it."

"He's not the kind of guy who'd do it."

"What if it's not intentional, but he's just careless and something happens. Like Lydia."

"Someone killed Lydia," Sandy said. His color had returned. "Her carelessness is beside the point. Anyway, as messed up as Pete is, he's never careless."

"Everything's weird and out of control."

"He's tough. He's handled a lot over the years, and it's worn him out."

She felt the tears again. "I don't know."

"Honey, relax." He reached for her hand, and she balled it into a fist and put it in her lap. "How many ways can I say it? Pete's not going to wander into the woods like some old Indian and die."

She wanted to believe him. She didn't know why she was so sure something awful would happen to Pete. Maybe it *was* Lydia fever. It never occurred to her something would happen to Lydia. She seemed, by all accounts, one of the sanest and self-assured people on the planet. Pete was sane and self-assured, too, but the red flags were everywhere. She could hear them flapping, see them in her peripheral vision. Why couldn't anyone else? They were concerned, but fine with him disappearing into the wilderness.

Sandy tilted his face up to the sun. "Beautiful day. Maybe

summer's here for good." He tapped a drumbeat on the table, totally relaxed. Not worried at all. She could take that as a cue that she was worked up about nothing, or as a cue that he didn't care. She didn't like either choice. She tried to picture Pete in the woods, walking along the trail. Sure-footed and confident. She couldn't make it come clear.

"I hope he brought his whistle," Bernie said. The Christmas gift that had felt so right at the time, then seemed so dumb and corny she was embarrassed to give it to him. Now it felt important again.

"I'm sure he did," Sandy said.

"You don't even know what I'm talking about."

"Yes I do. He loves that whistle."

She couldn't tell if he was mocking her or sincere. He wasn't normally a mocker, but everything was sideways. "I hate this," Bernie said. "I hate feeling this. I hate living it."

"Everything'll be okay."

"How can you know that?"

"Let's talk about something else."

"Tell me about Lydia," Bernie said.

"Something else than that, too."

"What did you see? Come on, it'll make me feel better."

"You got me." He smiled, but then looked guilty. "This is totally between us. Off the record."

"Absolutely."

"I think she had CO poisoning. Her face was red. It's unmistakable. There were some other things, too. Little things."

She didn't want to say Dawna had already told her that. She'd expected more. Some big, solid thing. "How would someone kill her with CO poisoning out there? Why don't you think it could be an accident?"

"There was nothing in the tent that could have caused it," he said. "Think of it like she'd been shot. You want a murder weapon. Accident or suicide, the weapon's still there. CO poisoning just doesn't happen. Something causes it."

71

"But could it be something natural? In the atmosphere? Something she ate?"

"None of the above," he said. "Remember, I do CO workshops as part of my job, and I can't even figure it out."

Bernie was beginning to see why the state cops didn't think there was a case for murder.

"Here's a bonus fact, not something I saw, but something I heard them talking about," Sandy said. "It's not about the murder, just something really sad. She tried to text when she got lost, but, you know, no service. The texts stayed in her phone."

"Text who?"

"Clyde, hey Clyde." Fergus Kelley came down the steps from the street.

"Crap," Sandy said.

"Double crap," Bernie said. She focused on looking like she didn't want to pick up a rock and bash Feckless Fergus' pasty face.

"Not giving the *Watcher* an exclusive, I hope," Fergus said as he sat down next to Sandy. "Hi, Bernadette. Long time no see."

There were a lot of things she could say, but wasn't going to give him the satisfaction.

"Clyde, I wondered if I could talk to you in private."

"No one calls me Clyde," Sandy said. "Not even my dad."

"That's a shame. It's a fine name."

"What do you want?" Sandy asked.

"I'll tell you when we talk in private," Fergus said.

"I was just going. Something around here smells." Bernie knew it was a lame line, but she was already upset and if she really thought about how much she hated Fergus, she'd lose it and maybe never get it back. She got up.

"Don't go, Bernie," Sandy said. Then, to Fergus, "I already told you there's nothing to say. Get it from the state police."

"We can talk later," Fergus said. He got up. Bernie sat back down. "We're working on something pretty interesting at *Franklin On Call*. That's me and Sean. They've got a central office in Boston. Setting up online *On Calls* across New England. Print'll be gone by

2018, just wait."

"We could all be gone by 2018," Sandy said. "A lot can happen in eight years."

Eight seconds, even. Bernie felt the planes hitting the buildings. She tried not to think about Pete.

Fergus laughed, a big fake belly laugh. "Anyway, Clyde, you know we've got a hot scoop. Your input would really help. I know you haven't said anything to Bernie about it, because she wouldn't be sitting here all nice to you if you had." Fergus beamed at her.

Bernie focused on looking disinterested.

"Get lost," Sandy said.

"Journalism, you know?" Fergus said. "It's all about boots on the ground. See you later."

They watched him lumber back up the granite stairs to Main Street.

"Boots up his ass, more like," Sandy said.

"What's that about?"

"Nothing. He's bluffing."

"It seemed like something. What's with the Clyde business?"

"He found some old article from years ago, when I worked in Bangor. The papers used to ID me as Clyde C. MacCormack. He's just giving me shit."

"You were in the papers?"

"I was a lieutenant, so I got quoted."

"Why would Fergus Google you?" Maybe she'd Google Sandy herself.

"Not Google. I've been here fifteen years. That was pre-internet."

"He's acting like he's got one on you."

"He's an asshole, you know that better than anyone," Sandy said. "I gotta get back to work."

They walked back down Main Street. When they got to her office, Bernie tapped him lightly on the back. "See ya."

"Bernie." Sandy sounded serious, apprehensive.

"What?"

"Be careful about Lydia, okay?"

"Yeah, okay."

"Yeah, okay." He said it sing-song. "I mean it."

"Talk to you later." She'd decide what she was going to do. She was tired of people telling her to let it go, calm down, not to worry. She opened the door, feeling his eyes on her back. But when she looked, he was walking away, back to the public safety building.

She took a deep breath and walked into the office. The sky outside was impossibly blue, the day shimmering in the heat of real summer after the long winter and the dark, wet spring. It should have made her feel good. But the doom wouldn't let her. Something bad was coming in at three hundred miles an hour, and the bright blue sky didn't fool her at all.

*****

There was nothing left for Pete to see at Lydia's campsite. It wasn't cozy. It was tight and cold. Lonely. He worked his way through the trees back to the logging road, following a faint path that she'd probably followed, that Sandy and his search group had, that the guys bringing out her body had, too. Maybe he could figure out how Lydia got to that little patch in the first place. The AT was less than a mile away, but his maps—not Bernie's mega-map, but the standard topographical maps—didn't show a straight shot from the trail or any of its spurs.

His hike became increasingly difficult as he battled undergrowth and scrabble, circling the area. He felt heavy from lack of sleep and humidity. He followed an overgrown trail, but it faded, became rougher and more difficult, the terrain steep and pocked by ravines and drop-offs, uphills and downhills, with more rocky scrabble. The undergrowth grabbed and scratched at his legs—none of it blackberry. His T-shirt was soaked with sweat, the metal frame of his pack rubbing it against his back. As drained as he was, the heat felt good. So did the discomfort. The bugs, the branches grabbing at his legs. The sweat in his eyes. He wasn't trying to punish himself, he just wanted to feel alive.

He batted away the anger every time the package from his

father came into his head. He tried to think about Lydia, the case. Every time his mind went farther, it scared the shit out of him. He batted that away, too, and concentrated on the terrain. The same terrain Lydia had struggled with when she wandered off the trail, even if it wasn't the same route.

He was going uphill, away from her campsite. This couldn't be right. At least he wouldn't get lost, he had a compass and knew how to use it. That was one good thing that'd come out of his childhood, those summers with his Uncle Victor, camping in Michigan's Upper Peninsula. Never, ever without a compass.

Pete kept an eye out for blackberry, even though he knew he wouldn't find it where he was. It liked the sun and could spread like fire when it got enough, vines and bushes six or seven feet high and dense like barbed wire. He'd had to cut a huge tangle of it at his house when he first moved in last fall. This spring it'd burst back out of the ground like grass. That wouldn't happen here in the cool rocky darkness. Sandy had mused about where she'd wandered that her legs had gotten so tangled in it that she'd had to use her arms to bat away blackberry vines, the scratches criss-crossing her flesh. Not here. Nowhere near here.

Pete found the bare trace of another trail, unused and overgrown, harder to see and follow than the one he'd been on. It skirted a rise on his right, in places so vertical it was a wall of dirt, rock and brush. The other side was a steep drop-off, hard to see in thick growth. It startled him that at first what he thought were shrubs were actually tree-tops. The ground was rocky and uneven with gnarled roots, sudden steep climbs and piles of slides and downed trees. The area had eroded and collapsed over the years, the topography changed with nature and the brutal push and pull of Maine's weather and the rocky earth.

The trail narrowed as he climbed. At some points he had to turn sideways and inch along, his pack scraping against the wall, his boots kicking pebbles that skittered down the steep rock and dirt mountainside below. No way Lydia came up here. Yet he kept going. He knew part of the trail had been a logging road, still shown with a dotted line on the map when he'd looked earlier. It led to a fire tower on the summit, a high spot between the mountains. The fire tower was no longer in use, but like most in remote areas, never removed. He was going to take a break there, have a snack, get his bearings. Maybe hunker down for the rest of the day and stay the night, depending on what it was like. Now he wondered if he'd ever get there.

As he climbed, the trees got thicker and the trail less clear, steeper. Maybe he'd missed a turn. He reached into his pocket for his compass just as his heel slipped and his feet slid out from under him. The ground gave way. He was falling, and, despite the shock of it, he had a flash of wonder that it was a free-fall when he'd expect to be sliding down dirt and rock. Before he had time to think more about it, he slammed to the ground. He landed on his back, the wind knocked out of him, like being hit by a train from below and run flat under. That was his last thought, that and excruciating pain.

CHAPTER 9

Dawna tried to enjoy her coffee, but it wasn't easy. She had a notebook in front of her at the counter at Choppy's, more to make people leave her alone than anything else. She'd just needed to escape the office, where Vicki was more fidgety than ever with Pete gone. The whole town was fidgety. Ryan Grant had called looking for Pete and was pissed he wasn't there, as though it were her fault. She'd asked if she could help and he said no, he didn't think so, it was official town business. She doubted he even knew who she was, though they'd been introduced several times. Dawna had seen it before. It wasn't just older guys—Grant was in his thirties—he saw a bulky, dark twenty-something woman and dismissed her as someone he didn't have to pay attention to. Her to-do list was already too long to worry about it. If it was important, she hoped it'd come to him that he should tell her, since Pete was gone for a week.

Her sister, Debbie, refilled her cup. "I know you can handle things, but he's got a lot of nerve taking off like that," she said.

"I *can* handle things," Dawna said. "You should be happy I have a boss who thinks I'm good at what I do. I've come a long way in two years."

"I'm proud of you, but I can still worry."

"If you really want to help, pretend I'm not here."

Debbie patted her cheek and moved back down the counter.

The murmur of the diner washed over her. She caught snippets of conversation, the long vowels of Franklin County mixing with the clipped syllables of the people from away. Two little voices behind her wiggled their way to the front.

Dawna had seen her cousin Natalie and Natalie's friend Hallowell sucking sodas through straws in a booth when she came in. They both looked guilty, but she'd been eleven once. Looking guilty went with the territory.

"Yes, he is," Natalie was saying.

"No, he's not," said Hallowell.

"More than she is," Natalie said. "She's weird."

"No she's not, she's nice. He's weird. Anyway, you said they were friends."

"No I didn't. They just know each other. And you shouldn't be talking about him to her and I'm not going to tell you anything more if you're going to spy."

The loud-whisper argument had been going on for several minutes. They were a funny pair. Natalie, dark and stout, Hallowell, pale and all elbows and knee caps, thick glasses and a baby-bird tuft of fine hair that Dawna always had to fight the urge to slick down. The only thing they seemed to have in common was that they were both eleven and stuck in Redimere.

"You don't even know," Natalie said. "I've seen him, not you."

"Maybe I did, too."

"No you didn't. You even said so."

Dawna wanted to ask the kids who they were talking about. It could be nothing. But on the other hand, she'd asked Eli, Natalie's dad, to keep an eye out for Danny Fuller when he went up Route 27 on his dumpster runs.

She turned around. "Natalie."

The two kids looked at her. Guilty.

"Can you come down to the station with me? I have something I need you to bring your dad."

"Okay." Natalie and Hallowell exchanged a glance. Dawna thought his eyes narrowed in warning, but it was hard to tell behind the glasses. Natalie grabbed her backpack off the seat. "See ya tonight," she said to him.

"I'm going over there to watch *Wipeout*," she said to Dawna when they got outside. It was a never-ending lament of Natalie's that her dad didn't have a TV.

"I don't really have something for your dad," Dawna said. "I wanted to ask you about something, but I didn't want to in front of Hallowell."

"Okay. Can I have a Pepsi at the station?"

"Sure."

"So, Chief Pete is on vacation and you're in charge?"

"Yep."

"Oh."

"Did you have something you wanted to talk to him about? You can talk to me, you know."

Natalie shrugged. "Nope."

"I heard you and Hallowell arguing."

Natalie hitched her backpack a little higher and pursed her lips, her eyes straight ahead as they approached the public safety building. The doors to the firetruck bays were open, Sandy inside. He waved as they walked by. Dawna and Natalie waved back.

"Was the argument about Danny Fuller?" Dawna asked.

"No, someone else. I don't want to say until we get inside, so Chief Sandy won't hear."

"No one's bothered you, have they?" They were well out of Sandy's earshot. Dawna opened the door to the police department.

"You mean stranger danger?" Natalie asked.

"Anything that's not ordinary."

"We learned all about that stuff in school, believe me." Natalie said it like it exhausted her. "The fisherman isn't like that. He's just this guy I see around." She threw her back pack on a chair in the office.

"Vicki, I'll be talking to Nat in the kitchen for a few minutes," Dawna said. "What do you mean see?" she asked Natalie as they went down the hall.

"Just see, like around." Annoyed. "I see him around when we go to the dumpsters. I don't want to talk about him in front of people anymore."

"You're sure it's not Danny Fuller?"

Natalie sighed, a drawn out world-weary sigh. "I'm sure. My dad would tell you if we saw him."

"Who's the fisherman?"

"Like I said, he's just this guy. We wave to each other. But I don't want everyone asking about him, because people will bother him."

"Where do you see him?

"All sorts of places."

"Who's going to bother him?" Dawna handed Natalie a can of Pepsi and got herself a water. She'd had easier interrogations with career criminals. "Is that what the argument with Hallowell was about?"

Natalie was opening cupboards, looking for a straw. "The argument was just dumb stuff. He's doing odd jobs for people, like Walt at the store and the lady, Crystal, who's a friend of Lydia Manzo."

"Why would he or anyone else bother your fisherman?" Dawna got her a straw from the box on top of the refrigerator.

"Because people are dumb and do dumb things."

"Can you be more specific?" Dawna knew it was probably a silly children's argument, but it felt like there was a subtext of something that wasn't, whether Natalie realized it or not.

Natalie slumped against the wall and rolled her eyes, and sighed, the whole world on her shoulders.

"Natalie?"

"When's Chief Pete coming back?"

*****

Pete remembered falling. Slamming into the ground. Pain. He'd blacked out, not sure if it'd been for a few seconds or twenty minutes. Probably seconds, because he was breathing hard, the world still spinning. He took inventory. He lay awkwardly, his legs higher than his torso, his backpack under him, the frame digging into his back. He was elevated several inches off the ground, on top of something. Maybe rocks? The embankment he was on when the earth crumbled under him rose to his right. The bright blue sky

80

peeked through a thick tangle of trees above him. As the ringing in his head faded, he heard birds, a squirrel chattering, far off, then louder. The leaves rustled in the breeze. It would be tranquil and soothing if it weren't for the red-hot pain, so intense he couldn't identify its source.

He lay as still as possible. Each beat of his heart brought a hammer of agony. He closed his eyes and took a deep breath. Held it, then let it out. His back was sore, but didn't feel like he'd broken any ribs. He took another breath, shallower, eyes still closed. Started with his toes. Pain there? Hard to say. His left foot and lower leg felt stiff and detached. The pain was coming from there, somewhere. He mentally inched up his leg. He didn't dare look, afraid he'd see it broken or twisted, or grotesquely torn away. He tried to shift the leg, just a little. The pain jolted him. It was nothing he'd ever felt before. The leg was stuck; moving it hurt. Eyes still closed, he tried, in tiny increments, to move the leg and figure out the source of the pain. This time he was ready for it. As it burned through him, he focused on its epicenter. The middle of his thigh.

He opened his eyes. The toes of his hiking boots were visible beyond his stomach, which was rising and falling without rhythm below his wet T-shirt. He put his palms on the ground, and raised the top of his body, his arms trembling. Beyond his legs, a little past, trees and a jungle of undergrowth were wrapped around a long rusty tangle of metal that poked up through it and stretched yards into the distance. That's what he was on top of, what his leg was stuck in.

He raised up more. The leg of his shorts was torn and bloody. A pointed rusted metal rod twisted high above his thigh, which was pale and clammy, wedged against the metal rod. That's what he wanted to believe. Just like people who stumble upon a body, the rational part of his mind told him. It's a mannequin, or a pile of clothes. But it never was. He was buying time until he could put together the truth.

The metal rod wasn't next to his thigh, it rose through the center, splitting the puckered flesh beyond the torn shorts leg.

81

He was impaled.

"Shit. Holy shit." He looked around, as though help was something he could grab. Nothing but trees, brush, the embankment. The blue sky. Now that he knew what the problem was, the pain was worse. Much worse. His words were a whisper, but inside he was screaming.

The rod rose a couple feet, tapered off and twisted, bent at the top. The dark rust was streaked with bright blood. He could feel it heavy in his leg, huge and on fire. A sharp, deep throb pulsed from it with his heartbeat. He lay back, vomit spreading up through his chest, burning his throat. He twisted sideways to throw up, the movement pulling the leg. Pain knifed from his thigh up his spine.

He lay back and tried to be still. Breathe. Think. He knew legs should be elevated above the head to ease shock. At least he had that part right. On the other hand, he was balanced awkwardly on top of his pack and the tangled metal below. Any shift could send him backwards or sideways. The weight of his body would rip the leg.

"Hey!" he yelled. "Help!" It was weak. He tried again, louder and stronger. Then he couldn't stop. Each bang of his heart, each yell rang against the rod. Sent rockets of pain. He yelled louder. Screamed until he was hoarse. Until he couldn't breathe. Then he lay silent, the screams echoing in his head. Relax. Take slow, deep breaths. Yelling was pointless. There was nothing for miles but trees, rocks, undergrowth, mountains, animals and birds who didn't give a shit. That's why he'd come out here, wasn't it?

He knew the shock would get worse. He had to get free, separate his body from the metal. If he could do that, anything else would be easy.

His position didn't help. The backpack was caught, making it harder to lift the top half of his body very far. He unbuckled the belly belt, his hands clammy, trembling, barely usable. He eased his shoulders from the straps. He lay back down. It was a little better. Shock could kill him if he didn't figure this out. Dying from shock, his organs shutting down, his heart and brain stopping, though, would probably be better than dying of thirst and starvation, deteriorating in pieces as he lay pinned like a bug to a board.

Neither of those things were going to happen. He'd freed his arms—a small victory. Now for another one. One little win at a time, just like pitching a baseball game. Don't think about the nine innings, think about the next pitch, the next out. He reached underneath and felt metal, then soft wet dirt half a foot below. He lifted his torso and pushed himself up with his good leg, raising his body, hoping for enough leverage to slide his leg up and off. The tiny movement—he'd barely moved—sent a piercing stab through the constant throb. Interesting how there can be so many different types of pain from one injury. It was pointless to try to lift the leg up far enough to free it. He knew before he tried that it wouldn't work. The end sticking out of his leg was too long.

He was thirsty, his mouth and lips gritty and dry, his throat tight. When a person was in physical shock they shouldn't eat or drink, but if he was going to have the energy to figure it out, then do it, he needed water.

His water bottle was heavy-duty aluminum and should've survived the landing. The pack, though, was still twisted at an angle, and he couldn't move it enough to reach the bottle. The effort jarred his leg again. He stopped, lay back, took deep, slow breaths until the pain faded enough to try again. A trickle of blood oozed onto his thigh, joining the blood that was drying there in the dappled sun, some puddled and drying, some in rivulets down the sides or soaking into the torn hem of his shorts. Not a lot of blood, considering. At least it was bright red, not dark arterial blood. It didn't fool him—he knew where his femoral artery was. Any wrong move, any clumsy lurch, could be fatal.

Fatal. The word sat there. The sky was blue blue blue beyond the green trees. So many different types, more than you'd think. How many could he name? The dark white pines, balsams, and the brighter deciduous trees, sugar maples and beeches, some poplar. Birch in clusters. A hundred shades of green against the blue sky. When he was a teenager he'd constantly reread the scene in *War and*

Peace when Andrei, wounded, lies on the battlefield staring at the sky, so captivated that when his hero Napoleon looms over him, he doesn't care. Now here Pete was, more than two hundred years after Andrei, staring at the same bottomless blue sky. High definition. That's what Bernie calls it. His mind was drifting, the shock taking over. He knew this as well as he knew where his femoral artery was. The pain was a giant pulse, dark red, pounding with his heart. Would it be so bad to give in? He'd been fighting a long time. Ever since he could remember. He didn't believe in an afterlife, knew he wouldn't see his mother, or his brother Joey, or Baba, but the pain would be gone. Not only the physical pain, but the other pain, made acutely worse in the last twenty-four hours by his goddam father. Being free of all that would be a gift.

Pete closed his eyes, tried to relax, wondering how long it would take for the shock to win. He considered one of Baba's Czech resistance tricks: Start from the first thing you can remember, then try to remember every moment of your life in order. Pete couldn't do it when he was thirteen, and he sure as hell didn't want to now—it'd be trading one kind of pain for another.

He wasn't Andrei, he was more like the guy in *Castaway*. The movie had been playing at the town's only movie theater for more than a month—one screen, movies that were making their second, or third, or hundredth run. He asked Bernie if she wanted to go, back when it first opened, before their breakup, but she refused. "I hated it ten years ago, and I hate it now," she'd said. "Tom Hanks talking to a volleyball, 'Wilson! Wilson, I'm sorry!'" She did it in a mock agonized wail. He went by himself. He'd seen it before and something in him wanted to see the scene where Hanks' character decides not to kill himself. The guy was never going to get off the island. The only thing he had control over was how he'd die. Pete wasn't sure why he remembered the scene so vividly from years before, why he'd wanted to see it again. As he sat there in the dark, the scene where the character explained the need to die seemed hollow. Pete had been relieved.

It turned out his relief hadn't meant anything. A week later, on

84

Memorial Day, home from the weekend in Phippsburg, he'd been exhausted from no sleep and terror, and from trying to hide it, trying to fight it. He wasn't going to sleep that night either, so he went for a swim, despite the soft rain. He went way out, past the middle of the lake. He'd gone that far before, but only when he was strong and rested. Floating in the misty half-moon light, he thought how easy it would be to sink. Four days earlier, he'd battled a riptide to save a child without any fear or doubt, but now, in the calm lake, he was going to sink down and let it take him.

What had stopped him? Bernie, of course. Asleep in her own bed across town, she'd still elbowed her way in, the way she did. Laughing, soft and warm, but absolutely determined. Telling him to get his head out of his ass and get home. He gathered energy he didn't know he had and swam back. As he pulled himself up on the rocks, drained, the horror of what he'd almost done knocked him sideways.

Bernie was with him now, too. She wouldn't believe he'd give in any more than she'd give in herself. He could hear her, incredulous. "You're going to lie there and wait to die? At least make it a fight."

He forced his mind through the haze. Think. The *Castaway* guy hadn't killed himself. His attempt failed, and he took it as a sign that he had to hope, even though there was no reason to. Pete waited for the same inspiration. Nothing. Okay, what about Shackleton? When Shackleton and his men were stranded at the South Pole, he made them prepare every day as though it was the day they'd be rescued. It'd been Pete's philosophy through his teen years. It's what got him, with no money or any support aside from the love and faith of his mom, to Penn. That wasn't much help now, either. He forced his mind to stop drifting. He had to find a usable example.

There was the guy who was trapped by a boulder in the desert canyon and freed himself by cutting off his arm. Pete tried to remember how he'd done it. It didn't really matter, an arm wasn't a leg. Even with a tourniquet, cutting through his thigh would kill him. If by some miracle it didn't, he'd have to get through miles of bushwhack, boulder falls, scrabble and centuries of underbrush—probably crawling, dragging a useless stump, trying not to bleed to death.

Doing something, though, was better than doing nothing.

His leg pale, clammy, and trembling, looked like someone else's. It'd be easier to cut into someone's else's leg. That's how he'd do it. Tell himself it wasn't his.

He tugged at his backpack beneath his wet back, and twisted, fumbling for the side pocket while trying not to move the leg or shift the pack to a worse angle. He worked the zipper down with his worthless bloated fingers and felt for the knife. He was stupidly giddy at the first touch of cold metal, then realized it wasn't the knife, it was the whistle.

He gripped it, the edges cutting into his palm. Bernie had been so sure of its power to save him, symbolically if not literally. It was so small in his hand. Sorrow, sudden, worse than the pain, made him want to never let it go. It wouldn't help now. He dropped it on his stomach, reached, the strain pulling his leg. *It's only pain.* He stretched farther and his fingers touched the leather sheath. They slid across it, but he tried again and pulled it close enough to grab. He laid it on his stomach next to the whistle as he rearranged himself, the muscles in his leg clenching as he tried to keep it still.

The knife's weight comforted him as he watched it rise and fall. Once he took it out of the sheath, touched the blade to his leg, there'd be no turning back. He hoped it'd be quick and he wouldn't have time to regret it or think about what he was leaving behind. At least this death wouldn't be as pathetic as being found pinned to the ground like fate's joke. Like he had waited for death the way Lydia had.

The guy who cut his arm off had to break his arm bones because his knife wouldn't cut them. He remembered that now. There was no way to break his femur. Maybe the metal rod had already done it. It was hard to tell, with the pain. The thigh was hugely swollen—it was possible it was broken. It didn't really matter. He'd bleed to death before he got that far, tourniquet or no tourniquet. The tourniquet was just going through the motions, anyway. He knew from experience that most people didn't tie them tight enough to do any good, and he didn't have the strength to. He needed something to use as a winch to tighten it, but the thought of figuring that part out was beyond him. He'd make a half-assed tourniquet, useless, but a sign to Bernie—because that's who this final fight was for—that he'd gone down thinking he'd survive.

He slid the knife out of its sheath. In two quick motions, he cut the belly belt from his knapsack. He'd do it that fast when he cut his leg. He wouldn't think about it, just cut. He wondered if his skin would feel like the nylon straps, make the same soft sound.

He put the knife down on his stomach again, its rise and fall faster, shakier than before. He pulled himself up to as much of a sitting position as he could, ignoring the agony as muscles pulled against the rod. Soon, the pain wouldn't matter. He leaned forward and wrapped the piece of strap around his upper thigh.

CHAPTER 10

How well do you know Sandy?" Crystal asked Bernie.

"We're pretty good friends," Bernie said. She'd almost forgotten herself and said "In the biblical sense, hardee har har," but then realized how wrong that would be. Crystal probably wouldn't get it anyway. Bernie tried to sort through whether Crystal could know she and Sandy had a fling, but everything was so tangled. This was the longest Tuesday ever. "Why?"

"Fergus Kelley was asking me about him, and I just wondered."

Bernie, for what seemed like the millionth time that day, tried to act like she wasn't screaming inside. "What did he ask?"

"I know you have a history with Fergus, and Sean too, they told me about it," Crystal said. "I feel kind of bad talking to them, which is why I'm telling you up front. I think you do a great job, but they're working on different angle than you are. Fergus has a lot of experience and Sean is a prize-winning photojournalist."

How many times had she heard the phrase "prize-winning photojournalist"? Friggin' Sean Speck. The effort to keep her face impassive, to not pick up her iced coffee, the one Crystal, as usual, had brought for her, or her keyboard or computer, and heave it through the window, almost made Bernie dizzy. Crystal hadn't even answered her question.

"What's going on?" Bernie asked.

"There's no reason I shouldn't talk to them, right? I mean, if you were asking me the same things they're asking, I'd be talking to you about it. You've asked me in the past not to talk to other journalists about what we've discussed, so I think it's only fair to give them the same courtesy."

Bernie tried to think of a good negotiation point, but negotiating wasn't one of her talents. "That's true."

"They said their article is going to have an in-depth approach that tells the story in a new way," Crystal said.

It sounded like bullshit. Bernie's only hope was that Crystal would realize it and not fall for their act. Bernie knew there were things she could pry out of Crystal that Crystal didn't think were important. She knew that Fergus, despite his feckless laziness, had an innate instinct for a good story, too. And Speck, though lazy too, was a sneaky bastard. Combined, they were a dangerous weapon if their laziness didn't get the best of them. She had a suspicion that their mutual dislike of her was helping them power through.

Annette, Shirley, Guy, and Carrie—Tuesday! All hands on deck!—weren't even pretending they weren't listening. When Crystal had come in, Bernie had made the tactical error of having the conversation at her desk. They'd already talked that day. She figured Crystal was stopping in for some chit-chat. People did that a lot.

"Sean was showing me some of his pictures, he's really good," Crystal said.

"Yes," Bernie said. She hoped that Crystal had said "pictures," to Sean because it'd make him nuts. He'd told Bernie repeatedly that he didn't "take pictures," he "made images." She smiled, hoping it looked sincere. "If they want to talk to you, you have every right."

Guy made a strangled noise. She wished they'd all get back to work.

"I also wanted to talk to you about Colleen Sullivan," Crystal said quietly.

"Who?" Bernie's phone rang. It was her brother. Normally she'd let him leave a message, but she needed to put a halt to the conversation so she could catch her brain up. Where had she heard that name?

"This'll just take a sec," she said.

"Bad Ronald's back," Sal said.

"That's such good news."

"I told you before, I can climb up on the roof and find how they're getting in and patch it up."

"And I've told you, let's wait until I can afford to hire an exterminator, because I don't want you imprisoning squirrels in the walls of my house."

She hung up. "Where were we?" The conversation hadn't helped her catch up at all.

"Crystal, isn't your husband an exterminator?" Annette asked. "Maybe you can help Bernie."

"No, he works for our town's public works department," Crystal said, annoyed.

"I thought LeeAnne said something about that, last time we were talking about the squirrels," Annette said.

"She was referring to an incident related to getting rid of rats in sewers," Crystal said.

"It was in the paper where you live," Annette said, in a drifty way, like she was trying to remember.

"That's correct." Crystal turned to Bernie. "Bad Ronald?"

"Bad Ronald after the movie," Bernie said.

Crystal shrugged. "Don't know it."

"Made for TV. 1974. The kid was living in the wall of a house, spying on the family." Bernie wanted to add that everyone in their generation had seen it. But maybe other people didn't watch as much TV as she had. She was still trying to buy time, figure out a way to turn the conversation around, or off.

"They can get through the smallest holes," Annette said. "Squirrels."

"Yep," Bernie said. It was like there was a script for when you had squirrels. Everyone said the same thing every single time.

"They'll eat your wires," Guy added. She shot him a look and he winked. "Red squirrels are worse than gray squirrels," he added.

"I have to go," Crystal said. "But we need to talk later about that other topic." She mouthed the word "Colleen."

Bernie'd wanted to take her down to the picnic table. Negotiate the Fergus/Sean thing without an audience, find out now, not later, why she wanted to talk about someone whose name barely registered with Bernie.

Crystal gave a little wave to a chorus of goody-byes and was out the door before Bernie could get it out. She slumped in her chair, exhausted. She'd also forgotten to ask Crystal if Lydia's cellphone had been with her stuff, and if the unsent texts were still on it. If so, what they said. And, oh yeah, can you not tell Fergus about it, if that's okay.

"Gotta keep moving forward, like a shark," she said to the room. She faced the problem she always did, the one she was still getting used to after three years as editor/owner of the *Watcher*. It was a weekly and she had to find a way to keep a story almost a week old fresh. She wished she knew more about the texts, or had it on the record. She knew what Sandy told her was just between them. She could write about the lack of GPS and compass, at least. She went through her notes from the interview before Memorial Day weekend, trying to remember why she'd been so bothered. Oh yeah. The half-dozen or so letters that'd come to the newspaper office, addressed to Lydia. She should have asked Crystal if she had those, too.

She texted her. "pls cll when u cn. Got ?s" She wondered if Crystal would get she meant that she had questions, not that she was asking if Crystal had something mysterious.

She double-checked the story to make sure she didn't include anything she shouldn't have. Sometimes lack of focus let things slip through the cracks. It was a good read, but not nearly as good as it should've been.

A SAD END TO 'LIVING THE DREAM'
By Bernadette O'Dea

Lydia Manzo had started her Appalachian Trail thru-hike on Springer Mountain in Georgia earlier in March than many hikers do, but she lucked out because it'd been a mild winter. She wanted to be sure to finish in time for her son's July wedding.

She'd been preparing for the hike for more than a year, and though she was 55, she was in the best shape of her life. She'd gone on extensive and intensive hikes, power hiking with her two best friends, and alone, too.

Manzo had taken hiking courses, including one that focused specifically on long-hiking the AT.

She'd set up a blog so people could track her hike. She and her friends had strategized on how to best get it the attention they thought it would deserve.

It wasn't so much that Lydia wanted publicity, she'd told the Weekly Watcher in an interview before her hike began in March. It was more that she thought people would enjoy the story, that it would inspire women her age.

She stressed in her first blog post the day before she began, that both writing and hiking the trail had been long-time dreams.

"Two dreams coming together — and I'm living them!" she wrote.

In her second post, she revealed she'd been given a trail name by fellow hikers: Nursedreamer.

How had those dreams turned into a nightmare that caused Manzo to apparently take her own life?

Bernie wondered if she should strike the word "apparently." Nah. She was feeling constrained enough.

Lydia had been upbeat, articulate in person and her blog posts. One of those positive go go go people who were usually in real estate or ad sales. She wrote the blog in her notebook, and Crystal transcribed it on the laptop when they met up every few days. Before they got to Maine, Bernie dealt with Crystal mostly, with an occasional Skype with Lydia.

Bernie printed a map of the trail every week, showing Lydia's progress. Carrie made it interactive, so readers could hover over sections and read excerpts of what Lydia wrote while she was at that part of the trail. It had been fun. Right up until it wasn't.

When Lydia got lost, the worst part of the entire trail—western Maine's high peaks—was behind her. But she still had 70 miles of mountainous and remote terrain before she got to the famed 100-Mile Wilderness. Bernie couldn't believe Lydia wouldn't be concerned about not having the GPS, particularly with the stunning fact she didn't like using a compass and didn't have one. Maybe she was, but didn't want her friends to worry.

That night in the Pour House, LeeAnne had said the rest of the hike would be a cake walk. Lydia had already conquered thirteen states—2,000 miles—faster and earlier than anyone thought she could.

Lydia had smiled wearily and said, "Well, maybe not a cake walk." Crystal and LeeAnne had laughed. Lydia hadn't.

She was happy she was going to finish in time for her son's wedding. She had the girls to help her, just the way they had since the beginning, making sure she had her supplies, shopping for her while she was on the trail. They were going to meet her at Abol Stream outside of Baxter Park and hike the last fifteen miles with her, summiting Katahdin and shouting "woo hoo" out to the vast stretch of mountainous Maine, where it would echo down the 2,176 miles to Springer Mountain, Georgia, and the 750 west to Buffalo, New York, and tell the world that Nursedreamer had made it.

Aside from the lost GPS, the lack of compass skills, the foolish idea she could rely on a cellphone for help, Bernie felt like there were other things Lydia hadn't told her. She obviously wasn't going to find out today. Crystal hadn't called back. Pete wasn't here to try to pry information out of. The story was done.

*****

Pete couldn't do it. The cold blade had become warm as he held it against his thigh. He didn't know how long. He'd even poked, ever so slightly, into the skin, letting a drop of blood ooze around it, bright against the blood that had dried there. The prick of pain was almost welcome, so different from the thundering throb that had become his life. It was later afternoon now, he guessed from the sun. He'd been lying on the tangle of metal for hours, much of it with the knife poised to cut off his leg a few inches below the hip.

He knew not cutting it off meant death, too. He didn't believe that bullshit the guy was throwing around in *Castaway* about there being hope even though it seemed impossible.

He threw the knife into the weedy tangle of brush. It wasn't a strong throw, not one of No-Hitter Novotny's blazing fastballs. The pain, the shock, were taking over. He didn't have any leverage, pinned in place like a bug. Still, it was far enough that any second thought would be just that—a thought.

As he'd played with the knife, the loop that was his life settled on a scene. It'd been the thing that made him throw it away. He and Bernie, very early in the relationship, after a lot of wine, on his couch in front of the pellet stove fire. One of those moments that seem painfully corny when you hear about them, but not when you're in them. It'd started out not corny. A challenge to see who could recite how many complete poems. It'd been fun. She did *The Raven;* he did *Jabberwocky*. She did *Annabel Lee*, warning him not to challenge her on Poe, because she had the guy down. He'd tried to do *Rime of the Ancient Mariner*, but failed horribly as she collapsed into laughter. Then he realized the possibilities. He took her hand and looked into her eyes and recited the most romantic poem he could think of, John Donne, right down to the end: "Thy firmness makes my circle just, and makes me end where I begun."

She'd actually cried. Yeah, they'd had a lot of wine, but it felt like a big moment. Turned out it was. For Christmas, she gave him the stainless steel whistle, engraved, "End where you begun - B."

She'd been embarrassed. But it was perfect, a simple declaration of love.

Now, stiff and shaky, he ran his hand on the ground below him, looking for it. It'd fallen off his stomach as he'd debated over the knife. I'll get it later, he'd thought. Then, oh yeah, there won't be a later. Now there was, for what it was worth.

He searched the damp ground, his fingers barely reaching. It couldn't have gone far. He'd barely thought about it when it fell, but now he was desperate to have it. It'd become the most important thing in his life. His forty-five years had telescoped to this moment, this tiny universe. His leg screamed as he strained to find it. He almost wept with relief and gratitude when his fingers finally touched metal.

He wiped it on his shirt then brought it to his lips and blew. His mouth was dry, and he had little lung power. All that came out was a peep. He took a deep breath. Put aside the pain, the nausea, the exhaustion. Everything focused on the whistle. He gave a sharp blast. Then another. Bernie was right. It was a lot easier than yelling. He blew it long and loud. Blew it with everything he had.

CHAPTER 11

The more Bernie thought about what she couldn't put in the paper, the fact Crystal hadn't called her back, that Pete was gone, that Feckless Kelley and useless Sean Speck were poking around her town, the more pissed off she got. Screw all of them. She was going to add more Lydia stuff. Every single thing she could think of. The best excerpts from Lydia's blog, a bigger map. Photos. She'd throw every goddam thing she had at it.

"I'm adding four pages," she said to the newsroom. For a moment, there was silence. Bernie knew that's how they'd react. The size of the paper is determined by ads, not how much news there is—cost versus revenue. Shirley usually had worked out how many pages there would be shortly after the noon Monday ad deadline. A page on the press was, front and back, four newspaper pages, the minimum amount that could be added. Adding four pages times 5,000-plus papers with no ads to back it up was going to skew the budget, but Bernie didn't care. Adding it this late was going to skew everyone's day, but that didn't bother her either.

"It's Tuesday afternoon," Guy said.

"Aren't we pros?" Bernie said. "Aren't we the A-Team? We can do it!"

"We don't have the ad support," Shirley said. "That means four more layouts, and someone has to call the printer and let them know it's going to be bigger than what I told them yesterday."

"I have enough copy to fill, and I'll call the printer. Come on guys, it'll be great."

Annette and Shirley looked at each other. Bernie could

practically hear their eyes roll. She didn't care. She had too much to do to worry about what everyone was thinking.

· The phone rang. Sal again.

"Damn it," she said. She picked up the phone. "What now?"

"Washing machine's broken again."

"What's wrong with it?"

"Same as last time. It's not gyrating."

"Do you have money for the laundromat?"

"No. You?"

"No."

"I can go on payday." Sal said.

"You have a payday?"

"I'm doing the best I can, Bern. Maybe there's some change lurking somewhere in the house."

"Yeah, ask Bad Ronald." She hung up. She'd been planning to do laundry that night. Had put it off until she didn't have one clean thing. She couldn't wait until whenever Sal got paid. She took her salary monthly, and payday wasn't until next week. She was broke. Actually, she was whatever you are when you're worse than broke.

Think about it later, there was work to do.

Guy had edited her story, so that was done. She'd already gathered all the extras she was going to put in. She was ahead of the game. She hadn't been squeamish about putting in what was now public about Lydia's mistakes, her miscalculations. It was part of the story. She'd even got a brief interview from the lead Warden Service guy for a sidebar about smart hiking.

"A hiker who goes into the woods without a compass is a lost hiker," he said. Good quote! Perfect.

She'd asked him in general about using cellphones when you're lost, even though she didn't let on that she knew Lydia had tried to use hers.

"Biggest mistake we see," he'd said. "Everyone thinks they can call or text for help. The best defense against getting lost in the woods is knowing how to take care of yourself and being prepared."

It bothered Bernie that Lydia, who'd seemed so on top of

things, had been so unprepared.

The fact she'd apparently tried to text hurt. It made Bernie think of the twin towers, even though it wasn't the same. People thinking they'd be saved, hoping. Then taking that leap when they knew they wouldn't be. Lydia hadn't taken the leap. She had to keep reminding herself. Despite her mistakes, she may have been saved if someone hadn't killed her.

She'd gone maybe ten minutes without thinking about Pete. He was lost in those same woods. *Not lost.* Why did she keep thinking that? Pete didn't have a GPS either. All he had was his flip phone, as old and clunky as Bernie's, but it wouldn't work in the woods no matter how modern it was. He didn't need GPS. Didn't need his phone, only brought it so he could text when he got out. All he needed was a compass, maps, and a brain. That's what he always said.

Bernie's father, who took them camping every year—no Disneyworld for the eight O'Dea kids, too fake, cost too much—would tell them that if they got into trouble, "You have to be the most enthusiastic participant in saving your own life."

He'd give the same speech every time, sure one of them would do something stupid and disappear into the wilderness of Baxter, or wherever they were.

It was a joke to the kids, a catchphrase—driver's ed, being asked out by creeps, having to tell Mom and Dad about a bad grade, choking down a meal another sibling had prepared—everything applied.

She whispered it now. "You have to be the most enthusiastic participant in saving your own life."

She and her brothers and sisters had laughed, but deep down she always liked the sound of it. She wondered if she'd ever said it to Pete. She hoped she had.

*****

Blowing the whistle had exhausted Pete, a waste of the little energy he had. The woods were dead quiet. There wasn't another person for miles, and it would be dark soon.

When he first heard the rustling, he thought it was his brother again. Joey had come to him a couple times. Or maybe it was one in the endless crawl of rotted Philly and Redimere corpses that'd been visiting him as he drifted in and out.

He forced his head to clear. It was behind him. Too loud for a squirrel; maybe a deer. He'd caught a flash of one earlier, flitting beyond the trees, startled by the whistle blast. This was no deer, though. It made too much noise, breathed too heavily. It carried a cloud of very human body odor and something fouler. Pete tipped his head back until he could see, just feet behind him, camo cargo pants torn off at the knees into crude shorts, muscled, tanned legs criss-crossed with scratches, ending in combat boots with filthy wool socks. He tipped farther. A dirt-encrusted T-shirt. A face, sunburned and unshaven. It stared down at Pete, expressionless.

Inside, Pete was begging for help, pleading, but the blank eyes pinned him just like the metal did. Andrei seeing Napoleon above him on the battlefield surfaced. It wasn't Napoleon, of course. Not even close. It was Danny Fuller. They stared at each other. Pete's leg pulsed with pain as his heart pounded. He'd been found. Instead of elation, he felt fear. *No, he'll help me.* Pete could imagine how he looked—helpless, pathetic. Fuller was a human being, after all.

"Help lift me off," Pete said, his voice a dry croak. It was so obvious, so easy. Let's just do it, his brain screamed.

Fuller's eyes left Pete's and locked on the twisted spike of metal.

"Straight up and off," Pete said. *So fucking obvious.*

Fuller looked back at Pete's face, then squatted down next to him and yanked the knapsack. Pete yelped as his body dropped backwards, pulling his leg. He put his hands down to brace himself. Fuller, as though Pete weren't there, pulled things out of the pack. Pete's extra T-shirt, his fleece pullover and flannel pajama pants. He tossed them aside. He grabbed Pete's dried fruit, the ramen packets, the trail mix, and stuffed them into his rucksack. He was quick, methodical. He pulled out Pete's burner and paraffin can, along with the collapsible pot, took them, too.

"Help me," Pete said. He was beyond pride, beyond anything but desperation. If Fuller didn't save him, there was no one else. "Please."

Fuller pulled the knapsack farther out, but Pete was ready, and steadied himself on his arms.

He took Pete's flashlight. Found the water bottle Pete had tried to reach earlier. Fuller opened it, his eyes on Pete's face as he drank, a smile behind the bottle. Water dripped down his chin, wasted. He wiped it off with his arm. He put the bottle in his duffel. He yanked free the bedroll, jarring Pete on purpose. Pete gritted his teeth, suppressed the scream.

He dropped Pete's cellphone on a flat rock and crushed it with the heel of his boot.

"Help me off. You can just leave me and go," Pete said.

Fuller reached into Pete's pockets, hissed when he found them damp with urine. He pulled his hand out before reaching the compass that Bernie had given him for Christmas along with the whistle. Pete would never need it again, but he was still relieved. Fuller pushed him sideways, and Pete bit back another scream. He pulled Pete's wallet from his back pocket, then let him drop. Pete had his arms out, ready. He wouldn't be able to hold himself up for long. He'd shifted enough that his body weight pulled the leg constantly. He pictured falling the inches to the ground, the rod ripping through his thigh, his femoral artery shooting dark blood like a geyser.

Fuller emptied the wallet, dropping the contents on the ground. He laughed. He'd seen the badge. He held it up so Pete could see, then spun it into the woods. He took the bills, maybe forty bucks, shoved them into his pocket.

He grabbed one of Pete's arms and jerked it. Pete fell sideways, steadying himself with one arm. Still, he thought for a split second that Fuller was going to help him after all. But Fuller pried open Pete's fingers and took the whistle that Pete had been clenching, hadn't even realized had been digging into his palm, held tightly even when he'd pressed the hand against the ground to hold himself up. Fuller took it and left a huge empty chasm.

Fuller dropped the whistle on the rock that was littered with the cellphone shards and ground his heel on it. The whistle, stainless steel, stayed intact. Fuller cursed.

"Give it back," Pete said. "Please."

Fuller put it in his pocket. He shouldered his pack and left the same way he'd come.

"Don't leave me." It was a whisper. Pete knew it was too late.

CHAPTER 12

Bernie's washing machine had been broken on and off for months. Pete had been happy to let her use his, even when he wasn't home. Before. She'd assume it was okay now. He never asked for his key back, and she put off returning it. Moot point, now, she reminded herself.

A floodlight burst on, flooding the dooryard, as she walked to the door. She dropped the basket, startled. Motion sensor. Her hand shook as she unlocked the door. She didn't know why—it wasn't like he was going to show up and catch her. She'd confess when he got back. He'd probably laugh and say it was fine. She wished she could fast-forward to that moment.

His tiny house—smaller than Bernie's, basically one room— was neat as always, smelling like wood smoke and sun-warmed lumber, just like when she'd last been there more than a month before. In the laundry nook, tucked behind the kitchen, she dumped the whole load into the washer. Making it all just one load made her feel less guilty.

She put her bag on the table, next to a box that had a Milwaukee return address. C. Novotny. His birthday was in early May, so maybe it was a late birthday present from a relative. His parents were dead, she knew that. She wasn't going to be nosy. New era. She could sit in his house for a couple hours without looking at his personal stuff. Definitely. The fact that she'd looked to see who it was from meant nothing. Anyone would do that. She opened the slider to the deck, and the warm night air drifted through the screen, smelling like summer. The lake lapped the flat rocks beyond the little patch of grass. Nice, relaxing, she tried to convince herself. She sat on the couch, poking at the laptop keys.

The quiet night picked up a rhythm. The washing machine chugged. A loon cried, then another one. A burst of laughter, rising and falling voices, echoed somewhere across the lake. The box on the table had its own whisper: Come and see. She'd seen a cassette player, a tape, a pile of papers next to it. She shifted so they weren't in her peripheral vision.

Come and see.

Who the hell was she kidding? She went to the table. "JCN, November 1980" was written in faded pen on the cassette's label. She put the cassette into the tape player and hit play. It whirred to life. She turned it off. She looked back at her laptop. The monitor had gone to sleep. Her eyes wandered to the folded papers next to the tape player. So inviting. She unfolded the top piece, old notebook paper, dirty at the creases.

"Mom, Sorry I couldn't be better. Please don't ever tell Pete about Gerry. Love, Joey." No date.

Too personal. She popped open the player, ejecting the tape. She looked at her laptop. It was dark, boring. She opened another piece of paper. Yellow legal paper, fresh and crisp with Pete's familiar neat printing.

"Chuck, You are not part of my life. If we never said goodbye, consider this it. Pete."

She picked up the last one. White computer paper.

"Son, I know we haven't talked in a long time. Since your mother's funeral..."

She was sure Pete had told her his father was dead. The root of her anxiety about Pete warred with common decency. Leave it alone.

The cassette player had grown larger, buzzing at her. Play me. *Play me.* She pushed the tape back in, closed it, pushed play.

"This is November 13, 1980, coming to you from Milwaukee, Wisconsin." A young boy's voice, using the tone kids use when they try to sound like TV announcers. "This is episode one of Meet the

Novotnys. I'm Joseph Charles Novotny, age twelve. I'm in seventh grade, and recess is my favorite subject." He imitated the sound of a drum rim shot, punctuated with laughter.

"We're going to meet another member of the family, my brother, Pete." A knock at a door.

"Go away." Irritated.

"Let me in a minute."

"I'm doing homework."

"Just one minute." Then, into the microphone. "Pete is a sophomore in high school."

A door opened. "What do you want?" It was a teenage boy, but Bernie could hear Pete's voice. Her heart leapt.

"I want to interview you for my project."

"I'm busy."

"Just a few questions, then I'll leave you alone. Pleeeeeaaaaase."

"Okay." Reluctant.

"First say your name and age."

Loud sigh. "Pete Novotny. Fifteen."

"Pete's a star of the cross-country team and a star baseball player and a star student."

"I'm not a star, doofus, I just play. Is that it?"

"Pete, tell our listeners what you'd like to be when you grow up."

"Someone who doesn't have an annoying brother bothering him."

"That's a good career goal." Suppressed giggle. "What else?"

"A lawyer."

"Good. You'll be rich."

"Are you done?"

"Tell our listeners what you think of your little brother, Joseph C. Novotny."

"I think he's a moron who needs to leave me alone."

Scuffling and giggles. "Let the record show I'm being thrown out of Pete's room," Joey was laughing. Bernie laughed too. It reminded her of her brothers.

The door creaked back open. "Listen." There was affection in Pete's whisper. "I wouldn't bug Gerry with that, okay? Could be the last time you see your recorder." The door closed.

A click, static, another click.

"This is November 14, 1980. It's morning in Milwaukee. I'm talking to a very pretty lady. Can you tell our listeners your name?" Joey's voice again, with TV announcer intonation.

"Jan McElroy." A woman's voice, amused. "Eat your breakfast and get ready for school."

"Just a couple minutes, Mom." Joey said, the announcer voice gone. "Say who you are and then I'll turn it off."

She sighed, just like Pete. "I was born Jan Marsalek, in Milwaukee. I graduated from high school in 1961 and got an associate degree in accounting from Milwaukee Tech. I met your dad, Chuck Novotny, when I was working in payroll at State Fabricators, where he was a machinist."

"Was it love at first sight?"

"No, though he was very handsome, I thought he was too full of himself. But I guess he grew on me. We got married in June 1964. And in May 1965, your brother Pete was born, and in November 1968 you were born. Now get ready for school."

"You have to say the rest."

"Like what? You're going to be late."

"What happened since I was born?"

"The world fell off its axis."

"Be serious, Mom."

Another Pete-like sigh. "Your dad and I lived in our old neighborhood until we got divorced in 1976. I got a job as a bookkeeper and desk clerk at McElroy Motel, where I still work, and it's where I met my new husband and your stepfather, Gerry McElroy, who's the owner. We got married May 5, 1978."

"On Pete's birthday," Joey said. "Stinko de Mayo."

"We didn't plan it that way, as you know. It was just a day Gerry was free. We moved into Gerry's house, which is very nice,

105

and you boys each have your own room instead of sharing. Gerry takes very good care of us. Now get ready for school."

The recorder clicked again. "Later that same night," said Joey, whispering. "The nature of this report has changed. Pete and I took a blood oath to follow Baba's rules from when he fought the Nazis." Joey hissed Nazis. "Baba said the secret to surviving torture is you don't let it bother you." There was a long pause. "Pete says not to tell Mom, because she'll get mad at Gerry, and he'll be even meaner. This recording is for when I turn eighteen and can tell, and Mom can come live with me."

Bernie felt strongly she should turn it off. Then again, it was a way to understand Pete.

"Baba said he was scared, but he fought the Nazis because he had enough. I've had enough, too. What happened is, Pete's supposed to make supper. He made chili in the crock pot because he had cross-country and the state meet is Saturday and Gerry said Pete couldn't do sports if it got in the way of making dinner. Gerry said the chili was shit, which was stupid, because he didn't even try it. He dumped it in the garbage, then pushed Pete's head in to make him eat it. Then Gerry ordered a pizza for just me and him and wouldn't let Pete have any. I didn't want to eat any either, but Pete told me to. Then he went to do his homework and acted like he didn't care. I was going to save a piece for him, but Gerry sat there the whole time and made sure it was all gone. Then Gerry made Pete take the pizza box outside to the garbage. It still had cheese and stuff on it, so it smelled good, like pizza, but Pete was cool and threw it out like it was nothing. Then he says, 'Is that all?' and went back in his room. Stuff like that happens all the time. Gerry pushes our heads in the toilet and call us shits if we make a mess in the bathroom. Sometimes Pete says it's his mess when it's really mine. I told him not to, but he says it's because he's bigger and not to argue. Gerry's only mean with words when Mom's home, so she doesn't know."

Joey's whisper got lower. "Gerry did something with Pete's accordion, the one Baba left him. Uncle Victor bought Pete a new one, but it doesn't matter because Gerry won't let Pete go to Sokol or be in the band."

He was speaking so quietly Bernie had to put her ear against the recorder, the plastic hard against her cheek. "There's the worst thing, that Pete doesn't even know. Gerry says if I tell, he'll kick us out and fire Mom. Anyway, he says no one will believe me, and he's right because I get in trouble a lot."

Turn it off. Bernie couldn't make herself push the button.

"This recording will prove I'm not lying. It happens after the sports on the news when Mom's at work. I used to go in Pete's room, but Pete got mad and got a lock. Pete doesn't know. If he did, he'd try to kick Gerry's ass, and then everything would be worse, because Gerry's like five times bigger and says if Pete finds out, me and Pete'll both be sorry."

A pause. "The TV went off. I'm putting this under the bed."

Bernie tensed, her finger on the "stop" button, frozen.

There was rustling, then a door opening. "I know you're awake." It was a man's voice. Quiet, but Bernie could feel the menace. "I know you're awake you little shit."

"Leave me alone," said Joey, in a loud whisper.

"Shut up." Then a slap, a muffled cry. "Any more noise and it's the last sound you'll make."

Bernie turned off the recorder and scrambled away from the table knocking over her chair. She shouldn't have listened. It hadn't helped at all.

*****

Dawna sat back and put her feet up. She took a long swallow of beer. She didn't drink much, but it'd been her first full day of being in charge, the sheriff's department had taken over for the night, and she was going to relax.

Before Pete, she'd been treated like a secretary. Things could change a lot in less than two years. Still, she'd be glad to give the title back to him. It's not like it'd even been an eventful day. Still, there were a lot of mosquitos buzzing around, and it was up to her to swat them.

She wished she could call Bernie and talk about Pete looking into Lydia Manzo, the fact that he told her he had the case file. But Bernie was stressed out about making sure there was no conflict of interest, she'd been even during their breakup. Dawna got that, but it was a small town, and there were so many layers to professional roles and friendships. Bernie should chill out, but Dawna knew tonight wasn't the night she was going to, Bernie was too worked up about Pete leaving.

Dawna wanted to talk to her, too, about the annoying call from the mayor looking for Pete, and another call, from Colleen Sullivan, saying she and Pete had talked the week before, and had a lunch appointment, but she hadn't heard from him.

It wasn't like him to blow someone off, but he'd been in a rush to get to the woods. Dawna didn't tell Colleen that. She just told her Pete was off for the rest of the week. Neither of the callers wanted to talk to her. She wasn't sure whether to be hurt or relieved, whether to wonder if there was police business that wasn't going to be taken care of or just accept that people thought they had important things that only the man at the top could deal with. She wanted to run it by Bernie, but again, it'd all probably just upset her more.

She was in a vacuum. Was this what it was like to be chief? Wanting to run things by people, but not being sure how much to say about what to who? Pete confided in her a lot about the department. She saw the logic in that now, the need to have a right-hand person. With him gone, there wasn't anyone in the department she could confide in. She felt the need to talk to someone about something, anything. Her sister was asleep, and she'd just lecture her anyway, not really listen. There was one thing she could take care of at least. She called Eli Perry.

"Has Natalie mentioned someone she calls the fisherman?"

He laughed. "Oh yeah. He's a guy she sees around when we're hauling rubbish. One of her people. You know how she is. They wave to each other."

"Does he have a fishing pole or something?"

"No. Floppy fisherman's hat. You've probably seen him. I think he lives out toward Kingfield, or maybe farther up, Carrabassett. Early riser. We see him walking. I think he hitches with the logging rigs. Seen him getting out of them on 27 a couple times. He's a night owl, early morning guy. Saw him this morning, as a matter of fact, up by the Lazy Logger."

"I think I know who you're talking about," Dawna said. "Big guy? Maybe as tall as you? Glasses?"

"Yeah, leaner though." Eli weighed a good three hundred pounds. Everyone was leaner. "Why?"

"Just wanted to make sure it wasn't Fuller and if you think there's anything hinky about the guy."

"Naw to both. I woulda said something to you. Like I said, one of Nat's people."

Dawna heard a peep in the background.

"I thought you were in bed," Eli said. "We've got an early morning." He came back to Dawna. "I better go. She gets pissed when I talk about her. We're going up to Eustis on a new job."

"Keep your eyes open when you go through the valley."

"You know it."

Dawna had people too. It must run in the family. She added the fisherman to her list.

※ ★ ★ ★

Bernie was shaken by the tape. She wasn't sure what she'd imagined Pete's childhood to be like, and hadn't thought of his brother much, except for how the loss must've hurt Pete, but now her perceptions were blown up and the new ones were horrible. She blew her nose and threw the tissue in the wastebasket underneath Pete's desk. Or rather, at it—it hit the rim and fell on the floor. As she picked it up, she saw crumpled balls of legal paper in the basket. In for a dime, in for a dollar. She took them out, smoothed them on the desk.

"Chuck, whatever the reason you sent me this, fuck you. I don't want to see or talk to you again. Thanks for putting the final nail in my coffin."

109

Another one, "It's your fault Joey's dead, it's your fault Mom's dead and I wish you were dead, too. Thanks." That one had a big X across it, drawn so hard the pen had ripped the paper.

There were a few others, with varying degrees of anger. None sounded like any part of Pete she knew, but they were all in his neat printing, just like the watered-down one on the table.

She ran her finger over the recorder, thinking about the monster that'd come with the tape. No wonder Pete left. God, she wished he was here.

A flash of light and a loud knock at the door spun her around. The door opened. She screamed and threw the recorder.

It bounced off the wall, missing Colleen Sullivan by inches. As Bernie watched the recorder fall to the floor, she thought, "Oh yeah, that's who Colleen Sullivan is."

They both froze, confused.

Bernie was the first to react. She crossed the room and picked up the recorder. The top had broken. She tried to jam it back on.

Colleen watched from the doorway, wary.

"I guess there's no standard response for a situation like this," Bernie said.

"No."

"Close the door before the mosquitoes get in."

Colleen closed the door. "I'm Colleen Sullivan. I was looking for the police chief." She stood by the door, hand on the knob.

Bernie put the recorder back on the table, on top of the notes. "He's not here. I'm Bernie O'Dea. Do you have a key?" That would explain a lot. Maybe Colleen was from Pete's past. Now she'd come back to claim him, so he fled rather than face the wrath of two competing women. One pretty, cool, composed, despite the fact that she'd just had to dodge a flying cassette recorder; the other with a coffee stain on her blouse and a mouth that wouldn't stop. It would explain the breakup. Explain Colleen in Redimere. Actually, it wouldn't. It was idiotic. Bernie tried to detour the half dozen tracks in her head—Joey's voice, Pete's voice, the work she should be doing—onto a side track and figure out what was going on in

110

front of her.

"A key?" Colleen asked.

"You came right in."

"The door was ajar. It opened when I knocked."

Bernie let out her breath. "Sorry. I'm having a weird night. Would you like to sit down? Can I offer you something to drink?"

"Sure." Colleen sat on the couch, but on the edge.

Bernie looked in the refrigerator. "Allagash White. Geary's Pale Ale. I don't know why he can't have normal beer. Bottle of white wine."

"White wine's good."

It was one of Bernie's. From before. He hadn't touched it. Should she feel good about that or bad? "In case you're wondering, Pete and I are partners. Partners in love. Not business or something." Bernie felt stupid, but it was too late to rewind.

"Ah. Okay."

"I'm doing my laundry." She handed Collen a glass of wine. "What are *you* doing here?" She was going to make a joke about it obviously not being laundry, but stopped herself. She'd been rude and babbly enough.

"He and I were supposed to talk today, but I haven't been able to reach him. Someone told me he lived here."

"Someone?"

She put her wine glass down on the coffee table. "Since he's not here, maybe I better go. You seem agitated."

"Stay," Bernie said. "I feel bad about how this started out."

"This seems like a bad time."

"I'm sorry," Bernie said. She was. None of her anxiety was Colleen's fault. That she knew of. "Like I said, I'm having a weird night. Are you visiting Redimere?" Bernie felt silly, trying to be socially polite, but she couldn't figure out anything else.

"I'm here on business, more or less." Colleen sipped her wine.

There wasn't a lot of business in Redimere. The college, maybe. Colleen seemed wary. Though there *was* the recorder thing. "I'm the editor of the newspaper," Bernie said. "What kind of business are

111

you here on? I'm just nosy."

Colleen smiled. It seemed genuine. "Oh, the *Weekly Watcher*. I'm a big fan. Maybe you can help me. I'm here for research. I'm a forensic sociologist. I study how social issues interact with legal issues. I'm working on a study of people who isolate themselves from society and the impact on their lives and others, including criminality."

The penny dropped. "The Midnight Rambler."

"Yes, I've been following your articles online."

"Where are you from?"

"I'm from Buffalo."

Their eyes met. "Given Lydia Manzo, that's quite a coincidence."

"It is." Colleen smiled. "Though not really. I'd been interested in Lydia's hike, so saw that your paper was featuring her. Then I saw your extensive series on the Midnight Rambler and since it was exactly what I was researching, I thought I'd come up here and see what else I could find out."

"Are you a friend of Lydia?"

Colleen's eyes held Bernie's. "No."

"Look, I'm not good at this type of thing," Bernie said. "I don't believe you, about Lydia at least. I can't figure out what you're doing here." She stopped herself, her face hot. "Sorry, I don't mean to sound racist or something."

"I don't take it that way."

Bernie couldn't tell if she was joking or angry. "Your story doesn't make sense. It's too much of a coincidence. Crystal Corson, Lydia's friend, knows you." Bernie tried to remember what Crystal had said. "What do you want to talk to Pete about that you can't talk to him at the station? Don't say the Midnight Rambler, because that's something you could talk about in his office, and anyway, he doesn't even believe he exists."

Colleen was on the edge of the couch, perched to fly. She drained her glass. "I think my story's pretty believable." Her self-assurance had faded. Bernie felt they were on more of a level playing field now.

"I have news for you, it's not. I mean, is your name even Colleen Sullivan?"

Now Colleen was mad. "Of course it is. Why would I lie about my name?"

Bernie got the bottle and poured Colleen and herself more, then set it on the table with a thump. "Maybe we can help each other," Bernie said. "You're from Buffalo. I think you know Lydia. If you're really interested in the Rambler, I'm your girl. If it's not about him, then we still have something to talk about."

Colleen was thinking about it, Bernie could tell by the way she swirled her wine around in the glass. The way she sat farther back on the couch. The way the tightness in her face softened.

"You tell me your story," Bernie said. "I'll tell you mine."

CHAPTER 13

Fuller was gone, a fading rustle through the underbrush, then nothing. Pete was alone, his one chance at rescue lost. He tried not to panic. It'd sap what little energy he had left. He worked his pack so he was more comfortable. It was a victory that didn't matter. The afternoon faded, twilight came, then it was dark.

Fuller had taken his water, his food, the whistle. Smashed his phone. Not the knife. That was in the brush where Pete had thrown it. He had nothing.

As he faded he kept hearing Joey, the tape. How could he not have known what Gerry was doing? He'd been trying not to think about it. But now he was trapped and he couldn't stop. After his dad left, the three of them had moved from the familiar city block of duplexes, family, and friends, to a one-bedroom apartment, the boys crammed onto twin beds so close together you couldn't walk between them, his mother on the pull-out sofa in the living room. Pete was happy to have his own room when they moved to Gerry's house, a three-bedroom ranch, even though he hated Gerry from the start. Pete and Joey had shared a room all their lives, so when Joey started coming into his room with a blanket and pillow and sleeping on the floor, Pete thought he was being a baby. It seemed odd to Pete at the time that Gerry—so controlling, so ready to demolish any ounce of happiness—would let Pete put a deadbolt on the inside of his bedroom door. Pete wondered now if he'd been so selfish, so stupidly grateful for the privacy, that he ignored the obvious.

He'd cried like he hadn't in years when he listened to the tape for his lost brother—the sunny kid he'd been then, not the angry, fighter, thief, dropout, drug abuser he became. He wept for his tired, loving mother who'd married Gerry thinking she'd found a savior, only to find it was another ring of hell. He cried for himself, too. How determined he'd been to be like Baba, how he thought he was protecting Joey by taking the brunt of the abuse. Gerry had the last laugh.

Chuck, he didn't even think of him as Dad anymore, but Chuck, had been in some bar, or with his new girlfriend. It didn't matter, he hadn't been around. They hadn't talked for more than twenty years before the box came. It was decades too late.

Pete drifted, scenes sparking, then fading. In his lucid moments, he wondered if this was what they meant by your life passing before your eyes. It wasn't the entire forty-five years in a linear stream, but snapshots, startling in their detail and clarity.

There'd been this girl, Angie Pavano. She sat behind him for four years in homeroom and most of his high school classes— alphabetical order. She was funny. Smart, too. Was she a lot like Bernie, or was that just his fading brain, everything melting into something else? He'd had a crush on her. She knew a lot about baseball. Loved the Braves, not the Brewers, just like his dad, even though the team left Milwaukee when she was a baby. Knew every Monty Python sketch by heart. She'd sit behind him in class and make wise-ass remarks, and he'd try not to laugh. "Bloody 'ell," she'd say in a bad British accent, then kick his chair. Her family owned a bakery. No, wait. Bernie's mother's family owned a bakery. Did they both? Senior year, on his birthday, she brought him a cannoli. She blushed and made a joke when she gave it to him, like it was an afterthought.

He'd never wanted a girlfriend in high school. He was focused on getting straight A's so he could get into a college far away, focused on sports so he could escape his life for a couple hours, focused on his jobs. He knew, too, he didn't want to have to explain his home life, expose some nice girl to the ugliness that was Gerry. He had that crush on Angie, though. She had dancing dark brown eyes and a dumpling-sweet shape and treated him with an honesty and affection that no one else did. No, dammit, that's Bernie. Maybe both. He finally got the nerve to ask her to dance at the graduation dance. He'd never danced with a girl before. Okay, polkas at the Sokol, mostly with his mom, or jumping around with his cousins and girls from the neighborhood at weddings. That didn't count. Angie made a joke, but then she'd leaned into him, put her head on his shoulder. Stopped talking. Her warm breath brushed his neck, and her heart beat against him. He felt it now, here in the woods. She'd been soft and warm, and he'd wanted to hold on forever. *So this is what it's about.* The sweat on his hands soaked through the back of her dress, but he was afraid to move them. She kissed him lightly, right below his ear, and he'd squeezed tighter. Then the song was over and her friends, laughing, dragged her away.

He wished he'd told her how much he liked her. He wished he'd known, the way he knew now with shocked clarity, that she'd liked him, too. His friends called her Laverne. Could that be right? Maybe that was Joey. He kept thinking Joey was with him. It was because of the tape, he knew that, but he'd still open his eyes and scan the darkness, hoping he was there. There was only silhouettes of trees, stars visible through the canopy.

The Angie scene sparked another one. It came back so sharp and real it shocked him into full alertness. He used to think about it a lot in the years after Joey died, wondering if he should've understood what his brother was saying and could have done something to change things. It'd faded over the years; he got tired of trying to change the script.

But now, here it was. The two of them on the couch, a stifling summer night a few weeks before Pete left for Penn. Pete was reading. Joey—a pale, fidgety teenager, no longer the sunny twelve-year-old of the recording—watching TV. Stupid line, laugh track, thirty seconds, stupid line, laugh track. *Laverne & Shirley.* It was driving Pete nuts.

"I don't know why you watch that stupid show," he'd said.

"I like it." Everything with Joey was that simple. I like it, so I

116

watch it.

"It's dumb."

"They're funny. Wouldn't you like to live in their Milwaukee instead of ours?" Joey asked. "Hang out with Lenny and Squiggy, have a dad like Frank?"

"It's not real. Anyway, they moved from fictional Milwaukee to fictional California. Then they got canceled."

"There'll be reruns forever," Joey said, chuckling along with the laugh track as though he hadn't seen it dozens of times.

It was a quiet night, Gerry and Mom both working. It was a luxury having the house and TV to themselves without worrying about the next swinging fist or nasty remark.

"Do you think people who die can contact living people?" Joey asked.

Pete looked up from his book. Lenny and Squiggy mugging it up, exasperating Laverne. The question wasn't prompted by the show.

"No."

"I think they can," Joey said.

"If they could, then Baba would have contacted us."

"Maybe he did, and we just didn't get it."

"If people could do that, everyone who died would do it."

"Maybe you can only do certain things and living people are too numb to get it."

"This is stupid. Let me read," Pete said.

"Let's have a signal if one of us dies."

"Let's not."

"Let's."

"Okay. Every time I hear something really stupid, I'll know it's you trying to contact me."

"It can be *Laverne & Shirley*."

"What? Like when it's on TV, that's the signal? Like I said, dumb."

"No. Duh. How about, say I die, I'll send you *Laverne & Shirley* signals and eventually you'll get that it's me because it'll be too many to ignore."

"Dumb dumbness from a dummy." The conversation bothered Pete, more than just the usual annoyance of Joey poking at him.

"I'm gonna do it. I'll send you *Laverne & Shirley* signals all over the place. I'm even gonna send you a girl just like Laverne to marry, because I know you have the hots for her."

"Shut up."

"Just wait, you'll see." He started singing the theme song. "We're gonna make our dream come true!"

"I'm trying to read."

Joey pulled Pete's book away from him. He put his face right up to Pete's, laughing. "Doing it OUR WAY."

"Turkey." Pete grabbed him and flipped him, pinning him to the floor. His brother, a few months away from fifteen, was small and too skinny, but still wiry strong, like Pete. Pete had a few pounds on him, though. Joey convulsed into giggles, still singing.

"I'm not going to let you up until you shut up," Pete said.

"DOING IT OUR WAY," Joey sang. "Pete and Laverne, sitting in a tree, K-I-S-S-I-N-G."

"You're a moron." Pete let Joey go.

"Just wait," Joey said as Pete went down the hallway. "You'll see."

It had been the first time in a long time his brother had acted like his old self—silly, normal. It was also the last real conversation they had. When Pete came home for Christmas, Joey was rarely around, and when he was, he was sullen and snarly. Pete avoided him.

That March, Joey died. Pete couldn't help it; he started looking for *Laverne & Shirley*.

He'd been right, though. It was dumb. He didn't marry Laverne. Karen, his wife, who he'd started dating right after Christmas freshman year, had been tall, slim, and elegant. She was smart and funny, but in a quiet way, not the sarcastic nasal hee-haw of Laverne, or Angie Pavano. Eventually, he stopped looking. Once, years after Joey died, he was clicking through channels and stopped at the familiar theme song, almost knocked over by sorrow. Karen was there, a rare night she wasn't working. She grabbed the remote. "We're not watching this dumb show." She changed the channel.

She was right, dumb.

Now, impaled, in pain, shock taking over, his life running through his head, Pete felt like he should've looked harder. He wondered what signal he'd send Bernie. Wondered if she'd notice it. She was Laverne, kind of. More like Laverne than anyone he'd dated. A lot like Angie. Funny, sarcastic, big-hearted. One hundred percent true blue. He should've talked to her about signals. She would've thought he was nuts, though. It's the kind of thing she'd go on about, not him. They hadn't had enough time, and he'd wasted what they'd had. Tears wet his face, ran into his ears and mouth. He barely noticed. He was pissed off. He wasn't sure if the anger was keeping him alive or sapping his strength. Since he'd made the decision to live, he had to keep trying, even though it was pointless. He'd be the one person in his immediate family who wouldn't give up. He knew when he died he'd simply cease to exist, just like everyone before him had. There'd been times when that thought had been comforting. Now, when it mattered, it wasn't comforting at all.

For every loop of his brother's voice, there was also Bernie's, reassuring him, telling him she didn't blame him for anything. Sometimes she turned into Laverne, and that pissed him off, too. He wanted Bernie so he could explain, apologize, get on solid ground and move forward.

He wept for the loss of the whistle, now fouled by Danny Fuller's dirty, scratched hands. Taken for no other reason than he didn't want Pete to have it, to have that tiny, impossible hope. Just like Gerry throwing away Baba's accordion. The whistle had been Pete's charm, even in his darkest days when he'd stupidly—he'd been so fucking stupid—panicked and sent Bernie packing. He'd still carried the whistle, feeling its strength. Fuller had taken from him the one thing he could hold dear as he slid into death.

He tried to remember how long they thought Lydia had gone without food and water before she died. It had seemed incredibly short to Pete, too short to make sense, one of the things that made him wonder what really had happened. Lydia had been missing for almost a month when she died. He wouldn't last that long, given his injury. No one would start looking for him for a week—he wasn't expected back until Monday. The thought of being pinned to the tangle of rusted metal for even that long seemed impossible, but he had no way to speed it up. Where's a fucking Ziploc bag when you need one?

He took a deep breath, held it, and let it out. Anger and panic would only make it worse. He tried to think of something pleasant. He didn't have any control over the loop playing in his head, though. It just wanted him to see regrets. Missed chances. Fuckups. When he and Bernie were driving home from Phippsburg Memorial Day weekend, she had him drive past the house in Augusta where she grew up, pull over across the street and stop. It was raining, and despite the fact it was late morning, the lights were on.

"Don't you look at houses and feel good when the windows are lit like that?" she'd asked as she'd leaned past him to look. "It's all cozy, like when you come in from the rain on a cold day, and it smells like what your mom is cooking for dinner, and there's music playing somewhere, and everyone's there, talking, hanging out. It's like the house has saved that feeling, even though someone else lives there. Know what I mean?"

"No," he'd said, starting the car. He drove down the tree-lined hill, Augusta's ancient wooden houses sagging in the rain. He'd turned onto Route 27 to go north. The houses gave way to peeling clapboard triple-deckers and vacant storefronts, convenience stores and old men walking dogs. The pot-holed bumpy road and gray little city depressed him.

She hadn't responded or argued like she normally would. He knew at the time he'd hurt her feelings, and he felt bad. But he hadn't lived the life she seemed to think so happily existed for everyone. The one she thought they could lead. He was collapsing into a dark hole and didn't have the energy to fight it or even examine it. That's how he felt that day. How foolish he'd been. How self-indulgent. He saw that now. If he'd only gotten his head out of his ass and seen that she was offering the gift of the kind of life he'd never had, not asking him to pretend he'd lived it.

Now, in the dark woods, the pain a dull red throb that ticked away his final hours, it crept in, all on its own, that warmth. There was a dining room; it was soft and glowing. It smelled like wood smoke and food. His mom was there, bright and happy, like she'd been when he was a kid. So was Joey, bouncing around. Baba, too, his eyes shining, nodding and talking. Bernie was there, too, laughing, looking across the table at him with her big dark eyes, that look of faith and love that he'd found he couldn't live without. Walt was there, his buddy; so was his old partner Sid. Dawna and Sandy, too. Talking, eating, laughing. Dubya danced around, nudging his legs. He couldn't make out the words, but it felt so good as it drew him in. He could almost reach out and touch them. They were happy to see him. Arms reached out, beckoning, smiles. He didn't feel pain, or panic, or sorrow. He walked into their embrace, feeling nothing but warmth.

*****

Bernie and Colleen contemplated their wine.

Colleen spoke first. "I'm not sure I can trust you."

"At least we have that in common."

"I don't even know what we're talking about."

"We have that in common too," Bernie said. She didn't know where to start. Everyone had been weird. It was claustrophobic, the voices, the irritations, the horrors. Pounding from every direction. She had no idea what was going on or who she could believe. If she said that to Colleen, it'd sound stupid, or like an evasion. Or nuts.

"Why don't you start by telling me what you want to talk to Pete about, and why you have to do it at his house instead of the police station?"

"This is just between us," Colleen said.

"Definitely."

121

"I *am* a friend of Lydia's."

"Why aren't you hanging with the Woo Hoos?"

Colleen drained her wine glass.

"Want some more?" Bernie asked.

"No thanks, I have to drive. In fact, could I have a glass of water?"

Bernie got her some and poured herself more wine. "You know them, right? But you're not friends."

"The short version is, they're an impediment to the truth. They mean well, but keep messing things up."

"The truth about what?"

"How much do you know about what happened at their hospital?"

"About how they became friends?"

Colleen waved her hand, impatient. "Did anyone tell you about the murders?"

"No." Bernie took a long gulp of wine. She would have remembered someone telling her about murders. Plural.

"I have to trust you. Seriously."

"You can," Bernie said. She almost said "cross my heart and hope to die," almost made the gesture, would have if she didn't have a glass of wine in her hand.

Colleen looked Bernie in the eye, assessing. Bernie tried to look like someone who could keep her mouth shut.

"I'm not really on leave," Colleen said. "I didn't get tenure last year. Kind of like being fired, but reeeeaallll slooowwwwww."

"I'm familiar."

"Part of it was school politics. A bunch of old white guys, and they'd just given tenure to a black woman a couple years before. Can't have too many, you know. No offense."

"None taken. I'm not an old white guy."

"It was kind of a relief, not having to act like I thought they wanted me to, trying to keep my mouth shut so I wouldn't be perceived as stepping above my place."

Bernie had been the victim of the boys club, too. It's why she was self-employed. "I feel your pain, kind of. Not as bad, though. I can't even imagine."

They clinked glasses. Bernie was starting to like her.

"I was originally going to write a paper," Colleen said. "One of their complaints was that I didn't publish enough."

"There'll always be complaints, no matter how hard you work or how perfect it is."

"Oh yeah. But what I was looking into for my paper became more complex, so I decided to write a book."

Bernie nodded. She wanted to get to the murders.

"When I submitted an outline, my department head said that true crime books weren't what we did. Bottom line, the book is more important than working for some stuffy old Irish Catholic college that doesn't respect black women."

"Bravo. The topic?"

Colleen put her water glass down, her eyes bored into Bernie. Bernie got hot, suddenly nervous. Maybe it was the wine. Her medication was definitely wearing off. Some of it, too, was the effect of Joey's tape, which was still running in the back of her head. Focus.

"I was originally looking into corporate reaction to employee malfeasance, and chose the hospital affiliated with the college I taught at. I wanted to know how hospitals handled things like nurses who put patients' lives in danger through mistakes or carelessness. There had been a big case a couple years before—have you heard of Charles Cullen?"

"No."

"It's funny how few people have. You know who Ted Bundy is, right?"

"Oh yeah."

"Everyone knows Bundy, but no one knows Cullen. He was a nurse in New Jersey and Pennsylvania who between 1987 and 2003 may have killed as many as four hundred patients at nine hospitals."

"No way."

"It's true. He's in prison. But the big thing was, when a

hospital became suspicious, they'd quietly let him go, and he'd get hired at the next one."

"Really?" Bernie thought of how hard it was for her to get a job after losing her last one.

"Hospitals were more interested in covering their butts. Granted, that type of murder's hard to prove, and they didn't necessarily even know he was doing it. But there were red flags all over the place. They just wanted him to be someone else's problem. He never got a bad reference."

"You found a similar case in Buffalo?"

"Not at first. I started the original study three years ago. I really wanted to talk to nurses. They're the ones who know what's going on. I met Crystal and got her, LeeAnne, and Lydia through their union. They were a little reserved at first, but once they got to know me, they told me about Herman Czarnec."

"Never heard of him."

"No reason you should've. The hospital suspected he killed at least four patients in 1995. Crystal, Lydia, LeeAnne, and other nurses at the time kept notes, records, noting patterns."

"The hospital gave him a pass?"

"Yes and no. It took a while for the administration to take it seriously, but the nurses were persistent and the hospital started putting the heat on him. Then he took off. They found his car parked at the Route 20 bridge over the Hudson, across the state, and it looked like he killed himself. Problem solved. More than ten years later, the nurses I talked to were still upset. They felt like, even dead, he should've been publicly fingered as a murderer, or at least privately, within the hospital."

"'Looked like' he killed himself."

"I believe he's living in the woods a little north of here."

"Really?"

Colleen looked at her, waiting. Bernie knew she was being slow, but it'd been a long day. "You really can't guess?" Colleen said. "The Midnight Rambler."

CHAPTER 14

When Pete woke up, it was still dark, but the birds were loud, which meant morning was coming. There was pain, incredible thirst, nausea. He wondered if he was in purgatory. He tried to move, and the dull throb exploded. Must be hell, because he was still impaled.

He was thankful he was still alive. He almost laughed at the paradox. He didn't want to slowly die like this, but yet he was thankful he was still here, slowly dying.

When he saw the figure standing nearby, a hulking silhouette against the trees, he knew Fuller had come back to kill him.

"Kill me." Pete's voice was a croak, barely audible.

The figure loomed, silent.

"Kill me." Louder this time. He wished he hadn't woken up. The relief he'd felt moments before at being alive was a lie. He didn't feel it now. He had no fight left, nothing.

He felt a hand on his thigh, next to the metal. He was surprised he could feel anything there that wasn't pain.

The man squatted next to him, studying his leg. Not Fuller after all.

"Are you real?" His throat felt closed, the words painful.

The man looked at him through thick glasses, then quickly away. Pete's eyes had adjusted, and he could make out his face, a white oval, the mouth a thin line. Ghostlike. But the hand on his thigh was warm and firm.

The man took a deep breath, cleared his throat. "Yes." His voice sounded more unused than Pete's. He ducked down and looked under Pete's leg.

125

"Will you help me?" Pete asked.

The man took a water bottle from his fanny pack and held it out. Pete struggled up and tried to take the bottle. His hands were swollen and numb. The man, expressionless, looking above Pete's head rather than at him, held the bottle as Pete drank. He'd never been so thankful for water in his life. He barely tasted it before the man took it away.

"Please," Pete said.

"Shock," the man said, low. Then, louder, "Shock. Don't want a lot of water."

"Will you help me?" Pete asked again.

"If it's possible."

"Who are you?" There was no logic left to Pete's shrunken life. It's last vestiges had vanished when he held that knife to his thigh. The fact he'd thrown the knife into the woods was a disconnected blip of logic in a chain that started when he'd angrily started packing Monday, Joey's tape ringing in his ears. A lifetime ago. Nothing existed before he fell. This was his reality, this odd man just one more thing. He wasn't a hiker, or an outdoorsman—not a poacher or logger. He looked like a suburban dad on his way to mow the lawn. He wore a floppy fishing hat, no hair poking out. He was clean-shaven. Pale as the ghost he'd seemed at first. His clothes were clean, but ill-fitting. The T-shirt had creases as though it had come out of a package, the jeans looked new. He wore hiking sandals with socks. Pete wondered at his ability, though the fog of pain and shock, to still take in details. Maybe he had something left. Maybe this guy would save him. Maybe.

Gray light filtered through the trees. Pete's savior—whether he was going to free him or kill him, either one would work—studied Pete's wound. He bent to look underneath again. He looked for a long time, then, with a quick glance at Pete, touched the skin near the impact, pressing gently.

"Does this hurt?"

"The whole thing hurts," Pete said. "I'm Pete. Who're you?"

"Max," he said, after a pause. He cleared his throat. "May I?"

"Sure." No idea what the guy wanted, but at least it was something.

Max's large, long fingers pressed the skin around the wound, this time closer to it and with more purpose. The pain, which had been a general throb, sharpened. Pete gasped.

Max eased the pressure but kept his fingers there. "I want to see if your leg's broken. Tell me how this feels." He pressed his full hand harder on the meat of Pete's thigh.

The pain was intense, but it wasn't that sharp electric feeling Pete knew from experience came with a broken bone. "Sore. Maybe not broken."

Max nodded. "It's swollen. Hard to tell."

"Are you a doctor?"

"Nurse." Max took a multi-tool out of his pack. It was a Gerber, less popular than the Leatherman that many of the men and some of the women in Franklin County carried, but with more blades. Pete was mostly familiar with it from domestic violence attacks, which seemed to be its most popular use.

"You're going to cut my leg off?"

Max ran his finger up the metal spike from where it had ripped through the top of Pete's leg to its rusty, jagged end. He did it lightly, but the movement made Pete cry out.

"I can't tell if your femoral artery is impacted," Max said, as though he hadn't heard the question. "The instrument may be blocking the hemorrhage, or it could be close enough to the artery that movement will cause a laceration to it. Removing the instrument may kill you."

"Staying here will kill me." Talking had exhausted him. The burst of energy and adrenaline from the water and possibility of rescue was gone. He fought to stay alert. Maybe he'd be saved. Maybe he'd die. He just wanted it to happen soon.

"The instrument may have impacted the femoral nerve. Removal could also impact the nerve. There could be avulsion of either the nerve or the bone."

"Fine."

Pete's lack of concern seemed to annoy him. "It could be extremely painful and permanently inhibit the use of the leg."

"It's inhibited now," Pete said. Pain and nausea spun the world around. "Do whatever."

"It's mandatory I tell you the possible consequences."

Pete watched Max lay the multi-tool on the ground and gather the clothing that Fuller had scattered. He picked up the torn strap.

"Tourniquet." Pete said. "Was one."

Max dropped it and took a bungee cord out of his pack. He expertly wrapped it around Pete's upper thigh, using a stick to twist it tighter, ignoring Pete's gasp. "This will do if the femoral artery isn't impacted. If it is, it won't matter."

"Are you going to cut off my leg?" Pete asked again.

Max looked at Pete. Or rather, turned his eyes toward Pete, looking above his head. "That would definitely kill you. I don't have the means to amputate a leg and keep you from dying."

"Not sure I care."

"You don't now, but if you live you'll be glad." Max folded the two T-shirts into squares and laid them on Pete's stomach, with the flannel pants.

"You're in shock," Max said. "You need to be warm." He took Pete's fleece pullover and, lifting Pete slightly, pulled it over his head, putting one hand on his back to steady him. "Put your arms through."

Pete's arms were dead weights as he tried to work them through the sleeves. Max held Pete up with one hand on his back and pulled the fleece down his arms with professional efficiency. He shifted the knapsack under Pete and eased him down. It was higher and straighter that it had been, metal no longer pressing into his spine.

"Thanks," Pete said, pitifully grateful for that one small thing.

Max looked Pete square in the face without flinching for the first time, his eyes large and round behind the glasses. "I'm going to cut the metal below your thigh with the hacksaw blade. There'll be vibration, and it'll heat the metal, causing you considerable pain. I'll hold the metal steady, which means I can't hold your leg still. You must try, and I can't stress this enough, to keep the leg and your body as still as possible despite the pain. Once I've cut all the way through the rod, I'm going to pull it through your leg. I'm going to have to do it very slowly, to cause as little damage as possible. I expect this, too, to cause pain. You must keep still. A fraction of an inch could kill you. Once the rod is no longer protruding from the bottom of the wound, I'm going to pause briefly to press one of these bandages on it." He pointed to the T-shirts. "I won't be able to steady your leg. It's up to you to keep it still. If you bleed out, there's nothing I'll be able to do, but I'll try to make you as comfortable as possible in the last moments of your life."

Max's voice was flat and matter-of-fact. When he finished, he looked away. "Are we agreed?"

"Okay." Pete couldn't muster any more.

Max faced the rod, as though he were talking to it instead of Pete. "Once it's removed, I'll press the other bandage on top of the wound. You'll have to hold it while I wrap the flannel pants around your leg to secure the bandages. It won't work unless you're able. I'll remove the tourniquet, and secure that around the pants, to hold the bandages in place."

"Fine."

"I don't feel comfortable not explaining the procedure."

Pete didn't care. They were just words, pinpricks in the throbbing pain, the weakness, and exhaustion. He wanted to live, but more, he didn't want to be in this limbo.

Max took a small piece of PVC pipe, a few inches long, out of his pack and held it to Pete's mouth. "Bite down."

Pete stared, not understanding.

"To save your tongue. For the pain, too. It'll help. I use this to isolate bug bites, but I can assure you I sterilize it after use."

He put the pipe in Pete's mouth, and Pete bit down. The throb in his thigh was so familiar now in the hours, almost a day, he'd been living with it, he couldn't imagine the pain being worse. Maybe worse would be better. At least it would be different.

129

Max picked open a blade on the Gerber. It looked too small to do any good. "Lie back."

Pete lay back, the pipe loose between his teeth, palms flat on the ground below, the sides of his forearms pressed against the twisted metal under his backpack. He dug his fingers into the cool dirt and looked up at the sky through the trees, lighter now, a soft gray.

Max gripped the rod and Pete's muscles clenched against the slight movement, a shocking wave of pain. He bit harder on the pipe.

"Stay still," Max said. He started to saw. At first the vibration sent small sharp simmers through the roaring throb. Not too bad. As the sawing increased, the shimmers got closer together and intensified. Pete's teeth dug into the hard rubber of the PVC, his fingers clawing the ground.

"It's okay to make noise. It may help," Max said. "Pain management studies show that a release may divert attention from the pain."

Pete didn't need permission. The sound of the metal on metal was a counterpoint to the heavy searing burn that grew with each bite of the blade. Max talking didn't change the rhythm of the steady back and forth. Pete, soaked with sweat, squeezed his eyes shut and bit down, tried to focus on biting, not caring that he was crying in agony. Baba's rules. It's just pain. He repeated it in his head. Just pain. It's just pain. He lost track of time—the sawing, Max's breathing, the white-hot grip of pain, all were one thing. Pete had never wanted anything in his life more than he wanted it to stop.

Max stopped, and the pain eased back almost to what it had been before. Pete pushed at the pipe with his tongue, took a deep breath. His jaw and teeth ached.

"I'm going to pull," Max said. "This could hurt more, particularly if it's against the bone or the bone is broken, or it impacts the femoral nerve. Again, if the femoral artery is impacted, this will kill you."

Pete took the PVC pipe out of his mouth. His fingers were caked with dirt from clawing the ground. He wiped saliva from his chin with his forearm. "Go ahead."

"Would you like to pray first?"

"No." He put the PVC back in his mouth and looked up at the sky, imagining he was Andrei. It didn't help. He wasn't Andrei at all. No big philosophical breakthrough. He was Pete. Instead of Napoleon, he saw Bernie. He cared, cared intensely. Hugely and desperately. Painfully. He wasn't Baba. He was that boy with his face in the garbage, or the toilet, or the couch as the belt or cigarettes did their damage, trying hard to be brave, but knowing that he wasn't. He silently apologized to Bernie for everything, all of it. For not having enough faith in her love, or in himself. Not saying goodbye. Not caring right now if he died. That wasn't true. Just like when he swam out into the lake Memorial Day night and almost sank. He'd gathered his strength and swam home. He didn't want to die. He dug his fingers into the dirt.

Max put his hand on his thigh next to the wound. Pete's leg jerked.

"Hold still."

Pete took a deep breath around the PVC, bit harder.

The metal slowly moved through the wound with pain like Pete had never known. He screamed, his back arched, he grabbed at the wet dirt below him, trying to get away from it.

"Don't move," Max said sharply. He stopped pulling. Pete tried to catch his breath. Max took his hand from Pete's thigh and he felt the firm touch of the folded T-shirt pressed on the underside of his leg. Then cool air again as Max took it away. "Not too much blood. It's bright, not dark. That's a good indicator."

Pete opened his eyes, but they were wet and gummy and everything was a blur. He had no strength to lift up to see for himself. He felt the pressure on the bottom of his leg again as Max pressed the T-shirt against it.

"We can rest for a minute," Max said.

Pete dreaded the return of the pain. "Keep going," he said

around the PVC pipe.

Max began to pull again. Pete could feel every fiber, every muscle, tendon and piece of tissue the rough metal scraped against as it slowly moved through the mass of his thigh. The pain increased with each millimeter. It was bright red behind his eyelids, searing his eyes. It had a color, a taste, an odor. He tried to say the alphabet backwards in his head. Couldn't. He started with the first varsity game he'd pitched, when he was a sophomore in high school, tried to remember the first pitch, the first batter. Nothing. *Sorry, Baba.*

"Stay still," Max said.

Pete knew the rod was out when the pain eased enough that the train screaming through his head stopped and he could think. Max pressed the other T-shirt to the top of the wound. It still hurt, but for the first time since he'd fallen, the pain was something familiar that he could live with. Blood puddled across the white jelly of his thigh, the hairs shining in it. It dripped down the side, much more than there'd been before. It seemed like a lot. He didn't care. Even if he bled to death, he was free, and he wouldn't die impaled on a piece of metal, alone, in the middle of the woods.

"Hold the bottom one."

Pete's fingers still clung to the dirt. He stretched his left hand out, black with dirt, the nails broken. Max took his hand and wiped off some of the dirt before pressing it against the bottom cloth.

"That's not arterial blood," Max said.

"It seems like a lot," Pete said. His hand pressing the cloth shook. His whole body did.

"It's not," Max said. He pressed his hand against Pete's. "Please continue to apply pressure. You can still bleed out. I'll be quick."

Pete took a deep breath and focused on his shaking arm, the sore, swollen hand pressing against what he'd once thought of as his leg, but now saw as a bloated, jellied thing attached to him, heavy and painful. He'd felt giddy, but it had been brief. Like every other positive emotion he'd felt since he fell, it was barely there before it was replaced with a smothering weight.

Max pulled Pete's hand away and wrapped the flannel pants around the bandaged hole. He removed the bungee tourniquet, and Pete was jolted out of wherever he'd been drifting as blood flowed back. Max's eyes were on the bandage, one hand lightly on top of the wound. He moved the other underneath. "Not much leakage. I have real medical supplies at my camp and will replace this with sterile bandages as soon as I can."

Heaviness pushed Pete somewhere dark and black.

"I need to move you and treat the shock." Max came around behind Pete and put his arm around his chest, slowly pulling him from the tangle of metal. "Try to steady yourself with your good leg so the injured one doesn't hit the ground hard."

Pete was fading, limp and boneless. Both legs hit with a thud. He cried out, but Max didn't stop. He pulled him clear and laid him on the undergrowth.

Pete's backpack was under his head, no idea how it got there. The leg throbbed, but the nausea and inability to breathe were worse.

"I have to treat your shock," Max said again, poking around in his pack.

Pete was drifting, but not so far that he didn't notice a hypodermic needle and small brown bottle in Max's hand.

"What's that?" Adrenaline, no idea he had any left, kicked in, along with his inner cop.

Max measured liquid from the bottle into the hypodermic.

"We have to get me out of here," Pete said. "I don't authorize you to inject me."

Max focused on the hypodermic, expressionless. "I'm a nurse." He tapped it, the way nurses do.

"Don't give me a shot." Pete tried to lift himself up farther, but his arms trembled with his weight and the brightening day became dark again. He closed his eyes and took a deep breath, trying to find a place to pull some strength from.

"This'll help," Max said as though Pete hadn't spoken. He took

Pete's arm, anchoring it between his own and his side. Pete couldn't even struggle. He didn't have anything left. "For the pain and the shock." Max rubbed something cold and wet on the inside of his elbow.

"Wait," Pete said, trying to struggle. He had a flash of Gerry with the lit cigarette, pushing him down. Instead he felt the prick of the needle and cold, then warmth, rushed through him. The world faded before he could say anything else.

CHAPTER 15

Bernie's initial wariness with Colleen was gone. Sure, a lot of it was the wine. But it was also nice to have someone to talk to who was on the same track. She told Colleen there was evidence Lydia was murdered. She didn't tell what it was or who she'd heard it from. She didn't tell Colleen her suspicion that Pete might be looking into it, even as they sat there. That the case file was probably within feet of them. Bernie didn't know where, but it was a small house.

She could tell Colleen wasn't telling her everything either.

Colleen said Herman, the suspected murdering nurse, and Lydia were friends. Rather, Lydia was the only person who was nice to him. A couple weeks after Bernie's first feature about Lydia's plan to hike the trail was published, Lydia got a letter with a Redimere postmark and no return address. In the envelope was a clipping of one of Bernie's Midnight Rambler stories and a brief note on paper that had "Redimere Drug, Here to Serve You!" printed at the top.

The note was simple. Colleen showed Bernie a photo. "I'm the 'Midnight Rambler.' - Herm C."

Lydia hadn't told the Woo Hoos.

"Did you think it could be a hoax?" Bernie asked.

"I considered that, but not Lydia. She was stunned, but thrilled. Happy he wasn't dead. She's a very compassionate person. Was. I was worried it was too weird, especially given the coincidence she was going to be hiking the trail, and out of all the places he could be, there he was. She wasn't, though. She wanted to find a way to meet him, but couldn't figure out how to contact him."

"Ahhhh," said Bernie. Things, at least some things, were making sense.

"I'm afraid she tried to find him. That's how she got lost."

*****

After Colleen left, Bernie wandered Pete's house, trying to think. She had two tracks: Colleen/Lydia and Pete/cassette. Colleen/Lydia was too hard to sort the threads out. Pete/cassette was just too hard.

She picked up the letter from Pete's dad. It was sad, apologetic. Didn't give much information, except where the box had come from. Pete's mom had asked Chuck to keep it after Joey died and he'd kept it all these years, hoping he could give it to Pete in person when the time was right. Chuck wanted Pete to call, and he'd tell him more. There was a phone number.

She wandered into the bedroom, separated from the rest of the house by a shoulder-high partition, and lay down on the bed. She looked through the skylight at the stars—was Pete looking at them too? Ugh, corny. She got up and cranked open the big window that looked out over the lake. The warm breeze drifted in, smelling like cedar.

She turned on a light, and bugs banged against the screen. The room was a soft sage green, a contrast to the whites, grays, and tans of the rest of the house. It'd been white last time she was here. She and Pete had different opinions about color—she couldn't get enough. If she saw a white wall, she had to paint it. He liked things neutral. That was before. Now his bedroom was green, her favorite color, with an orangey-tan trim. The paint matched a new rug on the hardwood floors she watched him labor to refinish over the winter. The rug had darker greens and corals, an abstract, almost floral pattern. It made her suspicious, just a flash. But no, he wasn't the one who'd strayed during their breakup, she was. She shouldn't have to keep reminding herself.

On top of the pile of books on his nightstand was one about the effects of PTSD and suicide. She put it down as if it were on fire.

She turned out the light and went back into the living room. Pete's police scanner was on his desk, off. She turned it on and it crackled to life with the deadpan voice of the county dispatcher. Bernie didn't know his name, or the names of any of the others, but they felt like friends, their voices winding through her days and nights at the office and home. "Subject says neighbor took his lawnmower," the dispatcher said. He gave a New Sharon address, far from Redimere.

"Car operating erratically on Route 2, just before Wilton," the dispatcher said. "Caller says," Bernie said it along with him "car's all over the road." She laughed. Scanners had been the soundtrack of her career. She opened a folder on the desk as she listened. It held neatly sorted papers, dated Sunday. An insurance beneficiary change form with her name as beneficiary. A letter, looked like to a lawyer, outlining Pete's assets. She was stunned at how much money he had. Neither document made sense. Neither made her feel good, just apprehensive and guilty.

She should go home, but she'd forgotten to put her laundry in the dryer until Colleen left. She could take it home to finish, her dryer worked fine, but the thought of lugging the wet, heavy basket defeated her. Everything did.

"Anyone near Redimere?" the dispatcher asked.

"I am," Bernie said. She looked at the scanner as the numbers blinked across its screen.

"I can be," said a voice.

"Caller advises vandalism at neighbor's house. Landlord's in Florida. Racial in nature. Caller's concerned. Tenant's not home."

"I'm wrapping up something in Weld. Is the caller concerned about immediate danger, or can Redimere talk to subject in the morning?"

"Caller didn't seem concerned about any imminent threat."

"Why don't you copy Redimere PD?"

Bernie'd check with Dawna tomorrow. A hate crime. That's all they needed. She was too tired to play scanner roulette, the old newsroom game of standing by the scanner waiting to hear more.

She turned it off.

She'd been trying to avoid the box on the table, but it pulled her. She'd seen a manila envelope inside earlier. She opened it. Why not? She'd already listened to the tape. What could be worse? There was a bundle of photos, report cards, newspaper clippings. She'd been under the impression Pete had a miserable childhood, but the photos said otherwise. One of a man Bernie assumed was his dad, looking painfully like Pete, only robust, not wiry, holding a tow-headed baby caught in mid-squirm on his hip as a curly-haired older one held his hand. They were laughing. On the back was written "Chuck, Pete (5) and Joey (18 months), 1970." Another of Pete, in a necktie, playing an accordion, biting his tongue in concentration. "Pete, 10, wins Sokol talent show." Another photo of a little boy on a piano bench with a young dark-haired woman, both were playing as they smiled at each other. "Jan and Pete (4) Heart and Soul, 1969." Report cards showed all A's. The teachers loved him. "A very bright boy!" "Polite and helpful! A joy to have in class!" A newspaper clipping showed him in a high school baseball uniform in mid-pitch windup, curly hair sticking out from under his cap, biting his tongue just like in the accordion photo. The headline said, "Novotny tosses second no-hitter as win skein continues." Skein. She'd only seen that word in sports headlines, and probably not for a decade.

She was tired and sad. Agitated. She couldn't shake the PTSD book, the crumpled draft notes to his father. The beneficiary form and list of assets. The tape.

She wandered into the bathroom. Spotless, as usual. Opened the medicine cabinet. No surprises. She looked behind the door of the walk-in shower, half expecting to see Dubya, who liked to curl up in there. Before. She wandered out and opened the closet and buried her face in Pete's black wool overcoat, smelling wood smoke and soap. Pete's smells. She willed him to appear, but when she opened her eyes, it was just the coat.

She turned on the TV. The Red Sox were playing Tampa Bay. She watched for a few minutes, but the players seemed sluggish, the game something everyone just had to get through.

She clicked through the channels, stopped at the familiar "1, 2, 3, 4, 5, 6, 7, 8, schlemiel..." She hadn't seen *Laverne & Shirley* in years. It was dumb, but what she needed—a world where the biggest problem was Lenny and Squiggy seeing Laverne in her slip.

She snuggled into the couch. The girls were getting ready for a big date as a fire raged in the neighborhood. They were oblivious. Shirley had to dry her hair in the oven, which set off a bunch of suicide jokes without anyone actually saying suicide.

Suicide. She hadn't been able to believe Lydia had done it when they first thought she had. It was hard for Bernie to get how someone could have that little hope. She knew people did it. Joey did it. Pete's draft notes to his father, the PTSD book on his bed, the insurance beneficiary form all stabbed at her. Think about it later, just watch TV. The girls getting ready for their big date, a burst of laughter every thirty seconds.

She woke up to darkness, a different episode of *Laverne & Shirley*, the voices and laugh track a muddle. Three a.m. Her dreams had been a tangle of laugh track hilarity, ovens, fire, Laverne saying "Shirrrrrrl." A box with big red letters "CASE FILE" sitting in the middle of the room. Little boys crying. A man crying. Pete.

She turned off the TV. She didn't look at the tape recorder or the insurance form or anything else. She didn't check to see if there was a box anywhere that said case file in giant red letters. She got her clothes and left, desperate for her cats and dog and her own bed.

*****

The alarm on Dawna's phone buzzed under her pillow at three Wednesday morning. She'd been alert for it, waking up seconds before. She got dressed in the dark and left quietly, so she wouldn't wake her sister, who still had another half hour to go.

She eased her Jeep down the driveway, hit the gas and headed for Route 27, then north. Half an hour later, she pulled into the lot that abutted the Lazy Logger, used this time of year to store snowmobiles on trailers. She pulled up between a couple. She had a perfect view of the back of the Logger and its dumpster. She could also see the parking lot and trailhead where they'd brought Lydia down from the mountain, fifty yards away, the porta-potty and trail info kiosk glowing in the moonlight. She could watch the Sugarloaf Airport, too. Not that there was anything to watch. It was a wide dirt strip along the edge of the woods, a small cabin at the far end. A herd of deer nibbled at grass nearby, their legs gracefully bent.

Every once in a while a logging truck roared by, or a pickup, an early riser on the way to work. The Logger was in the woods on the southern edge of Carrabassett Valley. There were few homes or businesses around, just woods. It made perfect sense Fuller would choose this dumpster to look for food.

The mountains loomed on three sides. Pete was in there, somewhere, asleep under a tree likely. She was envious. She didn't get into the woods as often as she wanted to.

As she waited, she sorted through the day ahead. She'd have a lot on her plate when she got back to the office, and that was aside from getting ready for the busy Fourth of July weekend. There'd been a vandalism incident in Redimere the night before, the sheriff's department told her. An ugly racial epithet written on someone's door in what looked like dog poop. "Not a big deal, probably kids," said the deputy.

Why did people think kids spewing hate wasn't a big deal? As a Passamaquoddy, she'd heard and seen enough casual ignorant or hateful references growing up to know the damage it did, and what people who'd do that as kids grew up to be. The victim was Colleen Sullivan, the woman who'd called looking for Pete. Her neighbor called it in. She'd worry about what was going on in Redimere later. She watched the dumpster at the Logger, waiting for the shadows to change. She knew that note left on the cruiser windshield last week wasn't a hoax. She could feel it. She knew, sooner or later, Danny Fuller would show up.

CHAPTER 16

T here she is," Bernie heard Sal say from the kitchen as she came in.

"Here I am." It'd been a long Wednesday at work getting the paper done, longer than normal, given how little of her Tuesday she'd spent doing it. She'd started the day with a hangover and hadn't slept. Now here was Sal chopping vegetables for the entertainment of Chloe Houten, who was sitting at the table drinking a glass of Bernie's wine.

"Hi," Bernie said, trying to remember if they'd been introduced or she just knew who she was.

"We're brainstorming," Sal said. "Chloe, do you know my sister?"

"I've heard a lot about you," Chloe said.

"Uh oh," Bernie said, forcing a smile. She wasn't in the mood. All she wanted was to collapse on the couch with a beer until she fell asleep.

"All good," Chloe said.

Bernie got sandwich stuff out of the refrigerator.

"I'm making a salad. We're going to grill salmon," Sal said.

"I'm just gonna have a sandwich and go to bed."

"It's not even six," he said.

She shot him a look. He should know how exhausted she was. On top of it, he knew she hated unexpected company—she had to get her head into a different place and act a certain way, and she didn't have the energy.

"What we're brainstorming about, since you're so interested, is

141

Chloe's new business venture."

"Hmmph," Bernie said, spreading mustard on turkey.

"My art career is on the upswing, but I need something more immediate," he said.

"What are you going to do? Sell caricatures on Main Street?"

"Harsh," Sal said.

Chloe watched, alarmed. Bernie wanted to tell her this was normal, but she was too tired.

"We're thinking of going in on that old gas station building that's for sale on Main Street. It's pretty cool, art deco. It'd make a great restaurant," Sal said.

"Le Filling Station Bistro," Chloe said, like that would make Bernie think it was a good idea.

"I've got bad news," Bernie said. "Opening a restaurant means a huge capital outlay, and even a successful one doesn't make a profit for years."

"My parents are going to loan me the money to get it started," Chloe said.

What was she? Forty? Bernie picked up her sandwich and beer and headed for the porch.

"Ryan Grant, you know, the mayor, he's also the real estate broker Chloe works for, has been trying to unload that building for two years," Sal said, in that cheerful-come-on-get-on-board way he had. "It's in good condition and priced to sell. I'm going to make a wrought iron fence for the outdoor seating, wrought iron tables."

"For the six weeks a year that people can actually sit outside," Bernie said. The introduction of Ryan Grant into the conversation didn't make her like it any better.

"We'll have tables inside, too," Chloe said.

"Success assured."

"Once Chloe knows you better she'll realize this is what you're like, and that she shouldn't take it personally," Sal said. "Sorry, Chloe. I don't know why my sister is being such a rhymes-with-witch."

Bernie came back from the porch doorway and put her

sandwich on the counter. "Sorry. Long day." Week. Month. Year. "We could use another restaurant in town."

"That's what Sean says," Chloe said.

Sal broke in before Bernie could react. "Chloe's dating Sean Speck."

Bernie's resolve of thirty seconds before to be nice disappeared. She couldn't think of one nice thing to say. Maybe change the subject. "Would you still sell real estate?"

"No, it's not really for me," she said.

"Grant's an asshole," Sal said.

"I second that," Bernie said.

"He's okay," Chloe said. "It's just hard working for a guy that much younger."

"That's why I'm self-employed," Bernie said. "Let me guess, he doesn't really listen to you, but thinks he's a great listener. No matter how hard you work, he gets the credit for what you do. But if something goes wrong, it's all your fault, even if it wasn't. He doesn't read or answer your emails, even though they're about things he wanted you to do. Then he gets mad if you ask again, or the thing gets done wrong. But he thinks the men in the office are brilliant."

"Some of that, yeah," Chloe said. "Maybe not everything."

"Just wait," Bernie said.

"Don't encourage her," Sal said to Chloe.

"Well, there was this one thing," Chloe said. "It bugged me. I'd spent weeks working up a new spreadsheet for us to keep better track of properties and their status. Every time I mentioned it to him, he didn't say much. Then, the day I finished it, he announced to the office we were getting new software, and it made everything I'd done useless. He'd known about the software for weeks, but hadn't said anything."

"Ha," said Bernie. "Doesn't surprise me."

"Now look what you started," Sal said.

"I was really upset, but he brushed it off," Chloe said, like she was just realizing it. "He said he never asked me to do the

143

spreadsheet, but he knew I was doing it and never said not to. It would've been great, too. We have a lot of property to keep track of."

A spark of recognition flicked in Bernie's dead brain. "Hey, you live next door to Colleen Sullivan."

"I got her the rental," Chloe said. "Did you hear about the graffiti?"

"A little." Very little. Colleen hadn't wanted to say anything when Bernie called her that morning about it. Dawna was too busy to fill her in.

"Someone wrote 'N word go home' in dog poop on her front door. Only it wasn't 'N word.'"

"That's really disappointing. I thought this town was better," Bernie said.

"I'm the one who reported it," Chloe said. "She wasn't home. She's nice. I'm glad she finally made it here. I was afraid the rental was going to fall through and give Ryan something else to be mad at me about. She called up at the beginning of June and booked it for the whole summer, but then didn't show up until last week. She'd paid first and last month, all of June, too, but Ryan was all, 'You should've gotten all the money up front.'"

"Did she say why she didn't get here until last week?"

"No." Chloe shrugged. "Ryan was all antsy to get a tenant for that house, now that I have one, he's annoyed."

"I could never work in real estate," Bernie said.

"I couldn't be a reporter," Chloe said. "To hear Sean talk about it, it sounds so hard. They're doing a story about the fire chief, and it's just very hard to get the right information."

"Ixnay on the iefchay," Sal said.

"I understand pig latin, Sal," Bernie said.

"I don't get it," Chloe said.

"I already know about the story, anyway," Bernie said.

"It's funny, I thought he and the police chief were a couple, until Sal told me that you date the police chief," Chloe said.

Bernie laughed. "Sandy and Pete a couple?"

"I saw them at the bean supper at the Congregational Church a month or so ago, then the next week, I saw them at the bean supper at the VFW."

"Were they holding hands or something?" Bernie asked.

Chloe took it seriously. "No, but they laughed a lot. They looked like they enjoyed each other's company. They were cute together." She shrugged.

"They go to all the bean suppers," Bernie said. "Community relations thing." She forgot, sometimes, what good friends Pete and Sandy were. They had a bond over their shared responsibility for the town, Sandy told her once, totally without self-consciousness. She wondered if they'd ever be friends like that again. Assuming Pete came home.

"Where's Dubya?" She'd been too tired to notice until now that he hadn't greeted her at the door, hadn't been banging against their legs in the kitchen.

"I thought you had him," Sal said.

"Does it look like I have him? He was asleep on the couch when I left this morning."

"He must've gotten out."

Bernie stuck her head out the porch door. "Dubya! Here boy!"

"You know how he is," Sal said. "He'll be back when he's hungry."

"I saw him walking down Main Street one day like he owned the place," Chloe said. "He looked so funny, with all that big round fuzzy body on those short little legs. So proud of himself."

Bernie knew she was trying to be reassuring, but it didn't help.

Sal nodded. "He likes adventures."

Bernie took her beer to the porch. Her dream of relaxing, slowing her head down, was crushed. Now the dog was gone. She couldn't deal with one more thing, say one more word to one more person.

After a while, Sal came out with the salmon.

"Where's Chloe?" Bernie asked.

"Calling Sean." Sal laughed, a little hollow. "You know how it is, 'You hang up,' 'No you hang up.'"

Bernie could hear Chloe's voice rising and falling, faintly. Laughter, too loud and bright. She'd gone into the guest room to make the call. Bernie watched Sal fiddle with the grill, brush his curly black hair back. He was definitely a better catch than Sean, even if he was her annoying little brother.

"You laugh, but the restaurant's a really good idea," he said. "The real estate thing sucks for her. She's just not the type, you know? She has a culinary degree. She's worked at restaurants all over Maine."

"Why isn't she working at one now?"

Sal waved his hand at her. "Circumstances. Thanks for not giving her a hard time about Sean. She'll figure out he's a jerk."

"Here's hoping. Doesn't look like she has a great track record."

"She's had a rough time. Her husband died of a stroke two years ago, and she has the three kids."

"Where are they? With Dubya?"

"Hallowell's babysitting."

"Seriously? With a baby? He's eleven."

Sal shrugged. "You guys babysat at that age. Younger."

"That was in the wild seventies, when parents raised their kids to be feral animals."

"Hallowell's pretty responsible, and with cellphones it's easy. She's also kind of an airhead."

"You want to rescue her."

"Just helping out with the restaurant plan. We're already business partners since she's renting me the studio."

"You have no money. Her parents can't pay for everything. I can't believe they'd be on board with this, and I don't even know them."

"Shut up, she'll hear you. They're concerned about their grandkids."

"What about the baby daddies?"

Sal sighed. "Why are you so judgmental? Hallowell's dad was an asshole, and he's not in the picture. Carl, Corinna's dad, was a

146

great guy, but he's dead, like I said. She doesn't know who Richmond's father was. She went through a rough time after Carl died."

"What's with the names?"

"Towns they were conceived in."

Bernie spit beer down her chin. "No," she said, wiping it with her hand. "Please. No."

Sal grinned. "I'm not making it up. Though Corinna may be the Dylan song, I can't remember. Or both. Maybe she was conceived in Corinna while the Dylan song was playing."

"Stop." Bernie was laughing too hard to say anything else. "Good thing she didn't conceive any of them in Coburn Gore. Or Mechanic Falls."

Sal was laughing too. "Stop."

"Cornville."

"Don't make fun of her. She's got a huge heart, and the restaurant's a great idea."

"I hope she chooses you over Speck."

They could hear Chloe saying good-bye.

"I have faith. Her liking him better than me would just be weird."

Bernie swallowed the last of her beer, scanned the woods for Dubya. "Everything's weird, Sal. So fucking weird, I don't know which way is up."

*****

Dawna's cellphone rang as she was getting into her Jeep to go home. Bernie.

"Have you seen Dubya in your travels?"

"No. He's missing again?"

"Yeah."

"He'll turn up."

"Yeah." Bernie didn't sound so sure.

"I've got a question," Dawna said. "Off the record-ish."

"Ish?"

"Just something I wondered if you'd know."

147

"Okay."

"I've had two calls now from Ryan Grant. Yesterday he was looking for Pete, didn't say why. Today he wanted to know if we kept criminal files on town personnel."

"Really?"

"I told him all the personnel files are in the town office, and he said, 'Not personnel files, criminal files.'"

"That's not good."

"I mean, there's no such thing, as far as Pete or Sandy or anyone else who works for the town is concerned."

"Chrissake. I bet it's whatever Feckless Kelley and Speck are doing."

"But criminal files?"

"I don't know. I have no idea what they're after. Feckless was giving Sandy a hard time yesterday, but Sandy didn't seem concerned."

"The state guys were pissed Sandy went up there and found the body without them knowing, so maybe it's got to do with that," Dawna said. "But criminal files? And why would Grant care?"

"They're just fishing," Bernie didn't sound very sure. "And you know how Grant is, one of those guys who doesn't give his own people any credit, but the minute an outsider has a criticism, he jumps right on it."

Dawna laughed. "You are so down on that guy."

"He just reminds me of people I've worked for. I'm tired of guys like him always calling the shots. Why isn't Gert Feeney mayor?"

Dawna started driving out of the parking lot. Sandy was sitting on the bench by the firetruck bays, Heidi at attention at his feet. Dawna waved. He smiled and waved back. She couldn't understand how anyone could have an issue with Sandy.

"Grant wouldn't say any more about what it was," Dawna said to Bernie.

"It's all about control, because he's in over his head, but too egotistical to want anyone to figure that out. Did you ask Sandy?"

"He said it's bullshit and not to worry."

"He said that to me, too. I guess we shouldn't worry," Bernie said. "We've got lots of other things to worry about, anyway."

"Yeah," Dawna said.

Bernie sounded worried though. Just as worried as Dawna was.

CHAPTER 17

Bernie couldn't sit still after the conversation with Sal and Chloe. Talking to Dawna had made it worse. She hung up and sat in her car in the driveway. Maybe she'd go to Pete's and see if the case file was there, like in her dream, only not as obvious. She'd meant to ask Dawna about it, but she had a feeling Pete hadn't told anyone. Although Crystal knew about it, so maybe everyone but her did. She was tired of all the bullshit and innuendo. She had enough on her mind with her missing boyfriend and missing dog. Okay, her boyfriend wasn't missing, it just felt like he was. She was going to start getting to the bottom of things. All things. Everything. She called Sandy.

"Can we talk?"

"What's up?"

"I don't want to talk on the phone," Bernie said. "Where are you?"

"Is your phone bugged?" he asked. "Are they on to us?"

"Don't mess with me."

"Sitting in front of the station."

When she got there, Sandy was on the bench, legs stretched out, face turned up to the early evening sun. Heidi sat at his feet, doing her large German shepherd regal pose thing, disguising the fact she was as goofy as Dubya. Sandy was leaning back against the bricks, his tanned arms crossed over his crisp white uniform shirt.

"Have you seen Dubya?" she asked.

"I haven't. Heidi?"

The dog took her cue and rolled on her back, tongue out and legs wiggling. Bernie rubbed her tummy.

"He'll come back," Sandy said.

Bernie leaned back against the brick wall, too. Heidi put her chin on Bernie's thigh. Bernie stroked her head, looking into her deep brown eyes. Heidi sighed, a little bit of dog drool wetting Bernie's pants. She didn't care, she kept petting.

"Pete'll come back, too," Sandy said.

"My bad feeling's getting worse."

"I dread to think what you're going to be like by Saturday."

That's right, it was only Wednesday. She couldn't tell him about the package from Pete's father, the anguished crumpled replies, the insurance policy, the PTSD suicide book. Her deep fear. The anxiety that had become a being, buzzing through her.

"What the hell is *Franklin On Call* writing about?" she asked.

"*Franklin On Call?*" His eyes were closed, his posture hadn't changed. He didn't seem upset or surprised or anything else.

"Don't pretend you don't know what I'm talking about. Speck and Kelley."

"That sounds like a bad nineteen-thirties bank robbery duo."

"What's it about? Lydia?"

"I don't know. Some shit."

"You don't seem worried."

"I don't have anything to be worried about."

· "Here's what you should be worried about. The mayor's poking around now. Those guys could get something totally wrong and write a really damaging story; it doesn't matter if it's false, the damage would still be done. It could wreck your life."

"I highly doubt it would wreck my life."

"You've got to be the most easy-going person I've ever met."

"You say that like there's something wrong with it."

"I can't imagine what they could be writing about. Why the mayor would care. Gert Feeney said Grant was asking about Pete, too. It must be because those guys put a bug in his ear," Bernie said.

Sandy sat up. Heidi abandoned Bernie and flopped her head onto his lap, pulling at his hand with a giant paw. "Silly dog," he said, rubbing her ears. "It's not about the steamy Redimere love triangle if that's what you're worried about."

"I'm not," Bernie said. "I'm worried about it having to do with something about you finding Lydia, and somehow mixing in Pete's issues, and they'll get it totally wrong."

"I don't believe it has much to do with that."

"If it's not about Lydia, then why is Crystal talking to them?"

"Let's just drop it."

The public safety building was at the end of Main Street, right before it faded into woods and farm fields, but Bernie could still hear voices, bursts of laughter, coming from the Pizza Bowl's roof deck a block away. An occasional car went by, racing way over the speed limit on the empty street. Across the street, the empty gas station that Chloe and Sal wanted to buy glowed in the setting sun. It was stucco, with arched bays. Kind of cute. It pissed Bernie off. Everything did.

"I just feel like if I could figure out what happened to Lydia, everything else will make sense," she said.

Sandy snorted.

"Okay, not everything, but it would be one less thing that didn't."

"You know Pete has the case file, right? At his house."

So Sandy knew, too. She was probably the only person in town who he hadn't told. "How do you know?"

He leaned back again. Heidi flopped down, her snout on his foot. "They'd decided by Saturday it was suicide. Pete was over at my house that afternoon having a beer and telling me about his big plan to go over and win you back when Libby called to tell him."

"Don't be mean about Pete," Bernie said. "They decided Saturday? It's like they didn't even think about it."

"Yeah, right after the autopsy. Said it was pretty obvious, just confirmed what they knew. Pete asked if he could have the case file, and Libby told him he'd have to go to Augusta to get it. As far as I know, he went Sunday afternoon. Monday, when I asked him about it, he said it was at his house. By then he'd done his turnaround on the whole thing."

Saturday afternoon. Sunday afternoon. In between, Pete had come to her house, they'd made up, he'd spent the night. He never mentioned the case file. She tried not to feel hurt. After all, they hadn't talked about Lydia at all.

"It just pisses me off," she said. "How fast they decided."

"You know how it goes," Sandy said. "They've got enough to do without borrowing trouble, looking into a case with no evidence of murder."

"I wish you were more pissed off."

He shrugged. Bernie swatted at a mosquito. A dog barked in the distance, and Heidi jumped up, ears forward. "It's not Dubya, Heidi." Bernie could tell by the bark. Too yappy. Heidi didn't care who it was. She panted happily, rotating her ears.

"Do you think Heidi could find Dubya?" Bernie asked.

"If he was standing right in front of her with a salami in his mouth," Sandy said.

"How did that happen, you guys going up there?" So much had happened since Friday, she hadn't asked him. She wondered how his version would match Crystal's.

"Crystal called Friday morning. She knew I was trained in search and rescue. She and LeeAnne were pretty sure Lydia hadn't gotten as far west as the searchers thought. You know that. The two of them wouldn't shut up about it."

"Oh yeah, I remember."

"So when Crystal got that call from the woman in Millinocket, the hiker who'd just finished the trail, I think Crystal was pissed no one took her seriously and just said to hell with it. You know? Just find her ourselves. Me and Jamie met them up at the trailhead, the one by the Sugarloaf Airport, not the AT one up at Wyman Township, around seven-thirty."

"I'd think you'd go earlier."

"I'd been at that conference in Bangor the day before. Sleeping in."

Bernie remembered. Thursdays were usually one of their "date nights," but that one wasn't.

"I didn't tell Pete we were going. I figured it was probably a wild goose chase."

"So what did Wilson the tipster tell Crystal?" She didn't want to let on Crystal had already told her, because then he might leave things out, assuming she knew. Old reporter's trick.

"She caught up to Lydia shortly after the trailhead. They hiked along for a while, got around West Carry Pond, and Lydia turned off, saying she'd heard there were old logging camps all overgrown and it was kind of cool and she wanted to check them out."

"She's right about that," Bernie said. "They're all on my Rambler map, as you know."

"Yep. We found that old logging road you'd told Lydia about almost right away."

"I never told Lydia about a logging road."

"When you interviewed her at the Pour House."

"Sounds like me. But I'd remember."

"Did she see your map?"

"No."

"Maybe someone else told her, and by the time I heard about it, the info was crooked." He shrugged. "Crystal knew about it, and LeeAnne. Don't look so surprised. You've blabbed about it a lot, with your Midnight Rambler obsession. A bigger surprise would be if you hadn't told her."

"My interview with Lydia wasn't that long, because it was right before Memorial Day weekend and Pete and I were going away the next morning." Bernie poked the bruise a little. Yep, still hurt. "Lydia was tired and wasn't really talkative."

"When did that ever stop you?"

"Crystal didn't tell me Lydia heard about that stuff from me. How does Wilson remember it in such detail?"

"From Crystal's description, picture Rain Man's personality, only a woman in her fifties with a build like Big Bird."

"I'm trying."

"She also remembered a cairn where Lydia split off, and she was right. We found it easily. You can barely see the tote road in the growth, but it's a quicker route to where Lydia was found than where the official searchers went. Where they went, the terrain was too tough. I think they figured she wouldn't have gone up there."

"She would've still been alive when they were looking up there."

"Yeah, sad." Sandy said. "Which is why the state guys aren't keen on us being heroes."

"I wish I could get hold of Wilson," Bernie said. "I don't care how odd she is. I can do odd. She wouldn't give Crystal her info, though, not her real name or anything. Crystal said she was waiting to catch the shuttle to the Bangor airport and fly away to whatever 'I' state she lives in. The phone number she gave Crystal wasn't in service when I tried it. Area code 361 something."

"You sure about 361?"

"Yeah, it was our house number growing up."

"361 is Texas. Corpus Christi."

"How does a Franklin County farm boy know that?"

"I was there in the Navy, way back when."

"The stuff I don't know about you. So Wilson just gave Crystal a fake number. She didn't want to be bothered."

"Possible."

"Maybe she's the killer."

"Except when we found Lydia, she'd been dead less than a day, so she was probably killed the day Wilson told Crystal where to find her, and Wilson was in Millinocket, nearly two hundred miles away as the trail crawls."

"It doesn't make sense," Bernie said.

"Question everything that doesn't make sense, a top investigator we both know says."

"Sherlock Holmes?"

"Only smarter." He waited. "Pete. Sheesh. Get with it, Bernie."

"You know what I think when I hear 'Wilson?' *Castaway*. 'Willlsonnnnn! I'm sorry, Wilsonnnnn!' You know, Tom Hanks' volleyball? God, I hate that movie."

"Maybe Millinocket lady looked like a volleyball."

155

"Do you think Crystal is misdirecting me?" Bernie asked. "She doesn't want me to talk to Wilson, so she gave me a fake number to placate me."

"Maybe. Why, though?" He didn't sound like he cared.

Bernie was annoyed. "How would I know?"

"Good point." He knocked her upper arm lightly with his elbow. She looked at him, and he smiled at her. She jabbed him back.

"You don't have to figure it all out tonight," he said. He looked tired, despite the smile. Everyone did these days.

"You're really not upset about those useless fucks writing some bullshit story about you?"

"I really am not."

"Why?"

"Bernadette, sweetheart, this too shall pass."

They sat for a while, wordless, as Heidi panted at the bugs banging against the light on the wall. The sun was almost gone, and the mosquitoes were getting worse.

"I feel claustrophobic," Bernie said. "Everything's crowding me, making all this noise. There's too much of everything." She felt a tear on her cheek but didn't wipe it because she didn't want him to notice.

"This too shall pass," Sandy repeated, almost a whisper. "I promise."

Bernie wanted to find her dog. Eat something. Sleep. She patted him on the knee. "Goodnight, Mr. Zen. I wish I knew your secret."

As she got in her car, she thought she heard him say, "No you don't." When she looked back, his eyes were closed again, head back against the wall. Heidi watched her, anxious.

She started up the car and drove home. Tomorrow was another day. She couldn't be Zen about it, but as long as there was another day, things could get straightened out.

CHAPTER 18

When Bernie got home, Sal and Chloe were gone. Sal had left a note. "Dub not back. See ya tomorrow."

Her exhaustion had turned into anxiety. Or maybe it'd been anxiety all along. She was having trouble telling the difference. Every twenty minutes or so she'd call Dubya. She heard crickets and cicadas, a loon, the peepers and the breeze. The occasional car or truck whooshing somewhere on its way somewhere else. Firecrackers here and there. But no happy bark, no anxious whine.

She turned on the TV, but everything was boring. The Red Sox were sluggish again, every batter taking forever, every pitcher fidgeting and walking around the mound. The commercials were loud and way too long. She found the channel that showed endless loops of *Laverne & Shirley* and watched that for a while. Her panic about Pete had reached crisis level. Full-on red alert. She tried to tell herself, had been telling herself all day that she was just tired and jumpy and her dog was missing and everyone was being weird. Pete not being here was something to focus her anxiety on. That didn't make it go away. She knew she couldn't go into the woods and look for him, but she had to do something. She searched her bag for the paper she'd written Pete's dad's number on. It was nine-forty-five, so in Wisconsin that would be, what? She couldn't begin to think. Sometime earlier than it was here, in any case.

She got an answering machine, Chuck's pleasant rumble a little deeper and Wisconsin-accented, but similar enough to Pete's to make her cry. She had no idea what to say.

"Hi, you don't know me," she said after the beep. "I'm Bernadette O'Dea, a friend of your son Pete. He's," her voice cracked, and she took a shaky deep breath. "He's not doing well. He went for a hike, and I'm just really worried." She laughed, but it came out more like a cry. "He got your package and took off. He's been in bad shape. He has PTSD. I'm worried. Sorry, I know I said that." She was openly crying now. "I'm sorry to bother you. I know you can't do anything. I'm just so worried. I don't want to upset you, just, okay. I'll let you know when he comes home that he's okay. Sorry to bother you. Bernie."

She hung up. Her family made fun of her habit of signing off messages with her name, like it was a letter. She didn't do it on purpose. She could call again and take it back. The rest of the message, too, but that would make her feel even dumber.

She went into her bedroom and lay down, listening to the night through the open window. Listening for Dubya's tell-tale bark. She was listening for Pete, too. The chug of his Volvo, even though he didn't have a Volvo anymore. He had a Subaru like everyone else. Any car coming down the street could be him. This time of night there weren't that many, and none stopped, no sound of tires on the gravel driveway. She didn't know why she was listening. He wouldn't come out of the woods and drive up to her house. Someone had to pick him up at the trailhead. He wasn't due home for days. It was only Wednesday. Well, Thursday now. He hadn't even been gone three days.

She went into the kitchen. It was three a.m. The cats, alerted to a possible food situation, wound around her legs. "Where's your brother?" They didn't care. She poured them some food, then took a beer out of the fridge. It tasted horrible. She dumped it down the sink and got dressed. She propped open the door to the backyard and put bowls of dog food and water on the porch. She knew she was as likely to have a new raccoon or skunk pet when she got home, but she'd take the chance.

She drove down the hill, even though it was just half a mile, so she'd have her car if there was an emergency. She wasn't sure what type, but she felt like there was bound to be one. One where she could get in her car and race to it and solve it. The town was dead quiet, except for the crickets and early morning birds. Everything was wet with humidity. The office smelled musty and damp, like it had aged another century overnight. She opened the payroll file on her computer, but the numbers didn't make sense and she kept losing track.

She took out a legal pad and started a list. A row for Colleen's story, one for Crystal's, one for the official story, one for Sandy's. One for what she knew to be true. One for Wilson. She made columns: the facts about Lydia, the facts about her remains being found. She circled things that contradicted each other. Was there more? One for the Midnight Rambler and one for Danny Fuller. Though even if either of them had done something, how would she know? She could put down what was likely about them, though those wouldn't be facts. Maybe she needed a separate column for speculation.

It was a mess.

There was a knock at the door. Colleen.

"I was going for coffee but saw you through the window," she said. "You start early."

It was five-thirty. "Yeah, sometimes. I've got a pot on. It's pretty fresh."

"Thank you. That would be nice."

She led her to the coffee maker and couch in the back.

"I have a request," she said. "I wonder if I could look at your archives, your research into the Rambler, as well as newspapers covering his time here."

Bernie wanted to protest, but she'd shown the entire world her archives, if that's what they were.

"I know they're not for public use," Colleen said. "But if I found information I'd want to use in my book, maybe we could work together, and it would be beneficial to both of us."

"Okay." Bernie was too tired to weigh the pros and cons. Even if Colleen hadn't told her everything, it would only help to have another brain looking at the Rambler stuff, now that Colleen thought he was Herman Czarnec, the killer nurse.

159

"Can we talk about the racism incident?" Bernie hadn't intended to make it sound like it was part of a deal to let Colleen look at the archives, but realized when Colleen flinched, it probably had.

"I'd prefer not to make a big deal about it," Colleen said.

"I'm sorry it happened," Bernie said. "I'd expect more from our town."

Colleen shrugged.

"Why don't you want to report it?"

"I'd just as soon move forward."

"Reporting it shines the light on things like that."

"Can we talk about something else?"

"What do you want to look for in my archives?"

"Any little thing about Herman, or that could be him, anything that no one thought of that would help me find out what he's been doing, and maybe even what happened with Lydia."

"How much do you think he's connected to Lydia disappearing?"

Colleen opened her bag. It was a courier bag, kind of like Bernie's, only more organized. She handed Bernie the note that Herman had mailed to Lydia all those months ago. "I feel like this is the key to everything."

His handwriting was block print, but kind of rounded.

Bernie went to her computer and opened the photo of the Danny Fuller note Dawna had shown her.

"It's the same handwriting?" Colleen asked, looking at the photo.

"I'm not an expert, but yeah."

"What is this?"

"Someone left it on the windshield of the town police cruiser."

"Herman must want Danny Fuller out of his hair. And yes, I know who Danny Fuller is. I read your paper." Colleen's smile was genuine, and Bernie smiled back.

"The thing is, the notebook paper is steno paper, the same kind Lydia used, and the handwriting is Herman's, if it's the same as on the one he mailed Lydia."

"Was this note before or after Lydia was found?" Colleen asked.

"Everything's such a muddle," Bernie said. She counted back days. "Before."

Bernie took out her phone and scrolled through the photos as they walked back to the lounge. She settled on one and showed it to Colleen.

"What's this?"

"About a half-dozen letters came here for Lydia before she got to this part of the trail," Bernie said. "I took a photo of the envelopes to use with a story. Then I forgot. I don't use the phone as a camera a lot."

"The one on top looks like the same handwriting."

"That's what I think. Lydia read them that night in the Pour House. She didn't say much, but she was really quiet after. Nervous-acting. It bugged me."

Bernie sank into the chair; exhaustion was setting in, despite the gallon of coffee.

"Where is it now?" Colleen asked.

"I assume, if she kept them with her, Crystal has it. She was given Lydia's belongings."

Colleen rolled her eyes.

"I can ask her," Bernie said. "So that means if the handwriting is Herman's, he wrote a letter that Lydia received here right before she disappeared, and that later, after she disappeared, he had her notebook paper, or paper that looks like hers, which would mean he was in contact with her." Bernie was proud she'd been able to connect those dots, given her mental state.

"That's something," Colleen said.

Bernie nodded. "Something."

"Did I mention the other night that I think Herman was falsely accused?" Colleen asked.

"No."

"He was an easy target. Everyone thought he was weird. His

161

nickname was Herman Munster, but the evidence wasn't any stronger for him than anyone else."

"Did the murders stop when he left?"

"They seem to have stopped when the investigation started."

"That could mean anything. Were they mercy killings?"

"No, they were random. Some of the people were pretty sick, but none were terminal."

"What killed them?"

"Someone spiked IV bags, totally random. No one realized it was happening at first. The theory was they were spiked while they were set up before the beginning of the shift. They could go to anyone."

"Murder roulette," Bernie said. "Why was Herman a suspect? There must've been something besides no one liking him."

"The victims all died on his shift, but he worked a lot of shifts. There were a good eight or nine people with similar shifts, including Crystal, LeeAnne, and Lydia. No one nurse was there for every single murder—remember, these are just ones we know about—but they all could've accessed the IV bags. They didn't have to be there when someone got the IV."

"Hard to figure out," Bernie said.

"I've done extensive research into Herman's past," Colleen said. "He'd been a foster child, abused, and it's known childhood abuse can cause PTSD and other issues that emerge in adulthood. But he's also methodical and organized, a creature of habit. Total rule-follower. There were no red flags."

"That anyone knows of."

"True. It's also hard to get records or accurate information. The information about shifts and the four patients they think were victims was in a very thin report someone from the hospital finally gave me a copy of, but Lydia told me there should be records of drugs that nurses signed out and that type of thing. When I asked the hospital administration, they said most of those records weren't around anymore. That's about where it's at."

"Why don't I show you the archives?" Bernie said. They went

up the creaky wooden stairs to the second floor. Bernie led her to the back, stifling despite the high ceiling and the fact the sun was barely up. It smelled like a century of baking wood and old newspapers and ink. Bernie breathed deep.

"I love that smell," Colleen said.

"Me too. Sorry it's so hot." Bernie turned on a box fan. "This just blows the dust around, but at least it feels like it's doing something."

She showed Colleen the stacks, and how the papers are in order of year, month and day, as well as the index card system and clipping files. Then she led her behind the stacks to the far wall.

Bernie had gotten a lot of different reactions to what Sandy called her Rambler exhibit. He'd laughed and shook his head the first time he saw it, months ago, but had also been fascinated. Lydia's friends, Crystal and LeeAnne, seemed overwhelmed, but became more interested as Lydia's disappearance dragged on. The map was their guide as they endlessly hiked the section of trail she'd vanished on, trying to figure out where she'd gone.

When Bernie had shown Pete, back when their relationship was still new, she couldn't tell if he was impressed or worried about her sanity, but he'd been sweet about it. "Boy, if he doesn't exist you'll at least have the most detailed extensive map of Franklin County in the world." Then he kissed her.

Colleen was definitely impressed. "Wow."

"I know," Bernie said as they took it in.

Bernie had nailed the largest topographical map of Franklin County she could find to the wall. She'd marked trails, and anything she could find about former logging camps and other old communities in the woods. She had different color pins for burglaries, the colors representing less than five, less than ten and more than ten, with labels showing addresses.

"As we get closer to now, 2010, it's more complete," Bernie said. "The farther I go back, the less specific the stats are, but these basically go back ten years. These are burglaries I think he could be responsible for. See how each label is numbered? I have a list here."

163

A color-coded list of addresses, some annotated, filled the wall next to the map. "I have a separate list of items taken as a computer file. Clothing, books, food, anything people reported."

"This is fantastic," Colleen said.

"These boxes over here are the reports I've gathered and clipping files and stuff," Bernie said, trying to sound like, hey, everyone does this kind of thing. "I have a request in to Redimere police for more information on specific burglaries in town. He seems to have targeted the town, even though Kingfield is closer to what I believe is his base. The burglaries radiate out from here." She pointed to a circle around Redimere and its nearby lakes. "His base, or what I think is his base, is more than twenty miles from here, but you can see the different areas of his focus and how it connects. See all these camp burglaries up there around Flagstaff Lake? I think that's when he doesn't stray far from home."

"So the same territory where Lydia was found."

"Yeah," Bernie said. "I'd been thinking it was just a coincidence."

Colleen ran her fingers over the map, like it was Braille. "I wish it told us what happened."

"Maybe it will," Bernie said.

Colleen was going to have breakfast, then come back. Bernie walked with her down the stairs.

"Did you and Lydia text while she was hiking?" Bernie asked.

"Not regularly, and not about Herman," Colleen said. "She didn't want to take the chance Crystal and LeeAnne would see. It would upset them. They really disliked him. They thought he was a murderer, after all. They thought Lydia was too easily influenced by him."

"Do you think Herman killed Lydia?"

"I hope not," Colleen said. "I wish I'd told the police chief more last week, but she was still only missing and I didn't want to, I don't know, seem like a crazy woman with crazy ideas or something."

"He would've taken it in stride," Bernie said.

"He said at first he wasn't the right guy to talk to, and that made me even more reluctant. But the more I thought about it after she was found, he felt like the right guy, like he'd listen to me."

"Yeah, that's him." Bernie's heart sank a little more.

*****

After Colleen left, Bernie got back to work. Actually, back to staring at her computer. It was Thursday. She should take the day off. The paper was out. She couldn't imagine even thinking about putting out another one.

"Good news," Carrie said, deadpan, as she came in the front door.

"What?" Bernie never knew if Carrie was joking. The delivery was always the same.

"I got those burglary stats from Dawna."

"Anything interesting?" Burglary stats were interesting, but now that Bernie knew, or thought she might know, who the Rambler was, there were so many things that were even more interesting. If only they were as easy to find out.

"One big thing," Carrie said. "Redimere Drug over the past ten years was burglarized forty-seven times. That's as far back as Dawna's stats go. Most of those were before Pete became chief in August 2008. The old chief used to scrub the police log—you know, not make them public. Dawna said he didn't want people to panic. Once Pete started leaving them in, they dropped off."

"The burglar realized someone noticed after all," Bernie said. "Did you say forty-seven in ten years at Redimere Drug?"

Carrie nodded.

"Holy crap, that's a lot of times for one business to be burgled."

"Dawna says the building was old, and Herb didn't want to invest in more security. The back door lock was easy to pick, I guess." Carrie was bouncing a little. She usually didn't get this excited. Bernie perked up. This *was* good information.

"There's more," Carrie said. "The burglar always took similar things, which would make you think it was the same guy. He took

165

stationary supplies, batteries, candy, and specific drugs."

"Gotta be the Rambler. They kept records of what drugs he took?"

Carrie came over to Bernie's desk with a pile of papers. "Some. Antibiotics, mostly. But the last one, the one a couple weeks ago, he took a load of morphine, remember?"

"Yeah. Jamie tried to convince me it was a different burglar because that's the first time morphine was stolen."

"Dawna said, too, since Herb's been gone for eight months or so, the new owners, they're in Portland, and since there haven't been that many burglaries since they bought it in January, they haven't done much for security. They got a new door last week, though."

Bernie felt better. In fact, she felt great. She didn't know how, or even if, all this was connected to Lydia. Maybe the morphine was, somehow, though it didn't cause carbon monoxide poisoning. She knew that much. She'd Googled CO causes and got all the things she expected—faulty furnaces, generators in the house, grills in the house. Nothing that could've killed Lydia.

Her cellphone rang. Redimere PD. Jesus, it wasn't even seven. The anxiety rose so fast she realized it hadn't been gone after all. Just waiting.

It was Dawna.

"Is Pete okay?" Bernie asked.

"This isn't about Pete," Dawna said. "I thought I'd tell you before the state police get their press release out. Danny Fuller's been arrested here in Franklin County."

"Wow. What happened?"

"I'm not sure how much I'm allowed to say, so this is off the record. I've been staking out the Lazy Logger in the early mornings. He showed up this morning. So, I arrested him."

"Wait, you're the one who arrested him? Talk about burying the lead. And you make it sound like it was easy as pie."

"I think he was just tired of living in the woods." Bernie could almost hear Dawna blush over the phone.

Bernie was getting Fuller and the Rambler mixed up. She waited a beat for it to sort out. "Can you tell me anything on the record, so I can get it on the web before the whole world gets the release?"

"I wish I could," Dawna said. "I can give you some exclusive quotes after the release comes out, if that helps."

Bernie gave Carrie, who was listening, a thumbs-up. "Where's he now?"

"Farmington. The county jail."

"There must be something you can tell me."

"Bernie." Dawna was throwing the flag that Bernie was used to hearing from Pete. "I don't want to mess things. I didn't even talk to you, okay? Everything's coming from the state."

"George Libby?"

"Maybe. I think the release will be out around eight."

"Okay. Then I'll call you for some quotes."

"You'd have to ask him." Dawna paused. "We're not their favorite people, with the Lydia thing. I don't want to fuck up with the chief gone."

Dawna rarely swore. Bernie reined herself in. "No problem. I'm glad for the heads-up."

CHAPTER 19

The press release finally came at eight-thirty. It didn't say much except that Fuller was arrested. Nothing about Dawna's stakeout or that she's the one who made the arrest. There was a press conference at two in Farmington. "So we have to go to Farmington? Why even send the press release?" Bernie asked the room. She had a bad feeling about it.

Around noon, her cellphone rang. It was Crystal. She got right to the point, none of the usual friendly small talk. "I know you've been talking to Colleen Sullivan."

"Excuse me?"

"I didn't get the chance to tell you the other day, but I heard she's been talking to people, and now I heard she was there at your office today," Crystal said. "I want to be sure you're aware that she's a very smart woman, but she has some strange ideas. I hope you're not getting drawn in."

"We haven't really talked much about anything. She wanted to look at the newspaper archives."

"She may tell you she was Lydia's friend, but they weren't really," Crystal said. "Be very careful with how much you say to her."

"It's not my first rodeo," Bernie said.

"Sorry," Crystal said. "I know you know what you're doing. It's just that Colleen has made life difficult for a lot of people, including Lydia. I don't think it's appropriate for her to be here."

"I understand."

"I also wanted to tell you I remembered something Wilson said."

"Shoot." Bernie grabbed a pen and flipped the legal pad on her desk to a blank page.

"She told me she'd lived in Niagara Falls in the early nineties, before moving to whatever 'I' state she's from," Crystal said.

"Let's just say Indiana for the sake of calling it something," Bernie said. Or Corpus Christi, Texas.

"Her mother had been a patient at our hospital. She and Lydia had chatted about the coincidence as they hiked. I think it could be more than a coincidence."

"Definitely."

"You might want to find out more."

"Yeah, just gotta find out who Wilson is. On yet another note, with the stuff they gave back to you, did they give you Lydia's phone?"

Crystal thought about it. "You know what? I don't think they did. I hadn't even thought about it."

"Anyone say anything about it?"

"No one said a word to me," Crystal said. "Now that I think about it, that bothers me. I wonder where it is?"

After Bernie hung up, she tried to make the Wilson timeline work. The timing would be off, as Sandy already had pointed out. Wilson would've talked to Crystal in Millinocket on Thursday, more than a hundred miles away. They'd found Lydia just after noon Friday. The ME couldn't pin down what time of day Lydia had been killed, but the report said it was likely eighteen to twenty-four hours before she was found. Pete, who'd seen so many dead bodies, told Bernie even that was a guess, but probably in the ballpark. It might be less than that, but not likely more, he'd said. "It's not like on TV." He was always saying that.

On the other hand, who's to say Wilson hiked to the end of the trail after she parted from Lydia? She could have hopped back down to the trailhead and driven to Millinocket. Maybe she had a friend helping her, just like Lydia did. A friend with a car who picked her up after she murdered Lydia and drove Wilson to Millinocket, where she talked to Crystal.

She'd have to ask Crystal just when it was Wilson called her, and what time did Crystal get to Millinocket. That reminded her—she hadn't asked Crystal about the well-wisher letters either.

Bernie wondered if any of that would be in the case file. She wanted to run to Pete's house that minute and look for it, but she and Carrie had a press conference to go to.

*****

The press conference ended up being a waste of time. Not only didn't they say anything Bernie didn't already know, but they said even less. They didn't give Dawna credit for arresting Fuller until Bernie asked about it. Bernie wanted to press them on it, but the state police spokesman called on one of his old friends, one of those reporters who'd been around for years and would rather kiss up to the cops than get a good story, was guaranteed to throw a softball and change the subject. She didn't disappoint.

"Can you tell us how hard law enforcement worked all these weeks to bring Danny Fuller to justice?" she asked. That was the end of Bernie's line of questioning.

When she got back to the office, Bernie called Dawna, pissed off, and also looking for a quote.

Dawna said it was okay. "It's their case, go with what they're saying." She didn't want to say much if they weren't going to.

"It's bullshit. They didn't want to give you credit."

"It's okay, Bernie. The important thing is he's been caught. I don't need a parade or anything."

"If it weren't for you, he'd still be out there."

"I know. It's frustrating, but I'm used to it. There's no point. Everything's too sensitive and I don't want any problems. I'm focusing on the weekend."

Bernie left it alone, once again writing a story for the website that she knew was only partially true. She wondered if she was ever going to be not pissed off again.

She closed up the office, trying to figure out what she was going to eat. It was almost seven. Late for her on a Thursday. She usually knocked off mid-afternoon. She sat in her car behind the

Watcher, watching the sun go down behind the mountains.

She wondered were Dubya was. She wondered if Pete was okay somewhere in those mountains, glowing in the evening sun. She wasn't even mad at him about leaving early any more, just desperate for him to be okay. She tried to pick up the thread of where she'd been with Crystal and the Rambler and Colleen and Lydia that was all jumbling around. She wondered for a second if she'd locked Colleen in, but then remembered she'd checked an hour ago and she was gone. Bernie wanted to get her reaction to what Crystal had said, but she could barely remember it now. Her medication wearing off and not eating since late morning were a bad combination. She was hot and jumpy. She needed peace and quiet on her porch with a beer and no people. It was just two minutes away.

Her cell rang as she put the key in the ignition.

"Can you come to the station?" Dawna asked.

"Did Fuller kill Pete?" It sprang up, felt so real. She felt faint, sick.

"Nothing like that. I'd just as soon you come over here."

Everything around Bernie cracked. She'd gone from okay to insane in ten seconds. It didn't even surprise her. "Just tell me."

"It's not bad. Probably," Dawna said. "We'll talk when you get here."

"Is it Dubya?" Bernie had a vision of him, hit by a car, bloody, needing to be identified. It wasn't as bad as what she pictured happening to Pete, but almost. She tried to put on her seatbelt and start the car and hold the phone at the same time.

"Danny Fuller had something of Pete's. I want you to take a look."

"Oh no no no."

"I'm sure it's okay," Dawna said.

Bernie heard Sandy's voice in the background.

"She's fine," Dawna said to him.

"Sandy's there?" Bernie said. "What's going on?" She started the car and shifted into reverse but forgot to clutch and the car stalled. "Shit goddam shit."

171

"I'm hanging up so you can drive."

*****

In the one minute it took Bernie to get to the police station, she'd convinced herself Pete was dead. What else could it be? There was no other possibility.

Sandy and Dawna turned to look as she walked in. Their faces blurred, but what she could make out was pale and tragic.

"What is it?" She sat down.

"They found this on Fuller," Dawna said.

Bernie tried to focus on what was in the evidence bag in Dawna's hand.

"The whistle," she whispered. "Oh no."

"Bernie, it's probably okay," Dawna said.

Bernie reached for it. "Can I?"

"Don't take it out of the bag."

"Why's it bagged?" She was trying to sound calm and reasonable, hoping the feelings would follow.

Sandy started to say something, but Dawna gave him a shut up look.

"What?" Bernie asked. The whistle looked so small in the bag. She wanted to rub her finger across the engraving.

"They don't think Fuller did anything to Pete," Dawna said.

"How would they know? Why's it in an evidence bag, then? How did he get it?"

"He says he found it."

It was something Pete wouldn't lose. But that was Bernie's assessment. Maybe he *would* lose it. "Do you believe him?"

"I don't have any reason not to," Dawna said. "The state investigators believe him."

Sandy, his butt propped against the edge of a desk, kicked his foot backwards. The burst of clanging metal made Bernie and Dawna jump. "Is anyone concerned that Fuller is a lying, murdering sack of shit?" he said.

"I don't think he'd be dumb enough to kill a cop, then let himself be arrested so easily," Dawna said. "He didn't even put up a fight. He was done. He wasn't acting like a guy who'd killed a cop. I wonder, even, if it was him who wrote that note just so he'd be caught rather than have to give himself up."

"That note was the Rambler," Bernie said, her thoughts on the whistle. She tried to take comfort in the fact Dawna was calm. She was more of an expert on this kind of thing than Bernie was.

"Fuller was really dirty, but there was no blood on him or anything that would indicate he'd been in a scuffle," Dawna said. "It was a blessing he was so dirty, in fact. If he'd had any hard contact with someone, it would've disturbed the dirt and been noticeable."

"You're assuming Pete fought back," Sandy said. "You're assuming Fuller didn't ambush him."

Dawna stood taller. Her eyes pinned Sandy. "I'm not assuming anything. Especially not assuming Fuller did anything to Pete. All we have is the whistle. Pete could have easily dropped it."

Sandy was pacing now. "If Pete dropped the whistle, it's because he was holding it. You don't hold it unless you need it."

"Maybe he was getting something out of his pocket," Dawna said. "Any number of reasons he could've dropped it."

Bernie ran her thumb along the engraving through the plastic. *End where you begun -B.* That's all it was, he dropped it and Fuller picked it up. "Maybe the whistle didn't matter to him," she said out loud, hoping that if she stared hard enough she wouldn't cry. She could take the whistle not mattering to Pete if it meant he was okay.

"It mattered," Sandy said. His voice shook.

That was it. "What happened to him?" She tried to stifle a sob. "Where is he? I knew something was wrong. I've known all this time. Ever since he left. I kept telling you."

"We don't know anything's wrong," Dawna said. "It's just a whistle. Fuller didn't have anything else of Pete's that we know of."

"That you know of," Bernie said. "I'm gonna go find Pete."

Sandy put his hand on Bernie's shoulder and squeezed. "Jamie and I are going first thing tomorrow. It's better if you stay here."

She knew it. *Knew it.* They didn't want her to go because they thought he was hurt, or dead. "How are you going to know where to go?" His grip on her shoulder told her he was scared.

"We have an idea of where Fuller was running around and an idea where Pete was going. We'll find him," Sandy said. "He'll be pissed off that we wrecked his vacation, too."

CHAPTER 20

Bernie called Sandy when it was still dark Friday morning. "I feel like I should come."

"Bernie, it's tough terrain and we can do it more easily ourselves."

He was right. She was horrifically out of shape. As much as she was desperate to find Pete, she didn't want to be dragged around the mountains out of pity. She could picture it, Sandy carrying her, like a Sherpa carrying a millionaire up Everest, people dying in their wake because they couldn't get past them before the avalanche comes. "Please find him."

Neither of them had to say how big the Maine woods are, how little a person is, especially if the person is hurt or unconscious. It felt worse to Bernie than Everest. Colder and more remote. She pictured Pete's body, frozen into a glacier even though she could feel the morning humidity sticking to her in her dark kitchen.

"Don't worry," Sandy said. "It'll be okay."

She wanted to believe him. She knew Sandy felt guilty. He'd told Pete to get lost in the woods. He was as desperate for Pete to be okay as she was. If anyone would find him, he would. She had to get to work, anyway. She'd slowed way down in the past twenty-four hours and no one was going to get paid next week if she didn't get her shit together.

Dubya still hadn't come home. She wondered if she should make posters, but posters seemed too final. Whenever she saw a missing dog or cat poster, she knew the pet was gone forever.

When she got to the office, she tried to remember what she had to do. Nothing seemed important. She hoped Colleen would come in, but she didn't. Bernie thought of calling her, but didn't have the energy. She had the office to herself; Friday was everyone's day to take it easy. The paper was out, the advertisers were happy. Monday would come soon enough. She called up the payroll account and tried to make sense of the numbers, but they just kept slipping away.

When her phone rang, she considered not answering it. Voicemail was invented for a reason. Then she saw the name on the caller ID. Manzo.

"Bernie O'Dea," she said, trying to sound upbeat and professional.

"This is Georgia Manzo, Lydia's daughter."

"I'm so sorry about your mom. How are you?" They'd talked a couple times when Lydia was missing, but hadn't talked since she'd been found. The family wanted privacy. Bernie was fine with that. Someday they'd want to talk, and they'd remember that she didn't badger them while their grief was still raw.

"Not well," Georgia said. "That story you did on my mom was a total hatchet job."

Bernie tried to remember how old Georgia was. She was in college. Stanford. Had she graduated, or was she going to be a senior? In any case, she was young. "I'm sorry you feel that way."

"I'd rather you were sorry about writing such an inaccurate article," Georgia said, her voice shaking.

Bernie didn't think what she'd written was inaccurate or a hatchet job, but there was no sense dueling with a grieving child or reminding her that the family hadn't wanted to talk. She'd had a million conversations like this in her career. Okay, maybe not a million, but enough to know not to argue.

"Why don't you tell me what I got wrong, and I'll fix it."

Georgia sputtered. Bernie knew she'd been expecting a fight.

"I based everything in the article on the information available to me," Bernie added. "But I don't like getting things wrong, so help me out."

"Okay, first of all she knew damn well how to use a compass, and she actually had a real one."

"I was told she didn't," Bernie said. "On both counts. So that's good to know. They didn't find a compass with her—" *body* Bernie almost said. "With her belongings."

"We'd gone on lots of camping trips and hikes, and she even taught me how to use one. I don't know why they didn't find one, but I'm a hundred percent sure she had one."

"What else?"

"She knew what she was doing. She wasn't some idiot, like the story made her sound."

"I'm sorry."

Georgia started crying. "She wouldn't kill herself. I know she was unhappy, but she just wouldn't. She was almost done."

"What was she unhappy about?"

Georgia took a deep breath and hiccupped, trying to stop crying. Bernie was familiar with the signs. "I don't want to say this for the paper."

"How about all of this is off the record, you can tell me what you feel I need to know, then we can figure out what to say in the paper."

"Okay." She sniffled. "Her back was bothering her, but she didn't want to take her medication because of the way it made her feel. It wouldn't be good to be in the woods with it. I think she was depressed, too. Something was bugging her that she wouldn't say."

"I wonder what?"

"I don't see how she'd get lost," Georgia said. "She was smart and had a lot of common sense. I talked to her on the phone Memorial Day weekend, the night before she left Redimere, and she was all 'I've just got to get this done, then I'll be home.' Very determined."

"Did she say anything to you about plans to go off the trail?"

"For what? I mean, she did, you know, to use the bathroom, but that was it. She was definitely just anxious to finish."

"What was she taking for her back?"

"Tylenol on the trail, or maybe Aleve."

"When she wasn't hiking?"

"I don't know. Some prescription for spasms. She didn't like the side effects, though; it made her loopy."

"Is it possible she had some with her, and finally took it because she was in pain?" Bernie was seeing some possibilities.

"Absolutely not."

"You sound pretty sure."

"She didn't even like taking it at home. I can see Crystal and LeeAnne trying to get her to, but I know she wouldn't."

"Do you think they'd do that when they knew how she felt?"

"You know how nurses are," Georgia said. "They all think they're the biggest medical experts and everyone should do what they say."

Bernie talked to Georgia for another half hour, getting some of it on the record. Like most complaints that a story is "totally wrong" or "full of errors," there was only one factual error, the compass. Bernie didn't blame Georgia for being upset about the rest, but Bernie had written the story with what she'd had to work with.

The conversation had been a distraction from obsessing about Pete, but now it was done and Bernie had nothing else. She pictured him at the bottom of a ravine, leg broken, calling for help, or worse, a head injury. Wasting away like Lydia had. Before someone killed her. A couple times, her mind drifted to imagining him dead, killed by a ruthless and sadistic cop-hating Danny Fuller, who snatched the whistle out of Pete's dying hand for a trophy.

A car pulled up out front, and a man came to the door. Great. She wasn't in the mood to be Miss Customer Service. She made a deal with herself—take care of whatever he wants, then drive around and look for Dubya.

As he came in out of the bright sun, Bernie recognized him. He was older than in the photos, bigger than Pete and with flyaway white hair, but he looked enough like Pete that she wanted to hug him.

"I'm looking for Bernadette."

"Are you Chuck Novotny?"

His smile bloomed, the way Pete's used to. The big face-cracking smile she hadn't seen in months. "Bernie." She held out her hand.

His was warm and dry, like Pete's, but lumpy and calloused. "I recognize you from *Dateline*," he said.

"*Murdertown: USA*."

He shrugged. "I don't watch a lot of TV."

"You came here." She was confused.

"I was going to anyway, sooner or later," he said. "Then I got your call. Is he back?"

"No." She was desperate to get out of the office. "Why don't we go to his house?"

"Sure," he said. "You seem better than the other night on the message."

"I'm all right. Can you drive? I walked here."

"I flew into Portland and rented a car. Didn't realize how far this was," he said as they got in.

"That's what everybody says."

A few minutes later they were bumping down the dirt road to the end of the peninsula, Pete's little forest-green house shining in the sun, trees on one side, long flat rocks into the water on the other. A picture postcard that felt false.

Muffled barking came from the house as they got out of the car.

"Dubya?" She unlocked the door as he scratched and whimpered on the other side. She pulled it open, and the dog ran out to the grass and did the world's longest pee.

"Pete's dog?"

"Mine." Dubya had rambled to Pete's a couple times, including one excruciatingly awkward time right after they broke up when she'd looked out the window to see Pete's car turn into her driveway. Her heart leapt, thinking he was there to make up. But no, he was just returning Dubya.

"How did you get in?" She got his food out of the cupboard,

surprised Pete hadn't tossed it. Dubya ate like he was starving.

"What kind of dog is he?"

"Corgi, some Australian shepherd. Maybe something else. He's one of a kind."

Chuck was at the table, reading Pete's note. "I shoulda brought this in person," he said. "Mailing it was a mistake."

"It wasn't going to be good no matter what," Bernie said. "Can I get you something? Beer?"

"Not for me thanks. I don't drink anymore."

It was morning, anyway. Duh. "Water?"

"That works."

"Let's go out on the deck."

The sliding door was unlocked. She realized she'd left it open Tuesday night.

"Is this how you got in?" she asked Dubya. He panted at her and jumped onto a lawn chair. She shooed him off and sat down. The dog wouldn't have closed the door behind himself, though. The house seemed in order, but she'd look around later when she was alone.

The morning was warm and still, the sun climbing into a cloudless blue sky, the lake flat glass, mist rising off, the way it was in the morning. But she felt that chill. Someone had been in the house.

"You must've thought I was nuts when you heard that message I left," Bernie said.

"I wouldn't be here if I did." Man, he sounded like Pete. Same warm, low voice, even the same mannerisms, cocking his head to the side when she talked, smiling slightly. Sitting in the morning sun, her dog nearby, her worry felt false. Unearned. Except for the fact someone had been in the house, the whistle in Fuller's dirty pocket, Sandy and Jamie in the woods right now looking for Pete. Pete changing his insurance beneficiary, listing his assets. Those were just the things she knew about.

"There was a fugitive in the woods," she said. "He killed his ex-girlfriend." She tried to think of a way to tell the story without a dozen tangents. "He was arrested yesterday, and he had something of Pete's."

"Not his gun, I hope."

"No. He doesn't carry it unless he's working. It was a whistle, like hikers carry in case they get in trouble. It was a special one. Unique."

"But just a whistle. Not one of his ears or toes."

It was just like something Pete would say. "Just a whistle."

"He's a tough kid. I bet he's okay."

Bernie tried to take trembly little breaths instead of big gulping ones.

"He was always his own man, even when he was a kid," Chuck said. "I used to do handyman work on Saturdays to make an extra buck. I'd take him with me, you know, when his mom and I were still together. He was a great helper. People used to call him 'little man.' It made me kind a proud, but it bothered Jan, his mom. She'd say, 'He's just a kid.' I finally figured out what she saw, that he felt like he was responsible for everyone and it was too much pressure."

"He has nightmares, panic attacks. I think I only see a small part, because he's good at acting like things are okay."

"I wish I'd done things differently."

"I don't think it's your fault."

"Who knows? It's a lot of things. He was so smart, good at music. Math, like his mom. He had this way about him. Something that stayed with me all these years was this time, he was maybe ten, he and some of his friends were playing whiffle ball in the street and there was a girl visiting her grandmother or something, never seen her before. She had Down syndrome—mongoloid we called it then, if you can believe it—she was sitting there on the stoop watching. She had a baseball glove with her and it was obvious she wanted to play. One of Pete's friends made some remark to her, you know, you don't need a glove to play whiffle ball. Mocked her. But Pete made them let her play. Didn't make a big show out of it, wasn't condescending or anything, just, you know, 'We have room for her.' I told him later how proud I was, and he said something like, 'It

181

wasn't a big deal. It didn't hurt anything to let her play.'"

"Yeah, Pete in a nutshell."

"And he was just ten. It wasn't an act," Chuck said. "I thought he was going to do great things. Jan was the worrier. She said it was going to make everything harder for him, to be that smart and care so much, feel like it was up to him."

Two loons landed on the water, flapped around, then tucked their wings in, gliding on the still surface. One warbled a cry, and the other answered. It sounded to Bernie like a warning.

"Now here's a story about his brother," Chuck said with a laugh. "He's more like me. Both the kids were good athletes, but Joey was always goofing off. This is a story one of his friends told at his funeral, but I can see it. When he was in middle school, he and his buddies joined the cross-country team. There's this practice run they had to do, and if you did it in a certain time, you got your name on this wall. One day Joey decided, what the hell, he wasn't going to goof off. He broke the time limit by a good two minutes. The bigger kids were even cheering him on. But the next day, his name wasn't on the wall. He didn't say anything, too much pride, you know? But one of his friends asked the coach, and the coach said, 'Novotny never woulda been able to do that, he must've cheated.' The kid told Joey and Joey walked off right then, never ran cross-country or played any organized sport again."

"Pete would've gone out and done it again," Bernie said.

"Exactly," Chuck said. "They were the same in a lot of ways, but hugely different. I only worried about Joey, but I should've worried about Pete, too. Do you think he's depressed?"

"I don't know," Bernie said. "That's a co-occurring disorder with PTSD, right?"

"You're asking me?"

She was embarrassed. "I'm just thinking out loud."

"Depression runs in the family," Chuck said. "I don't know how much he's told you about his childhood and me."

Nothing. Nada. Zilch. "Not much."

"I didn't realize it at the time, but I had it bad. I was on the edge anyway, but I had a thing happen at work. I was a machinist. Spent months on my off time inventing a process to make something run more efficiently. Showed it to my boss, and he blew it off. Three weeks later, he's showing it to his boss and taking credit."

"That sucks."

"I walked out. You know, 'Screw you.' It started me on a bad slide and that's when things fell apart with Jan. Had some bad years."

"I'm sorry."

"I'm better, more or less. Found a good woman—not that Pete's mother wasn't—but she helped me get sober. I sound like a pamphlet or something." He laughed. He looked just like Pete did when he was embarrassed.

"I'm worried he's going to hurt himself." She expected Chuck to brush her off, like everyone else had.

"Me too. His mother and brother killed themselves. I could've. Easily. It's just by the grace of God I didn't. When I saw him on TV, I saw my little boy in a lot of pain."

Chuck's validation shook her. He seemed shaken too.

"What's the Sokol?" Bernie asked after they'd watched the loons glide on the lake for a few minutes.

"An organization, kind of a Czech community center, in Milwaukee," he said. "It had everything, music, gymnastics, parties. Great place."

"He plays in a band. Guitar, banjo, accordion. He's a good singer."

"You know, Pete didn't have a bad childhood," Chuck said. "We had this whole community the kids could depend on, a real family. His mom and I fought a lot, but we loved each other. We loved our kids. I didn't realize how they'd end up, pulled away from the community, off on their own. I thought Jan's new husband was a good provider and would give them a good life."

"You couldn't have known."

Bernie made sandwiches. She and Chuck chatted about other

183

things. The Red Sox, the economy. It felt like they were waiting for something. She checked around a little more to see if anything looked out of place. Nothing looked different from when she'd been there a few nights before. The door to the big closet was open, but she'd probably left it like that. She shifted the hanging coats to get to the cupboard in the back, almost invisible. The gun case was in there. She hefted it, and it felt heavy. It was locked. There was a cardboard banker's box back there, too. She lifted the top; it was full of documents and files. It didn't have big red letters like in her dream, but it was the case file. She couldn't look at it with Chuck there. She closed the cupboard and brushed against Pete's overcoat. She buried her face in it. "Please come home safe," she whispered. She wiped her tears with the sleeve and closed the door.

CHAPTER 21

Pete woke to bright light, but he was still in what he thought of as the cave. He could see now it was a basement, with dirt walls and floor, maybe a root cellar. He had no idea how long he'd been there, had no linear memory of the time since Max freed his leg. There'd been snapshots of things, ghosts, terror, pain. The needle and the cold chill going through his veins, then nothing. He couldn't remember how many times

There was an open trap door above, morning light streaming in. It hurt his eyes. He'd seen the room by battery-lit lantern, but it'd been hazy and dim. Now he saw neat piles of books and magazines, other supplies, organized in crates and on two-by-fours. A large mattress made up like a bed. Pete was on a smaller cot mattress. There was a radio. Two Coleman stoves. A memory of Max saying, "I don't light them in here; I'm not interested in dying of CO."

Pete wondered if one had been used to kill Lydia, if a tent was air-tight enough. But there'd been the Ziploc too. He'd dreamed of a stove inside the bag, Lydia's eyes wide in horror.

He was thirsty as hell. There were plastic two-gallon jugs of water against the wall a few feet away. Pete got up, holding the wall for support. He hadn't stood since Max had freed him. Hadn't been this lucid either. The pain in his leg was searing. He stood, willing away dizziness and nausea, tried to get used to being vertical. When he felt like he could move, he inched down the wall to the jugs. He wondered where Max was. As far as he knew, he hadn't been left alone before. It was hard to remember through the fog. He wasn't going to worry about that now, though. He picked one up, took off the top, surprised at how weak his arm was, how heavy the jug

185

seemed. He lifted it, holding onto the wall with his other arm, and drank until it spilled out of his mouth onto his T-shirt. It was cold and wet and heaven. There were a couple empty hiker-type water bottles next to the jugs, and he filled the largest one. He wasn't sure where Max got his water. Definitely not the grocery store. Pete knew he was sick enough that bad water could kill him. Max seemed organized and smart about things. Sure enough, on a shelf at Pete's shoulder, next to medication and first aid supplies, he found water purifier. There was a pack of tablets and a couple small bottles in liquid form. He didn't want to wait for the tablets to dissolve, so he emptied one of the bottles into the water.

He drank about half the water, then filled it up again, emptied another bottle of the purifier in. He couldn't focus enough to read the small print, but he knew it was less dangerous than bad water would be. Now, how was he gonna get out? There was a wooden ladder attached to the wall leading up to the trap door. Two-by-fours spaced about two feet apart for rungs. It'd be easy with two good legs. He let go of the wall and put his weight on his bad leg. The pain was almost unbearable, but he could do it. He had to. He made himself walk to the ladder without using the wall. *It's only pain.*

He stepped on the first rung, bad leg first. The leg buckled. He pressed his forehead into the rung in front of him until the pain faded, then stepped with his good leg. He reached up a couple rungs and pulled himself up. His arms shook, but he was able to step onto the next rung. He could do pull-ups forever at the gym, but wasn't sure if he could do this the four more times it would take to get through the opening. He leaned against the wood until he'd stopped shaking enough to grab the rung above him, then he did it again. Halfway there. Did it again. Then he was pulling himself through the trap door.

He lay on the floor of a kitchen in what had once been a house. As he waited for the second wind he'd need to get up, he took it in. Bare wood walls, an ancient rusting sink pulled halfway off, a wood stove, the stove pipe rusted and fallen. Probably had once been a logging camp. The roof was half caved in and the window glass was long gone. The floor was littered with leaves and pine boughs; they'd drifted into the corners and against the walls.

Before he'd climbed, he jammed the water bottle into the pocket of his shorts, which were stiff and rancid. He didn't care. He was free. He pulled himself up and took another long drink of water. Then, holding onto the doorjamb, he stepped into the sunshine. The light burned his eyes. He shaded them with his hand and could see enough to tell that there was no dooryard. A thick wall of blackberry bushes towered over the house, pressing against it, surrounding it. The berries were still small and green, just a tinge of lavender. He picked a few and ate them. They were sour and hard and didn't ease his hunger. There was a narrow path between the bushes and house. Max didn't have any scratches that Pete had seen, so there must be an opening. He slowly circled the house, holding onto the wall for support, ignoring his throbbing leg, until he found it in what had looked like solid rock. It was actually two rocks, one leaning into the other. Pete took another long, long swallow of water, then eased through the narrow opening. The rock was cold and he fought the urge to stop, lean against it and close his eyes. He squeezed through. Then he was in the woods.

He found a stick to use as a cane, but it wasn't enough. His leg hurt more with every step. He was woozy, probably from the heat and sun, being vertical, the pain and lack of food, and coming down from the morphine. He took another long drink of water.

As he made his slow way, the world tilted. It wasn't making as much sense as it should. The woods began to fade into terror and shadows the farther he went. How had he been so stupid? He'd thought he was free. Now he knew he wasn't going to make it out alive.

*****

Dawna had been through two tours in Afghanistan and knew how to keep her head. She was known for it, alive because of it. She knew better than to panic.

She took a deep breath and focused on the evidence bags that had been laid in front of her by Tyler, the new part-time officer who'd had the bad luck of starting his job in Redimere on what was turning out to be a very bad week.

There were shards of cellphone, possibly Pete's; the mangled frame of a backpack that looked a lot like Pete's; some scraps of material, sharply cut. A knife that also looked like Pete's, with a tiny bit of blood on the tip. And something that was definitely Pete's—his badge, which had been found in the woods near the knife.

Tyler told her there was blood on the ground, too. A puddle of it, then drips. "Looks like an old fire tower collapsed years back," he said. He looked like he was about twelve, with pink cheeks and a blond buzz cut, and, right now, eyes wide with wonder. "It was all sticking up out of the weeds. Pretty dangerous, when you think about it. Spikey."

Spikey. Exactly. In one of the evidence bags was a length of rusted metal, about three feet long. Half of it was smeared with blood, the bottom was bright, freshly cut.

Sandy had sent Tyler back with the evidence bags while he and Jamie forged ahead on what Tyler said looked like a deer trail that had recently been used by more than deer.

Dawna told Tyler if he said one word to anyone he could kiss his days-old job goodbye, and sent him off on patrol.

She called the state police and told them what she'd found. They said to let them know if something more turned up. She got it. They weren't going to run into the woods on a wild goose chase. She probably should've called the Warden Service instead, but she'd wait to hear from Sandy first.

She was stuck staring at a puzzle that she couldn't figure out, but knew it was bad. The most optimistic thing she could say was that, though they'd found blood, it wasn't a lot. And they hadn't found a body.

"What's that?"

Bernie was in the doorway, her eyes on the evidence bags.

"Nothing."

"It's not nothing," Bernie said, coming closer. "That looks like Pete's pack. What's that?" she asked pointing at the bloody metal spike, her hand shaking.

"I don't know," Dawna said. "There's probably a good explanation."

"Where's Sandy?"

"They're still looking."

Bernie sat down. "Oh shit."

"We don't know anything right now," Dawna said. "Why don't you go back to work, or home, and I'll call you when we know more? Want me to call your brother or someone to get you?"

"No."

"Bernie." Dawna made her voice as steady as possible. Not talking down to her, just making sure Bernie knew she wasn't panicking. "We don't know anything. I'll let you know when we do. You'll drive yourself nuts if you stick around here. Find something to do."

Bernie seemed to pull herself together. "You're right. I'll find something to do." She left.

*****

Pete didn't know where his compass was, but more than that, the world was too bright and tilted. He wouldn't have been able to read it if he had it. He'd walked despite his leg, something driving him, the pain there, but disconnected. The shivers and cramps that he'd been so sure were withdrawal had been joined by something else. His skin crawled. Bugs were coming out of the wound in his leg. He could feel them. When he looked, they changed to the red and brown that was spreading on the bandage, but he knew it was bugs.

The trees were crawling, too. He had to be careful. They knew he was there, and they were waiting.

The sun was setting him on fire. He'd lost his water bottle, but there was water somewhere. He could feel it. All he had to do was dive in and put the fire out. If only he weren't so exhausted. If only he weren't shaking so much. If only the bugs weren't eating his leg, making it so hard to walk. He sat on a rock and closed his eyes, hoping it would make the noise stop, but it got louder. Whispering.

189

Talking. He'd had dreams he couldn't save Bernie, or Joey, but now he knew they weren't dreams. He'd seen them die, heard their cries of pain. He was an idiot to think he could escape it. Someone did this to him, but he wasn't sure what they'd done. It kept slipping away.

He looked around, feeling something cool through the fire. There it was—he was just yards away from a lake. How hadn't he seen it before? It was beautiful and clear and spread to the far mountains. It was a little behind him and to his left. His bad side, the one with the bugs. Once he found some strength, in a minute, he could get to it.

He was sick, but worse, he was in trouble. Something wanted to kill him. He had to get out. He took a deep breath, trying to gather the strength to move to the lake. If he could get in, he could hide, or swim across. Or sink, like he was going to do that rainy night in his own lake. It seemed long ago, but he could still feel it. How cool the water was, how he knew he could sink and no one would know where he was. Sorrow gripped him, rising in a wave, just like that night.

The voices were louder. There was rustling. He stood up. Or thought he did, but then realized he was still sitting and he'd just thought it. The world was terrifying hazy slow motion. He had to move, get into the lake.

"Pete."

There were two men and a dog. He stood up, this time he made sure, holding the rock for balance.

"Stay back," he said. It sounded shamefully weak.

They stopped.

"Pete." It was Sandy, but Pete knew it wasn't. "What happened, buddy?"

"I don't know you," Pete said. He couldn't let them see the terror.

"He's on something," the other one said.

Pete had to get away. Get into the lake and disappear. He couldn't move. If he let go of the rock, he'd fall, but in the wrong direction. It was so close. One sideways lunge would bring him to the edge, then he could roll over and in.

"Pete." Sandy took another step toward him. He was pulsating, on fire.

"Don't," Pete screamed. "Stay away. I DON'T KNOW YOU." The long arms were stretching toward him. He put his weight on his right leg. One good push would roll him toward the water, away from them. The trees were closing in, so was the fire, just like in his dreams. The tall one was stretching higher, his long arms coming toward him through the flames.

"Pete, you know us. It's Sandy and Jamie."

He felt for the rock. He tried to focus on the distance to the lake without taking his eyes off them.

"We're your friends. Bernie sent us to look for you."

It was a trick. "Bernie's dead," Pete said. The terror was paralyzing. He fought it off. "It's my fault."

"No. Pete. She's fine. We're here to bring you home."

"I don't know you," Pete said, no longer a scream. They were too close to him. "You're lying." He was too terrified to scream. He inched closer to the lake.

"Pete, don't move. You're too close to the edge."

Another trick. He didn't need to look, he knew it was there. It was beautiful, glimmering in the sun. Sandy took another step. The dog barked fire.

"I don't know you." Pete yelled it as loud as he could. Why didn't they understand?

"I can prove it," Sandy said. He'd stopped coming toward Pete, but his rubber, burning arms were still stretching toward him. "Here's something only I would know. Last year, when things got bad, I told you I'd always have your back, and you said, 'We'll go down in flames together.' We drank to it. It was our inside joke. Remember?" He didn't look like he was playing a trick. He looked as terrified as Pete was. Pete hesitated. The words were familiar. But this pulsating thing, this being who wanted to kill him, couldn't be that guy.

191

"I don't know you," he said. His voice was thin. It shook. He knew they heard it.

"Yes you do, Pete. I love you, brother. Let's go home."

Pete was closer to the lake now, but he was melting, the terror melting with his body. He was overwhelmed by relief that he'd be in the water, where no one could get him. Relief and sadness. In seconds he'd be in it. He'd drift to the bottom. It'd be like that, quiet and cool, like a dream. He pushed with all the strength he had, and fell toward the lake.

CHAPTER 22

Bernie went back to Pete's. She didn't want to be anywhere else. She thought of making a deal with the fates, "I don't look at the case file, and you bring Pete home safe," but she knew that was bullshit. She'd look at it—she had to. The fates couldn't care less what she did. They'd do with Pete what they would.

She dragged the box out of the closet. Things were just piled in, no order to it. She guessed Pete hadn't gone through it, because he wouldn't have left it like that. There was a checklist of contents on top, and it listed a hiker roster. Good, at least that was going her way.

She sifted through, trying to separate things. Reports on the search, printouts of email exchanges, interview transcripts. It was overwhelming.

She found a copy of the medical examiner's report, without redactions. It said Lydia's pre-death deterioration indicated possible drug intoxication, but there were no needle marks, no signs of obvious drugs in her system, no drug containers with her belongings.

A note in a margin, in Pete's handwriting, said, "no CO mention/check if blood test/other CO indicators." So he had gone through it.

There were also copies of Lydia's unsent texts, two of them, both to Colleen, according to a handwritten note, not in Pete's writing, that said "# Colleen Sullivan, Buffalo friend."

At 8 a.m., an hour after the girls dropped her off: "GPS good, terrain not."

At 9:13 a.m.: "Feel sick."

On it, in Pete's handwriting, "PN notes."

Bernie had seen that before. It meant his own notes. She didn't see any in the box, though.

She also didn't find any notes that made it seem like investigators were concerned about the texts. Once they determined it was suicide, things like that didn't mean anything. Bernie knew that much.

There was an email from a state police investigator to Pete in the early days of the search making him the liaison with Lydia's friends. "Keep them engaged & out of our hair," the guy had said. Bernie guessed it was to keep Pete on the fringes, too.

She found the letters from the well-wishers. Not all of them, though. The envelope with Herman's handwriting wasn't there.

She couldn't find anything that looked like a hiker roster.

She went back to the closet to see if she'd missed something. Sure enough, on the floor, leaning sideways next to Pete's winter boots, was a manila folder. It must've been next to the box, maybe under it, and fallen when she pulled it out. She tried to remember if she'd looked down there the day before—maybe it fell when whoever had been at the house had pulled it out.

The folder and a bunch of papers in it. One was a page with notes, Pete's handwriting, dated June 22. An interview with Colleen. That would have been the Tuesday before Lydia was found. Colleen's cellphone number was written at the top of the page. He'd written she was worried Lydia's disappearance was connected to something from Buffalo. "Wants to say more; agitated; scared. Didn't press. Follow up." The last two words were underlined.

There were also printouts of Lydia's texts from before she was lost. Typical trail stuff she'd sent to LeeAnne and Crystal. A couple to her kids. "NH mtns awsm!"

Bernie was getting overloaded. It felt like there was so much there, but nothing that meant anything.

Pete's notes had questions, too. "Why bag if CO?" Good one.

He'd made some points under it, likely his own speculation: "Didn't want to engage w/ L?; CO no contact; No neck scratches;

194

prints?"

He'd done a lot more thinking about the murder than Bernie thought he had. That might have pissed her off a few days ago, but now it gave her hope. For a second. Then she pictured the awful, heart-shredding collection of Pete's broken belongings on the table at the police station.

She had the worst thought yet, piled onto all the other ones she'd had the last couple days. Someone came into his house Wednesday and likely went through the case file. What if that person felt Pete was getting too close and went into the woods to kill him?

She couldn't tell if that was really stupid or she should be scared shitless.

Everything felt hopeless. The piles of paper, impossible to decipher, scattered around her on the floor. It felt like chaos, nothing. It wouldn't bring her closer to the truth, or to Pete.

Her phone rang. Dawna.

"They found him."

*****

The shaking wouldn't stop. Pete's stomach cramped, and his skin crawled. He was waking up on the damn ground again. The pain in his leg ripped through him, worse than before. He opened his eyes and the light knifed into his already throbbing head. He closed them, bracing for the needle he knew was coming, dreading it, but knowing at least the pain would ease.

"Are you awake?"

Sandy. Maybe. Pete had no idea what was real and what wasn't. He wanted this to be real.

"Pete."

Pete opened his eyes.

"Do you know who I am?" Sandy asked.

"Sandy," Pete croaked. His throat was so dry it stuck together.

"Thank God. We're getting you out of here. Jamie went to get help. He's been gone a couple hours, so hopefully not much longer. We think we can get you to a good spot a short ways away for the helicopter so we don't have to carry you out."

Pete put his arm over his eyes.

"This'll help." Sandy lifted Pete's arm and put a cold, damp cloth over his eyes, then put the arm back.

"What are you on?"

Pete didn't understand. He was too tired, in too much pain.

"Pete, listen. What drug are you on?"

"Don't know."

"I have Tylenol, but I don't want to give you anything until I know what you're on." Sandy sounded kind. Pete wanted to answer. He was just too tired. "What happened to your leg?"

Pete concentrated. His head throbbed. His throat burned. It would hurt to talk. "I didn't take drugs."

"Let me give you some water. Can you lift your head?"

Pete took the bandana off his eyes. His arm felt like it weighed a hundred pounds. He propped up on his elbows, his arms shaking. Sandy held the back of his head with one hand and held the water bottle with the other.

"Just a little," Sandy said. "Until I know what you've got going on. It's okay, whatever you took, but I need to know."

The cold water felt like it was seeping through Pete's organs into his skin, relief, but short-lived. Sandy took the bottle away. "Bring me to the lake." If he could only get in that cold water, he'd feel better.

"We'll get you home as soon as we can."

Pete tried again. "Over there." He pointed. "I was going to jump in." Then he'd been attacked. No, that was wrong. It'd been Sandy and Jamie who tackled him to keep him from the lake. He had to get back to reality.

"That's a three-hundred-foot drop-off. There's no lake. Jesus, is that what you thought?"

Pete took a deep breath. Held it.

"I thought you were trying to kill yourself," Sandy said.

"No." The terror had felt so real. The lake had seemed so real, too. He took another deep breath.

196

"Tell me what you're on."

Pete's head was killing him. So was his leg. The cramps, the nausea. Sandy's voice was soft, pleading. Pete tried to think. "Morphine. Something else. I don't know."

"You took something without knowing what it was?"

Pete licked his lips, concentrated. "Given. Against my will. Same person who dressed my leg."

"What happened to your leg? The dressing is soaked through, but I don't want to change it here. Are you in pain?"

"Yes."

"Well, you must be pretty bad, because that's the first time I've ever heard you admit it."

Sandy was rummaging, just like Max. "No." Pete tried to get up, but Sandy, hand on his chest, eased him back down. Pete had no strength to fight back.

"Don't go nuts on me again. Everything's cool."

Pete fought panic. Sandy would help him. He wasn't Max. Heidi whined and put her snout on Pete's stomach. He'd forgotten about the dog. As sensitive as his skin was, the weight of her warm head felt good. He put his hand between her ears, and she sighed.

"Sorry," Pete said.

"It's okay." Sandy was wrapping something around him. Pete tried to get up again.

"Easy," Sandy said. "Mylar blanket. You've got the shakes. How old is the injury?"

"Tuesday."

"Jesus, Pete."

"What's today?"

"Friday."

Pete wanted to be somewhere dark and silent. Ride out the pain and sick.

"What happened?" Sandy's voice wasn't as gentle this time.

"I don't know."

"You need help. I feel for you, but I'm mad, too. And scared shitless, honestly."

197

"I can't."

"Can't what?"

"Sorry."

"Don't be sorry, just listen. It's selfish as hell. I know what I'm talking about."

"Can I have water?" Pete took the cloth off his eyes and shimmied back until he could sit up against the rise of earth behind him. The world spun, pain and nausea combining. Sandy handed him the bottle. He looked stricken, not mad. Pete wanted to say something, anything, but he wanted the water more. After less than a mouthful, Sandy took it away.

"You're going to make yourself sick."

"I am sick," Pete said. He tried to smile. Even that hurt.

"What happened?"

"I fell."

Sandy sat down next to him. "I was scared shitless I was going to find a body."

"But you didn't."

"You own a fucking gun. What do I do when we get home? Nobody can watch you twenty-four hours a day."

"You don't have to do anything," Pete said. He was shaking. His stomach cramps were more severe, overlapping each other, and his leg screamed with pain, but his head was clear. "I just want to go home."

CHAPTER 23

Bernie had talked to families of people who'd been accused of murder, or lived through a horrible accident, or been lost in the woods. Frequently the family would say, "I don't know what happened. I haven't talked to him about it."

She could never understand. How is it not the first thing you talk about? How do you not talk about it every second of the day?

As she sat in the hospital Saturday afternoon, watching Pete sleep, she finally got it. She had little idea what happened to him. He was alive, breathing and here, and that's what was important. He'd been impaled. He'd been clear on that in the little time they'd had alone. He'd somehow, in four days, had enough morphine to be in withdrawal—the doctors and nurses were clear on that.

He'd also been on something else that made him nearly dive off a three-hundred-foot cliff. She'd heard that part from Sandy, his voice shaking as he told her how he'd tackled Pete, both of them nearly falling over the edge. How Pete had struggled, trying to go over, but had been too weak, and how Jamie grabbed Sandy's legs as Sandy struggled to get Pete back. Then, thankfully, Pete had passed out.

Pete had talked to the state investigators, and from what she gathered from their asides and from what they'd told Dawna and Sandy, they thought Pete was full of shit. They believed he'd taken drugs, gotten hurt, possibly had a psychotic break and then told them a story that was almost comical in its unbelievability.

She wasn't sure what to say or ask, given his condition. The time may not have been right, but she did confess to listening to the tape. It felt like the most important thing.

"I didn't listen to all of it," she said. "I stopped when I realized where it was going."

"I listened to all of it," he said, then turned his head away. That was the end of that conversation.

Now he was asleep.

"Hi." Chuck was at the door. Crap. She'd forgotten about Chuck.

"Oh my God," he said as he came in and got a good look at Pete.

Bernie's instinct was to run out of the room and let the chips fall without her there, but that would be babyish. It was too late, anyway. Pete was awake. His eyes moved from Chuck to Bernie.

Pete had five days growth of beard. His face was pale and thinner than it'd been before the woods. None of that hid the confusion, then the anger.

"I called him," Bernie said. "I was worried."

"She didn't ask me to come," Chuck said. "That was me. How are you, son?" He leaned toward Pete to hug or kiss him.

"Bernie, can you leave us alone?" Pete said, as he angled away from his father.

Chuck pulled back.

"Okay," Bernie said. "I'm not going to apologize, though."

*****

Pete hadn't seen Chuck in nearly thirty years because he hadn't wanted to. He was too sick, though, to be as mad as he should. The anger was muted, wrapped in the woods, the things from the box, the years.

"Don't be mad at Bernie," Chuck said. "She loves you very much."

Pete felt like he was a teenager again. *Don't tell me how to feel.* He was too tired. "I'm not mad at her."

"It's good to see you, despite the circumstances."

"Why are you here?"

"You're my son. I love you, and I want to talk."

A nurse came in. "I'm sorry. I can come back," she said.

"He's leaving," Pete said.

Chuck got up, to Pete's surprise. "We can talk when you feel better. I just wanted to see my boy. I've missed you."

Pete was glad the nurse was fiddling with his IV, blocking his father's view. He didn't want him to see the tears. They didn't mean anything, just a byproduct of pain and drug withdrawal. That's what Pete told himself, anyway.

"Take care," Chuck said when Pete didn't answer.

The nurse gave Pete a hard look after Chuck left. He looked away, out the window.

*****

Bernie was on her way back with a coffee when she saw Chuck farther down the hall, walking towards the exit. Boy, that was fast. She'd better go back and face the music.

A nurse turned to her as she walked into Pete's room. His eyes were closed.

"Are you the one he's being discharged to?" the nurse asked Bernie.

"What?" Bernie asked. Being in the hospital reminded her why she hated hospitals. The nurses were great, for the most part; the doctors professional, but distant. But no one communicated. She wasn't sure if they all thought someone else was keeping her informed, or if they just didn't think her knowing what was going on was important. They seemed even less interested in telling Pete what was going on. Bernie had no idea what "being discharged to" even meant.

It was too soon after Chuck left for Pete to be asleep, but he didn't stir.

The nurse tried again. "He's being discharged tomorrow. I have in the chart that he's being discharged to Bernadette O'Dea. His wife."

"That's me," Bernie said. Denying she was his wife seemed like it would complicate things. "He's being discharged tomorrow?" He seemed so sick, so hurt, so broken. That couldn't be possible.

"These cover care and other requirements." The nurse had

201

about a pound of paper in her hand. "The withdrawal isn't too bad, because he apparently hasn't been dependent on morphine that long, but the symptoms will probably last several more days and he shouldn't be left alone."

"Great."

"The other drug, as long as he won't tell us what it is, we don't know if he's still going to have effects. You need to look out for that. Any signs of hallucinations, irrational behaviors, psychotic behaviors. If he seems like a danger to himself or someone else, don't hesitate, call 911. He hasn't shown any signs in twenty-four hours, but since he won't tell us what it is, we don't know what the long-term effects are."

"I think he doesn't know what it is, it's not that he's refusing." She looked at him again. Nothing. Bernie hated it when people said "behaviors" instead of "behavior." She hated it more that everyone assumed Pete was a lying, suicidal drug abuser. She didn't know exactly what had happened, but she knew he didn't inflict it on himself. Now that he was back, that was clear.

"The dressing on his leg will need to be changed every twelve to twenty-four hours. There's a list of supplies you can get in the pharmacy."

"Wait, I have to do that?"

"Keep it clean and dry. He can get a plastic sleeve to cover it for the shower, but don't let him shower alone, he's too unsteady, between the leg and the withdrawal."

"I don't know how to dress a wound." She had a vision a World War I battlefield, shielding Pete's body as bombs went off, wrapping a dirty, ragged bandage around a leg being held on by tendons and skin. But, of course, that wasn't what it would be like at all. It would just feel like it.

The nurse handed her the papers, telling her what they were in a rapid-fire monotone that Bernie couldn't follow. "He'll be discharged around nine. You want to get crutches from the PT. She had him up on them today."

Pete had been up on crutches?

202

"She said he was resistant and would rather not use crutches. You need to stress to him he could injure his leg worse than it is now if he puts weight on it. He has to stay off of it, keep it elevated. One of these tells you how to check for infection when you're changing the dressing."

"I'm pretty sure I shouldn't be the one doing that."

"It's all right here. His physician will let you know when he needs to come back. Once the swelling and inflammation go down, they want to assess the damage for possible surgery. They also haven't determined how badly the femoral nerve was impacted, which may have long-term effects."

Bernie had more questions, but as she tried to sort them in her head, the nurse left. She looked at the mishmash of papers. Who the hell told them she was Pete's wife?

"I can change the dressing myself."

Pete pulled his pillow up behind his back and sat up. He looked better not lying down.

"That sucked." Bernie said.

Pete laughed. Weak, but still a laugh.

Bernie swatted at him with the papers as she sat down. "Why didn't you rescue me?"

"You were handling it."

"How do you feel?"

"Fine, considering."

"Always with the fine," she said. She tried to make it sound light, but her voice broke.

"Come here." It was soft, a whisper. She was close to the bed, and he took her upper arm and pulled her toward him. She bent forward and kissed him. His grip tightened as their lips met. It didn't loosen as she sat back.

His eyes were glassy and red-rimmed, his hand clammy, and, as tight as it held her arm, trembling. His lips were dry and cracked. But he was smiling. "Do you have any idea how happy I am to see you?" he said.

"Me too. Are you mad about me calling Chuck?"

"I'm mad at Chuck for a few decades worth of shit," he said. "Not you."

"Did you guys talk?"

"Can I have another kiss?" He smiled again, tired and sad. She leaned forward and kissed him, gently, one hand on his chest to feel the reassuring thump of his heart, his hospital johnny damp under her hand.

"I missed you," he whispered against her cheek.

"I missed you, too," she said. She sat back. "What happened?"

"I'm not sure. It's all jumbled. Reality, dreams, nightmares." His voice was hoarse, but matter-of-fact.

She kept waiting for her anxiety to go away. Why were they letting him go home the next day? She was supposed to take care of him? Did he even want her to?

"Don't worry," he said. "It could be a lot worse."

"Don't sit there smiling," she said. Maybe it was the stress of the past four days, or weeks, or the past year, but she couldn't pretend to be okay. "Don't be so fucking smug about being alive. You scared the living shit out of me. Jesus, Pete." She started to cry.

She leaned forward and put her head on his chest. He put his arms around her and pressed his face to her hair. "It's okay," he whispered. "I'm okay. I'm back and in one piece. Everything's okay."

*****

Bernie lay in bed as morning seeped into her room. She'd almost nodded off on the dark deer-pocked drive home. Then, as usual, she hadn't been able to sleep. She was trying to decide whether to get up when her brother made the decision for her.

"Bernie," he called from down the hall.

"What the hell, Sal? It's five a.m. on Sunday."

"Happy Fourth of July," he said, opening her door. He sat down on her bed. "How's Dudley Do-Right?"

"Aside from the giant hole in his leg, the shakes, the vomiting, the memory loss, and the multiple near-death experiences, he's great," Bernie said. "Don't call him that. Why are you up so early?"

"Chloe and I wrangled some booth space for today. We're going to sell some of her food."

"You woke me up to tell me that?"

"You're obviously already awake. Do you have a cooler?"

"In the basement. Why?"

"Styrofoam? I need to pick up some dry ice at Walt's."

"Glad you woke me up for this. No, it's not, just a regular old cooler."

"Cranky this morning."

"I thought she was seeing Sean."

"We're just friends and business partners."

"Don't let her take advantage of you," Bernie said.

He laughed. "You forget who you're talking to."

Right, she thought as she got dressed. When she went out into the kitchen, Sal was washing out the cooler as Dubya supervised.

"I'll be at Pete's for a couple days," she said. "They're discharging him today, but he needs a baby-sitter. I guess I'll bring Dubya. They have a bond."

"I can't see him doing well with a baby-sitter."

"He's going to have to, isn't he?"

"I've got something for him." Sal went into his room and came out with a long piece of iron.

"What's that?" Bernie asked.

"It's a cane. I sculped it, custom for Pete." He handed it to her.

"Heavy." She turned it over. Strands of wrought iron were twisted, vine-like, around it. The grip was smooth and soft, the bottom a heavy ball, but flat at the end "Scary looking, but kind of neat. Just hope it doesn't give him flashbacks. You know, with the impaling and all."

"I didn't even think about that. Sorry."

"The nurse said he has to use crutches, but I'm sure he'll like it."

"I gotta go. Give him my best."

"Be careful with the dry ice," Bernie said. "Remember that thing when we were kids? Maybe you better see if Walt has

Styrofoam. Don't close the lid all the way if you use that one."

"Stop lecturing. One exploding cooler and you guys never let me forget it."

"Two, if I remember right."

Sal opened the front door. "I'm stunned we all turned out so normal."

*****

Dawna walked between the booths set up on the grass by the river. In a couple hours, the park would be hopping, but now, with the dew shining in the just-risen sun, it was quiet.

Her job—her first job of the morning, out of a million that would come that day— was to check out the park before the festivities started and make sure everything looked okay. When she and Pete had talked about it last week, he'd said, "You're not looking for anything specific, but if there's something wrong, you'll know it when you see it." It embarrassed her that he seemed so sure she'd be able to figure it out.

She hadn't had the time, but she'd made the run down to Farmington the day before anyway. The story Sandy and Jamie had told was so shocking, so not Pete, she wanted to see for herself that he was all right. He was, more or less, but she knew how good he was at faking it. He wasn't worried that the state police didn't believe him. It wasn't them she was worried about, though. She was more concerned about the mayor and selectmen, the people who could kick him out of his job. She had his back, and she knew Jamie and Sandy did, too, but she wasn't sure that mattered.

"Knew I'd find you here."

Fergus Kelley and his mascot, Sean Speck, had come up behind her. "Wondering what you can tell me about what happened with your chief," Fergus said. Sean took a photo of her. She caught herself adjusting her uniform pants. She hooked her fingers under her utility belt to avoid the temptation to do it again.

"I can't tell you anything aside from what you've been told."

"It isn't much," Fergus said.

"He got hurt hiking, not much more to it." She knew better

206

than to get into a back-and-forth, but she could feel it sucking her in.

"There has to be more to it than that."

"There was. Danny Fuller had something of his, and that concerned us, so Chief MacCormack and Officer Paradis went to check."

Sean fiddled with his camera, not looking up. "Funny how MacCormack found Lydia, then found Novotny," he said.

"I've got work to do." She started walking faster.

"We're doing a story no matter what," Fergus said. "It's coming out tomorrow. You can talk to us, or you can get dragged down, too."

"I'll take my chances."

"Don't you want to know what it's about?" he asked.

"No."

Fergus laughed. "You seem like a nice girl, but one who's in a little over her head. Maybe you really don't know what's going on."

Dawna scanned the booths, watching the few vendors who'd arrived.

"Right now the story is mostly about MacCormack," Fergus said. "Lots of shady things there."

Sean walked backwards in front of her. "If the police department would comment, that would prove they're not complicit."

"Nothing to say."

Fergus shook his head, looking fake sad, as Bernie would say. Dawna could tell he was enjoying himself. "You know, since Bernie is screwing the police chief, and, if you believe rumors, MacCormack, too, that makes us the only news source in this town that can be trusted."

"If you have a story to write, you better go write it," Dawna said. "You're wasting your time harassing me."

"Did you hear that?" Sean said, his voice rising. "Why are you so angry? We're just doing our jobs."

She kept walking.

"Really, why are you so angry?" Sean asked. "Come on, we're just trying to talk to you." He was in front of her again now, walking backwards. She knew she could tackle him and pound his skinny aging Peter Pan frame into the wet morning grass, but it wouldn't accomplish anything.

She turned to Fergus. "The two of you need to let me do my job, or I'm going to let the sheriff deal with you. It could take all day and you'd miss your deadline."

"Come on, Sean," Fergus said. "Let's go."

"She can't kick us out of here. It's public property."

"Don't worry about it. We'll be the ones laughing tomorrow."

CHAPTER 24

Everything at the hospital was hurry up and wait. Bernie had brought Pete clean clothes, agonizing over the choices until she realized she was going to be late and grabbed shorts, a T-shirt, boxers, socks, and sneakers. He insisted on getting dressed himself as she hovered around him, desperate to help, feeling like an inept mother with a willful toddler.

As they prepared to leave, someone handed her a plastic bag with the clothes he'd been found in. Everyone was rushing around, coming in and out, occasionally having Pete fill out paperwork, then disappearing. He was silent and irritated. Once he was dressed, he sat on the edge of the bed holding the crutches as they waited for someone to give them the go-ahead. Bernie made small talk about the Red Sox, Dubya.

His tremors weren't as severe, but they were still there. He was pale and sweaty. If he was suffering the stomach cramps that had been doubling him over the day before, he didn't show it. He leg was swollen under the large bandage around his thigh, his foot propped on a stool. He looked strained, in pain, but he didn't mention that, either.

"I just want to go home," he said at one point, out of the blue, when her stream of chatter slowed.

Finally, whatever bureaucratic magic that had to be done to free him was done. A nurse asked if he wanted a wheelchair.

"No."

"Okay, I have to escort you." She put a sling around his waist. It seemed worse to Bernie than a wheelchair. Pete nodded, grim but polite, and swung himself forward on the crutches.

"I always wondered why people can't walk out of the hospital under their own steam," Bernie said, walking on his other side, her hand on his elbow more to make sure he didn't vaporize than for support. "My sisters in health care can't adequately explain it."

"It's policy," the nurse said.

"I mean, patients are treated like invalids who can't operate under their own steam right up to the door, then you dump them into the street to fend for themselves."

"That's not what we do," the nurse said. "Please slow down," she said to Pete.

"Sorry," Pete said. "Anxious to get home."

"I know they've already told you this," she said. "But you have to take it easy. Stay off the leg, keep it elevated. Drink a lot of liquids. You're fighting a couple different things, your injuries and withdrawal. Let your wife take care of you."

"Wait here while I get the car, hubby," Bernie said as they approached the door.

The small hospital parking lot was half-empty on a Sunday morning. She kept her eye on Pete, waiting at the door, as she threw the paperwork and plastic bag of ruined clothes onto the backseat and pulled the passenger seat back as far as it would go to make room for his leg and crutches.

Pete was moving toward the car before it stopped.

Bernie started to get out, but he already had the door open and was pulling himself in, the nurse trying to hold his crutches with one hand and help him with the other.

"I've got it," Pete said.

The nurse put the crutches in the backseat. "All set?"

"We're good," Bernie said. Pete nodded.

"Remember, take it easy," the nurse said.

"Got it," said Pete. "Thank you."

"Finally, home," Bernie said as she pulled onto Route 2.

He shifted in the seat.

"Are you okay? Is there enough room?"

"Fine."

The fact it was Fourth of July had been a vague concept to Bernie, but the long line of stopped traffic made it real as she rounded the turn onto Main Street in Farmington.

"Parade," she said.

"Yeah."

"Why does everyone at the hospital think I'm your wife?"

"I think it was something I said when they bought me in. I was pretty out of it."

"You would've had to be." It annoyed her the way he qualified it so fast.

The parade bobbed up ahead, beyond the line of cars. The tinny sound of bands, punctuated by firetruck siren blasts.

"It always seems like every firetruck in Maine is in these. What if there's a fire?" Bernie said.

"That'd be a problem."

She cast around for something that they could talk about. "Did you think about the stuff I told you last night, about Colleen and the nurse killings, and Herman and someone being in your house?"

"Little bit."

"Any thoughts?" She tried to remember the part last night where he'd told her he'd missed her, the way he kissed her. Today he seemed like he wished she wasn't there.

"Hard to say."

"Do you think Herman could have killed Lydia?"

He sighed. "I don't know."

Brake lights flashed up ahead. She shifted into first gear.

"I'm having trouble focusing," Pete said as Bernie eased the car through the stream of parade-goers.

"You're talking to the right person." She made a drum roll sound.

Pete didn't say any more for the rest of the ride.

*****

When they pulled into Pete's dooryard, they were greeted by Dubya's happy barks.

"Your welcome home party."

211

Pete smiled as he maneuvered out of the car and took the crutches from Bernie. Dubya bounced around him, panting and yipping, nearly tripping Pete up as he crutched into the house and sat on the couch. The dog jumped up beside him, licking his face.

"Dubya, off," Bernie said.

Dubya ignored her. "I know, boy, I know," Pete said, burying his face in Dubya's neck.

"Hey, look, gift from Sal." Bernie held up the cane.

"Good God, what's that?"

"A cane."

"Looks like a murder weapon."

"Could be, yeah." She leaned it against the wall by the door. "Do you think you can eat? I have some homemade chicken noodle soup and Saltines."

"What I really want is to take a shower."

"The nurse said you need help in the shower."

He eased off the couch. "I'll be okay. Do we have that thing to put around the bandage?"

Bernie got it out of the bag of supplies and handed it to him. She'd forgotten about his old clothes. She opened that bag and took out the shorts. They were stiff, torn and bloodstained. "Want me to wash these?"

"Throw them out. Throw out the whole bag." He headed for the bathroom.

She reached into the pocket of the shorts. His compass was in there, so was his wallet. "Hey," she said.

"Max must've picked that up," he said when she held the wallet up for him. "Fuller dumped it all over the place."

She held up a thumb-sized bottle in a baggie. "What's this?" The label was torn, but she could still read part of it. "Baclofen." She handed it to him.

"I don't know." He frowned, thinking. "I found this at Lydia's campsite. I put it in my pack, not my shorts."

"Is it Lydia's?"

"I don't know."

"Her daughter told me she took medication for her back, but not on the trail. Maybe it's the mystery drug Max gave you."

"Look." His eyes held hers.

"What?"

"Don't get all excited."

"Don't worry. I'm not excited at all."

He went toward the bathroom. "Put it on my desk, okay? I'll figure it out later."

"Let me know if you need help." She put the bottle next to the folder with the insurance form. He hadn't mentioned it, and she wasn't going to ask. The box, tape recorder, notes and everything were still on the table. "Can I put this away somewhere?"

Pete barely glanced at it. "In the closet." As though it were yesterday's newspaper. He went into the bathroom and closed the door. After a minute she heard water running.

She put the box in the closet and took a second to bury her face in the overcoat. Last time she'd felt hopeless. Now she should feel relieved, but she didn't.

As she heated up the soup, she heard Pete clunking around in the bathroom.

"Need any help?"

"No thanks. I'm fine."

She took out her cellphone and dialed her sister Amy. Of her three medical siblings, she was the one who'd most likely know the answers, stick to the facts, and not make small talk.

The name of the drug felt familiar. Maybe Lydia's daughter, Georgia, mentioned it, but Bernie didn't think so. "What's baclofen?" she asked when Amy answered.

"It's a muscle relaxant and anti-spastic, chemical name 4-amino-3-4-chlorophenyl butanoic acid. It's used mostly as treatment for Parkinson's, though it's also an anti-flu medication and can be used for other spasticity indications." She paused. Bernie waited, knew she was searching the encyclopedia that was her brain for more information. Bernie pictured her standing in her lab coat, her curly red hair up in a bun, her glasses askew. "I believe it's most

213

often taken orally, most commonly by tablet, but also as a powder. There's also a cream or gel that can be applied externally, and it's available IV."

"Does it have side effects and stuff?"

"There's a long list. Which ones are you interested in?"

"I don't know. What are the worst ones?"

"Hallucinations, lightheadedness, muscle weakness, nausea, confusion, depression, nightmares, mania."

"Ugh."

"Coma, death."

"Geez."

"That's if more than the recommended dose is taken."

"It's for Parkinson's?"

"As I said, it's commonly used for Parkinson's but can be used for other musculoskeletal complaints involving spasticity, particularly related to the spine. It's also sometimes used as a flu medication, but I believe that's falling out of favor."

"You didn't really say all that before."

"I was trying to simplify it."

"Thanks."

"Does that help?"

"I'm not sure."

"Why do you want to know?"

"It relates to something going on here. It may have been used inappropriately."

"That's bad. The side effects can be very severe."

Bernie hung up, trying to grab what had been tripped in her memory. *Spinal. Baclofen.* She'd seen it in Sandy's medicine cabinet. It was a box that had another container inside. She could feel it rattle around when she picked it up to read the label. In an unusual fit of self-control, she didn't open it or ask him about it. She'd planned to Google it later, but forgot. Until now.

She ladled soup into a bowl and put it on the table, a sleeve of crackers next to it. She made a bowl for herself, too. They'd told her his stomach was sensitive and to make sure he didn't overdo it. She had no idea what to feed him, so she was going with what her mother did when someone was sick.

He came out of the bathroom, a towel wrapped around his waist. "I couldn't shave," he said. "Hands too shaky."

"Did everything else go okay?"

"Fine," they both said at the same time.

"That smells good," he said. "Who was on the phone?"

"My sister Amy, the doctor at Mass General."

"ALS research."

"Wow, you're good."

"It's the last few days I'm having trouble with, not the rest of it."

"She says baclofen is used to treat muscle and spine things."

"Hmm." Pete crutched into the bedroom.

Should she mention she'd read in the case file about Lydia's possible drug intoxication? She sat down at the table. She'd told him she'd gone through it. He didn't seem bothered. She added it to her list of things to worry about, that he seemed okay with her poking her nose where it didn't belong.

A soft swear came from the bedroom, then a clatter. Crutches falling, she guessed. She broke crackers into her soup. "Sure you don't need help?"

"I'm sure."

It'd been a shock when he came out of the bathroom. His skin was almost gray. He'd lost weight. His back was bruised. Then, of course, there were the cigarette burn scars on his hip and lower back, rising above the towel. She'd never gotten used to those.

He came out of the bedroom in shorts and a T-shirt, bare feet. Almost himself except for the crutches and the facial hair. "Thanks." He sat down, laying the crutches on the floor. He broke some crackers into the soup, then dipped his spoon in. His hand shook as he lifted it.

"Good," he said after what looked like a painful swallow.

He'd barely touched his hospital food, but the nurse told her people in withdrawal rarely felt like eating. Bernie had made a joke that maybe she needed to be in withdrawal, it sounded like a great weight-loss plan. The nurse had frowned. Inappropriate.

"Did you eat in the woods?"

"I'm not sure."

"Not sure if you ate?" She couldn't imagine it. She watched as he lifted another shaky spoonful.

"It's a blur. Hard to know what's real."

"Oh." She watched as he swallowed.

Pete took another spoonful. His hand jerked, and he put the spoon down. "I want to eat, but it would be easier if you weren't staring at me like that."

"Am I? Sorry."

"You're goggling," he said, with a little smile.

"Sorry." She knew the smile was meant to reassure her, but it didn't.

They ate in silence; the only noise Pete's spoon clinking against the bowl each time he dipped it in, then the stream of dripping soup as he raised it. Dubya panted next to him. Smart dog, Bernie thought. Usually it was her he sat next to.

Pete was home. He was alive, but what happened to him had been horrible. It hit her as she watched him. She thought him being home would make everything okay, but it didn't.

"Why are you crying?" He said it gently, but it didn't make her feel better.

"Why aren't you?"

"Would it make you feel better?" He made it sound like a reasonable question, not an accusation.

"I meant figuratively."

"In that case, I've got it covered."

She brought her dish to the sink, almost tripping over the dog, who expected her to put it on the floor so he could lick it. Maybe he wasn't that smart after all, because he hadn't figured out they only did that at their house, not Pete's.

"That was good," he said. "Let's hope I keep it down."

"Do you want to try some scrambled eggs?"

216

"Later. I'm going to take a nap." He made his way to the bedroom.

"Do—"

"I've got it, thanks."

She went out to the deck. It was early afternoon on a beautiful Fourth of July. She could hear voices from across the lake, the sound of a motorboat, laughter. She wondered if the fireworks were visible from here. She wondered if she should tell Pete she'd seen baclofen in Sandy's medicine cabinet. That would raise the question of what she was doing in Sandy's bathroom, though. She wondered if Sandy could've dropped it at Lydia's campsite when they found her. That didn't seem likely. It didn't seem like the kind of thing someone would tote around unless they had to. Like if they were hiking the Appalachian Trail, for instance.

Lots of wondering, but, as usual, no answers. She got her work stuff out and found her notebooks about Lydia. Instead of the crazy-making chart from the other morning, she'd keep it simple. On a fresh piece of paper, she wrote:

1. Where's the hiker roster?

2. Who was in Pete's house Wednesday & did they take it?

3. Did that person read Pete's notes?

4. Did they see his note about the CO on the medical examiner's report?

It was more like one question. The bigger one was, if this person had seen all that, what did it mean? The obvious thing: They knew that Pete at least suspected Lydia had been murdered. Would that be good news for that person, or bad news? More likely bad news. If the person thought it was good news, they wouldn't be sneaky about it.

She went through her Lydia notebooks, looking at the things she'd marked and underlined, and things she'd ignored. In all caps, underlined, a few days before Lydia was found: CRYSTAL AND LEEANNE DON'T BELIEVE SHE'S DEAD.

It made her sad. Bernie had been pretty sure at the time that she was. The irony was, at that point, she was probably still alive.

217

There was a note from the night she talked to Lydia: "Smiled/tired when I gave her letters." She'd have to ask Pete if he'd seen the Herman letter with the others. She should ask where Lydia's phone was, too. She wondered if he cared anymore.

CHAPTER 25

Despite the hot day, a cool breeze blew through the open windows in Colleen's house. The kitchen smelled like cinnamon. Dawna almost felt like it wasn't official business.

Colleen offered her an iced tea, and they sat down at the table.

"How's the police chief?"

"He's doing well," Dawna said. "He's home from the hospital."

"Glad to hear it."

"This is nice," Dawna said.

"It came furnished, so luckily it's nice stuff."

"Why rent a house? Aren't you just visiting?"

Colleen smiled, polite but guarded. "I wasn't sure how long I'd stay. I have a lot of research to do, and it seemed like a nice place to spend the summer."

"I'm sorry, it usually is. You wanted to talk about the vandalism?"

"Yes. I know you're busy with the holiday, but there was more," Colleen said. "I debated saying anything, because I don't want to make a big deal."

"What now?" Dawna hadn't seen any more graffiti. The ugly, hateful smear of dog poop was gone, and the house was as pristine outside as it was inside.

"I found a dead rat in the front seat of my car."

"When?"

"This morning. And this was not road kill. It was still warm, with no visible sign of injury, but like it had been killed just for this purpose. It was in my front seat. There was a note. 'Go home, nigger.'"

Dawna flinched. "I'm really sorry. I know this doesn't help, but we haven't had anything like this, at least this overt, happen here since I've been here."

"I'm sorry, too."

"Did it happen here?"

"No, I was at the self-storage place, up by the dump. I have a unit there."

"Someone did it while you were right there?"

"I'd been distracted. The little boy next door and his friend were riding their bikes, and I heard one of them yell, and it didn't sound like kids having fun. I went to see what was wrong."

"That would be Hallowell and my cousin Natalie."

"He fell off his bike. It took several minutes to determine he was all right."

"Was anyone else there?"

"I didn't see anyone. It's usually pretty deserted when I'm there. I do see Natalie, often, sweeping out empty units and picking up, but she's normally by herself."

"Her father owns it," Dawna said.

"I think the children were distracting me on purpose. Hallowell isn't a good actor. Natalie didn't seem concerned about him, more like a reluctant participant."

"That sums her up. So there was a third kid, who put the rat in your car." Dawna tried to figure out who it would be.

"Possibly."

"Do you still have it?"

Colleen led her out the back door. "I used a piece of cardboard to slide it into a box."

The rat, definitely dead, a little bit of mucus dried on its snout, lay in a shoebox on Colleen's patio table. Next to it, the note. It was on steno paper with rounded corners, a red double line down the middle. Dawna felt a shock of recognition. "I'll take these. Can we talk later? With the Fourth of July, I've got a lot on my plate."

"I understand," Colleen said.

220

"Are you going to be okay?"

"I'm definitely okay. I've got something else." She went into the kitchen and came out with a baggie. Inside was a blue latex glove.

"What's this?"

"I found it in my front bushes. It has dog poop on it. If I had to guess, I'd say it was used to write on my door."

*****

Dawna put the rat, note and baggie in her cruiser, then stood in front of Colleen's, considering.

Union Street was a narrow dead-end, with no sidewalk. Its five houses, all on one side, faced a thick growth of woods that stretched down from the last block of downtown. Colleen's house, next door to Chloe Houten's, was the last one on the street before more woods. Someone could have come through the woods to leave the dog poop message, but they would've had to work at it. There were more woods next to Colleen's leading to the river fork. Whoever did it would've had to walk down the street and, since the houses were close together, do the deed in full view of Chloe's house.

The sound of a TV and piping voices came through Chloe's open windows. Dawna knocked.

Hallowell opened the door. "Do you want Natalie? We're watching *Star Wars*."

The living room behind Hallowell was tiny, hot and dim, the shades drawn. The floor was littered with toys and magazines.

Natalie waved from the couch. She and Hallowell looked at Dawna, waiting, a set of big black eyes and gray ones huge behind thick glasses. They both looked guilty as hell.

The four-year-old, Corinna, was on the floor coloring. The baby, Richmond, was in his high chair, tomato sauce smeared around his mouth, pizza crusts on his tray and the floor around him.

"It's Fourth of July, why aren't you guys at the park?"

"It's boring," Hallowell said. Natalie nodded.

221

"Can I talk to your mom?" Dawna asked.

"She's at the park. They have a booth."

"Who's babysitting?"

"We are."

The baby squealed and threw a pizza crust. Dawna knew that when she was a kid, eleven-year-olds babysat all the time. Debbie, when she was younger than Hallowell, had been left with Dawna and her younger brothers. That didn't make it a good idea.

"The two of us together is like a twenty-two-year-old," Hallowell said, reading her face.

"That's not how it works," Dawna said. "We need a grownup here."

She called Eli as Hallowell rolled his eyes.

"Not my dad," Natalie said. "Great." She slumped deeper into the couch.

When Eli answered, Dawna explained the situation.

"I was going to pick up Nat and bring her to the park anyway," he said. "I had no idea the kids were alone."

"It'll just be for a bit," Dawna said. "I'll go talk to his mother."

Hallowell turned to Natalie. "Thanks a lot."

"I didn't do anything."

"While we're waiting for Natalie's dad to get here, I want to talk to you guys," Dawna said.

Richmond shrieked.

"Hallowell, the baby's making a mess," Corinna said without looking up.

Dawna turned off the TV and went into the kitchen to find paper towels. She wiped the baby's face as he gurgled, crushing fistfuls of pizza crust in his hand.

"How old is your brother?" Dawna asked.

"Eighteen months," Corinna said. "He's a love child."

"Corinna, that's not appropriate," Hallowell said.

She stuck out her tongue, still not taking her eyes off her coloring.

"Okay, guys," Dawna said to Hallowell and Natalie. "I want to know what happened at the storage units."

"When?" Hallowell said.

"Earlier today, with Ms. Sullivan."

"Nothing."

"I heard you had a bike accident."

"See, I told you," Natalie said.

"Shut up," he said.

"You might as well tell me the truth."

"We were just playing around, and she thought we were serious," Hallowell said. "It was a joke."

Hallowell looked her in the eye, face passive, a little smug. Natalie looked at her hands, tight little balls in her lap.

The roar of Eli's pickup sounded out front, then silence, the engine pinging and a door slamming.

"Great," Natalie whispered.

"If you two can think of anything you want to tell me, you know where to find me," Dawna said.

CHAPTER 26

Bernie put a plate of Saltines on the coffee table. She'd taken them out of the plastic sleeve and fanned them out.

"Nice presentation," Pete said.

"I think it's important food is as pleasing to the eye as it is to the palate." She sat down. "That's my Martha Stewart impersonation."

"Sounded more like Eleanor Roosevelt." He chewed a cracker, swallowed. She tried not to watch. Normally she'd fire off a smartass answer, but everything felt so precarious. She had no idea what he was thinking, what the aftershocks were. No idea what the script was.

"Hey Eleanor," Pete said. "If you see my good friend Bernie O'Dea, tell her I'm looking for her."

"I don't get it."

"I don't blame you for walking on eggshells, but the best thing you can do is be yourself," he said. "That'd be my best medicine."

"No one's ever said that to me before," she said. "I feel like it's some kind of trick."

He smiled, but it was still that tired one. "Let's try to act like everything's normal until it is."

"I wish you could tell me what happened with Max," she said. "Herman. We can't even settle on a name."

"I just don't know."

She got him a glass of water. "You're supposed to be hydrating. At least you're keeping the crackers down. Maybe we can graduate to scrambled eggs for supper."

He took the glass, his hand was steadier than it'd been earlier, but his fingernails were still broken and torn. She couldn't imagine how that happened or what he'd been through. How was she supposed to act normal?

"Let's talk about who might have killed Lydia," Bernie said. "You know, from your point of view as a homicide detective. It's not really normal conversation, but it's something"

He sat back. "Yeah, okay. Let's do that. Here's how I approach it: You start with the evidence and work toward a suspect. So, doing that, it was someone who knew her. The scene was staged."

"How so?"

"It was made to look like suicide. The only reason to make a murder look like it's not is if the killer can be tied to the victim and wants to hide it. Fuller or a random hiker wouldn't have bothered."

"It's not like her ex-husband or some old boyfriend would come up from Buffalo, hike the Appalachian Trail, find her and kill her, then stage it to look like suicide," Bernie said. "Or even a stalker that we don't know about. I can't think who it would be."

"There's Max, LeeAnne, Crystal, Colleen."

"Except none of them killed her, at least not the three women."

"You don't know that."

"I can't see any of them killing someone."

"That's why you follow the evidence," he said. He seemed more sure of himself, less shaky. "Take the baclofen. It was at her campsite. What does that tell you?"

"It could have been hers. One of them slipped it in her pack in case she needed it. They helped her pack, helped her with supplies, so that's plausible. Maybe she brought it herself. "

"Let's say it was planted at the campsite."

"Someone had to have access to baclofen and her campsite either when they killed her or after she died," Bernie said. "Herman could've, if he stole it from Redimere Drug, though it wasn't on the list of stolen medication. I don't know who else."

"Sandy."

"How do you know he takes baclofen?" She tried to remember

if she'd said something. "I can't believe you'd even bring him up."

"This is an exercise, okay? Look at the evidence. He has access to it. He found her body."

"If he killed her, why find her?" She couldn't believe she'd had to use the phrase "if he killed her." Pete looked unaffected, like it was the exercise he said it was.

"I know he has it because he told me a few weeks ago he was given a prescription, but didn't want to take it because he never knew when he'd have a fire call and he didn't like the effects. As to why a killer would put himself in position to find his victim, it happens a lot. If they're controlling, as many killers are, that's another way to control the investigation. There's also, 'Hey look at me, I found the body, so therefore I didn't kill her.'"

"Oh my God. You're serious. He didn't even know Lydia."

"The night you interviewed her at the Pour House, Sandy was there. He talked to her. He told me."

"They talked for a minute."

"That's what he said, but who knows?"

"What would his motive be? Why would he tell you all that obvious stuff if he killed her? This is ridiculous." Her voice was climbing. She took a deep breath. "I don't want to talk about it." She wanted to accuse him of accusing Sandy because of their fling, but he didn't know about it and this definitely wasn't the time for him to find out.

"Do we know he was really at that conference in Bangor the day she was killed?"

"Why are you doing this?"

He gave her a long look, that old familiar laser stare that could see everything she was thinking. She burned with self-consciousness.

"I don't think Sandy did it," Pete said after way too long a pause. "I'm just making a point. The victim and the evidence speak. Personal feelings about people aren't evidence."

"I don't want to play anymore."

"Welcome to my world."

226

"You can have it."

"I need to finish that nap," he said. "My head is killing me."

She opened her laptop as he went into the bedroom. She closed it again. No way she could work. Evidence. She couldn't begin to separate real evidence from everything else. She went out to the deck with her cellphone and called a high school friend who was an officer in the state fire chief's association.

After an excruciating couple minutes of chit-chat and Augusta gossip, she asked how Sandy's panel at the conference went.

"Would've been better with him there," he said. "He had an emergency. Never showed."

She fumbled through some more small talk, then clapped the phone closed. She peeked in at Pete. He was lying on the bed, one arm over his eyes, Dubya snuggled beside him. She went back to the porch and slumped into a lawn chair. The lake glittered in the afternoon sun, the party somewhere along the shore had ramped up the music, the laugher raucous. She hated them. Hated the Fourth of July. She stared at the lake and tried to imagine everything that happened to Lydia from the time she got to Redimere that rainy Thursday afternoon in May until she was killed. There wasn't much there—the night at the Pour House, the interview, the letters from well-wishers, one of them obviously from Herman, the texts that never got where she was sending them. She tried to picture any of her friends killing her. She couldn't.

She heard Pete in the living room. "How was the nap, besides short?"

"Okay." He went to the refrigerator.

"What are you doing?"

"I'm going to make those scrambled eggs I've heard so much about."

"Let me."

"Let me. I'm tired of being treated like I'm helpless."

"You're being treated like someone who's sick and hurt and is supposed to be resting and staying off his leg."

Pete struggled with his crutches as he pivoted to put the eggs on the counter. The carton flopped open, then fell on the floor. "Shit."

Dubya was on it, lapping up the broken eggs, shells and all. Good. She didn't want to watch Pete defiantly try to clean it up. She picked up the soggy carton and threw it in the trash.

Pete made his way to the couch. "Who was on the phone?"

"Work." She sat down next to him as he lifted his leg onto the coffee table.

"The windows are open. I heard the conversation."

"Then why'd you ask?"

"I wonder where Sandy was, if not at the conference?"

"I have no idea, but I know where he wasn't—in the woods killing Lydia."

Pete shrugged and picked at his dressing.

"I think we're supposed to change that at some point," she said.

"Later."

"Now I have to figure out what we can have for supper since eggs are off the menu. How about spaghetti if I just put butter and parmesan on it? Think that'll be okay?" She didn't want to talk about Sandy. Didn't want to think about it.

"Sounds good. I'm not hungry yet."

"Me neither." All she'd had to eat since breakfast was soup and Saltines. Her stomach growled. "We're just going to eat yellow and beige food from here on out."

Her cellphone rang. Her heart sank. "Speak of the devil."

She cringed at Sandy's cheerful hello. "He wants to know if you're taking visitors," she said to Pete.

"Sure, why not."

*****

Sandy arrived in uniform, a reminder that it was Fourth of July. Bernie kept forgetting.

He and Pete made small talk about how Pete felt, then about how things were going in town—uneventful. They danced around, stiff and awkward. It was making Bernie lose her mind.

"There's going to be an article tomorrow in *Franklin On Call* I wanted to tell you guys beforehand," Sandy said when the small talk ran out.

"What about?" Pete asked.

"Fergus Kelley got a tip there's something fishy with Lydia being found and I'm the fishy part."

Bernie's heart sank.

"He asked if there's any reason Lydia would have carbon monoxide poisoning," Sandy said. "He said he wanted to give me a chance to fill in the blanks."

"What blanks?" Bernie asked.

"That doesn't sound like much of a story," Pete said. "There's no way Kelley could know about the CO, and there's nothing else, right?"

"If he'd looked at the case file, he'd know," Bernie said. She hoped Sandy didn't notice that Pete was using his friendly interrogation voice. Neither of them reacted to what she'd said.

Sandy leaned over with his arms on his thighs, looking at the floor. "There's more."

Bernie wanted to stop him. Pete squeezed her arm. Sandy caught it, then looked away, his ears red.

"I don't know exactly what the article is about, but I have an idea," Sandy said. "I want you to know the real story."

Bernie gave him an encouraging smile, but she didn't feel encouraging. Pete squeezed again, and she sat back.

"Kelley asked if the CO with Lydia and with my ex-wife and kids was a coincidence."

Pete's grip tightened on Bernie's arm. He was looking at Sandy, but she got the message. She kept her million questions to herself.

Sandy looked at Bernie. "I've never told this before, so let me tell it my way. I got married right out of high school. Joined the Navy, was a Navy corpsman. When I got out, in '88, we moved to Bangor. We had two kids by then. I was a party boy." He paused. "I was a bad husband, but I loved my kids."

Bernie's eyes burned. She could feel Pete breathing next to her,

229

but didn't dare look at him.

"We got divorced, but I wanted to be sure they knew I loved them, because when I was a kid, it was all business at the farm, kind of a cold place, with Dad and my brothers. My mom died when I was eight, and my next brother's ten years older than me. I didn't want them to ever feel that lost. I feel like I need to explain that to you guys." He cleared his throat. "Unfortunately, I also loved partying and being out all night, and girlfriends, and being a fireman."

"You're being too hard on yourself," Bernie said. She dreaded where this was going.

"I'm not." He took another deep breath. "Sorry. I didn't think it would be this tough."

"Sandy, you don't have to," Pete said in his calm cop way. She knew he felt for Sandy, but Bernie was shaken by their conversation earlier. She knew, too, there was a part of him that was looking at the evidence.

"I have a point," Sandy said. "Sorry it's taking me so long to get to it. Winter of '93, there was a storm, knocked out the power for days, weeks in some places, you know how they do. Tammy and the girls lived out in the country, toward Garland. I could've had the kids stay at my place in Bangor—my power was only out a couple hours—but Tammy didn't ask, and I didn't offer. I'd already burned through my second marriage, had a new girlfriend. The kids would've cramped my style. So I got this generator, used, a buddy of mine got a new one and was getting rid of it, so I should've known it was probably a piece of shit."

Bernie wanted to make him stop. Pete's eyes were steady on Sandy, his face blank.

"I went over to their place, hooked it up. Told Tammy to keep it outside. You know, 'Hey babe, be sure to keep this outside, okay?' Like it was a pail of rubbish or something. They had an attached garage. Guess I should've made it clear garage doesn't count as outside." He paused, took a deep breath. "It was cold that weekend, so fucking cold. She called me a couple times because the generator was crapping out and she had to keep restarting it. I told her, 'What do you want me to do about it? Come out there from Bangor every time?' Just like that. 'Go out and fucking restart it if it needs restarting.' I guess she got tired of going out into the cold and hauled it into the garage."

"Sandy," Bernie whispered. Pete's hand was still on her arm. He squeezed again, maybe in sympathy, maybe to shut her up. She couldn't tell.

"The phone rang all morning. I didn't answer, figured it was Tammy bitching, and I had a hangover and my girlfriend was there. When I finally answered, it was my captain. Tammy's neighbor heard the generator going in the garage and tried to get them out. Too late."

"I'm so sorry," Pete said. Bernie was relieved that he sounded it. Had she really been thinking that he was such a cop he wouldn't feel for his friend? She wiped her eyes as she watched Sandy's hand, large and tan, on Dubya's head, scratching through the riot of fur.

"CO poisoning signs wear off after a bit, but when I identified the bodies, they were still red. I've seen it plenty of times as a fireman, but nothing stays with you so much as seeing it on your own kids, the mother of your kids."

Bernie kept her eyes on the dog, Sandy's hand.

"You know how people talk about dreaming of the day they can walk their kids down the aisle and whatnot? Dance at their weddings? You know what I used to dream of? I mean, before they died? Just watching them grow up. See who they'd be. Shooting the shit with them in the kitchen. That was my dumb-ass fantasy." He wiped his eyes on his arm.

"I'm sorry," Pete said.

"I'm not telling it for you to feel bad for me. There was an investigation, like maybe I'd given them a faulty generator on purpose, or told her to put it in the garage. It was bullshit. I was never charged, but they jerked me around for months first. I lost my rank. I think they worried that if I couldn't make sure my family didn't die, they couldn't trust me."

"That's not fair," Bernie said.

"No, it is. I was a good firefighter, didn't bring the partying to work, but they started looking at me funny. No one talked about PTSD back then, not that they do much now, with firefighters, but back then it was worse. People knew I was edgy because of Beirut. So when I partied, it was 'What do you expect? Let the guy blow off steam.' That was the attitude."

"Beirut?" Bernie asked.

"The bombing," Pete said.

"Right. The one in October '83. I was twenty. I was part of that cleanup crew, if you want to call it that."

"I don't get what this has to do with anything," Bernie said. "Fergus thinks you gave Lydia a generator?"

"He got an email after I was in the paper for finding Lydia that said I wasn't a hero and 'ask MacCormack's dead wife and kids.' He told me about it couple days after we found her. Then someone told him about CO with Lydia and got him all jacked up."

"Fergus could find out the real story about your family and see there are no similarities," Bernie said.

"There's nothing online," Sandy said. "It was 1993. It was an internal investigation, and there was some vague stuff in the stories in the paper, but no one was putting stories on the internet back then. You know that, Bernie. It was all the way across the state, anyway. No one out here even wrote about it, except the obituaries. A year or so later, I high-tailed it back here to Franklin County, where all anyone knew is I was Clyde MacCormack's kid from the farm."

"I still don't get what he's writing about," Bernie said. "It doesn't seem like he can connect the two things. They're totally different." She looked at Pete. He still had that cop look.

"They can't write a story based on that bullshit," she said when neither of the guys responded.

Sandy laughed. "That was George Libby's territory back then. He wanted to pin it on me, bad."

"But the investigation showed you didn't do anything," Bernie said.

Sandy sighed. "Bernie. Doll. Do I really have to spell it out for you? All that matters is that I was implicated, and Kelley has a tip that there's something to do with CO with Lydia. He doesn't know what, but doesn't need to. He's not you, he doesn't have any ethics. You know that. Look what he did to you last year. All he needs is that thin little thread, probably with Libby's blessing, to weave a pile of shit."

He was right. Of course Fergus would write a story without any solid information or attribution.

"Kelley also asked Ryan Grant if he realized they had a fire chief who'd been accused of killing his ex-wife and kids, and asked Grant if he knew Lydia may have died of CO, just like the wife and kids. That I knew about the CO with Lydia, but didn't report it, so by the time they got the body in Augusta, the red had worn off and no one checked her blood, because I didn't tell them."

"That's wrong, you did tell them." She turned to Pete. "You were there when he told them."

Pete nodded. Still unreadable.

"I got grilled by Grant and the town attorney the other day," Sandy said.

"Why didn't I know that?" Bernie asked.

"You were a little distracted this week." He shot a look at Pete.

"Just have to prepare for damage control," Pete said.

Sandy nodded. "Right. Bottom line, there's a story coming out tomorrow that's going to make me look like crap. There's nothing I can do about it. I wanted you guys to know the truth, though."

He got up, gave Pete's ankle a gentle shake. He leaned down and cupped Bernie's chin with his hand, his palm warm, fingers tangling in her hair. He pressed his lips against her forehead. "Don't worry about me, sweetheart," he said. "I've already had the worst day of my life. They can't even touch it." He let go, his hand brushing her cheek.

"I have a question," Pete said as Sandy walked to the door.

233

"No," Bernie said.

"Where were you the day before you found Lydia?"

"What?" Sandy had his hand on the doorknob.

"I don't believe you," Bernie said to Pete. She jumped up and stood between them. "How could you?"

Pete cocked his head, waiting for an answer.

"What the fuck, Pete?" Sandy said.

"You didn't go to the conference."

"So I killed Lydia?"

"I didn't say that."

"I didn't even know her."

"You met her."

"For thirty fucking seconds at the Pour House. 'Hey, good luck, you'll love Katahdin.' Then I hiked into the woods and killed her? Shoved a Coleman stove into the Ziploc bag or something?"

"I just wonder why you didn't tell the truth about where you were."

"I didn't think I had to answer to anyone about where I go."

"Stop," Bernie said. She wasn't sure what she wanted to do first, push Sandy out the door or pummel the hell out of Pete.

"Fuck this," Sandy said, opening the door. "Sorry sweetheart," he said to Bernie. Then he slammed out.

"I don't even know what to say to you," she said as Sandy's truck roared away.

Pete picked at his bandage, not looking at her.

"He tells us about his wife and kids dying, and it's like this giant open wound that's going to bleed all over town tomorrow, and you pull that cop shit?" She wiped her eyes on her arm.

He didn't look up.

"I'm going to make that spaghetti." She clanged around in the kitchen, pissed that she was crying. How many times had it been today? Pete's eyes were closed, his head resting on the back of the couch. Dubya had joined him, his tail wagging, Pete's hand on his head. Stupid dog.

"You're being really unfair to Sandy," she said. The fact he wasn't responding pissed her off more. He usually didn't play that game.

She stood in front of him until he opened his eyes. They were bloodshot and wet.

"What just happened isn't you, cop or not. You wanted to hurt him. If it wasn't fucking obvious, he's in plenty of pain as it is. You don't believe he had anything to do with Lydia dying any more than I do. He won't even kill a spider."

"I'm sorry." He sounded like he meant it.

Bernie wiped her eyes. "I don't understand anything."

"Me either."

Her anger melted. He reached out and she sat on his lap, trying not to put weight on his bad leg. He wrapped his arms around her, and she put her head on his shoulder.

"I'm sorry I keep making you cry," he whispered.

"I'm making me cry."

His whiskers were wet against her cheek. He took a long breath in, then let it out slow, then did it again. She tried to match it. She'd wanted to ask if he knew about her and Sandy, but she couldn't now, as he sat there and breathed. The heat of his hands burning through the back of her blouse. She'd been so anxious to feel his strong arms around her like this, his heart beating against her. But all it felt like was a break in the action. She wasn't worried about the planes anymore, they'd already hit the buildings. Now the building was falling, and there wasn't anything she could do about it.

"Sandy's a brother to you," she said. "He loves you. Don't break that. You're both such good men."

He pressed his face harder into her shoulder. "I'm sorry."

She could feel his tears seep through her blouse. Did she really have to remind herself what he'd been through? She guessed she did. "I'm sorry, too." She hoped he knew it was for a lot of things. For everything.

Dubya whined and danced in the kitchen, then barked. The pot rattled on the stove. She slid off Pete's lap, giving him a quick kiss on his wet cheek and went to see. The water had boiled away.

She filled the pot up with cold water and it hissed, sending a cloud of steam into her face.

"I don't know what to do," she said. "You're not okay. What happened to you had to make your PTSD worse. I'm obviously not an expert, but it must've." It was easier to say it from the kitchen. "I don't know who you are. I mean, you're you, but I'm worried you're not anymore."

"I'm tired, sick, and in pain. That's all."

She grated cheese onto a dish, the sharp points of the grater hitting her fingers, the cheese scattering on the counter and floor.

"Bernie, look at me."

She looked up, stopped grating.

"I promise, I'm still me."

He looked like him. Stronger than he had when she was on his lap, the tears gone. He smiled. It still wasn't the big one she missed so much.

"Okay." What else could she say?

"Make enough for three," Pete said. He limped to the phone.

"Are you calling Sandy?"

"No, my dad."

CHAPTER 27

Chuck was there in minutes, like he'd been waiting by his door with his keys in his hand for Pete's call.

"Don't get excited," Pete said to Bernie before he got there. "I'm going to go talk to Fergus and I need a ride. You can't bring me. There's no one else."

"Why do you keep thinking I'm getting excited?"

He put his arms around her and kissed her. "It's what you do. I love you for it."

She wanted to argue, ask questions, but Chuck arrived and all she could do was send Pete angry messages with her eyes that he either ignored or smiled at. Pete's sudden change of mood didn't make her feel better. Talking to Fergus wouldn't fix anything; it would only make it worse. Bernie knew how he operated.

The men awkwardly shook hands. Chuck made the approach for a hug, but Pete deflected as though he hadn't noticed, nimble, even on his crutches.

"How are you feeling?"

"Fine," Pete said.

"Fine," Bernie echoed.

"That's good," Chuck said.

"Dinner is served," Bernie said.

The two men sat down. "It's not very glamorous," Bernie said to Chuck. "Do you want a salad or something? I feel bad just giving you this."

"It looks great," Chuck said. Bernie liked that he twirled the spaghetti on his fork, the Italian way. Just like Pete.

"If you want something more than water, I can get you some

iced tea or something," she said. The silence was getting to her. She wished Pete would at least tell Chuck the plan, instead of letting him think he'd asked him over to talk.

"Water's fine, thanks," said Chuck.

Both of them seemed content to eat, Chuck twirling away, Pete's shaky hands doing his best to do the same.

"I need you to drive me somewhere," Pete finally said.

"Sure, no problem." Chuck didn't seem curious or surprised. He was as good at the poker face as Pete was.

"A reporter is doing a story about the fire chief, and I want to talk to him in person about it," Pete said.

"Why don't you go with him?" Chuck asked Bernie. "I don't mind, but it seems more like your type of thing."

"She can't."

"I'm the guy's competition and former boss," she said. "If I show up, it'll make things worse. Worse than it's already going to be made by Pete showing up."

"It'll be fine," Pete said. "Do you still have his number?"

Bernie cycled through the numbers on her cell, found Fergus, and handed the phone to Pete. She wanted to refuse, but there was no point.

He fumbled with the phone. The shakes were back. "Let me." She pushed the button and handed it back. She cleared the dishes as Pete, all business, told Fergus he wanted to talk. Fergus must have said something about Pete calling from Bernie's phone.

"Mine's broken," Pete said. "She doesn't have anything to do with this. She doesn't even know I'm calling." Pete smiled and rolled his eyes at her. She smiled back, but she knew anxiety made it more of a grimace.

Pete hung up. "He's burning the midnight oil finishing a story on deadline, as he put it. He's happy to talk. I'm going to change."

Bernie washed the dishes, making small talk with Chuck, who insisted on drying. He was easy to talk to, just like Pete.

"Does he need help?" Chuck asked after a thump from the bedroom.

238

"He's fine."

Pete came out wearing khakis and a short-sleeved shirt. Police chief summer casual.

"I guess I can't shave, my hands are shaking too much."

"Why shave for Fergus?" Bernie asked. What she really wanted to say was "Why go?" But she'd already made her point and it hadn't worked.

"I wonder if I can do without the crutches," he said.

"No, you can't," Bernie said.

"I got through the woods on the leg. I can stand on it." He put his weight on it, bent it a little. "It wouldn't be too bad for a few minutes."

"Why?" Bernie asked.

"I don't want to be at a disadvantage," Pete said. "I don't want to look pathetic."

"You look awesome," Bernie said. She tried to sound like she meant it. "Use one at least." She tucked a crutch under his armpit, took his hand, and put it on the handle.

"Let's go," Pete said to Chuck, who was by the door jingling his keys.

"I love an adventure," Chuck said.

"You're just driving me. That's it," Pete said as he went past him out the door.

"Be careful," she said, but it was too late. The door shut behind them.

*****

Bernie flopped down on the couch. It wasn't even dark out yet. "Longest day ever," she said to Dubya.

He jumped up next to her. She turned on the TV. The Boston Pops pre-fireworks extravaganza was in full swing. Oh yeah, Fourth of July.

She watched with no interest. It was a different universe.

"Hey."

She jumped. Sandy was looking through the screen door.

"Where's Pete?" he asked, coming in and sitting next to her.

239

"He went somewhere with his dad. He shouldn't be gone long." She looked at the clock. They'd been gone half an hour.

"Mind if I wait?"

"Back for round two?"

"Something like that. I have more to say."

"I'm sorry," she said.

"Don't apologize. It's not you."

"I'm sorry about your wife and kids. I never knew."

"It's okay. It's not something I talk about."

"Sorry anyway. Don't you have to be at the fireworks?"

"Yeah, but it's not until nine-fifteen, so I've got an hour and a half."

She wanted to ask him where he was the day Lydia was killed, but didn't. Her life in the past hour had become a pile of unsaid important things.

"I thought Pete's parents were dead," said Sandy.

"Me too." She couldn't think of anything to add.

They watched the Pops, making small, obvious remarks about things that didn't matter. She'd never felt awkward with Sandy before, and she didn't like it. She'd expected Pete's trip to be quick. Downtown was less than ten minutes away. She couldn't imagine they'd have anything to say that would take more than a few minutes. The whole thing should've taken twenty-three minutes round-trip.

"Aren't you going to be late?" she asked.

"I already looked everything over. Anyway, some of the other guys are there. I still have time."

An hour had passed and Bernie was beginning to panic when they heard tires on gravel.

Chuck opened the door, and Pete came in on the one crutch. His left upper pant leg was dark with blood.

"What happened?" Bernie said, grabbing his arm and leading him to the couch. He was shaking.

"It's fine," he said.

"He insisted on not using the crutch," Chuck said.

"Hi," Pete said to Sandy. Sandy got up as Pete sat down. "This is my dad, Chuck Novotny."

"Nice to meet you," Sandy said. To Pete he said. "Did they give you dressing supplies?"

"I'll get it," Bernie said.

"I can take care of it," Pete said.

"Don't be stupid," said Sandy. "Take off your pants and lie down."

"At least buy me a drink first," Pete said, lying down.

It wasn't that funny, but Bernie laughed. No one else did.

"I can do this part myself," Pete said, undoing his belt buckle as Chuck and Sandy moved toward him. "Jesus."

Bernie stood by, holding the bandages and supplies.

Sandy took them from Bernie. "Why don't you two go outside?"

*****

"Thanks," Pete said as Sandy cut the tape holding the bandage in place. Sandy was being gentle, careful. It made Pete feel worse.

"Lots of blood," Sandy said. "It's stuck. What the hell did you do?"

"Just got ahead of myself some."

Sandy carefully pulled at the gauze. "The hospital expected you to take care of this yourself?"

"Worse, they expected Bernie to."

"Great."

"The wound is packed; they didn't close it. I don't know if that makes a difference," Pete said.

"Little bit." Sandy worked quietly, excruciatingly slow.

"Go ahead and pull if you have to," Pete said.

"I don't want to make it worse. It's soaked. I'll try to stop the bleeding, but if I can't, we might have to go to Farmington."

"I felt the wound tear or something when I was walking."

"I'm going to use saline, but it's still going to pull."

"Don't worry."

"At least it looks clean. The blood, I mean. No sign of

241

infection."

Pete's leg jerked as the gauze pulled at the edge of the wound.

"Sorry, sorry," Sandy said. He worked the last part off.

Pete felt cool air on the wound.

Sandy took a sharp breath. "Jesus, Pete."

"You've seen worse," Pete said. He kept his eyes shut and gripped the couch as Sandy removed the packing, reminding himself it was nothing compared to Max pulling the rod out.

"Sorry," Sandy said. "I'm trying to be careful."

"It's fine." Pete could hear Chuck telling Bernie some story, Bernie laughing. He took a deep breath and counted to four, then slowly let it out. He wished Sandy would stop apologizing.

"Everything isn't fine. You need to admit that," Sandy said quietly.

"I have admitted it."

"Don't kid a kidder." He tapped Pete's hip. "I need to look underneath. The bandage is stuck there pretty bad." Pete rolled onto his side.

"Hold this gauze on the top," Sandy said. He waited until Pete's hand pressed against it.

For a second, Pete was back in the woods with Max. He took another deep breath, held it four counts, then let it out. "Do what you have to do. Don't worry about hurting me."

"PTSD isn't something that goes away if you ignore it," Sandy said.

The dull ache turned into sharp pain as Sandy packed the underside of the wound.

"Sorry, sorry." Sandy stopped and steadied Pete's leg with his hand. "Almost done."

Pete held his breath, counted backwards, trying to make the hot dumpster smell go back to wherever it had risen from.

"I should have gotten help years before I did. Look what it cost me. I know people who specialize in it," Sandy said. "Usually vets, but they'd talk to you."

"It's different with you," Pete said, glad his face was pressed against the back of the couch, so he didn't have to face him. "You were in a bombing. Your ex-wife and kids died. How the hell do you survive that with your head straight? Nothing like that happened to me."

"You gotta get over thinking you don't deserve to be sick, so therefore you don't deserve to get better." He tapped Pete on the hip. "Roll back onto your back." He tucked Pete's leg against his side while he wrapped the gauze around it, then followed with tape, quick and efficient now that the bad part was over. "Remember who you're talking to. Guys like us, our jobs, we're the ones who march into a crisis, when everything's falling all around everyone, and we're calm and take charge. We're good at it, but we're human, too. It takes a toll." Sandy kept his eyes on what he was doing, not Pete, as he talked. "I didn't want to say it earlier and upset Bernie any more, but even now, if you're hurting and in our position, you don't want people to know. You don't want to be the weak link. It can cost you your job. I get that."

"I should be able to handle it," Pete said.

"You can't. I know a lot of people don't understand, but I do. I thought that was part of us having each other's back, you know? First responders together. I also know you care more than a lot of guys, and that adds to it. Maybe it goes back to you being a kid, wherever those cigarette burn scars came from. I don't know, I'm not a shrink. It doesn't matter why, it just matters it's happening."

"I'll deal with it." Sandy had rushed through the "have each other's back" part, but it still stung.

"People care about you," Sandy said. "Everyone's so worried. Bernie was a fucking basket case, thinking you'd kill yourself in the woods. Has she told you that? You can kick me around all you want. I don't care. Maybe I deserve it. But do you want to keep hurting her? Being embarrassed or thinking you don't deserve help is bullshit."

Sandy had finished and was rolling the dirty packing and bandage up, gathering the supplies. "Take some Tylenol or something, okay?"

Pete sat up, lifting his pale, useless leg onto the coffee table. The pain had been unrelenting since he'd come out of the woods. But since he'd walked in to Fergus' office without his crutch, feeling it tear, but standing on it anyway, for however long—half an hour? More, maybe—it was searing. He knew it was bleeding, hoped the blood wouldn't soak through his pants until he was done. He'd walked, knowing he was limping, but trying to look as steady, out to the street for the photo, then back to the car. That's when he'd fully felt it and collapsed into the car. He wondered if his leg was wrecked for good, if it was worth it. Too late to worry about it now.

"Thanks," he said to Sandy.

Sandy put the supplies on the counter. "Stay off it. I'll come by tomorrow to take a look and dress it again. Tell Bernie I said goodbye."

*****

Bernie and Chuck came in as Sandy's truck rumbled away.

"Sandy left?" Bernie asked.

"He had to get to the fireworks."

"Everything okay?" Bernie hadn't heard yelling, so that was good.

"Fine. I'm going to bed."

"Guess I better go, too," Chuck said. He and Bernie watched Pete struggle up from the couch.

"Are you going to be okay, Pete?" Chuck asked.

"Yeah."

"He's fine," Bernie said.

"Okay," Chuck said. "I'll check in tomorrow."

Bernie went into the bedroom after she walked Chuck out. Pete was sitting on the bed, his eyes closed.

"What happened?" Bernie asked.

"With Fergus?"

"No, with the fucking moon landing." She was tired and anxious. Her patience was shot.

He smiled at her and she sat down next to him. "I made a deal," he said.

"What kind of deal? You've read Faust, haven't you?"

"Can we talk in the morning? I'm wiped out. I can't think straight. Could you get me a couple Tylenol and some water?"

She brought him the pills and he took them, drank the water, then put the glass on the bedside table. Right next to the PTSD book.

He took her hand and tugged, and she sat down next to him. "I know it's been a long day," he said.

"The longest," she said. "At least you're home."

He lifted her hand and kissed it, then put his arms around her and pulled her close, kissing her long and hard. His whiskers scratched her face. "Things will be better tomorrow," he said. "I promise. I just have to get some sleep."

"I'll be up for a while. I still have work to do," Bernie said.

"If you want to watch the Pops, the TV won't bother me."

The fireworks had started, both in Boston and Redimere. Bernie half-watched the TV as she poked away at her laptop, taking care of work things she no longer cared about. Dubya circled the room, whining. Wandered into the bathroom, then came back out. He hated fireworks. She couldn't do anything about Redimere's, blasting in the distance, but she could get rid of the Pops. She flipped through the channels. Shopping show. Baseball. More fireworks. News. She watched for a minute. They were doing a story about the fireworks. She settled on the *Laverne & Shirley* channel.

"Doing it our way," she sang to Dubya. He stopped whining and panted at her briefly, then began circling again. "Making our dreams come true, for me and you," she sang to him. She heard a noise from the bedroom. She turned off the TV. "Sorry," she said. "You okay?"

"Yeah."

"I thought you said something."

There was a long pause. "It was nothing."

"Sure?"

"Yeah."

"Okay. Sorry about the noise. I'll be in in a bit. Unless." She got up and went to the doorway. He was lying on the bed in his underwear, his arm across his eyes. He was always doing that now. She picked his shirt and T-shirt off the bed, hanging the shirt and throwing the T-shirt in his clothes hamper with the bloody pants. He never left clothes lying around. She took the pants out to soak them in the sink.

"Unless what?" he asked, his arm still over his eyes.

"Do you want me to sleep on the couch? Maybe it'd be more comfortable for you since you don't feel great." She'd want a bed to herself if she was in his condition.

"No, I don't mind. Unless you want to."

"No, I don't mind."

She let Dubya out. The fireworks had stopped, but the party down the lake was having their own show. She hoped they'd wind down and go to bed soon. Dubya made it quick and scuttled into the bathroom.

She got in bed and snuggled up against Pete.

"What were you watching a little while ago?" he asked.

"*Laverne & Shirley*. Sorry. I know it's dumb, but they make me laugh."

His arm tightened around her.

"Have you ever wondered if the Pizza Bowl is named after their Pizza Bowl?" she asked. "Or maybe it's just the logical thing to name a place with bowling and pizza. I just always thought it was funny, two Pizza Bowls."

He was doing that deep slow breathing thing again.

"Sorry," she said. "I know you're tired. I'll shut up before you kick me to the couch."

"Never," he whispered, kissing her temple.

The fireworks down the lake popped. "You'd never know they were illegal," Bernie said.

"Over the town line. Not my jurisdiction."

She closed her eyes and listened to his heart beat. She curled her fist into the hollow of his chest. It still fit. He was here, not in the woods.

"It was inexcusable, me leaving for my hike without saying good-bye to you," he said.

"No, it's okay. You didn't know what was going to happen."

She was beginning to fall asleep when he said, "The night after we got back from Phippsburg, I swam way out. I just kept going."

"It's a big lake, but you're a good swimmer."

"I was so tired. It was raining, remember?"

She remembered. She lay in bed that night, listening to it against the roof, dreading work the next day and wondering how the weekend she'd looked forward to for so long had ended up such a disaster.

"I thought, 'I could just sink, it'd be so easy.'"

"Why?"

"I don't know."

"You wanted to kill yourself?" She tried to remember if anything that weekend would've been a sign he'd do that. She'd never considered it until he went into the woods. On some level, though, she must have known. It scared the shit out of her.

"No. I was just so tired of how I felt. I just wanted it to stop."

"Oh." Wasn't that the same thing?

He breathed in and held it. She counted in her head. One. Two. Three. Four. He let it out.

"When I broke up with you, I said I didn't want to burden you with my problems or some stupid bullshit. The truth is, I was so fucking scared I'd done that, I didn't want to know what was causing it. I knew you'd make me figure it out. I didn't realize that, though, until I was in the woods."

It didn't make her feel better. "That's why you broke up with me?"

"Sorry, baby," he said.

"It's okay."

"No it's not. But it will be."

CHAPTER 28

Dawna stopped at the Perry's trailer after the fireworks. Eli had called and said Natalie wanted to tell her something. Good. The more she thought about the harassment of Colleen, the more it bothered her. It really bothered her Natalie was involved. She gave her more credit than that.

"How did you like the fireworks?" Dawna asked.

"They were okay," Natalie said. "They bother dogs and other animals."

"As you kept saying," said Eli.

"Your dad says you want to tell me something."

Natalie looked at Eli.

"Go on," he said.

"It was Hallowell's idea."

"Don't go doing that," Eli said.

Dawna held up her hand. "Let her tell the story."

"He said it would be a good joke if he pretended to fall off his bike," Natalie said. "I didn't think it was funny."

"Who put the rat in her car?"

"I didn't know about that until later, when she kind of screamed."

"What about the dog poop on her front door?"

"I think it was Hallowell, but Lydia's friend paid him to, because he does odd jobs for her. I think she did the rat, too. He's not normally a racist."

"Which friend of Lydia's?"

"Crystal. Sorry, I don't know her last name."

"Start with the dog poop, and tell me what you know."

248

"That night, I was over there watching *Wipeout*. Crystal pays him to wash her car and pick up groceries and stuff. Since she's staying at the Four Seasons, she let him swim in the pool, too. That night with the dog poop, he was acting like he had some big secret and showed me she gave him twenty dollars. He had blue gloves that she gave him, too. I could tell he was supposed to keep it a secret, but he was too excited. His mom saw the dog poop word on the door when she came home, and called the police before Ms. Sullivan got home. I don't think Hallowell's mom knew he did it, though. She doesn't like racism."

"And the rat?"

"I'm not totally sure, but Hallowell came with me to the storage units. Usually he doesn't want to. Crystal asked him before to tell her when Ms. Sullivan was going there. Then he had the idea to pretend to fall. I thought it was dumb, so I just stood there like, whatever. There's rats around there from the transfer station, even though they try to keep it clean. Crystal talked to me about them sometimes, because she has a storage unit, too. "

"What did she say about the rats?"

"Just that they're dirty and not to play with them. As if I would. But it's not nice to kill them for no reason, either."

"Did Hallowell say how he knew Colleen would be at the storage units?"

"She told his mom she had to bring some stuff up there and he heard her and told Crystal. He was supposed to keep that whole thing a secret, but he thought it made him special, so he was bragging to me about it."

She got up. "I have to give you something." She went down the hall to her room and came back with a shoebox. "People are always piling stuff up by the dumpster instead of putting it in." She handed it to Dawna, smiling. "It's not a rat."

Dawna opened it. It was a GPS device and a fairly sophisticated compass.

"When did you find these?"

"Yesterday, when I was cleaning up. But I don't know how

long they were there. The rubbish was piled pretty high and this fell out when I tried to clean it up. I didn't think it was important, but then I remembered the story in the paper about Ms. Manzo and how she didn't have one, and that's why she got lost. It made me wonder if the fisherman put it there, because I've seen him there looking for stuff in the dumpster when we go really early."

"Did you find anything else?"

"Not like this. I mean there's a lot of junk because it was the end of the month."

"With how busy the weekend is, I haven't been able to empty it," Eli said, defensive.

"Can you hold off for another day or two?" Dawna asked.

"Sure."

"Natalie, why didn't you tell someone about this?"

"I was going to tell Chief Pete when he felt better."

*****

Bernie jolted awake. It took her a couple seconds to realize the outside light was on. Probably tripped by a squirrel or something. She couldn't remember what she'd been dreaming, but she was jumpy and scared. She watched the window, waiting for the light to go out. Pete, his arm draped over her, pulled her toward him in his sleep. She watched the window, feeling his heart beat against her back. The light faded, then brightened again, like something large had passed in front of it.

"Pete," she whispered. The windows were open, the rustle of the breeze and pre-dawn birds the only sounds. The shadow passed by the light again.

His arm tightened. "It's okay," he said, but she could tell he wasn't awake. She turned around, careful not to make any noise, put her mouth against his ear. "Pete," she whispered, as loud as she dared.

His eyes opened, instantly alert, just like the Pete she knew.

"I think there's someone outside," she whispered.

His eyes went from her face to the window behind her, his grip on her tightening. There was a quiet thump, then another one.

"Shh." He slid backwards off the bed tugging her arm. "Come here and get on the floor."

She followed him and eased onto the floor. He crouched above her, his bad leg stretched out. Another thump sounded, closer. From the deck.

He leaned down, his face white above hers. "Don't move until I tell you to. Whatever you hear, don't move. Wait until I say it's okay."

"Are you going to get your gun?"

"No time." He moved along the wall. Sal's cane leaned in the corner, and Pete took it as he crouched low, his silhouette lit by the window. Awkwardly, but without a sound, he moved around the partition.

Bernie held her breath. There was another thump, louder. She didn't hear Pete. She couldn't see the clock with her face pressed into the rug. Couldn't hear anything, not even the birds.

She wanted to call to him, had to force herself not to. She gripped the rug. Say it's okay. *Say it's okay.*

She could hear the clock tick now, slow, stretched out, a vast expanse of time between each tick. She was dying to look. She didn't know if he'd left the room seconds ago or minutes ago.

She was about to take a chance and look up when she was startled by his voice, normal, at her feet. "It's okay. You can get up."

"Who is it?"

He was smiling. "Come see."

She went with him to the window. A cow moose, lit by the moon, was stepping down the rocks to the water, her bulk moving delicately on skinny legs. A calf wobbled behind her. Bernie let out her breath.

"Guess we both have the heebie-jeebies," Pete said.

They got back in bed, and he wrapped himself around her, holding her tight, his bandaged leg thrown over her thigh. Within minutes, he was breathing regularly, asleep. She lay with her eyes open until dawn. There wasn't one thing, even Pete's arms around her, that was going to make her feel safe. Someone had killed Lydia. Bad things had happened to Pete. People moved through the night, doing things, whether it was dog poop on a door or worse. People who say they're perfectly fine swim out into the middle of the lake in the rain, wondering what it'd be like to sink to the bottom.

She wasn't going to get lulled into feeling like anything was okay.

*****

Dawna texted Bernie, asking if Pete was up, but she didn't get an answer. That was okay. He needed rest. She wasn't going to call the landline this early and wake him up. She'd tell him later. He'd understand.

She'd barely slept, but not like the nights before she'd gone to wait for Danny Fuller. This was different. Finally, a little before dawn, she called Sandy. He sounded way too awake for the time of morning.

"Did you have plans for today?" she asked.

"I was thinking of going fishing," he said. "Maybe just crawling into a hole somewhere."

"Want to go for a hike?"

"Not really."

"This is a hike with a purpose. Come pick me up, and I'll tell you about it."

She was waiting outside when Sandy pulled up. "I see you brought your fishing gear just in case," she said, climbing into the truck.

"That's from last week," he said. "I blew off that conference and went to Grand Lake Stream and fished until dark."

"Sounds like a good day."

"I thought so at the time."

"Head over to 27 and go north, up to Carrabassett."

He pulled onto the road. "Something wrong with your car?"

"No, but we may have a passenger coming back, and you have more room."

*****

When dawn broke, Bernie got up, as quiet as she could. Pete had slept peacefully and she wanted to let him keep on doing it for as long as he needed to.

She made coffee and went out on the deck with Dubya, her laptop, and her pile of notebooks.

The lake was glass, morning mist rising. It was going to be another hot day. Two loons glided nearby, every once in a while sticking their heads in. Just like Friday when she'd sat there with Chuck.

Bernie tried to picture Pete on that rainy May night, swimming out past Blueberry Island, out past the middle. The name of the lake was Patten Pond, but that was a Maine thing. It wasn't a pond the way people from away think of them, it was a good-sized lake. Deep and cold.

She found the notebook from when she'd interviewed Lydia on another rainy night that had come before something bad.

"It's not done yet," Lydia had said a couple times, trying to temper Crystal and LeeAnne's excitement. Lydia had been tired, had said something about her back. Bernie had made a note, hadn't thought about it since. "Taking Tylenol, old injury."

Nothing about a prescription. She tried to remember the conversation. LeeAnne and Crystal—had they said anything? Someone had said something about Lydia's back, its treatment.

The notes after that were a jumble. Bits and pieces of this and that. It wasn't really an interview at that point, just random talk.

She added it to her list of things to ask Crystal. At some point she'd written on the sheet "squirrel remedy." She wondered what Crystal's was.

She typed "public works rodent remedy" into Google. Then for good measure, "Corson," Crystal's last name.

Her cell rang. Guy. It wasn't even seven yet.

"Sorry, I know you're taking a personal day, but what do you want to do about the story about Pete?"

"What we said we'd do. Just he got hurt hiking, had to be Lifeflighted out. No embellishment."

253

"I thought maybe that's changed because of what *Franklin On Call* has," Guy said. "The Midnight Rambler stuff. Now we're kind of stuck. I mean if we don't write something, we look like we're either covering for him or out of the loop."

Goddam Pete. "Let me read it and call you back."

"Gotcha. I'll hold a spot on the front."

Feed the dog. Make more coffee. Wake up Pete and ask him what the hell he did.

She didn't have to, he was in the living room.

"I know I should have told you last night, but I was too tired," he said. At least he was using both crutches, like he was supposed to. "What does it say?"

"I haven't read it yet." She got her laptop and found the website as he sat down at the table. She didn't comment that he'd left a crutch propped against the counter so he could carry his coffee. His leg, his problem. That's the mood she was in.

"Read it out loud," Pete said.

"I haven't had coffee, I had no sleep, and my pill takes about forty-five minutes to kick in, and if you haven't noticed, I'm pissed off."

"Let's see how bad it is, then I'll explain."

It was spread across the *Franklin On Call* home page. A photo of Pete, taken the night before, standing on Main Street with his arms crossed as dusk settled on the mountains in the distance. Defiant, with a slight smile, the six-day beard giving him a touch of badass. Anyone who didn't know would think he was fit as a fiddle.

"Typical Sean Speck photo," Bernie said. "I'm surprised he didn't wait for the fireworks for full effect. He tell you to cross your arms?"

"Yeah." Pete crossed his arms, puffing out his chest.

"Don't," Bernie said. "You're not going to jolly me out of my bad mood."

"I wouldn't dream of it."

"You know, when you say that it just makes it worse."

He winked. It pissed her off even more that he was in a better

254

mood than he'd been in months on a morning that was bound to bring nothing but disaster. She read the headline in a deep bass voice:

"Redimere Chief, Midnight Rambler, Fuller in woods meetup."

"Great headline. Not," she said.

REDIMERE, Maine -- When they met, he didn't say, "Livingston, I presume?" yet no one would have faulted him if he had.

"Typical Feckless piece of shit lead," Bernie said.

Police Chief Pete Novotny, on a solo hike near the Bigelow Preserve, severely injured his leg, and while disabled, claimed he encountered both fugitive Danny Fuller, who has since been apprehended, and the legendary deep woods burglar known as "The Midnight Rambler."

"That's all one sentence, by the way," Bernie said.

While the nature of that injury wasn't made public earlier by law enforcement officials, Novotny claimed he slipped down an embankment and landed on a fallen fire tower, and had his left thigh impaled.

"You *had* it impaled?"

"This could take all morning," Pete said.

"I can't help it."

It was while he was impaled that Fuller happened by and stole Novotny's water bottle and some other belongings later found on his person. Officials haven't released what those belongings were. Novotny claimed he can't remember.

Novotny claimed he begged Fuller to free him, but Fuller declined.

"*Declined?* Jesus."

"I believe his intention was to leave me there to die," said Novotny Sunday night, in an exclusive interview in the Redimere office of Franklin On Call.

Novotny claimed a man named Max, who Novotny believes is the legendary Midnight Rambler, happened along some time later and was able to free the injured Police Chief.

Novotny said "Max" nursed him to a healthy enough state that he was able to try and make it back to civilization.

Novotny was found in the woods Friday by Fire Chief Clyde "Sandy" MacCormack Jr., his tracking K-9 "Heidi" and Police Officer and Reserve Fire Officer Jamie Paradis.

Ironically, MacCormack, "Heidi" and Paradis also found the body of lost Appalachian Trail hiking nurse Lydia Manzo just a week before, in a nearby area.

"That's not ironic," Bernie said. "And what's with the unnecessary quotation marks and capitalization? Doesn't this website have an editor? And that quote makes you sound like you have a stick up your ass."

"I'm really looking forward to your pill kicking in."

Ironically also, it's the second Fourth of July in a row that Novotny has had to explain bizarre goings-on in Redimere.

State investigators said Novotny told them a similar story.

"It doesn't pass the straight face test," said George Libby, the lead investigator into Manzo's disappearance. "We believe Chief Novotny means well, but that he was disorientated because of his injury and other factors and may have thought things happened that didn't."

Novotny, who was in the Franklin On Call office when the call to Libby was made Sunday night, didn't appear troubled that he wasn't believed.

"I know it sounds far-fetched," he said. "But as you can see, I'm up and about and fine. While I was in shock for some of the time and in some pain, I am not making any of this up or recalling hallucinations."

"Just so you know, he hasn't gotten one quote right yet," Pete said. "But he got the gist."

As to why he hasn't filed a police report on the Rambler, Novotny pointed out he was in the hospital after he was found and Lifeflighted out of the woods Friday and Saturday and was recovering at home Sunday.

The town has put him on paid indefinite medical leave, but aside from walking with a limp and claiming he was unable to drive, Novotny seemed healthy. He claimed that his father gave him a ride to the FOC office Sunday night. There was an unidentified man in a car that was not the Police Chief's personal silver Subaru vehicle as Novotny did his interview.

"Why do they keep using 'claimed'? It makes it sound like they don't believe you either."

When called for comment Sunday night, Mayor Ryan Grant said, "I can't comment on the chief's claims, but we will look into them." Grant also wouldn't comment on the reason for the indefinite medical leave, as it seemed that Novotny seemed to be healthy, and whether there were other issues which may not be physical.

"That's a personnel issue," Grant said.

Grant did say, however, he was concerned that Novotny hadn't told the town what he'd told FOC.

"I would think he'd tell his bosses before he'd tell the press," Grant said. "Especially with his history."

Novotny acknowledged that the selectmen had considered firing him a year ago, an action that took place in executive session and is on file as a "personnel matter," but isn't detailed. He wouldn't discuss specifics, except to their concerns were found to be unfounded.

Novotny appeared untroubled. "My history in Redimere and elsewhere speaks for itself," he said.

"Now the story goes into a long rehash, slightly inaccurate, about what happened last year and an unnecessary blow-by-blow of the change from a three-selectmen to five-selectmen and mayor system of government," Bernie said.

"Well, then," Pete said.

"How are you today?"

"Good." He smiled, his dimples showing through the beard. Not a hundred percent, but closer to old Pete.

"So, explain."

"I told Kelley I'd give him an exclusive about what happened—made it clear you didn't know the details—if he dropped the story about Sandy. He jumped at it after jerking me around for a little bit."

"Great," Bernie said.

"Now let me have it."

She took a deep breath. "First of all, they're my competition, so them getting an exclusive about the police chief in my town pisses me off, never mind that he's my boyfriend and I've been with him for the last two days and there are things I didn't know, like the indefinite medical leave."

"What else?"

"Second, you've exposed yourself to some bad potential fallout from the town, especially after last year."

"What else?"

She thought, letting the pieces sort themselves and drop into place. "Third, how can you trust those guys not to still go after Sandy?"

"Anything else?"

"Yeah." She didn't want to say it, but she had to. "Obviously, one of the reasons they jumped at it is because it makes me and my newspaper look bad, since we didn't have it first, and it tells the world that it was your choice to give the story to them instead of me."

"I know. I'm sorry."

"I can't think of anything else."

"Despite all that, you see it for what it is, right? Protecting Sandy. I know you'd sacrifice looking bad for that. You'll win in the long run, anyway."

"I don't see—"

He held up his hand. "Ah ah ah. Let me finish. Now you're free, your paper is, to do a better story, since someone else broke it but was half-assed about it. You've explained to me how that works. You've come out on top before doing that. I'll talk to Guy or Carrie and tell them anything they want to know, with the exception of anything related to Lydia, including the possibility she was murdered, and Max's tie to her."

"That's a lot to keep out." Bernie felt a little better.

"Maybe you'll have that story, too, at some point. If you do, you'll have the scoop of scoops."

"I guess." Her wheels were getting into gear, coffee and her pill kicking in.

"As far as this damaging me, I can take this hit better than Sandy can take the hit that they were planning."

"I guess you looking like a guy who's not copping to a drug-fueled woods bender is marginally better than the implication that Sandy's responsible for killing his family and possibly Lydia. If that's what they were going to do."

"Trust me, Bernie, it is," Pete said. "Now, on the third point."

"I can't remember what the third point was."

"They still may go after Sandy."

"Okay."

"Their attention is on me now and what'll happen next, which is meatier and right there for the taking. You know better than anyone they'll go for the low-hanging fruit rather than work to get something."

"I hope you're right."

"If they do go back on the deal, I'll find a way to defuse it."

She shook her head. It wasn't going to be that easy.

"Look at it this way," he said. "Libby is going to be gunning for me if I pursue the Lydia thing. This story?" He pointed at her laptop. "It's not a big deal, me telling what happened in the woods. Fergus and Sean were salivating, but that's mostly because you didn't have it. People can think I'm a doped-up nut if they want. That's their problem."

"You're really okay with that?"

He took a deep breath, then let it out, slow. She almost counted to four out loud. "I've made mistakes," he said. "If anyone's going to be made to look bad, I deserve it more than Sandy does."

"You don't deserve it," Bernie said. "Penance is for sinners."

"It's not penance," he said. "It's not about me, it's about Sandy."

She wanted to point out it could be both, but whatever it was, it was already done. "What about the real story? Lydia."

"Once we figure it out, I'll let Libby and company know what we've got. It'll be up to them to charge someone or not pursue it."

"Would they even listen to you?"

"Up to them."

"I don't need charges to write a newspaper story," Bernie said.

"I know you don't," he said. "But Bernie, look."

"What?" She knew what was coming. *Don't get all excited.*

"Let me do it, okay? Lydia was killed. It's not a game."

CHAPTER 29

Bernie called Guy and told him to have Carrie set up an interview with Pete. She was glad she was off for a couple days, it'd be better for everyone if she didn't have anything to do with it.

"I'm going to go home and get some more clothes, get some groceries and stuff," she said to Pete. He seemed fine. Healthier, as he worked on his laptop at the table, his leg propped up on a chair. The shakes seemed to be gone. He'd eaten cereal for breakfast. No sign of drug flashbacks in the twenty-four hours they'd been together.

"I'd just move back home, but I don't want to betray my word to the hospital," she said, half-joking.

"You should stay here at least another couple of days," he said. "I'm fine, but you never know."

Maybe he was messing with her, she couldn't tell. The thought of leaving him alone scared her, even to go to the store. She couldn't shake the vision of him swimming into the lake and not coming back. He seemed so normal today. He seemed normal then, too.

"I could call your dad to come over."

"I'll be fine by myself," Pete said. "I can finally read, my eyes have cleared up. I have work to catch up on."

"Aren't you on paid medical leave?"

"I'm still on vacation through Wednesday, as far as I'm concerned. I haven't heard a thing from anyone at town hall."

He didn't seem bothered by it, so she wasn't going to be. She hadn't told him her biggest errand, because she knew he didn't want her to get all excited. But she had questions and ideas of her own. Two heads were better than one. She'd convince him of it later. She couldn't talk on the phone and drive, so she drove up the peninsula until she knew there was no way Pete could see her from his house, then pulled over.

Her first call was to Colleen. She got voicemail. "Things are developing," Bernie said. "Call me when you can."

Next, LeeAnne, in Buffalo. She rushed through the small talk and her lame excuse for the questions she was about to ask, then jumped in. "What do you know about Wilson, the hiker tipster?"

"Geez, not much. I didn't meet her."

"Why didn't you go with Crystal up to Millinocket?"

"I was sick," LeeAnne said. "We'd gone to the movies the night before. *Castaway*. I think it was something I ate, or a twenty-four hour bug."

"Do you remember what time Crystal got the call from her?"

"I think it was when we were in the movies, and she called back or something. She told me about it, I wasn't there and then I got sick overnight. What does Crystal say?"

"Yeah, same thing. I just figured I'd check, because considering the shock of finding Lydia the next day, memory's a funny thing. Funny, too, how the hiker was Wilson and so was Tom Hanks' volleyball." Bernie couldn't help but say it, even if it tipped her hand.

"I know!" LeeAnne said, laughing. "I thought so, too."

Bernie finally got off the phone—way too much small talk—and called Crystal.

Crystal picked up on the first ring. "Interesting story about the police chief. How is he? He looks good in the picture, but honestly, his story seems a little off."

"He's struggling," Bernie said. A white lie for the cause. "I wonder if we could get together and talk? Not on the phone." It's too easy to evade on the phone. Too easy to hang up.

"I can't today. I have to bring my car to Augusta to a dealer to look at. It's making a funny noise. No wonder, with all the miles

I've put on it."

"Okay, tomorrow then."

Bernie was tempted to call the office, see how things were going. She felt like she should be doing something. Actually, forget it. She *was* doing something, and it felt good.

*****

Pete finished his coffee on the deck. He was still getting used to the fact he was at his own house, in one piece, not pinned to the ground or drugged in Max's root cellar. As Bernie would say, it didn't feel real.

He wondered why he hadn't heard from Sandy about the article. He knew he wouldn't be happy about it, but Pete didn't have any regrets. About that, at least. On the other hand, when he'd heard Bernie singing the *Laverne & Shirley* theme song the night before, just the way Joey had, it'd jolted him back to a vision he'd had of Joey during the dark days in the woods.

"I read somewhere that this one guy who jumped off the Golden Gate Bridge and lived, the minute he jumped, he thought to himself, 'Why the fuck did I do this?'" Joey said. "Remember how I told you I didn't care when I saw that brick wall coming, just gunned the throttle?"

"No." Joey couldn't have told Pete that. He was dead seconds later.

"I lied. I thought the same thing when I saw that wall coming. 'Why the fuck did I do this?' You know what my last word was?" He waited for Pete.

"No."

"'Mom.' Like I was some little kid."

Pete had remembered the vision, or dream or whatever, with a start the night before. He was shaken by it, that's why he told Bernie about the lake. He wished he hadn't. She was already worried enough and trying so hard to make everything seem okay.

There was something else he'd remembered too, something that Max had said about Lydia. He tried to grab hold of it. The phone rang and it was gone.

263

It was Jamie. "How are you?" He sounded nervous. Pete didn't blame him, last time they'd talked, Pete was accusing him of trying to kill him.

"I'm good. Sorry about Friday."

"It's okay. I'm glad you're okay. I have a message from Dawna. She didn't want to bother you before she left, but she's going to get the Rambler," Jamie said. "Up in the woods."

"Going to get him?"

"She said the coordinates are on the GPS. She'll explain when she gets back."

*****

The was a scattering of cars in the trailhead parking lot behind the Lazy Logger, and music coming out the open back door, but there wasn't a soul in sight. No audience for this big moment. Dawna was glad.

Her phone started buzzing and pinging the minute they got to Sandy's pickup.

"A lot can happen in ten hours," she said to Sandy. He'd been quiet all day. Pensive. She hadn't asked what it was. He'd tell her if he wanted to. She guided the Rambler to the passenger door. He'd been cooperative, but silent, wouldn't even give his name. All in all, it'd been a really quiet day in the woods for the three of them.

They'd found him right where Lydia's GPS coordinates had led them, in a tumble-down ancient logger's shack surrounded by monstrously overgrown blackberry bushes, an odd oasis in the middle of the pines and mountains.

"This is so close to where we found her," Sandy said as they'd approached it. "I'm talking fifty yards that way." He gestured to the undergrowth.

That didn't surprise Dawna. It was something to talk to the Rambler about, if they could ever get him to talk.

"You guys sit tight," she said, stepping away to listen to her messages.

She was right. A lot had, apparently, happened. There was a terse message from Ryan Grant wanting to talk to her.

There was one from her sister with a wry commentary on the *Franklin On Call* article, which, as promised by Fergus and Sean the day before, had been published that morning. She'd forgotten about it. The mystery of why Sandy was so quiet was solved.

One from Colleen: "Please call me when you can."

Pete with a similar message, as terse as Grant.

She'd deal with everyone when she got back. She was antsy, way more today, in the afternoon sun, than she was the dark morning five days before when she'd arrested Fuller. She got into the passenger side, squeezing next to the Rambler. The pickup was big, but so were the three of them. She felt him tense as their shoulders touched.

"Let's go home," she said.

"How'd you get back and forth from up here to Redimere?" Sandy asked him as they drove south on Route 27. "It's more than twenty miles."

Dawna almost said something. She didn't want any loose conversation that a lawyer could hold against them. On the other hand, the Rambler hadn't talked all day. He did now, though.

"Canadian loggers," he said, his voice almost a whisper. "They don't speak English and don't care who I am or what I do."

Sandy nodded. "Bernic'll love that."

"Let's save the conversation for back at the station, when I can get Pete involved," Dawna said.

"Gotcha," Sandy said. The rest of the trip was quiet.

As they turned into the station parking lot, the Rambler cleared his throat. Then, quiet, tentative, he asked, "How's your chief?"

"He's doing well," Dawna said.

"Considering," Sandy added.

"Good."

*****

Pete braced himself for the meeting with Max. *Herman.* He still thought of him as Max. He felt stronger. He hoped it was enough to mask the fear, ward off the dumpster smell and panic, if he had to. Dawna had said the Rambler would only talk to Pete, hadn't even

265

given his name. Pete didn't doubt it was Herman Czarnec, but he'd wait for Herman to tell him that.

Bernie had fussed and hovered as he shaved and got dressed. He'd discarded the shorts and T-shirt for police chief casual, as she called it. She gripped the wheel, white-knuckle and hadn't said a word on the drive to the station. He rested his hand on her shoulder; she was buzzing with tension. When he squeezed, she frowned.

"I'll be fine," he said.

"I hope so."

When he lurched into the conference room where Herman sat with Dawna, he did feel fine. More than fine, he felt the familiar mild relaxed feeling he got when he was about to interview a good person who'd done something bad. Compassion and empathy went a long way toward getting to the bottom of things when that was the situation, and he was relieved he still had it.

Herman stood up and put his hand out. Pete shook it as he leaned his crutch against the table and sat down. "Hello, Max."

Herman looked beyond Pete's shoulder. "Herman Czarnec." He blushed. "I apologize for lying."

"It's okay. Why lie though?"

Dawna caught Pete's eye. "Herman understands he can ask for a lawyer at any time," she said.

"I hadn't been Herman for a long time."

"I understand," Pete said.

"Did you follow up what I told you?" Herman asked. "Lydia."

"I don't remember much," Pete said. "I was drugged."

"You seemed lucid at times," Herman said.

"I may have, but as a nurse, you know how the drugs affected me. Morphine, and what else?"

Herman had been expressionless, aside from the blush, still hadn't made eye contact with either of them. His gaze switched from the wall to his hands. "I wasn't being a good nurse. I wanted to keep you comfortable and let you heal. It was just morphine, but too much."

266

"What did I put in my water that I thought was purifier?" Pete asked. He kept it soft, gentle.

Herman startled, looked at Pete, then away. "That was Lydia's."

"Did you leave the baclofen bottle at Lydia's campsite?"

"No. But if it was baclofen in liquid form, that would be an ampule, not a bottle."

"I don't know if it was liquid form. It was empty."

"I didn't kill Lydia. I told you that."

"I'm just asking about the ampule."

Herman, agitated, was looking at the wall above Pete's head again.

"Tell me about the water purifier," Pete said, trying to get the feel for how hard he could push.

"That wasn't from me," Herman said, impatient. "I gave you information."

"I don't know what you told me," Pete said. "I can't remember." It wasn't a trick—he wished it was—his memory of conversations with Herman was fractured. He could remember being scared, desperate, trying to sort out what was real and what wasn't. He couldn't remember much Herman had said.

"Lydia had a GPS device and a compass," Herman said.

Pete and Dawna looked at each other. "Did you see her with them?"

"Yes."

"Can you tell me what happened to her?"

"I can't talk anymore," Herman said.

Pete braced for him to ask for a lawyer. Dawna tensed—she was thinking it, too.

"I haven't thanked you for saving my life," Pete said.

"Yes you did."

"I don't remember, so I'm thanking you again."

"I'm sorry about the morphine," Herman said. Tears wet his cheeks, but he didn't wipe them away. "I'm sorry I didn't get you help. Lydia died. You almost did, too."

"It's all right. You were doing what you thought best."

Herman took a deep breath, then doubled over, sobbing. Pete looked away. He didn't want him to be embarrassed or defensive. Dawna looked at her notebook. Waiting.

"You don't understand," Herman said. "I could have gotten you help. Should have, after Lydia." His words were almost inaudible; the sobs huge. "I didn't want to."

Pete's neck burned. He took a deep breath, counted.

"You don't understand," Herman said. The sobs grew into a wail.

"It's okay, I understand."

"You don't," Herman cried. "She was so sick. I thought I could help her, but I didn't. Then you, too."

He doubled over, his head on the table, his large body heaving.

Dawna looked at Pete, but he was at a loss.

"It's okay," Pete said. "What happened to Lydia?"

"I'm so sorry," Herman sobbed. "Sorry I didn't help."

"What happened, Herman?" Pete asked, leaning forward, quiet, gentle. Just the two of them.

Herman sat back up, his hands covering his face. "I didn't mean to."

Dawna looked at Pete and he shook his head. He waited.

"Oh God," Herman cried. "I'm so sorry. It's just that I've been very, very lonely."

CHAPTER 30

Bernie caught a glimpse of Dawna leading Herman to the holding cell to wait for the sheriff as Pete came out of the office, leaning more heavily on his crutch than when he'd gone in.

"He didn't have much to say," Pete said, before she could ask.

"I hope he gets a lawyer," she said as they drove back to Pete's. She'd heard Herman crying, screaming actually, as she waited in the outer office. It'd unnerved her, and she'd fought the urge to run in and help him.

"Dawna says his camp was just yards away from where Lydia was found," he said.

"What do you think that means?" She could think of a lot of things.

"I don't know."

The sheriff's department only cared about the burglaries. The recording of the interview with Herman didn't even come close to a murder confession. The state police were involved now, too, and Herman's hideout would be a crime scene by morning, all his loot taken into custody. No one had asked Pete if he wanted to press charges except Bernie. No, he didn't.

"I don't think he killed her," Pete said as they drove down the peninsula. "When I try to replay it all, it's just bits and pieces. My brother. The needle. My leg. I don't know what he means when he says he gave me information."

"Maybe food will fix it." She knew it wouldn't, but she was hungry. "Think turkey burgers will go down okay?"

"As long as they're pale yellow and covered in salt."

"Hardy har har," she said. She was relieved. He seemed

269

relieved, too. Loose, like he'd been that morning. Almost normal. That word again.

"You know what else feels staged, besides the murder," he said as they ate. "Those racial attacks on Colleen. The rat note was written on Lydia's note paper. Someone with access to Lydia's belongings wants her out of town."

"So, Crystal. She doesn't like her because of her Herman Buffalo murder investigation."

"Exactly."

She wanted to talk more about the case with Pete. He seemed open to it. But he crashed on the couch after dinner, exhausted.

She woke him up when Sandy arrived to change his dressing.

"Thanks for falling on your sword, but it wasn't necessary," Sandy said.

"It was the best option," Pete said.

"The best option would've been to stay out of it," Sandy said. "Why screw up your life? I could've handled it."

Neither said much after that. Bernie tried not to flinch as Sandy pulled off the gauze, removed the packing. She didn't look at the wound, but Pete's leg, from what she could see from across the room, was swollen and mottled.

"Looks okay, relatively," Sandy said as he cleaned up. "When's the doctor going to look at it?"

"They said Friday," Pete said.

"I guess it'll be okay. Just try to stay off it more than you've been," Sandy said. "Talk to you guys later."

She'd expected Pete and Sandy to talk about Herman, how close his camp was to where Lydia was found. Or maybe, ridiculously, make up and behave like friends again. She felt guilty they were so awkward with each other.

After Sandy left, Pete got out his laptop. "Might as well catch up on paperwork."

She wanted to remind him he was on vacation, maybe even on paid indefinite medical leave, but now she was the one with no energy and the words seemed like too much work.

She wondered why she hadn't heard back from Colleen, and wondered if she should try calling her again, but she couldn't remember why she'd called her in the first place. She tried to read a book as Pete worked.

His hair, which had missed its weekly haircut two weeks in a row, was curly and uncombed. He was wearing his reading glasses. He looked adorable. He seemed okay. But his leg was propped up on a chair. There was the box in the closet he'd barely mentioned, and the father waiting at a motel three miles away for a conversation that didn't seem like it was going to happen. The specter of what would happen with his job hung in the air, untalked about, too. She tried to imagine the same scene—him at the table, working, her on the couch, reading—without the woods, the *Franklin On Call* article, the annoyed mayor, the leg, the box, the nightmares and terror. The midnight swim to the middle of the lake.

He looked up. "What?"

"What?" she echoed. "What, what?"

He smiled. "You're staring at me."

"I was thinking, and you're in my far-off gaze thinking zone."

"You look serious."

"You painted the bedroom green," she said. She thought of it every time she went in or glanced over the partition.

"You noticed." His dimples deepened, almost like his old full smile. Maybe it was just that he'd shaved and she could see them better.

"It doesn't seem like you."

"It wasn't for me."

"Between the time you broke up with me and we got back together you painted the bedroom a color you knew I'd like?"

"Yeah."

She was annoyed. She didn't understand it. "What's to say that sometime, maybe soon, we'll be sitting here in your spotless house after a perfectly cooked meal that you've prepared, watching *Jeopardy* and you're getting every answer right, while I power through a gallon of chocolate ice cream, reading People magazine and don't

271

know the capital of Arizona or some other obvious thing, and you go, 'What the hell am I doing with her?' Then you'll still have a green bedroom and hate it."

Pete's smile wavered. "That's how you picture us?"

"I don't know. It doesn't seem real."

"What doesn't?"

"Everything."

"I'm sorry I hurt you, Bernie. I wish I could go back and change it."

"I know. I'm just frazzled." Now she felt bad. Embarrassed, too.

"I want to show you something." He limped to the closet and brought out a carboard tube. He unrolled a blueprint on the table. "Come look."

She tried to make sense of it. It was the house, she could see that. There was an addition, a full bedroom, a screened porch added to the end of it, next to the deck, facing the lake. The partitioned area where the bed was now was labeled "Bernie's office."

"Remember the conversation we had in front of your old house in Augusta?"

She nodded.

"I never felt like that about anywhere I lived, that warm welcome feeling. At least not since I was a real young kid. After we broke up, I kept thinking about it. I got this vision about what a home would be like. I couldn't shake it."

She traced the lines on the blueprint with her finger. "I remember what I said, but I don't get this. You broke up with me, then decided to put an addition on your house?"

"I knew I'd made a mistake. Whatever issues I had—have—my life is with you."

Bernie ran her finger over the office, the bedroom.

"What *is* this?" she whispered.

He lifted her chin and looked into her eyes. "I would be so happy if this were ours."

"Me live here?"

"More than that, maybe. Only if you want it, too, though."

Bernie felt like the only thing keeping her upright was his eyes holding hers. The thought hurt too much. They were so far away from the possibility.

"I know it won't solve my issues," he said. "But I'm committed to you. I love you, chocolate ice cream, People magazine and all. You're brilliant and funny and brave and the best thing that ever happened to me. I want a life with you."

She looked back down at the blueprints, blurry through tears. "I love you, too. I want to live with you, maybe get married, but it's hard to think about. Nothing's been normal for so long. What if you realize this was a mistake?" She put her hand on the blueprint, fingers spread. "What if you're just really hurting and need someone to care, and it's me, just because I'm here?"

"Do you really think all these months have been me just settling for someone who cares about me?"

"I don't know."

"There's nothing more clarifying than being impaled in the middle of nowhere and thinking you're going to die. I'm positive about my feelings."

"I don't know why I'm trying to talk you out of it." She wiped her eyes.

"I do," he said. "But you can trust me to love you forever. I know that sounds like bullshit, but it's not."

"I guess I'll take your word for it. Can we talk about your mental health?"

"Okay." He limped to the sofa and sat down.

"I'm not saying I'll marry you if you do this or don't do that," she said. "But I've been so afraid for you for so long. I can't live like that. You're afraid too."

"I know."

She was still by the table, her hand on the blueprints, the cool paper crackling under it. It felt good, like a future that she hadn't thought of. "Don't you want to feel hopeful and happy? You have to feel that way because of you, not me."

273

"Come here." He held out his arms.

"You're not going to trick me with your manly ways."

"I wouldn't dream of it. Just please come here. I've spent too much time not holding you." He kept his arms out until she sat on his lap, put her head on his shoulder.

He wrapped them around her, tight. "When I was in the woods, I thought of so many things I'd never said," he whispered.

"Me too. It's okay. We've got time."

CHAPTER 31

Bernie was jolted awake by Pete's nightmare. He jumped out of bed, stumbling on his bad leg..

"Shit," he said.

"What's wrong?"

He turned on the light and starting pulling on his pants.

"What are you doing?" she asked. It was three a.m. She knew she shouldn't have believed everything was okay.

"I remembered something." He sat down on the bed, still pulling the pants on.

"What are you going to do about it at three in the morning?"

He stopped dressing. "Go to the station."

"What did you remember?"

He lay back. She put her hand on his chest. It was hot and wet, his heart pounding underneath.

"He had something he wanted to give to Lydia, but she was too sick."

"Medicine?"

"No. Shit. What was it? Something from Buffalo for her to take back. Did I dream that?"

"Let's go back to sleep. Or at least turn out the light and lie down."

He stared at the ceiling. "Lydia in the root cellar, or at least the cabin. We know that, because she had the blackberry scratches, and that's the only place I saw blackberries, and he kind of said that today, that he had her there. She was sick. Maybe she had something she wanted to give him. Does that make sense? Why can't I remember?" He jammed his fists into his eyes, the way she always did. "This is so fucking frustrating."

Bernie got up. "I can see we're not going back to sleep."

She went into the kitchen and opened the refrigerator. Dubya came to help.

"Everything okay in there?" she asked Pete after a minute.

"Fine."

He came out, on his crutches. "Let's get the case file out."

*****

When her phone rang at six, Dawna expected it to be Pete. He was an early riser, too. But it was Eli.

"Sorry to call so early. I'm on my way up north for the day's run. I was just at the storage area, and wondering if you could do whatever you're going to do with the dumpster. I really need to empty it."

"I'll take care of it first thing," she said.

"Natalie wants to talk to you," he said.

"Hi," Natalie said. "Sorry about the racist stuff, even though I didn't know much about it. Hallowell's grounded."

"So are you," Dawna heard Eli say.

She sighed heavily. "I think Crystal threw a lot of stuff in the dumpster. I just got the GPS and compass because they seemed important, but I saw her put garbage bags in there that were the dark green kind."

"Thanks, that's very helpful," Dawna said. "I know you didn't know what Hallowell was up to, but you're getting older and you have to use your good judgment. I know you have it."

Natalie sighed again, long and exaggerated. "That's what my dad said, too."

"You know how it feels when people make fun of you because you're Passamaquoddy," Dawna said. "Do you want to make someone else feel that way because she's a different color? I thought you knew better than that."

"I told you, I didn't know anyone was leaving her a note with the N word," Natalie said, her voice trembling. "I thought Hallowell was just doing a dumb prank."

276

"Dumb pranks aren't funny for anyone," Dawna said. "But they're a lot less funny when someone is also being treated like they're different."

"I know, I'm sorry. I was going to apologize to Ms. Sullivan, anyway."

"Okay. Be a good girl."

As she got in her Jeep, Dawna wondered if she'd overstepped. But Eli was white, and while Dawna knew he got it in theory, he didn't understand the constant hammer of slights, big and small that racism brought. It was stressful enough being Passamaquoddy. She could imagine how Colleen must feel, especially here in Redimere.

It reminded Dawna that she hadn't heard back from her. She'd returned her call after getting the message the day before, but got voicemail. Colleen hadn't called back. She tried again. Voicemail again.

Dawna wondered if she should call Pete and bring him up to date, find out if he'd talked to her. Better if she waited until she found something. She wasn't sure how much she could dump on him now, and anyway, he was on vacation.

*****

Pete's review of the case file was much more methodical than Bernie's. She marveled at his organized piles, his lightning-fast recall.

"I'm good at remembering details," he said. "It helped in law school."

"Too bad it doesn't help with the last week." She felt like a jerk the minute she said it, but he laughed.

He had piles for the search reports, the ME's report and autopsy report, which turned out to be two separate things; his notes; emails between officials; inventory of Lydia's belongings; interviews of trail hikers; interviews of friends.

There were a lot of things that surprised Bernie in the case file that Pete shrugged off. Different agencies not connecting the dots between each other, investigators ignoring tips from Lydia's friends and others that seemed credible.

"Things that don't seem to matter get ignored, and miscommunication happens any time more than one agency is involved."

"Colleen, for instance," Bernie said. "You thought she had more to say before Lydia was found. Wouldn't the guys in charge of the search want to know?"

"She didn't seem to know much at the time." He looked up at Bernie. "Wait."

"What?"

"Lost it." He looked back down at the papers.

"Try to go through the conversation backwards."

He shrugged. "It's gone. It'll come back." He pushed his reading glasses up his nose. She thought about kissing him, but didn't want things to get off track. Going through the case with him was almost as much fun. She'd wondered, but hadn't asked about, the fact he was including her after he'd warned her off. She'd ask later, when they were too far in for him to change his mind.

"I wish the hiker roster was here so we could check on Wilson," Bernie said.

"We don't need to. Wilson doesn't exist."

"How do you know?"

"The name. The fact that Crystal has details, but not the kind you'd expect from someone telling the truth."

"What kind of things would she remember if she were telling the truth?"

"How she felt, what she thought. Impressions as much as facts. Have you asked her about the drive? Remember when we took that ride out Route 16, and there was that spectacular view of the western mountains coming back along that steep downhill? That's the route she would've taken. I don't care how charged up someone is, she'd remember that. Ask her what the drive was like and see what she says. I bet she'll say she wasn't paying attention or doesn't remember."

"What does that mean about Crystal?"

"She'd been saying all along she thought Lydia was farther

west than where they were searching, closer to here. Maybe she made Wilson up so she could be more convincing about having someone help her look. Working theory."

"Makes sense," Bernie said. "She's a take-charge gal. But add to that the fact she's the person trying to scare Colleen out of town."

"That could be for a lot of reasons. Don't add two and two and get five."

"I do that all the time. Sometimes even figuratively."

She burned to talk to Crystal. She still had her list of questions. She was a journalist. Maybe that's why he was letting her do this with him, to keep her from doing it on her own.

"Let's hone it down to evidence, victimology, and what we know," Pete said. "Evidence is she had CO poisoning—I believe Sandy. But they didn't test for it and she's been cremated."

"When?"

"Yesterday," he said. "I got an email from the ME. The baclofen ampule is evidence of something, but we don't know if it's Lydia's or was dropped or planted by someone."

Bernie felt like she was on one of those police procedural TV shows. If only this could be solved in forty-two minutes with time off for commercial breaks. She'd say that to Pete, but he was always saying "It's not like TV." She'd make a crummy cop.

He wrote as he talked. "The autopsy report shows there was speculation she had drug intoxication because of how fast she deteriorated while alive, and they tested for some obvious ones—painkillers, that type of thing—but since no evidence of drug use was found, they discarded that. She had those blisters on her face and neck, but they could be something or nothing. No one could tell what they were—sunburn, bugs, an allergy, lack of nutrition."

Something was bugging Bernie, a question she wanted to ask, but she lost it. She'd try to be like him and just wait for it to come around again.

"We can discount Fuller," Pete said. "He was content to let me die, even though he knew I was a cop."

"Why would that discount him?"

"He would have let her die, too." He looked at her to see if she understood.

She did. It was a pretty simple concept. Something she'd even said herself. She'd been thrown, though, by how casually he'd said Fuller was content to let him die. Like it was about someone else. He hadn't ranted or raved or anguished about what happened with Fuller or any of the other things that'd happened to him. Like being impaled for almost a day.

"Are you okay?" he asked her.

She was crying again without even realizing it. "That must've been awful, him leaving you like that."

"Hey." He brushed her cheek. "It was, but it's over. I'm back."

She'd said it a million times, he'd said it a million times. He was back. It was okay.

"Now we look at victimology," Pete said. "Lydia wasn't high-risk, which means she didn't put herself in a position that put her in danger."

"Unless helping Colleen look into the Buffalo murders and meeting with Herman counts," Bernie said.

"Right, so we get back to what we talked about yesterday, or the day before, I can't remember." He smiled at her. She got it. Everything's okay, despite the horror.

"This was personal," Pete said. "Someone didn't want it to be obvious she was murdered, but they also hedged their bets. It was overkill. The plastic bag could've killed her, but they poisoned her with CO, too. Lydia was likely in such bad shape she couldn't fight back or wasn't aware, but the person wanted to double down."

"Seems like a lot of work."

"You see it a lot in homicides where the killer thinks it out in advance or tries to cover it up after. You know, someone's pissed, pulls out a gun and shoots someone, it's all pretty obvious. When someone takes the time to think something out, they overdo it nine times out of ten. Take the baclofen ampule. My guess is it was left so if baclofen was found in her system, it'd look like she drugged herself. Another insurance policy for the killer in case the Ziploc wasn't convincing or the investigation went in another direction."

"Slow down," Bernie said "My brain needs to process some of this. Did they check the Ziploc bag for prints?"

"No, it's been destroyed."

"Can we check the baclofen bottle?"

"Yeah, it's on my list to have someone do, but I bet the killer wore gloves."

"It couldn't be Herman," Bernie said. "He lures her there to kill her, but he couldn't know Colleen was looking into the murders and working with Lydia on it. Then he saves you, only to try to kill you, too."

"He didn't try to kill me. I put the baclofen into the water," Pete said. "Wait, do we know it was baclofen?"

"Well, there was something in the purifier bottles that wasn't purifier," Bernie said. "Maybe the state cops can check what's left in the bottles. It must be with the stuff they took from Herman's camp."

"I used it all."

"Were there empty water purifier bottles with Lydia's stuff?"

Pete sorted through the papers until he came up with the sheet with the inventory of her stuff. "No, they list her trash. A protein bar wrapper and some tissues."

"Maybe the baclofen was already in her water, and the bottles of it were more insurance by the killer in case she didn't get a big enough initial dose," Bernie said. "Which she didn't if the point was to kill her with an OD."

"She wouldn't put it in water she left here with, though," Pete said. "No need to purify bottled water, or tap water."

"That's right," Bernie said. "We don't know she was dosed with it, and we just have Herman's word that bad water purifier was hers in the first place, and we don't even know it was baclofen in the bottles. We're just assuming."

"You're right," Pete said. "We're chasing our tails. We need something solid."

*****

281

Pete cleaned up the breakfast dishes, trying to make things normal. Hard with a crutch. Bernie had gone to run errands. She probably just wanted to get out of the house. She hadn't brought up moving in this morning. He got it. She had to know for sure he was committed to getting better. The shame he'd felt over the years that'd kept him from seriously getting help was gone—one benefit of his ordeal. The fear was still there, but it wasn't as powerful as the shame, and he'd deal with it. The only thing that would convince her was how he dealt with it.

It'd felt good to discuss the case file with her, too. She'd joked he was Holmes and she was Watson, but she didn't give herself enough credit. Now he was trying not to think too much about the information, but let it sift through his head until a picture formed. He didn't have to wait for the picture, though, to know he needed more than what was in that box.

He called George Libby. "I'd like to talk more to Herman," Pete said.

"Why don't you hold off until we're done with him?" Libby said. "It's a complicated investigation. Your thing can wait."

Pete tried to sweep the floor while on the crutch, but it didn't work. He leaned the crutch against the counter and endured the pain. As he dumped the dustpan in the trash, he saw his shorts, and the unreality of the woods came back to him. He had a flash. Not a memory, but a blip. He picked them up, stiff and smelly and felt in the hip pockets, nothing. He unbuttoned the back ones, nothing. But in the front button pocket, there it was. A folded piece of yellowing paper. It was a computer printout with dates and times from 1995, abbreviations. The name Corson was at the top.

He went through the case file notes for Colleen's number. He got voice mail. "It's Pete Novotny. I have a question. Please call me as soon as you can. This is a landline, so call, don't text."

Text. As he hung up, one of the many things he'd been trying to remember came back to him. There were more printouts of texts than just the two Lydia had tried to send when she was lost. There were also ones from before then. The meaningless ones were there, but an important one was missing. It included a photo of a note that had a line of GPS coordinates, and the message from Lydia implied she was sending it to someone in Buffalo, but it'd been sent to Crystal. It didn't seem like it was intended for her, though, and Pete had planned, way back a week ago, to ask Colleen if it meant anything to her. It was easy enough with a flip phone to send the wrong person a text as you scrolled through names. Bernie did it all the time. Things like "By cat fd" and "wlk Dub hm lt." He got several while they were broken up and assumed they were meant for her brother. He didn't say anything—he was afraid they'd stop.

The phone rang, but it wasn't Colleen calling back. It was Natalie.

"Sorry you got hurt and stuff."

"I'm okay, but thanks."

"Dawna was asking me some things, and I've remembered more, but I tried calling her and she hasn't called back. I wanted to tell you, anyway.

"Sure, what's up?"

"I read that story in the paper about you and the Midnight Rambler and it made me think about something weird I saw. I didn't tell anyone because it's probably dumb."

"I'm sure it's not." He bumped Bernie's laptop and the screen came alive. About a dozen windows open, typical. He started closing them.

"I saw that friend of Lydia's, Crystal, when I was using the porta potty behind the Lazy Logger one morning. I thought she was bringing the Midnight Rambler a picnic. Back then I called him the fisherman."

"Why'd you think a picnic?" He was looking at an article about rodent extermination from a Buffalo newspaper. The name "Corson" caught his eye. He scrolled down; it was about a public works director in dispute with city officials in a suburb of Buffalo.

"She had a cooler, Styrofoam. You can't recycle it, and it's not biodegradable. I know it's what she had because I heard it squeak. I stood on the toilet and looked out the window. I think I saw her throw it out later at the storage area with her other stuff."

"Do you remember when?"

"Thursday. We go there on Tuesdays and Thursdays, but I know it was a Thursday because that's when we also do the KOA camp."

"Last Thursday?" He already knew the answer.

"No, because that's the day Danny Fuller was arrested. All the cops were there and we couldn't get to the dumpster. It was the week before."

"That's good work, Natalie. Thanks for letting me know." His heart was in his throat as he hung up. Everything was so obvious once the pieces fell into place, as usual. As he called Dawna, he scrolled down the article on the laptop. The word CO blazed from the screen. The public works director, Barry Corson, was reprimanded for using dry ice to kill rats in the sewer system. When it evaporated, it created CO.

Where did Bernie say she was going? It didn't matter. He knew she'd read that article and was going to talk to Crystal.

He called her cell. Voicemail. "Call me. Before you do anything or talk to anybody. Please."

He called the Watcher, praying she'd be there. Annette picked up.

"She's off today. She said she had to stay with you."

"She's running errands. If she comes in, can you please have her call me?"

He called Bernie's landline, realizing he should have done that first.

Sal picked up.

"Is Bernie there?"

"She was, but she took off. How are you? That story in FOC was nuts."

"Where'd she go?"

"Not sure. What's going on? You sound upset."

"I just have to find her."

"I'm trying to think." There was a sound of a baby screeching

284

in the background. "Sorry, I'm babysitting Chloe's kids. Dawna threatened her with arrest or something if she left them with Hallowell again. Bernie said something, but you know how she talks. It's hard to keep up."

"She was going to pick up Crystal," a voice in the background piped.

"What Corinna?" Sal asked.

Corinna said it again, drawn out, Sal obviously a moron. "She saaaaaiiiiddd she was gooinnnng to get Crystal."

"Did she say where?" Sal asked.

"How should I know? I'm four," Corinna said.

While Pete had been on the phone someone had left a message. Natalie again.

"I forgot something. One day at the storage units, it was really early and the fisherman was there, and Crystal was in her car watching him. It was the Thursday a week before I saw her with the cooler. He always went there on Thursdays to look in the dumpster."

CHAPTER 32

Bernie knew she should've told Pete where she was going, but they'd been up since three, he was tired, still sick but trying to act like he wasn't. She hadn't been totally sure of Crystal's role, so wanted to just look into it herself. She was sure of it now, though. It'd been an impulse not to tell him. A bad one. Her pill kicking in and the pieces falling into place made that clear.

One logical question that one of them should've asked came to her as she drove to the Four Seasons to get Crystal. If she made up Wilson, how did she know where Lydia was?

Bernie watched her walk across the parking lot, balancing an iced coffee and a box. Bernie could take off, roar out of the parking lot. Call Pete. But then Crystal would know she was on to her. This way, maybe she could play it cool and get some answers.

Crystal stowed the box in the back seat. "I've collected so much junk here, and have all Lydia's stuff, I have no idea how I'm going to get it all back to Buffalo."

"I bet," Bernie said as she took the iced coffee. She was all coffee-ed up, but if there was ever a time to be friendly to Crystal, this was it. She shooed Dubya into the backseat so Crystal could get in, and took a long drink through the straw. It was cold and sweet and felt good with the heat and her exhaustion. As she drank, she tried to figure out how to finesse this mess, now that she was in it.

"You have the chief's dog," Crystal said as Bernie started the car.

"He likes to ride in the car," Bernie said. Bingo. The only reason Crystal would think Dubya was Pete's is because she saw him at Pete's house.

"So, as I told you, I thought you'd like to see Lydia's things," Crystal said. "Her journals, the camping equipment they gave back. I have to find out from her kids what they want me to ship back to Buffalo, so thought you'd want to see it sooner rather than later. Thanks again for picking me up, by the way. They told me not to drive my car until that part comes in."

"How did you get back from Augusta?"

"I drove it, just didn't tell them." Crystal laughed.

"Why did you have to go all the way to Augusta to get the car serviced?" Bernie knew she'd gone to Augusta to get Lydia's cremains. She wasn't sure why Crystal would lie about it.

"Closest dealer. It's a warranty thing."

Bernie tried to figure out if the lie mattered or not. She was processing slowly this morning.

"Can you pull over a sec?" Crystal asked. "I need to discuss something of a serious nature with you."

They were on a winding two-lane that would eventually connect them with the road to the storage place. Nothing around but woods and squirrels.

"Why don't we just go to the storage area?"

"I'd like to talk privately. That little girl is often there. Other people, too. Colleen Sullivan, for instance."

That's exactly why Bernie wanted to get there. But she didn't want to agitate Crystal, wanted to keep her talking. Just like on TV. She pulled over.

"I think people need to start considering that Sandy MacCormack killed Lydia," Crystal said. "I don't know why Fergus didn't do the story he was going to about him, but all the evidence points to him. I know you two are friends, but you have to see the truth."

"What evidence?" Bernie asked. She sucked down a big strawfull of iced coffee. She could get out of the car and run. But Crystal so far didn't seem to see Bernie as a threat, and running would kill that. Crystal was in better shape than she was, too. They were in the middle of nowhere, the self-storage place was closer to the lake, near Pete's. She kind of wished she'd told him what she was doing.

"The fact he found her so easily," Crystal said. "It's not like that dog was really tracking. Then there's his history of killing people with CO, which was covered up. George Libby told me about what happened to his family."

"What does CO have to do with Lydia?" Bernie asked. She was proud of herself, she sounded conversational. She could pull this off for as long as it took to get somewhere more public.

"We both know the answer to that," Crystal said. "You're too influenced by your boyfriend and Sandy. Colleen Sullivan, too. She's totally full of shit. People in Maine bend over backwards to try to prove they're not racist, since there's no African-Americans here and they're so sensitive about everyone thinking they're racist, but I can tell you, as someone who's been around a lot of African-Americans, she's not someone you should give the benefit of the doubt to."

"How would Sandy have done it, do you think?" Bernie asked. "He obviously didn't bring a generator up there." She tried to say it like she really wanted to know, not argumentative, not skeptical. Bernie already knew part of the answer after reading the article about Crystal's husband.

"My guess is he used dry ice," Crystal said. "Pellets, not a big block. They sell them at the store. It would've been easy to bring a small amount up there, then put them in the Ziploc. They'd leave no trace and it'd look like suicide."

That would explain the blisters. Bernie almost said it out loud. Pete had once told her he'd ask suspects to speculate about how someone had committed a murder, and often the person would lay out exactly what they themselves had done. He said part of it was they secretly wanted to brag about how smart they were. Bernie was still stunned it'd been so easy.

"Why not just suffocate her with the Ziploc instead of lugging dry ice up there?".

"How should I know?" Crystal said.

"I'm just trying to think of how killing her like that would make sense."

"Maybe he didn't know the Ziploc would be an option," she said. "He saw it and took the opportunity, since it's more airtight than the tent would be."

"That makes sense. But then he didn't have to use the dry ice."

"Maybe he just wanted to do it that way, since that's what he planned," Crystal said, annoyed. "I honestly don't know."

"Colleen doesn't think Herman killed those patients," Bernie said. She didn't know why she said it, since she was pretty sure she and Crystal hadn't talked at all about the Buffalo murders. Bringing them up may have been a mistake. She was dizzy. Had she taken her pill? She couldn't remember.

Crystal leaned toward her, eyes narrow. "Let's cut the crap. What do you think you know?"

Bernie started the car. "We can talk and drive." She pulled out onto the asphalt, tires squealing, before Crystal could say anything. She looked for a place to turn around, so she could drive back toward downtown and the police station, or anywhere there were people.

"No you don't." Crystal reached toward her. Bernie, startled, slammed on the brakes. She wasn't sure what Crystal was going to do. Pull the keys out, maybe. Grab the wheel. The motion threw Dubya forward, and he was squeezed between the two front seats, whining, his front legs on Crystal's lap.

Bernie hit the gas.

Her phone buzzed in her pocket, but she was driving too fast. She couldn't remember where her pocket was. The road was blurry and it was hard to stay on it. Why was there never a place to turn around when you needed one?

Crystal tried to shove Dubya aside. His butt kept hitting Bernie's arm, making her swerve. Dubya, though, had nowhere to go. He snarled at Crystal, and she leaned away from him.

"Stop this car," she yelled at Bernie. "I'm warning you, stop now."

289

"I'm going to go to the police station," Bernie said. She was definitely dizzy, the road a wave of dark gray in front of her, blurry green melting in. She couldn't remember how to get to the police station. She was driving in the wrong direction, she knew that much. She wasn't sure what the right one was, though.

Crystal grabbed Dubya's collar and pulled him across her body, shoving his top half out the window. He yelped.

"Pull over now," she yelled.

Then what? Bernie couldn't think. Nausea boiled up her throat. Her head was hazy, filling with cotton. "You put something in my drink," she said, more in wonder than accusation.

"Pull over," Crystal screamed. Dubya yelped again, louder. His butt and back legs were in the car, the rest of him out the window. Crystal was holding him by the collar, her other hand on his rear. All she'd have to do is push.

Bernie looked back at the road just as a flash of turquoise flew towards her from the woods. Turquoise with a little dark blur on top. Natalie on her bike, coming down the hill from the self-storage units. Were they there already?

"Turn here!" Crystal screamed.

Bernie couldn't if she wanted to. Natalie seemed to float toward the car, like it was pulling her. Maybe Natalie was pulling the car. Bernie swerved as hard as she could, and the car rocked. It felt like it went up on two wheels. Bernie waited for it to roll over onto its roof. Natalie's shocked face was a flash, clear in the gray and green blur.

Crystal and Dubya both fell back into Bernie, knocking her against the door as she tried to keep the car on the road. Or what she thought might be the road. The gray in the green. She wished she'd thought to send some signal, yell something to Natalie, but they were rocketing north now.

Crystal and Dubya struggled to right themselves, banging into Bernie, the dog on top, trying to climb over Crystal to the backseat.

A logical thought pierced the haze in Bernie's head. She hit the window button now that Dubya was back in the car. The window

290

shot up. She hit the window lock.

That was as far as she could think.

Crystal screamed, banging on the armrest of her door, trying to make the window go down. Dubya tried to squeeze past her into the backseat, his body jammed against the gear shaft. Bernie could smell his hot breath, feel his drool on her arm. It was cold, not warm. It was her iced coffee. But no, that has spilled into her lap earlier. The whole car was cold. It was filling with haze. The drugs.

She didn't know how long she could keep driving. She couldn't form a thought into a plan. She knew they'd crash. Soon, likely.

"Open the windows, you stupid bitch," Crystal screamed. She pounded on the door while trying to grab Bernie with her other hand. Dubya kept knocking her arm away, his butt against Bernie's side. He whined as he tried to scramble over Crystal.

"Open the fucking window," Crystal screamed.

Bernie coughed. The car was filling with smoke. It was cold smoke. Dry ice. She'd seen the box when Crystal got in the car, but it wasn't a box. It was a Styrofoam cooler.

Crystal's hands clawed at her, but the dog was wedged between them, his front paws scrabbling against Crystal's face as he tried to free himself.

Bernie wanted to brake, but her foot felt disconnected, waving in the air. The coughing was making it hard to hold onto the steering wheel. Her head began to tighten, her vision darkening.

The car rocketed forward.

*****

Pete tried Dawna's cell. Voicemail. "I need someone to find Bernie's car," he said. "She's with Crystal. Crystal's dangerous. Absolute emergency. No idea where."

He tried Jamie, but got voicemail, too. Left a message, but shorter.

He tried Sandy. Same thing.

He called the sheriff's office. The nearest deputy was in Kingfield. Twenty minutes.

He tried Chuck. Voicemail. "Dad, I need a ride. It's an

291

emergency."

Shit. Shit. Shit. Maybe it'd be fine. Bernie would play it cool and Crystal wouldn't know she was on to her. Right. He was out of options. He grabbed his car keys and a crutch. Threw the crutch away and grabbed Sal's cane.

His leg screamed as he pressed the clutch. *It's only pain.*

He slammed the blue light onto the roof and roared up Loon Lane, no idea where he'd go from there.

When he screeched onto Pond Road, he almost collided with Natalie. She was on her bike, standing up on the pedals, flying at him. He hit the brakes as she waved furiously.

She was red and panting.

"Ms. O'Dea's driving out Route 145, and Crystal's trying to push Dubya out the window."

"Which direction?"

"Toward Bigelow Junction."

He hit the gas, blind to everything but the asphalt in front of him and Bernie at the end of it.

*****

A logging truck roared past them, horn blaring. Bernie could barely make it out through the fog. She had no idea how fast she was going. Dubya, crying, was jammed against her.

Crystal grabbed for the wheel, but couldn't get past the dog.

Bernie tried to stay alert enough to stay on the road. She had nothing left for anything else. Crystal seemed far away, at the end of a tunnel. She couldn't think of a way to stop the car and survive. Both she and Crystal were coughing. Vomit kept rising in Bernie's throat, burning when she coughed.

Her phone vibrated in her pocket. I can't answer. She wanted to scream it.

Crystal's screaming was nonstop and wordless. Bernie kept seeing her fingers in her peripheral vision, coming at her, then retreating. Bernie could feel Dubya moving, but he wasn't going anywhere. Crystal couldn't get around him.

Bernie's head pounded. Twenty minutes. She'd read

somewhere that's how long it took CO to kill someone. They wouldn't last that long because she couldn't keep the car on the road. She couldn't remember which pedal was the brake or the clutch, but since her leg wouldn't do what she wanted it to, it didn't matter.

The road was in a tunnel of woods. She imagined the car tearing through them, killing all three of them. She wouldn't be able to stop it from happening. She could feel the impact, hear it, hear the beeping as the car tick-tocked toward blowing up, like a bomb. Cars didn't beep like a bomb. In another miraculous moment of clarity, she realized it was the seatbelt warning. It pierced through the noise of the dog and Crystal, the roaring in Bernie's ears, the hiss of the dry ice. Her seatbelt was on, digging into her neck as she tried to avoid Crystal. That meant Crystal's wasn't.

Be the most enthusiastic participant in saving your own life. The order had never been clearer.

There was a break in the trees to the left, a meadow with a huge maple a couple feet off the road. She didn't even have to think about it. She said a quick prayer no one was hurtling around the curve toward them, and cut the wheel hard to the left.

The car lurched, tossing Crystal against the passenger door.

"Doing it our way," Bernie sang as the car shot off the road toward the tree.

*****

Pete heard the impact before he rounded the curve. He wasn't sure how he heard it over his siren, but he knew what it was.

No no no no no. The passenger side of Bernie's car was crushed against a tree. Steam hissed from the undercarriage and crumpled hood. He skidded to a stop. He took inventory as he grabbed Sal's cane and ran to the wreckage. He couldn't see inside—white smoke filled the car. Dry ice. He grabbed the door handle and pulled, but it was locked.

He banged on the window.

"Bernie!"

Dubya barked.

"I'm going to break the window," he yelled, hoping she'd hear him over the hiss of the steaming car and Dubya's barking.

He banged the end of the cane against the window. A web of cracks radiated from the small hole. Cold white mist snaked out. The barking was louder, more frenzied. No sound from Bernie.

"Bernie, are you okay?" He yelled it as he banged the window with the end of the cane. Nothing.

Come on, come on. He hit it harder, then harder still as the cracks spread. The hole expanded, little pieces of glass powdering his sweating arms.

Bernie was slumped against the deflated airbag. Dubya frantically pushed past him out the window.

She was warm and breathing. No blood. He reached in and unlocked the door.

"Bernie, it's Pete. I've got you. It's okay." She couldn't hear him, he knew that. It was more for himself. He tried to find the seatbelt buckle, pressing his cheek against her neck as he did to feel her pulse as he fumbled for it. Her heart was beating strong. Thank God. She groaned, then coughed. Half of Crystal's twisted torso and a blood-covered leg stuck out of the tangle of metal where the passenger seat had been.

The seatbelt clicked open and he pulled Bernie from the car and onto the grass.

He lifted her head onto his lap and pushed the hair out of her face as she coughed. Her eyes blinked open.

"It's okay, I've got you," he said.

"Someone get Crystal. She tried to kill me." Bernie tried to get up, but he held her tighter.

"It's okay. Don't worry," he said, rocking her.

He didn't have to go back to check on Crystal. He'd seen enough to know it was pointless.

CHAPTER 33

Wednesday morning went on its lazy way. Bernie tried to pretend it was just another normal summer day.

"Fine pair we are," she said to Pete as she looked out at the lake. When she woke up in the ambulance the previous afternoon, the first thing she'd felt was her hand crushed in Pete's. She could smell vomit. Her head was killing her. Worse than that was the terror. She could still feel Crystal clawing at her, see the tree as the car careened toward it.

Now, on another picture postcard perfect summer day by the lake, her headache fading, her aches and pains minor, it didn't seem real. She tried not to think about Crystal.

Pete had been attentive but quiet. Maybe he realized how stupid and impulsive she was. She agreed. He'd loved her anyway those times before, but maybe it was finally too much.

He put a glass of ice water down on the table next to her. "Drink this and eat some of these." Saltines.

"How the tables have turned."

Despite the chaos and uncertainty, she felt languid, calm. The frenzied anxiety of the past weeks was gone.

Pete had spent most of the morning on the phone. She'd heard bits and pieces as she lay on the chaise, Dubya at her feet.

Pete sat down, propping the crutch against his chair. She checked his bandage. No blood. They'd had to treat him at the hospital yesterday, too, after his wound had started bleeding and wouldn't stop.

He insisted it was fine.

"Herman talked more to Dawna," he said. She'd been in

Farmington the day before when Pete had tried to call her. She was horrified and apologetic when she found out what had happened while she was gone. She'd visited Herman armed with what she found in the storage area dumpster: a broken Styrofoam cooler, the missing documents from the case file, empty baclofen bottles, a box of blue latex gloves, Lydia's cellphone.

The biggest find of all had been in Crystal's car—a second GPS device with very similar coordinates to the other, just a little off. They'd put a person about fifty yards away from Herman's campsite, to the spot where Lydia was found.

Dawna didn't know when she went to Farmington what Pete and Bernie knew about Crystal, but she knew Herman had been at the storage area, that Crystal had too, and wanted to see if he'd help her connect the dots before she talked to Pete about confronting Crystal.

"Crystal took Lydia's GPS and compass?" Bernie's thinking was still a little fuzzy.

"To make it more plausible that she got lost," Pete said. "Lydia had them when Herman found her, but they were gone by the time Sandy found her."

"What did Herman say happened?"

"It's quite a story," Pete said to Bernie. "He said that when Lydia found him, she was really sick. He tried to take care of her at his campsite, stole the morphine in case things got worse. He didn't use any on her, though. She'd been there for a few weeks and wasn't doing well. When he came back from getting supplies, she was gone. He'd already left the note on the cruiser because he'd seen Fuller around and was afraid he'd find them. He thought at first maybe it was Fuller who took her."

"That wouldn't have made sense."

"No. Everything of hers was gone from Herman's campsite except the water purifier, which he'd put aside. He liked his own brand, so he didn't use hers. He didn't know it'd made her sick."

"I was thinking how anxious Crystal was when Lydia was lost," Bernie said. "It must've been because she couldn't be sure if she was alive or dead."

"Yeah, Crystal was driving me nuts during the search, because Lydia hadn't been found where she thought she should be," Pete said.

"You know what I remembered when I was in the car with Crystal? Lydia always purified her water, no matter where she got it, just to be in the habit. I even put it in a story months ago. I forgot all about it."

"So, yeah," Pete said. "Crystal knew Lydia wouldn't get far. Look how fast you got sick. Look how fast I did. Crystal knew Lydia should've been found sooner, so she began to worry. Natalie told Hallowell she saw the fisherman at the storage area, always on Thursdays, and Hallowell knew Nat saw him up by the AT, too, so he told Crystal because she paid him to tell her anything that would help find Lydia. Crystal checked for herself at the storage area. He's a distinctive-looking guy and I bet Crystal recognized him immediately. Colleen has a photo of him from when he worked in Buffalo, and he looks pretty much the same, only a little leaner now. Crystal must've freaked."

"She hid it well." Bernie tried to remember. LeeAnne had been a nervous bundle since Lydia disappeared, but Crystal was the calm, organized one. Task oriented, LeeAnne had said. Crystal had agreed.

"She was focused on making sure that what Herman knew about her from Buffalo didn't get out," Pete said. "It wasn't a bad plan—if it looked like he killed Lydia, and he was found, that would make him more of an obvious target for the Buffalo killings. If people thought Lydia killed herself, fine, too. I'm not sure what Crystal would've done about Colleen in that case, though, because she wouldn't have let things go. Then, after Lydia was found, Libby said some nasty things about Sandy to Crystal, Crystal saw in my notes in the case file Sandy knew about the CO, and now Crystal had another suspect to throw into it. Libby also told Fergus Kelley about Sandy, so when Crystal went to him with the CO angle, it fit, more or less."

"Less," Bernie said.

"It's like I said before, when there are too many possibilities, it means the killer overthought things. People think they're smart, but there's such a thing as being too smart."

"I wouldn't know."

He reached over and squeezed her hand. "Crystal went into the woods to get Lydia the Thursday after she saw him at the storage units, knowing Herman would be down here. She just moved her a ways—there wasn't much to move. AT hikers travel light—set up the tent, put her in it, did her thing and good-bye Lydia."

"I wonder if Lydia hadn't accidentally sent her that text meant for Colleen, Crystal would have known anything was up."

"Likely not."

"Natalie's turning into a good little detective."

"I shudder to think," Pete said. "She told Dawna she's trying to exercise good judgment by telling everything she saw with those two. I'm not exactly sure what she means, but she made the point that Herman wouldn't hurt anyone and Crystal was mean."

"Totally agree," Bernie said.

"It's all a theory, anyway. I don't know what happened in Buffalo, but Crystal was obviously desperate for Lydia and Herman not to meet. Or at least for Lydia to not live to tell about it."

"Do you think she had any help?"

"I called LeeAnne, she knew nothing."

"Do you believe her?"

"Yeah, she's devastated."

"What happens now?"

"Nothing. As far as the state is concerned it's still suicide. The DA says there's nothing that would support a strong case."

Bernie was worn out. Now that she was sitting in the sun, drowsy and only a little sick, she couldn't believe how close she'd come to not being here. She'd avoided those planes into the building. This time. Pete was close enough in his lawn chair she could feel his body heat, could smell that reassuring warm soapy Pete smell, could almost feel him breathe as they sat side by side, looking out at the lake.

It was time to march into the new era.

"I slept with Sandy when we were broken up."

"I know."

She glanced over. His eyes were on one of the loons as it coo-cooed and glided across the water for takeoff.

"I'm sorry," she said. Her voice shook.

"Don't be."

"It wasn't love," Bernie said.

"You don't owe me an explanation." She'd seen the flinch, though.

"Yes, I do. It was my idea, not his. I needed a distraction, something to just take me totally out of thinking about you. I wanted someone different from you, so it wouldn't be anything like us together." She was fumbling. She wished she'd thought more about what to say. She didn't want to have to go into detail.

"It's fine. I get it. I'm okay with it. Honest." He looked over and smiled, a little sad, though.

"How did you know?"

"Easy guess. His T-shirt in your dirty clothes basket."

"Oh." She'd seen it when she did laundry that Tuesday at Pete's, made an ephemeral mental note to give it back to Sandy. It never occurred to her Pete had seen it.

"You, um." He laughed and shook his head. "One time accidentally sent me a text, now I know it was for him."

"I don't want to know."

"I knew it wasn't for me. I think it was supposed to say 'Get your handsome self over here,' but it didn't have a lot of vowels. It took me forever to figure out what you were saying, then I thought it was something for Sal and I was deciphering it wrong."

She burned with embarrassment. "I didn't want to hurt either of you guys. I'm really sorry."

"You don't have anything to be sorry for."

"I am anyway."

"I am, too." He squeezed her hand. "I missed you."

His hand was warm and dry. Firm, not shaky like it'd been. She squeezed back. "I missed you too."

She was dozing, her hand still in Pete's, when he said something. "Sorry, what?"

"Write the story."

She drank what was left of the water, tepid from the sun. "What?" she asked again.

"Lydia," he said. "You have the case file. You have me and Sandy. Write it."

*****

Pete was content to watch the lake, let the voicemail pick up the phone, never talk to anyone again. He just wanted to sit with Bernie sleeping next to him in the sun.

Tires on gravel broke the spell. Two cars. Colleen and Chuck came around the side of the house.

Colleen was there at Bernie's invitation.

Chuck was uninvited.

Pete wished he'd go back to Wisconsin. He felt hopeful for the first time in a long time and Chuck's presence kept nudging it away.

"Let's go inside," Pete said to him, pretending he didn't see the look Bernie gave him. He'd caught it though. It was a plea.

"Brought you something," Chuck said, putting the accordion case he was carrying on the table.

"I don't need another accordion."

"God, you're a stubborn kid. Open it, okay?"

Pete opened the case. He hadn't seen Baba's accordion for more than thirty years, but he knew it immediately.

"I had it tuned," Chuck said. "The guy said it's in tip-top condition."

"Where'd you get it?"

"Your mother. She rescued it after Gerry threw it out. She didn't want him to know, so she asked me to keep it. All those years, I made sure it stayed okay, no matter where I was. Even got the new case for it."

Pete had mourned the loss of the accordion for years. He wiped his eyes, pissed at himself. It was his private sorrow, not

300

anything for Chuck to be part of.

"Play something," Chuck said.

"Later."

"Your baba was my father," Chuck said to Pete. "Joe was my son. I hurt, too."

"I'm not talking about this."

"I'm not leaving town until we do."

Pete sat on the couch. Bernie and Colleen's voices bubbled from outside. He wished Chuck would leave so he could join them in the sunshine.

Chuck sat across from him. "I never stopped loving your mother. It kills me every day the devastation I caused walking away instead of getting help. I know it hurt you. It hurts to see you like this. How many examples do you need of people who fucked up everyone's life around them because they were too proud to get help?"

"I don't need a lecture, especially from you." Between Dawna, Sandy, and Bernie, Pete felt like it'd been a week-long tag-team intervention.

"We were a family who loved each other, whether you admit it or not. You're still here, thank God. I'm here. I want a family. I want my boy back."

Pete couldn't look at him. He watched Bernie and Colleen through the window, the lake ripple in the sun beyond, clouds drift across the high definition sky. He didn't know if it was possible to get back something that had been so lost.

*****

"I didn't want Crystal to die," Colleen said, as she and Bernie sat on the deck.

Bernie could hear the murmur of Pete and Chuck from inside. She braced for it to get loud.

"Aside from the human aspect, a lot of information will die with her," Colleen said.

"What can you tell me that you couldn't before?"

"Is this off the record?"

"God, yes. Everything is off the record. My life is off the record." Bernie'd worry about getting her on the record later. Right now she just wanted to know.

"I believe Crystal killed a patient by mistake in Buffalo," Colleen said. "To cover up, she killed at least three more to make it look like a serial killer. No one would suspect her."

"She'd be the last person people would suspect," Bernie said. Crystal, the girl in charge, the go-to gal.

"She couldn't stand to make a mistake," Colleen said. "A mistake where she killed someone by giving them the wrong meds? No way."

"And that paper Pete found in his shorts that Herman gave him, that's evidence?"

"It shows she pulled the meds that killed the last two victims," Collen said. "He had two sheets—what she actually did, and one she altered. I don't think she knew he was on to her and that he'd printed out the original before she altered it."

"Good for him, but jeez. He carries that around for fifteen years instead of just telling someone?"

"I think he didn't have faith it'd help things. Crystal had campaigned pretty heavily against him. I remember an early conversation with her, before I started thinking she had something to do with the deaths, and I was saying Herman obviously had some mental health issues, but they weren't red flag ones, and she said something like, 'You have to understand, it's easy to be sympathetic until you have to work with a person like that. He was very annoying.'"

Bernie could empathize with Herman.

"He told Lydia that he thought the deaths were odd. He'd been on the shift the night of the first one with Crystal, and she altered the chart. But Lydia asked Crystal, thinking Herman had misunderstood, and Crystal said, yeah, damn right he misunderstood."

"She didn't think Crystal was guilty?"

"Not then. Crystal was a very competent nurse. She won the

302

excellence in nursing award at the hospital the year before. Lydia couldn't believe she'd make a mistake that would kill someone, then cover it up."

"Then three other patients died," Bernie said.

"Right. Herman was an easy target. No one to back him up. He'd had his eye on Crystal, though. That printout was his ace in the hole. He kept it all those years, but he didn't know what to do with it until he saw Lydia was going to hike the AT."

"Did Lydia know Herman had it?"

"No. She just wanted to talk to him and see if she could figure things out. I thought Crystal was guilty, but I never told Lydia. I figured if I was successful, she'd find out soon enough. I should have said something."

"She wouldn't have believed you or done anything differently," Bernie said. "She wouldn't, for instance, think her water purifier was tampered with. Look at me, I suspected her and still drank drugged coffee she gave me." Bernie would feel like an idiot for the rest of her life.

"One thing I've learned in my line of work," Colleen said. "It's hard for people who deal honestly with others to grasp someone they think is a friend will stab them in the back."

"True. People expect others to act like them. I've seen it the other way around a lot, people who are dishonest, or duplicitous, or manipulative, think everyone else is like that, too," Bernie said. "I'd still rather be stabbed than stabber."

"Me too." They clinked iced tea glasses.

"I wish Lydia had sent that text to me, not Crystal," Colleen said. "One little slip of the finger, and look what it cost."

It depressed Bernie. "Crystal will never have to answer for it. The case dies with her."

"It's not about Crystal," Colleen said. "It's about Herman. In Buffalo, they still think he's a murderer."

CHAPTER 34

Sal and Chloe insisted on bringing food over for the invalids, even though Bernie assured them she felt a lot better. She was sure Pete wouldn't want the visitors, but he said it was fine.

"There're the three kids, too," Bernie said.

"That's fine."

The only time all day Pete had been talkative was when they were discussing the Lydia case. Since Chuck left he'd barely said a word. She found it hard to believe he'd want a bunch of people in the house.

Sal and Chloe arrived mid-afternoon with tons of food. Bernie invited Colleen to stay. Fine with Pete.

"Why don't we give Sandy a call?" Bernie said. "He has to change your dressing anyway."

That was fine, too.

Sandy brought a case of beer and Heidi.

"Little secret," Sandy said to Bernie after a couple beers. "The reason I have her is my therapist told me to get a dog. She couldn't track her way out of a paper bag."

"It's a good thing Pete has Dubya," Bernie said. Dubya was lying across Pete's foot as he stared out at the lake.

"It's a good thing Pete has you," Sandy said, jabbing her with his elbow.

Pete sat removed from the others as they talked, drank beer, watched Hallowell and Corinna splash in the water.

Bernie was going to see how far fine went.

"Let's call Chuck," she said.

"Why?"

"He's alone. It's a beautiful afternoon. We have plenty of food. He's your dad."

Pete breathed in, held it. In her head, she counted to four with him. Counted to four when he let it out.

"We're both alive," she said. "If you want me to underline it with some big honking cliché, I can."

"Please don't."

She leaned over, so their faces were inches apart. "Because you're so captivated by my magical personality you'll do anything I ask," she whispered, giving him what she hoped was her winningest smile.

He smiled back, slight and thin. "That's true."

She kissed him lightly on the lips, then said, still a whisper, "Because I know you love him and he loves you, and too many sad things have happened."

"Fine."

"Thanks." She kissed him again.

"Are you sure?" Chuck asked when she called.

"It's fine."

And it was. Pete was cordial, the tension not obvious to anyone but Bernie. Chuck fit right in. When the sun began to set, no one showed any sign of leaving. Bernie lit some tiki mosquito lamps she'd bought at the Country Grocer. She knew they weren't Pete's taste, but when she showed them to him, he said they were fine.

"Pete, you got a new accordion?" Sandy asked.

"It's a very old one," he said.

"Play something?"

"Not today."

"Play us the accordion," Corinna said, clapping. "Play it!"

"I love a good accordion," Chloe said.

"Pleeeeeassseee," Corinna said, grabbing Pete's hand.

Pete smiled at her. "Sure, okay."

Bernie had been waiting for him to say he was tired, make everyone go home. But this was fine, too. "Bernie, do you mind getting it for me?"

305

"This leg thing is going to get old fast," she said. That got a smile out of him, too.

He strapped it on and played a riff. "Requests?"

"Anyone know how to polka?" Chuck asked.

"Don't look at me," Bernie said.

"I do," said Colleen. "I'm a Buffalo girl, after all."

"Polka it is," said Pete.

Chuck held out his hand to Colleen, and they went down the steps to the grass.

"I want to polka, too," said Corinna.

Sal held out his hand. "This way, m'lady."

Pete nodded a beat, smiled, then started to play.

Chuck and Colleen laughed as they polkaed around the small yard. Sal, with Corinna on his feet squealing with delight, tried to imitate them.

When the song was done, Pete started another.

Chloe dragged Hallowell out onto the grass. "Consider this part of your punishment," she said when he groaned. They joined Sal and Corinna, the four of them holding hands as they danced in a circle.

Colleen stepped over the dogs, snoring at the edge of the porch after an afternoon of chasing food scraps and each other. She sat down next to Sandy. "I haven't danced like that in ages," she said.

Chuck, winded and red-faced, followed her onto the porch. "Me either."

They watched Chloe and Sal wheel around the grass with the kids.

Colleen started singing along, clapping in time. "It's the theme song to *Laverne & Shirley*," she said, laughing. Richmond watched her with delight, then started clapping too, Sandy bouncing him on his knee in time to the music.

"What a great family this is," Chuck said. He was behind Pete, and he leaned down and kissed him on top of the head. Then he put his arm around Pete's chest, above the skipping accordion, and buried his face in Pete's hair.

Bernie waited for Pete to pull away, for the music to screech to a halt.

Pete, not missing a beat, tilted his head, his cheek against his father's arm. Chuck whispered something, let go, and went into the house.

Bernie caught Pete's eye.

He shrugged.

She smiled.

He smiled back.

"Fine," she mouthed.

His smile grew into the full, face-cracking smile, the one from the old days that she'd wondered if she'd ever see again.

She searched around for the familiar feeling of doom, the reason she shouldn't trust the moment. It wasn't there. There wasn't room for it as something warm took its place. Joy, maybe.

Pete's eyes danced, locked on hers. She felt her smile grow to match his.

"This is the greatest day ever!" Corinna yelled as she twirled across the grass.

Pete threw his head back and laughed, the accordion dancing in his hands.

-30-

Acknowledgements

I thank my excellent draft readers—Rebecca Milliken, Liz Milliken, Nicki Beauregard, John Radosta and Kathy McGrath Fitts—their suggestions made this book better. Miranda Mason did a wonderful copy edit of the initial draft and Sam Dunbar did an equally wonderful copy edit of the final (including correcting my pig latin). Also, thanks to my excellent audio producer Trudi Knoedler, who goes above and beyond with insight, suggestions and typo-catching.

Thanks as well to John Whitson, who allowed me to poach a story he told a long time ago over after-work beers. Though I twisted it around for my own purposes, the poignancy of the initial telling has stayed with me. Hope this is an adequate substitute for not getting the name on the wall.

Thanks, too, to Dr. Ken McKenzie, who, while skillfully treating my wrenched arm, cheerfully and without judgment answered my many, many questions about the effects of thigh impalement.

All writers are inspired by the works of others, and special recognition goes to *A Good Man and a Dog*, by Roger Guay and Kate Flora, which noted how blackberry scratches may mean more to a country cop than a city one, and also honestly and poignantly discussed the effects of PTSD on law enforcement agents. *Border Crossings: Coming of Age in the Czech Resistance* by Charles Novacek, was also a huge help.

This book was a long time coming, and I want to thank all those very special readers—a little mind-blowing how many—who took the time to tell me how much they were looking forward to it. I hope it doesn't disappoint.

About the Author

Maureen Milliken is a longtime journalist, who worked for daily newspapers in northern New England for more than three decades. She's a member of the Mystery Writers of America and Sisters in Crime, and blogs with other Maine crime writers at Mainecrimewriters.com. She also co-hosts a true-crime podcast, Crime & Stuff, with her sister, Maine artist Rebecca Milliken. She lives in central Maine.

For updates on Maureen's next book, go to maureenmilliken.com or follow her on Twitter @mmilliken47. Like her Facebook page facebook.com/maureenmillikenmysterywriter.

Made in the USA
Columbia, SC
27 October 2018